DEAD MAN
RUNNING

ALSO BY STEVE HAMILTON

NICK MASON
Exit Strategy
The Second Life of Nick Mason

ALEX MCKNIGHT
Let It Burn
Die a Stranger
Misery Bay
A Stolen Season
Ice Run
Blood is the Sky
North of Nowhere
The Hunting Wind
Winter of the Wolf Moon
A Cold Day in Paradise

STAND-ALONES
The Lock Artist
Night Work

STEVE HAMILTON

DEAD MAN
RUNNING

An Alex McKnight Novel

G. P. PUTNAM'S SONS | New York

G. P. Putnam's Sons
Publishers Since 1838
An imprint of Penguin Random House LLC
375 Hudson Street
New York, New York 10014

Library of Congress Cataloging-in-Publication Data
Names: Hamilton, Steve, author.
Title: Dead man running / Steve Hamilton.
Description: New York : G. P. Putnam's Sons, [2018] |
  Series: An Alex McKnight novel ; 11
Identifiers: LCCN 2018012928| ISBN 9780399574443
  (hardcover) | ISBN 9780399574450 (ebook)
Subjects: LCSH: McKnight, Alex (Fictitious character)—
  Fiction. | Private investigators—Michigan—Upper
  Peninsula—Fiction. | Murder—Investigation—Fiction. |
  BISAC: FICTION / Suspense. | FICTION /
  Thrillers. | GSAFD: Mystery fiction.
Classification: LCC PS3558.A44363 D43 2018 |
  DDC 813/.54—dc23
  LC record available at https://lccn.loc.gov/2018012928

Printed in the United States of America
1 2 3 4 5 6 7 8 9 10

BOOK DESIGN BY KATY RIEGEL

For Deborah Randall

ACKNOWLEDGMENTS

As ALWAYS, and more than ever, I am indebted to Shane Salerno, David Koll, and everyone at The Story Factory. Thanks, also, to everyone who's been with me since the beginning: Bill Keller and Frank Hayes, Maggie Griffin, Jan Long, Rob Brenner, and Nick Childs. And finally, my wife, Julia, who is everything to me; my son, Nicholas; and my daughter, Antonia. I will never be a good enough writer to express how blessed I am to have you as my family.

I found the following books incredibly helpful and highly recommend them:

The Manhunter, by John Pascucci and Cameron Stauth

The Anatomy of Motive, by John Douglas and Mark Olshaker

Advanced Fugitive, by Kenn Abaygo

The Devil's Dozen, by Katherine Ramsland, PhD

Ted Bundy: Conversations with a Killer, by Stephen G. Michaud and Hugh Aynesworth

Without Conscience, by Robert D. Hare, PhD

The Sociopath Next Door, by Martha Stout, PhD

You don't understand me.

You are not expected to.

You are not capable of it.

I am beyond your experience.

—RICHARD RAMIREZ, the Night Stalker

DEAD MAN RUNNING

THE ACT WAS DONE in a moonless desert darkness, but seen in the light, half a world away.

It was just before 4 p.m. on a bright February day on the Mediterranean Sea when a man named Frank Thompson logged on to his laptop. He was one of more than three thousand passengers on the cruise ship, midway between Sardinia and Sicily. His home in Scottsdale, Arizona, was six thousand miles and eight time zones away. Now that the ship's Internet service had finally been restored, Frank just wanted to know two things: That the video cameras installed in his house were working. And that his house was safe and secure.

The man's wife was up on the deck. She didn't think he should be worrying about the house. She thought he should be relaxing and actually enjoying this cruise, after waiting so many years to do this. After spending twelve grand to make this trip happen.

I'll start enjoying this, Frank said to himself, *when I can get a little peace of mind.*

He checked the first video feed. It came from the X10 Internet camera mounted on the bookshelf next to the fireplace. It was positioned so that the lens would look through the legs of a wooden elephant, and it communicated wirelessly with the server in the study, which in turn fed the images to the Web. Available to see anytime, anywhere in the world. At least when the Internet was working.

The live image, as Frank hit the key to bring it up, showed the front door and half of the living room. Everything looked normal to him, and yet *not* normal in a way he couldn't identify.

He kept looking at the image. The couch, the door, the little welcome mat to wipe the desert sand off your feet when you came in.

What's wrong with this picture?

Then it finally hit him. There was too much light.

It was early in the morning back home, which on most days would mean that sunlight should be coming through the big window in the kitchen. Just as it seemed to be doing here.

But when they had left the house, those curtains had been closed. Frank was sure of that.

He clicked the link to restart the video, which ran on a continuous eight-hour loop. The image jumped back eight hours to darkness, the only light a thin glow from the one lamp they had left on in the living room. He hit the fast-forward button and watched the image flicker, the minutes passing by in fast motion, with no movement.

Until there was.

It was just a flash. He backed the video up, then ran it at

normal speed. The front door opened. How could it be un-locked? This video would never reveal that secret to him—he could only go back eight hours, and as of eight hours ago, the door was obviously unlocked and any goddamned person in the world could walk right into their house.

Like this stranger.

Who was in their house.

Frank paused the video to get a better look. The man was tall and well built, a few years younger than Frank, with fair skin and long light brown hair that went down to his shoulders. He was dressed in black jeans and a black button-down shirt. Black shoes. Even a black baseball cap, his hair trailing down the back of his neck. Frank's mind caught on the hair first—he'd always hated long hair on men. Then on something else, a cer-tain quality about the man himself, how he moved with com-plete composure. No rush. No nerves. Like he was actually comfortable being in another man's house after dark. Frank watched as the man crossed the room, moving from the front door toward the hallway.

Frank hit the pause button again, sat there going through a series of emotions. Shock, anger, surprise. And if he was being honest with himself, a slight tinge of excitement.

This thing really works.

He switched to the kitchen feed, went back eight hours, ran it through at fast speed, watching for the same kind of flash. As he was doing this, his wife came back to their stateroom.

"Marion, look at this!" he said to her. "There's someone in our house!"

"What are you talking about?"

"Sit down." Frank went back to the living room feed, found

the time stamp when the front door had been opened. Just after midnight, Arizona time. Eight in the morning on the ship's time.

Marion watched the video, looking confused and skeptical until she saw the man walking through her living room. Her eyes went wide.

"How did he get in? We have to call somebody!"

"Just a minute," he said. "Let's find out where he went. Let me see if he..."

Frank didn't finish the thought. He had switched to the bedroom feed now. The camera was mounted on top of the armoire in the master bedroom, partially covered by the arrangement of silk flowers in a basket. It looked down on the bed and the dresser with the jewelry box on top. All of Marion's diamonds were in that box. He hadn't let her bring any of them on this trip, a pronouncement he was already regretting. The apology was half formed on his lips when the screen went from black to something else.

A light had been turned on. In their bedroom.

The stranger stood in the doorway, looking at a woman who was already lying on the bed. Waiting for him.

"That's our bed," Marion said. *"That's our bed."*

The man stepped forward. He stood over the woman and looked down at her for a long time.

Frank was about to pause the video. No need to see what came next. But Marion stopped him.

"What's wrong with her?" she said. "Look at that woman, Frank..."

He looked closely. The woman was lying on her back, her hands folded together on her stomach. She wasn't moving.

Her skin...

White. Like wax. Her mouth was open. Her eyes...

Staring at nothing.

"Oh my God," Marion said. "That woman, she's..."

She didn't finish the thought.

She didn't have to.

Frank and Marion Thompson sat in their cabin and watched the stranger in their bedroom as he began to take off his clothes.

CHAPTER ONE

THERE ARE SOME THINGS *a man should never have to see.*

Roger Halliday had an older brother who'd done three tours in Vietnam. When he'd asked him what had happened over there, that's what his brother had told him. Those exact words, and nothing more.

Forty-plus years later, his brother long gone, Roger Halliday was an FBI agent taking his last lap before retirement. He'd started as a probie on an Evidence Response Team, put in some time with the Behavioral Analysis Unit before going mainline with the Criminal Investigative Division. So he'd seen his share of dead bodies, shot or stabbed or thrown off a thirty-two-story building onto the hood of a car.

But he'd never seen anything like this.

"How many times did you watch it?" his partner asked. Agent Juwan Cook, in the Bureau for eight years now. He was black, with a smooth head he shaved every morning and a thin mustache. Cook kept his eyes straight ahead as he drove.

"Three times," Halliday said. The first time, it had been just a matter of getting through it. When it was done, he had watched it again. Twice. Looking for details. Doing his job.

Cook shook his head and kept driving.

The house was on the north side of Scottsdale, up by the Mc-Dowell Sonoran Preserve. One of those places you drive by and imagine yourself living someday, if you work long enough and are smart with your money. Spanish architecture, the standard for any house in this neighborhood. Clay tiles on the roof, an in-ground pool in the back. Five thousand square feet, one story, easier to keep cool in the summer. A single strip of grass, just a token amount of green for the dog to walk on. Everything else typical Arizona—rock, gravel, and cactus.

Once they turned down the street, it wasn't hard to find the Thompsons' house. There were already half a dozen police vehicles lined up on the street, and there were so many men walking through the yard it was raising a dust cloud you could see from two miles away.

Halliday had gotten the call just after eleven thirty, the last link in a long chain that had started somewhere on the Mediterranean Sea. It was almost noon now, on a clear February day, seventy-six degrees on the car's digital thermometer, the kind of day that makes Arizona feel pretty much perfect. Halliday wished the call had come in sooner, that he had had the chance to get here first, to see the house, to see the victim. He wasn't looking forward to pulling rank when he finally got here—that was the kind of thing that made the local cops hate the "feebs," if they didn't already. But this was going to be his case. He could feel it.

After chasing him around California, Utah, Nevada, and now Arizona, this UNSUB, the unknown subject suspected in the murders of at least five other women, had finally left a victim in the wrong place.

But why here?

Halliday tried to see this house the way the UNSUB would have seen it. A quiet street, not many neighbors. They had driven by a guard shack on the main road, but the UNSUB would have known this was just for show. With all of the trails in the preserve running along the backs of these property lines... There were plenty of ways to get to the house. You do it at night, and nobody sees you.

But as easy as it would be to get in, he had to know this place would have something else: a level of internal security that would make it different from all of the other places he'd used before. Sure, maybe the owner of this house put too much trust in the guard shack and didn't have an alarm, but those Internet cameras he'd installed—the cameras that recorded everything that happened inside that house... The UNSUB should have suspected they were there. And even if he'd decided it was worth the risk, he should have found them and disabled them.

He'd never been this sloppy before.

So maybe this is someone else, Halliday thought. But no. *No way.* He thought back to everything he'd seen on that video... *How many human beings on this planet are capable of doing something like that?*

It had to be the same man.

Cook pulled off the street and stopped behind a long line of squad cars. As Halliday led the way up the sidewalk to the front door, he was already getting the once-over from the uniformed locals. Everything about him, from the ground up, screamed *Fed*: his shoes, his suit, the expression on his face. Nobody tried to stop him. He asked the uniform standing by the door for the name of the man in charge and was sent in to see Detective Millens from Scottsdale PD. He found the man standing alone in the kitchen, in plain clothes, a gold shield shining on his belt. He was young for a detective, around Cook's age, and he was busy talking into his cell phone. As soon as Millens saw Halliday, he ended the call.

Halliday got out his ID and showed it to him. Then he introduced Cook.

"Back of the house," the detective said. "Master bedroom."

As Halliday followed Millens, he looked down at the carpeting in the hallway and saw the shoeprints.

"How many of your men have been in here?"

"Two," the detective said, looking back at him. "Maybe three."

Halliday scanned the rest of the hallway with a frown as the detective led them into the bedroom. That was where he saw the body on the bed. It was covered by a white sheet.

Halliday took a moment to walk around the room. He looked out the window at the backyard—more rock, gravel, cactus— and at the road that looped around the lot and started climbing up toward Dixie Mountain. He stood motionless for a full minute, looking at every window in the neighboring houses, every vantage point from the road, every spot on the preserve where a man could use a set of high-powered binoculars to peer right into this room.

He could be out there right now, Halliday thought, *watching us.*

But something tells me he's not there. Not now.

"Were these curtains open?"

"Yes," the detective said.

"Was the light on?"

"No, it wasn't."

Halliday left the window and went to the big jewelry box on the dresser, took out a pen, and used it to gently lift the lid. Nothing looked out of place. No conspicuous blank spots from which something might have been taken. So probably nothing stolen, even though, to his untrained eye, it looked like there were some real diamonds that would be worth putting in your pocket on the way out.

Halliday took a quick look in the bathroom, came back out and stood at the foot of the bed. The body lay in a straight line, perfectly centered on the bed, and even with the sheet over it he could tell that the arms had been folded neatly across the chest.

Five minutes in the house and he had already decided what needed to be done. Even if he knew it wouldn't be popular.

"Everybody out!" he said, moving to the doorway so that anyone else in the house could hear him. *"Now."*

"I understand if you need to take over the crime scene," Millens said, "but the ME's on his way right now and—"

"No," Halliday said. "We're not moving the body."

Millens took a moment to process what he was hearing. He looked back and forth between Halliday and Cook.

"You're not serious," he said.

"He'll come back again tonight," Halliday said. "She needs to be here. One more night."

He didn't feel like giving the detective a crash course on how a certain kind of "organized" serial killer works, the kind of killer who returns to the body several times after death for his further sexual gratification.

Like Gary Ridgway, the Green River Killer.

Like Ted Bundy.

"You're not leaving her here," Millens said. "You don't *have* to. Think about it, Agent Halliday. If he comes back, you can still catch him."

"You don't understand," Halliday said. "He'll know if the body is gone. He won't come anywhere near this place."

"I'm not leaving her here," Millens said, nodding toward the body under the sheet. "It's that simple."

"Not your call to make," Cook said, standing next to his partner.

"Get all of your men out of here," Halliday said. "Make everything look *exactly* like it did. I mean everything, right down to those footprints in the hallway. Which *never* should have happened, Detective. Find a rake, a brush, whatever it takes. In thirty minutes, I want this place to look *untouched*."

Millens just stood there, looking back and forth between the agents.

"The sheet over the body," Halliday said, knowing this would be the hardest part. "I assume you did that."

"No way," Millens said. "No ... fucking ... way."

"I'll do it. After you've left."

"When they find out you didn't let us take her away—"

"We can't help her now," Halliday said. "What we *can* do is stop this guy before he kills ten more."

Millens shook his head and left the room without saying another word. Halliday looked at his partner.

"Go," Halliday said.

"You really think he'd know if the body was gone?"

"You heard the man. The curtains were open."

"And the light was off," Cook said. "Even if he was on that road back there—"

Halliday put up his hand to stop him. He'd been taught long ago to trust his own instincts, the same instincts that went all the way back to the brief time in his career when he'd worked with the agents who had invented a new way to track serial killers. These agents studied them; they interviewed them; they took them through every case, going over every detail. They got inside their heads, even if that was the last place you'd ever want to be.

Thirty years later, Agent Halliday knew that the curtains had been left open for a reason. And that, lights on or off, the man they were looking for would never return to an empty house.

Cook knew his partner well enough not to press it any further. When he turned and left the room, Halliday was left alone with the body.

He had just talked to his daughter that morning. She was getting ready to come home from the hospital. If he had taken that retirement package, he'd be home right now with his wife, waiting to hold his first grandson.

But here he was. Two and a half hours after that phone call, standing in this bedroom.

He looked down at the still form on the bed. Then he lifted the sheet.

————

IT WAS ALMOST TWO A.M. They'd been waiting in the van for five hours. Halliday, Cook, Detective Millens, and another agent, named Pfeiffer, from the regional SWAT team. All four men were wearing tactical vests. Halliday's stomach burned from his third cup of coffee.

"The suspect was here around midnight last night," Millens said. "Don't these guys stick to a routine?"

These guys.

"Yes," Halliday said. "Maybe all that commotion around the house today…"

Millens gave him a look, like *Don't even try to pin this on me or my police department.*

Halliday was already starting to regret his decision to let Millens sit in on the surveillance. The FBI had quickly installed its own cameras all over the house, and had patched those into its own secure video feed, all relayed to a series of monitors here inside the van, which was parked in the courtyard behind one of the neighbors' houses. They were smart enough not to park it on the street. Smart enough to make sure everything looked exactly the same. *Everything.*

Millens was sitting next to Halliday, rocking back and forth with nervous energy. On the feed from the bedroom, the two men could see the body lying in the center of the bed, unnaturally still, the exposed skin glowing in the infrared light.

"I see something," Cook said. He was on the other side of the van, watching another monitor, with the feed from the external camera they'd mounted a mile away in the Sonoran Preserve parking lot. Halliday turned to look, but Cook's eyes were thirty years younger, so it took a few seconds for Halliday's to catch up.

Then he saw it.

The vague figure of a man, walking away from a vehicle, toward the camera they'd mounted on a light pole. As he passed under the light, his face was obscured by the baseball cap on his head. He was moving quickly. With purpose. Leaving the parking lot and entering the trail.

Heading toward the house.

There were two agents waiting in the closed-up rangers' building. They contacted Halliday now over the radio to let him know what he had just seen with his own eyes.

He's coming your way.

Another decision Halliday had made. *Let the man get to the house before we move. Let him come through the door. Don't try to pick him up in the parking lot.* It was a decision he now had twelve long minutes to wonder if he'd regret as he watched the next monitor with the video feed from the rooftop camera.

The man should be on the street by now, he thought. *Even walking in the dark, it's less than a mile.*

He got spooked. Now he's running. We'll never see him again.

But then Cook pointed to the monitor. "There."

Another movement on the screen. The same figure, growing larger.

Halliday could feel the adrenaline pumping through his body. He could sense the same in the other three men in the van. The SWAT agent was on his feet, ready to open the back door.

Halliday keyed the mic on his radio.

"Nobody moves until he enters the house."

"Why are we waiting?" Millens said.

"He won't touch her again," Halliday said to him. "I promise. But I want him in that house."

They watched the figure as he came close to the front door, moving quickly but without rushing. Like a man with no doubts, no worries.

Then he stopped. He seemed to be looking right at the rooftop camera. Looking right at Halliday with the blurred face of a pale yellow ghost.

Halliday keyed the mic again.

"Everyone hold," he said.

Halliday watched the still figure, holding his breath.

Open the door, God damn it.

Open the fucking door.

The figure disappeared from the rooftop camera's view. Halliday quickly looked to the other monitor, saw him stepping into the living room and turning on the light.

"Take him!"

The back door of the van was thrown open. Halliday was last out of the vehicle, his partner already halfway to the house. He saw the other agents converging—from a darkened house on the other side of the street, from another house on the property behind. Three directions, twelve men in total, all armed, including eight more members of the regional SWAT team. Halliday tried to catch up to them, hoping the lead men would stop the UNSUB in time.

He wanted to keep his promise to Millens.

When Halliday made it to the front door, he had to take a moment, half doubled over, to catch his breath.

There was a man on the floor, his hands cuffed behind his

back. Halliday bent down to see his face, pulling off the man's black baseball cap. Late forties maybe, long light brown hair, fair skin. He was wearing black jeans, black hiking shoes, and a black dress shirt that looked freshly ironed. Just in those two seconds, Halliday was already seeing a man who was smart, who was careful, who was so neat he made sure his shirt wasn't wrinkled when he broke into a house to visit a corpse.

The man looked back at him with something like a smile. No surprise. No anger. He was about to say something, but Halliday didn't want to hear it. Not yet. He left him there and went to the bedroom, thinking, *At least he didn't make it this far. He didn't even get a chance to turn on the light and see her again.*

Halliday stood in the doorway. In the dim glow from the window, he saw the woman's body on the bed. He opened the closet door and found the white sheet he had taken away from her earlier that same day. With great care, he unfolded it and placed it over her body.

"Thank you," he said to her.

He stood over her for a while, listening to the men in the other room, knowing exactly what they were feeling—how you wait and wait for hours and then in the course of a few seconds you're in motion, everything a blur. Even after you take your man down, your heart is still beating fast. The adrenaline has nowhere else to go. These men would be up for the rest of the night, pacing back and forth in their bedrooms, or sitting with open bottles at their kitchen tables.

We did it. We took down a serial killer.

For Halliday, the night would go differently. He'd go home for a couple of hours, just long enough to catch his breath, get up and make some coffee, put on some new clothes. Then come right back to the office. Years ago, he wouldn't have left the suspect, would have stayed up forty-eight hours in a row if he had to. But he knew he'd be back before anything important happened, and that his young partner would handle things in the meantime.

Besides, Halliday needed to be with his wife on a night like this, even if it was just slipping into the bed next to her for a few minutes. She'd wake up and ask him if everyone had made it home alive. After thirty years married to an agent, she knew that was the most important question to ask.

Yes, he'd say.

Did you catch him?

Yes.

Good. Just like that.

Then, while he stared at the ceiling, he would listen to her breathing as she went back to sleep.

BY THE TIME Halliday walked back into the FBI field office on Deer Valley Road, the UNSUB had a name: Martin T. Livermore. He was a robotics engineer—at least when he wasn't abducting women, killing them, and then violating their dead bodies for days at a time.

There were five open cases on Halliday's desk: two in California, one in Utah, one in Nevada, and one other case in Arizona, besides the one they'd just nailed him on. In all of the cases, it had been a woman between the ages of twenty-five and thirty-five. Three of those five women had been killed in their homes, two abducted and killed in nearby motels. In all of the cases, there were trace amounts of blood and semen found at the scene. And one other thing: rope fibers.

In all five cases, the women had been tied up. Here in the sixth case, where they finally had a body to examine, they could see the ligature marks crisscrossing her body, looped across her mouth like a gag, looped across her throat. The medical examiner's report on this woman would list asphyxiation as the official cause of death. There was evidence of sexual penetration, both before and after death.

She had been alive for six to eight hours after being captured.

Six to eight hours of torture before the ropes finally strangled her.

In each of the previous cases, the body had been moved to a second location, which had apparently been chosen with great care. Abandoned buildings, or houses that were unoccupied for weeks on end. In every case, this second location had been found eventually, by *someone*. If it was a house, the owners would finally come home and discover that someone had been sleeping in their bed—a perverse retelling of Goldilocks and the Three Bears, only this time with the evidence left behind by a killer. If it was an abandoned building, it would take longer, but eventually the location would be found. In one case, it had been a contractor visiting a long-vacant house, preparing an estimate for a renovation. He had found the victim's bloody clothing neatly folded next to the bathtub. In another case, a local police officer had gone into an old warehouse looking for a vagrant who'd broken in to steal copper wire. The officer had found a blanket neatly spread out on the second floor, near a window overlooking the street. Once again, there was bloody clothing nearby, neatly folded.

From each of these second locations, the FBI had gathered trace evidence and had matched that with the evidence from the kill site. A map was constructed for all five known victims, showing the progression from one to the next, moving from the first two victims in California to the single victim in Utah, then to Nevada, then Arizona. The second location would range from as little as twelve miles away from the kill site to over a hundred.

And then the bodies were never seen again.

When they reconstructed Livermore's movements through California, Utah, Nevada, and Arizona, they corresponded exactly with the dates and locations of the crime scenes. His DNA matched the samples taken from each location, in all five of the open cases.

Carolyn Kline, victim number six, had been killed in her own home on the north side of Phoenix four days before, had died on the floor of her living room before Livermore had brought her to the Thompsons' house in Scottsdale, the house he had returned to on the second night, at which point he was observed on the security video. If he hadn't been captured, he would have presumably followed the same protocol as the other five: after approximately one week of sexual contact with the dead body at the second location, the body would have been removed, taken to wherever he took them when he was done with them.

We've never come close to catching him before.

That video recorder. He should have seen it.

To Halliday, it didn't make sense.

That's why he was so eager to talk to Livermore. So he could ask the man himself.

THE INTERVIEW TOOK PLACE on the top floor of the Maricopa County Fourth Avenue Jail. Livermore was being kept here while they figured out which federal detention center could best hold him. Fine with Halliday, because he knew this was the most secure jail in the state of Arizona. Maybe in the entire country. Halliday rode up in the elevator alone, getting his mind into the right place.

Been a while since I sat across the table from someone like this, he said to himself. *I even let myself believe I'd be out of here before we caught another one.*

That thought was followed by another, the same thought he'd been revisiting ever since he'd gotten the call about the body found in Scottsdale.

There is no good reason to keep doing this to yourself. You've given this job enough.

The elevator door opened. Halliday walked down the hall. Two guards were waiting for him, and they nodded to him without saying a word. When they let him into the intermediate room, he had a moment to look through the small window in the door, set at eye level. He saw Livermore sitting at the interview table. His hair was pulled back and tied neatly behind his head. *He's just spent his first night in a jail cell,* Halliday thought, *but he doesn't look rattled. Even from here, the man's eyes are clear and focused. Like he can't wait for this interview to begin.*

Halliday thought back to the years he'd spent studying the work of Robert Ressler, the FBI agent who had essentially invented profiling. Then later John Douglas, who'd turned profiling into an art form. When Halliday had been invited to join the Behavioral Analysis Unit permanently, he'd told them he didn't want to move his family to Quantico. That had been the official excuse, anyway. The truth was he just didn't want to spend his career working with serial killers. He still kept in touch with BAU, and they had offered to send a man out here to talk to Livermore.

Maybe Halliday should have taken them up on the offer.

"This is what they do," his partner had said to him. "Why take this one yourself?"

Halliday hadn't given him an answer. Maybe he hadn't even known. Not really. Not until this moment, as he stood at the door and looked at Livermore through the little window.

There's one reason I'm here, he said to himself.

Carolyn Kline.

She was twenty-six years old, an optometrist's assistant, still taking classes at Arizona State University when she wasn't working. She was a daughter to two parents, a granddaughter to three surviving grandparents. A girlfriend to one boyfriend. But to Halliday she would always be the woman who helped him catch Livermore.

The second door was automatically unlocked with a loud buzzing sound. He took a breath and pushed it open. Livermore looked up at him with that same enigmatic smile he'd given him when he was first handcuffed at the crime scene. Now he was wearing the same orange jumpsuit every suspect was issued at intake, his hands not only cuffed but also attached to the chain that ran around his waist. His ankles were shackled with leg irons, with a ten-inch length of chain between them.

Halliday took a moment to gather his impressions of the

man. To study him at close range, now that he had the opportunity. He saw a man who'd spent most of his life indoors. Fair
skin. No sun damage. Not a surprise, given his job, but there was
little else about the man to suggest an engineer. He didn't wear
glasses. He wasn't soft around the edges. In fact, he looked like
a man who took care of himself. A man most women would call
handsome. Maybe even *striking*. Not musclebound, but lean
and athletic. He could imagine this man doing an hour of light
weightlifting, and then spending another hour on the treadmill.
And then maybe one more hour looking at himself in the mirror.

Halliday had brought a folder into the room with him. He
put that on the table and then sat down in the chair across from
Livermore. There was a video camera mounted high in the corner of the room. The light was blinking. Every word, every
movement, it would all be recorded.

"Congratulations," Livermore said. "I understand you have a
new grandchild."

Halliday had just opened the folder, was about to take out six
photographs. He stopped dead when he heard those words.

"How do you know that?" Halliday looked into Livermore's
eyes, really *looked* for the first time, and saw that he had green
irises circled with bands so dark they were almost black. The
eyes of an exotic animal.

Eyes you'd never forget.

Livermore shrugged at the question, gave Halliday that
same half smile again.

He overheard it in the hallway, Halliday said to himself. *One
of those guards outside, talking about me before I got here.*

*Ten seconds in this room and he's already trying to put me
off balance.*

I will not let that happen.

He went back to the six photographs, taking them out of the folder one by one and putting them on the table.

Six photographs.

Six women.

"Every one of these women," Halliday said, "you selected for a reason. Every step, every movement… it was all thought out. Where you took them to kill them. Where you took them after that. You must have watched those houses, those buildings…"

Livermore shook his head, giving Halliday the little half smile.

"You were just as careful when choosing your locations," Halliday went on, "as you were when choosing your victims."

Halliday pushed one of the photographs forward. It was the last victim, Carolyn Kline. Livermore looked down at the woman's face for just a moment. Then his eyes returned to Halliday's. The half smile was still on his face.

"Until this one," Halliday said. "Why did you break the pattern?"

Livermore shook his head again, and this time he let out a snort of laughter.

"This funny to you?" Halliday said.

"In its own way, yes."

"Last time I checked, you're the one wearing the cuffs and leg irons, and heading to death row."

"Do you honestly think," Livermore said, each word chosen with deliberate care, "that I didn't know there were cameras in that house?"

It was the last thing Halliday expected to hear, but this time he kept his reaction hidden.

"They were as obvious as this one," Livermore said, tilting

his head toward the video camera over his shoulder. "Or, for that matter, your interrogation techniques."

Halliday stayed silent, waiting for him to continue.

"The first camera was mounted on the bookshelf," Livermore said, "between the legs of the wooden elephant. The second was in the bedroom, on the armoire, in the silk flowers."

Halliday kept staring into the other man's strange green eyes. Kept waiting for more.

"I *wanted* you to see me," Livermore said. "Did you enjoy the performance?"

Halliday didn't move.

"Tell me, Agent Halliday, is it strange for you now? Sitting here across from me? After such an ... intimate experience as we shared? How many times did you watch it, anyway?"

I will not react, Halliday thought. *I will not give him anything.*

"I wonder if you'd even admit to yourself," Livermore said, "that in some primal part of your brain you may have enjoyed it."

Nothing, Halliday said to himself. *I am made of stone.*

"It's all right, Agent Halliday. It'll be our secret."

Halliday waited for another few heartbeats to pass. Then he reached down to the pile on the table and slowly pushed forward the other five photographs.

Livermore was still smiling as he studied the photographs, one after another. He had to bend his whole body sideways to touch one of them. Halliday was about to take it away, but then he saw that Livermore was simply straightening it, so that all of the photographs were in a neat, straight line.

He has a meticulous, ordered mind, Halliday said to himself. *Compulsively neat. He removes the bodies, takes them to a place where he can have his time with them. Someplace where he knows he won't be seen.*

Until this time.

"Where are the other bodies?" Halliday said.

"In a special place."

Halliday watched him for another moment, then took out the pad of paper from the folder and slid it across the table, with a felt-tip marker on top. Because you never give a killer a sharp object, not even a ballpoint pen. Not even when his wrists are cuffed to a chain around his waist.

"Write it down," Halliday said. "The exact location of this *special place.*"

Livermore looked at the pad for a moment, as if actually considering it. Then he tilted his body sideways again, took the marker, and wrote down two words.

Halliday leaned over the table and read the two words:

Alex McKnight.

"Is this supposed to mean something to me?"

"There is a small town in Michigan," Livermore said, "called Paradise. If you go there, you'll find this man living there. He's a retired police officer from Detroit. I would like you to bring him to me."

"Why do you want him here?"

"I understand Paradise is a very small town. He shouldn't be hard to find."

"If this is some kind of game, I'm not going to play it."

"I think you will," Livermore said.

"Why?"

"Because Alex McKnight is the only person I'll talk to."

Halliday sat there, watching the man. Waiting for more.

When it didn't come, he stood up and started to gather the photographs and put them back in the folder.

Livermore wrote two more words on the pad.

Halliday stopped dead. He read the two words. Then he stared at the man across from him. That same cold half smile stayed on Livermore's face as he dropped the marker on the table and leaned back in his chair.

"You should sit back down," Livermore said. "I don't think we're done here."

CHAPTER TWO

ALEX? IS THAT YOU?"

It was the last voice I ever thought I'd hear that night. Or any night, ever again. I was sitting at the Glasgow Inn, with a folder full of papers spread out on the bar top. A February night in the dead middle of a long winter. Jackie Connery, owner of the Glasgow Inn, was behind the bar, watching the Red Wings game on the television he'd hung from the ceiling. Vinnie LeBlanc, my closest neighbor, a member of the Bay Mills tribe, and a blackjack dealer at the casino, was sitting in one of the big overstuffed chairs by the fireplace. On most nights like this, I'd be sitting right across from him, warming my sore body after a long day of shoveling snow and chopping wood, nursing a Molson and listening to Jackie complain about driving all the way to Canada because I won't drink a fake American import.

But tonight I was sitting at the bar because I had all of these papers to look at and a stakeout date with my new partner in a couple of hours. My cell phone rang in my pocket and I took it out, expecting to hear Maureen's voice.

It was a woman, but not Maureen. It took me a moment to place the voice. That's how long it had been.

"Jeannie?"

"Yes, it's me."

I drew a blank on what to say next. I was counting up the years since I'd last talked to her, this woman I'd once been married to. I was just passing twenty years in my head when she broke the silence herself.

"I know it's been a long time," she said.

"Is everything okay?"

"Yes," she said. "It's…"

There was a long pause. I wasn't even sure if she was still on the line. The cell phone signal up here in the Upper Peninsula is always a crapshoot.

"It's good to hear your voice," she finally said. "I hope you've been well."

"Where are you living now?"

"I'm back in Grand Rapids. In my parents' house. How about you?"

"You remember those cabins my father built?"

"Up in Paradise?"

"That's where I am."

I had come up here a year after I had left the Detroit Police Department, just after Jeannie had left me. The most remote place I could find, maybe eight hundred full-time residents in this little town on the shores of Lake Superior, a good five-hour drive from Detroit. My stated reason was to sell off the cabins my father had built along an old logging road, just north of the one blinking light in town. The real reason was that I wanted to get away from everything else in the world, and I was wondering if Paradise would be the place to do it.

I'd been living here ever since.

"Listen," she said, "I know this is out of the blue, but there's a reason I'm calling you... You remember my grandmother?"

"I think so."

"She died, Alex. And she left some things... to both of us. You remember that place she had on the lake?"

As far as I could remember, I'd only been there once, right after we got married. I had a dim memory of a little house on an inland lake, maybe an hour north of Grand Rapids. The place had seemed like it was just about ready to fall down back then. Unless somebody had renovated it, I couldn't even imagine what it would look like now.

"Plus that old car she had, the big white Cadillac. Everything in the house. And some money. Not a whole lot... But it was everything she had."

"I don't understand. She left it for *us*?"

"Yes, to both of us. I don't know if she was just confused about the, um..."

She didn't have to say the word. The divorce. It was the only contact I ever had with her, after she had left. Those papers from her lawyer that had come in the mail. *Please sign and return.* Then it was done.

"Or I don't know," Jeannie said. "She was pretty sharp, right up to the end. Maybe she just had this naïve belief that it would be enough to get us back together."

"I'm sorry to hear about your grandmother," I said, trying hard to remember the old woman's face from the wedding. "But whatever you want to do with that house, and everything else… Just send me the papers and I'll sign whatever I need to. That stuff belongs to you."

"Gee, thanks," she said, and then she laughed. "That Cadillac is just what I need to drive to work."

Even after all of these years, it felt good to hear her laughing. When she stopped, there was a long silence.

"I have one more thing to tell you," she said. "It's something I should have said a long time ago…"

I waited.

"I never told you how sorry I was, Alex. All these years, I never got the chance to say it."

"It's all right, Jeannie. I know I didn't make it easy."

"That night you and Franklin both got shot," she said. "I remember being in the hospital, seeing you in that bed with all those tubes in your body… Not knowing if you'd ever open your eyes again. And then when I found out that Franklin was already dead… I just didn't know how to handle it, Alex. I walked away and I didn't even say good-bye. And I've never forgiven myself for that."

"I don't blame you for leaving," I said. "I let it go a long time ago. You should, too."

"Okay," she said. "I'll try."

There was another awkward silence, until she finally thanked me and said good-bye. I sat there on the barstool and looked at my phone, thinking about all the other things I should have asked her. This woman I once thought I'd spend the rest of my life with.

"Alex," Vinnie said from behind me, "what's going on?"

I turned and looked at him. Then at Jackie, who had stopped washing glasses and was watching me just as intently.

"That," I said, "was a phone call from another life."

I was still thinking about it as I left the Glasgow and got in my truck. It was twenty degrees, with two feet of snow on the ground and more on the way. I had just enough time to pick up Maureen and head over to Pickford, where we were hoping to find our man, a twice-convicted drug dealer who never showed up for his third court date in Iron Mountain. It was my latest case in my new job as a "fugitive recovery agent" for Superior Bail Bonds out of Marquette, a job that my former partner, Leon Prudell, once held—until he came home from one case with a knife wound. That was all his wife, Eleanor, needed to see. Now Leon was back working the copper kettles at the Soo Brewing Company full-time, and for some reason I had agreed to give the job a try in his place. It was a way to break up the long winter months, and I didn't have a wife waiting at home, worrying about me.

For liability reasons, Superior didn't let its agents carry firearms when recovering fugitives. As much as getting shot as a cop had put me off guns for the rest of my life, I still wasn't sure what to make of doing this job unarmed, especially when the fugitives weren't playing by the same rules. But tonight I was working with Maureen. She was a pro, and she really knew how to work the wives and girlfriends of the men we were tracking.

With a pair of handcuffs in my pocket, and no gun, I headed out into the cold Upper Peninsula night.

AGENT HALLIDAY watched his breath in the air, trying to remember if he'd ever felt air so cold it actually *hurt* to breathe it. After seven hours on a plane, they were walking down the stairs, onto the tarmac. The pilot told them he'd de-ice the wings and keep everything ready to go.

They walked into the one-room Chippewa County International Airport, skipped the waiting room, and went right to the parking lot. The rental agent was waiting next to the black Jeep Cherokee, which was already running. They verified the directions to a town called Pickford, and then they were on the road.

It was fewer than twenty miles. Cook was driving, and Halliday could tell he'd never driven on ice before.

"You get us killed before we even get there," Halliday said, "that would not be a productive evening."

Cook shook his head and kept driving.

When they arrived in Pickford, they found two roads and a traffic light. A few buildings and wide-open fields with snow blowing across the road. Halliday had already contacted the owner of the Superior Bail Bonds company, Alex McKnight's current employer, and had made two things clear: he needed McKnight's location, and he needed the owner *not* to warn McKnight they were coming.

"What else do we know about this guy?" Cook said.

"He was a cop in Detroit for eight years. Got shot on the job, came up here a year later. Rents out some cabins. He was a private investigator for a while…"

Cook looked over at him.

"Now he's a bounty hunter," Halliday said. "Excuse me, a fugitive recovery agent."

"Will he be armed?"

"According to his boss, no. But that's no guarantee."

Halliday checked his own weapon. He was one of the few agents still allowed to carry the old nine-millimeter Sig-Sauer P228, the same gun he swore he'd retire with.

"And as far as we know," Cook said, "McKnight has no connection to Livermore."

Halliday holstered his gun and looked out at the snow. "*That*, partner, we're about to find out."

MAUREEN HAD ALREADY knocked on the door, told the woman who'd answered she was looking for our man, playing the "other girlfriend" angle, telling her she was about to throw all of his clothes out into the snow. She came back to the truck and told me this wouldn't take long.

Maureen was ten years younger than me. She had dirty-blond hair she kept tied behind her head, clear nail polish on rough hands, the hands of a woman who lived in the Upper Peninsula. She was a good partner, even if I didn't know much else about her yet.

"You're even less talkative than usual tonight," she said to me. We were waiting in the driveway next door to the girlfriend's house, the heater in my truck going full blast.

I was still thinking about the phone call, but I wasn't sure if I wanted to tell her about it. That's when a flash of headlights hit us both in the eyes. I put the truck in gear and lowered the plow, scraping against the asphalt as I drove forward. To who-

ever was coming down the street, I would be just another plow-
man, the UP's best winter disguise. The truck on the street was
moving fast.

I felt the familiar rush of adrenaline, no different now than
on my first day as a Detroit cop. Maureen had her cuffs in one
hand, the other hand ready to open her door. If this went well,
we'd take him right there in the girlfriend's driveway, before he
even made it into the house. If it went badly, we could always
hook his cuffs to the back of my truck bed, take him to the
Chippewa County Jail, and see how frozen he was by the time
we got there.

The man's truck skidded as it slowed in the street, then
turned and finally came to a stop in the driveway next door. We
both hit the ground at the same time, covered half the distance
before the man even noticed us. It took another second for him
to process what was about to happen to him.

That's when the second vehicle arrived and blew everything up.

It was a black Jeep Cherokee, coming too fast down the icy
road and going right into a sidespin. Whoever was driving had
no idea what he was doing. When the vehicle corrected itself, it
came down the driveway we'd parked in, its headlights blinding
us. The driver hit the brakes too late, sliding across the ice and
slamming into the back bumper of my truck.

The vehicle backed up, spinning its tires and sliding sideways so that now all three of us were lit up in the headlights.

"We have a bond for your arrest!" Maureen said to our fugitive, who'd already stepped out of his truck and was now trying
to climb back inside. He kicked out at her with a booted left
foot, catching her in the stomach and sending her back into

the snow. I grabbed the door and held it open with one hand, reached in for him with the other.

That was when another man caught me from behind. I threw an elbow, pure instinct at that point, figuring it must be one of the fugitive's buddies jumping me. I felt the impact all the way up my arm, then sensed the man stumbling away from me. As I turned to face him, he had already brought out a Glock from his belt. I didn't know the exact model, but the important thing was he had it pointed right at my chest. I heard the other truck's door closing, the engine starting.

"FBI," the man with the gun said. "Do not move."

"That's a fugitive!" I said. "Stop him!"

But it was already too late. The truck spun its way back out of the driveway, the tires whining against the ice as it slid back onto the road. I caught sight of him behind the wheel, for one perfect split second, as he gave me the middle finger and then flipped the truck into drive and tore away.

"What the hell's the matter with you?" I said. A black man with a smooth, shaved head, he still had the gun leveled at me, so I made a point of keeping both hands where he could see them. Maureen was up on one knee now, catching her breath and brushing herself off. Another man appeared behind her, white and much older than the one who'd grabbed me. I noticed for the first time that the two men were dressed in identical windbreakers.

"You just let a drug dealer get away," Maureen said, pushing away the older man's hand when he tried to help her up. "Who are you guys?"

"We're looking for Alex McKnight," the older man said.

I looked back and forth between them. They were both

shivering in their windbreakers, comically underweight for a UP winter.

"What the hell is going on here?" I said. "Put that gun away."

The older agent came close to me. As he looked me in the eye, I knew exactly what he was doing, because I'd done it myself as a cop, more times than I could count. He wanted to see my immediate reaction to whatever he said next.

"We need to talk to you," he said. "About a man named Martin T. Livermore."

"Is that name supposed to mean something to me?"

"That's what we're here to find out."

He kept looking me in the eye until he nodded his head and put a hand on my back. "We'll talk about it on the plane," he said. "Let's go."

I pushed his arm away. "My partner and I are working here. You can talk to me tomorrow."

"I've got this," Maureen said. "Just go with them."

"I'm not going anywhere."

"This is not a request," the older agent said.

"Am I under arrest?"

"No," he said. "You are a person of interest."

That's not something you want to hear an FBI agent tell you, I thought. *If I were sensible, now would be a great time to keep my mouth shut.*

"I thought I was done with this a long time ago," I said, taking my usual pass on *sensible*. "Feebs messing up my whole life."

"Shut up and go with them," Maureen said. "Call me if you need me."

I took a long breath and watched it condense in the cold air.

"We've wasted enough time," the younger agent said. He had

put his gun away, and by now there was a thin line of blood running from his nose. I didn't bother to apologize to him.

"Just go," Maureen said.

I shook my head and then finally got in the backseat of their vehicle. The younger agent got behind the wheel, spun the tires as he backed out of the driveway, and then took me away.

CHAPTER THREE

'D SEEN THE FACES of killers before. But never this face. Not until this moment, sitting on the plane.

"This is his mug shot," Agent Halliday said, putting the photograph on my tray table. "Taken less than twenty-four hours ago."

We had just lifted off in a small commuter jet, which had been waiting on the runway at the Chippewa County airport. There were no official FBI markings on the plane. There was probably an elaborate cover story behind that, unmarked planes the FBI used in special circumstances, but I didn't bother asking because I knew I wouldn't get an answer.

Halliday sat in the window seat. I was on the aisle. Across the aisle was Agent Cook. The airplane was still climbing in altitude, riding the rough air over the half-frozen lake. The photograph shifted back and forth on the tray table, until I finally put my hand on it to keep it in place.

I was still catching up to everything that had happened. Still trying to understand how this night had somehow led to me sitting here on this airplane with two FBI agents, and no idea where we were even going.

"Take your time," Halliday said. "It could be years since the last time you saw him."

I looked carefully at the man's face. He had close-set eyes, intense and focused, even here while holding a mug-shot board with his own name spelled out in white plastic letters. His head was slightly tilted, and there was a half smile on his face.

"No," I said. "I don't know this man."

"I said take your time."

I kept looking. He was about my age. Long hair combed back. Clean-shaven. There was an intensity in his eyes that maybe I wouldn't have noticed at first glance. On closer examination, I could see that he was a smart, focused man. The kind of man you'd expect to be successful at *something*.

"A man can remember ten thousand faces," Halliday said. "A woman, possibly more. If this man was significant in your life in any way..."

"This face means nothing to me."

"You were a cop for eight years," Halliday said. "Is it possible that—"

"Did he ever live in Detroit?"

"We can't put him in Detroit, no. He definitely has no arrest record there."

"Then I don't know what to tell you."

"The man who shot you..." Halliday said. "We don't see any connection with Livermore, but—"

"He was a crazy fuck who lived by himself," I said. "He wasn't connected to anybody."

Halliday left the mug shot on my tray table. He put another photograph on top of it. A young woman. "This was his first victim," he said. "Three years ago, in California."

I shook my head. It was another face that meant nothing to me.

"A second woman in California," he said, putting another photograph over the first.

I shook my head again. He showed me three more.

Utah.

Nevada.

Arizona.

All young women.

Women I'd never seen before.

He put down the sixth photograph. "Arizona again," he said. "Phoenix. Just a few days ago. Her name was Carolyn Kline."

"He abducted every one of these women," Cook said. "Tortured them. Then killed them. None of the bodies were ever found, until this one."

"He's a highly organized, highly sophisticated sociopath," Halliday said. "We don't know his exact methodology yet, but he's clearly very good at manipulating people. I sat in a room with him twelve hours ago."

I picked up all of the photographs, one by one, and looked at them again. Six faces of women who'd suffered and died, and then finally the one face who was responsible for all of it.

Martin T. Livermore.

A stranger.

"I'm going to make this question as simple as I can," I said. "What does any of this have to do with me?"

"He asked for you," Halliday said. "By name."

I let the words wash over me, trying to absorb their meaning but utterly failing.

"He says you're the only person he'll talk to."

"That makes no sense," I said. "Why would he want *me*?"

"That's a good question."

The two agents stayed silent for a while. I knew exactly what they were doing, because I had done it myself a thousand times. This was the exact right moment to wait. To let the silence build.

I picked up the mug shot, holding it closer.

I looked at the man's eyes one more time.

Nothing.

Absolutely nothing.

"I don't know what to tell you," I said.

"So then *what*," Cook said, "he just picked your name out of nowhere?"

"I have no idea."

He stared back at me, looking for the lie behind my eyes.

I wasn't lying.

Halliday put one more photograph on top of the pile. It was yet another attractive young woman, late twenties. This was more of a candid shot, taken at a party, the woman with a plastic cup in her hand, her other arm around another woman. A little silver ring in her eyebrow, and a big smile.

"Who is this?" I said.

"Her name is Stephanie Hyatt," Halliday said.

I shook my head. Another face I'd never seen before. "Is she the latest victim?"

Halliday watched me carefully as he composed his answer. I'd already figured out the dynamic between these two agents— Halliday was the one with the experience and the even temper.

Cook had the raw energy, and he could obviously play the bad cop when it was needed. But now, as the overhead light painted every line in Halliday's face, he looked even older than I had first thought. Too old to be flying across the country and freezing his ass off in Michigan. Maybe too old to be doing this job at all.

"He claims to have met her two days ago," Halliday said. "I was not inclined to believe him, because it doesn't fit the pattern. He abducts one woman at a time, then he waits, sometimes for *months*, until he moves on to his next victim."

"So why do you—"

"He had details," Halliday said. "Knew she was from Mesa. Knew she had a tattoo on her left shoulder blade. It all checked out. She was last seen two days ago."

"I don't mean to be insensitive," I said. "But you just told me most of those other bodies haven't been recovered, either. How is this one different?"

Neither man said anything. I looked back and forth between them, saw them exchanging something without words. Some horrible truth that they both shared. Another moment passed, and then it came to me.

The one good reason they'd fly two thousand miles across the country to find me.

"Are you telling me…" I said.

"Yes," Halliday said. "We have reason to believe she's still alive."

CHAPTER FOUR

WHEN THE METAL DETECTOR went off, three different men drew their weapons on me. I froze and waited for them to pat me down. As if I'd actually be stupid enough to bring a gun into the jail. When they brought out the wand, it beeped when they waved it over my chest. That meant another pat-down, and eventually I ended up having to open my shirt and show them the scars.

"Twenty-two caliber slug," I said. "Next to my heart."

"You didn't set off the detector at the airport," Cook said from behind me.

"Airport detectors are set at a different level," I said. "This one's obviously cranked up to eleven, all right?"

We were in the Maricopa County Fourth Avenue Jail, where they'd driven me directly from the airport. It was early morning. The air was seventy degrees warmer than what I'd left behind in Michigan, even if I'd only felt it for the few yards between the airport and the car, and then the car and the jail.

I'd been surprised when we pulled up in front of the place, because you think of a jail as a place for drunk drivers to sleep it off, or for strung-out petty thieves to spend a week or two in holding cells, waiting for their trials because they can't scrape up the bail money. Not for one of the most notorious serial killers in recent history. But then two things hit me:

One, Martin T. Livermore—even though he was implicated in the murders of six women, and in the abduction of a seventh— was still officially an unconvicted suspect. That status would end about two seconds after his guilty verdicts were read in open court, but not before.

And two, this was Maricopa County, Arizona. So when it came to anything having to do with the apprehension and housing of criminals, right down to the county jail, these good folks did not fuck around.

As we got out of the car, I could see that the jail took up an entire city block, a hulking redbrick presence among the courthouses and other government buildings. There was a column of glass running four stories above the main entrance. The rest of the walls were broken only by the few thin slits that barely qualified as windows. It was as if the architect wanted to make sure anyone going into the place knew to leave all hope of ever seeing daylight again outside on the sidewalk.

"This is the most secure facility in the county system," Halliday had said as he'd closed the car door behind him. "The high-security floor is a vault."

We had come inside and met a half dozen of the detention officers who worked here. They all looked a little too amped up to me. But then here were two Feds, bringing in this civilian, this *stranger*, right into the heart of their facility, to ride in their elevator all the way up to their most secure floor, to interview a serial killer. So I couldn't blame them for being a little on edge.

Of all the men waiting for us, the warden was the one in the suit and the bolo tie. "This is my jail," he said to all three of us, after he'd shaken every hand. "I make the rules. I'll be watching on the other side of the window at all times. Nobody will make any physical contact with the suspect. No objects will be passed to him. Do we all understand?"

He looked each of us in the eye, one by one, until he was satisfied. Then I was led through the metal detector first, and that was when everything went sideways. It looked like they were going to drag me all the way out here from Michigan just to let three Maricopa County detention officers gun me down in the lobby.

But when the sidearms were finally put away and I had buttoned up my shirt, the warden took us to the elevator, put his special key in the control panel, and took us up to the top floor. He led us down another long hall. Everything was clean and functional and harshly lit. Like any jail, anywhere in the country, and yet everything felt different here. Even in the air itself, this sense that something big was about to happen, something that everyone involved would remember for the rest of their lives.

This is why you become a cop, I thought. *Or an agent. Or a guard or a warden, whatever you need to become to be a part of something like this. Whether you admit it to yourself or not.*

When we got to the interview room, Agent Halliday told his partner to wait with the warden on the other side of the glass. Agent Cook didn't look happy about it, but then I hadn't seen him look happy about anything, from the moment he had run into the back of my truck in Michigan.

Agent Halliday and I were led into a small intermediate room, the door clanging shut behind us. We waited there for a long moment, until we heard the buzzing sound on the second door. Halliday pushed the door open, and we walked into the empty interview room.

There was a table in the center. Two chairs on the near side, one chair on the other. A single video camera was mounted high in one corner. The red light was blinking.

Eight hours ago I was sitting in my truck, I said to myself, *freezing my ass off and watching for a petty drug dealer to show up at his girlfriend's house.*

Now I'm here.

Agent Halliday sat down. I took the chair next to him.

"Understand something," Halliday said to me. "I know you're an ex-cop. You think you know how to talk to a criminal…"

"I do."

"This man is something different."

"I'll be fine."

"I've interviewed psychopaths before," Halliday said, "but I'm still trying to understand Livermore. You're here because he asked for you. We want to know why. Let him go in that direction, but don't let him draw you in too deep."

"Just bring him in here," I said, feeling like I'd already waited too long for this. All of the confusion, all of the disorientation, it had been burned away on the long journey to reach this place. This moment. Now I just wanted to see this man face-to-face.

Another long minute passed. I heard the outer door opening,

then the buzzing of the inner door. When it opened, I heard the rattling of chains. Halliday and I stood up at once, like some dignitary was entering the room. By the time I turned around, he was already through the doorway.

Martin T. Livermore.

He was wearing an orange jumpsuit. His hands were cuffed and attached to a chain around his waist, so his hands were effectively pinned to his sides. Legs shackled. He was my height, a little leaner. Long hair tied neatly behind his head. Smooth skin, even with a little stubble around his chin, everything about him perfectly composed, like he'd spent the last hour carefully grooming himself for an important appointment, instead of sitting by himself in an eight-by-ten jail cell, waiting to be interrogated.

I kept looking at him, waiting for a bell to go off in my mind. Some hint of recognition. But my mind remained silent. I *knew* I had never seen him before, for the simple reason that having this man's intense green eyes on me was something I would never be able to forget.

I'd met plenty of killers before. I could remember running down at least two of them myself, literally chasing them and tackling them to the ground, putting on the handcuffs—*hooking* them, as we used to say in Detroit—and then dragging them back to my car.

But this man... Thirty seconds in the room with him and I was already starting to wonder if maybe Halliday was right. Maybe this was another kind of man entirely, something I'd never seen before.

There were two guards with him, two men who obviously spent every free hour in the gym, the sleeves of their uniforms pulled tight over their biceps. They looked just as amped as everyone else in the building. Probably making double overtime and drinking in every second so they could tell the story at the bar.

"You can leave him here with us," Halliday said to the guards.

"That's not happening," one of them said. "We stay with him."

"There's no danger," Halliday said. "He's chained up. There are two other men outside watching us, including your warden."

"We stay with him," the guard said, sneaking a look at the one-way glass. He'd obviously been given an order, and he wasn't even going to *think* about breaking it. "That's nonnegotiable."

Livermore had been watching the exchange with a slight smile on his face. He sat down on the other side of the table while the guards took their positions directly behind him. He didn't look comfortable—that would have been physically impossible—but he did his best to lean back in his chair as he kept looking at me. I'd sat across from five thousand men in interview rooms just like this one, and four thousand nine hundred ninety-nine of them had let their eyes wander to the ceiling, or had stared down at their own hands.

This was the first man who looked me square in the eye. Like he would somehow be the one leading this interview.

"Alex McKnight," Livermore said. "You'll excuse me for not shaking hands."

"Why am I here?" I said.

"Do you feel it? The gravity of this moment? The two of us finally sitting in the same room together?" He seemed to pick each word carefully, as if lifting it from a case lined in black felt.

I didn't answer him.

"Your whole life," he said, "has been leading to this moment."

His eyes remained locked on mine. The other men in the room didn't exist.

"What are you talking about?" I said.

"You and I are connected, Alex. Like two atomic particles hurtling in independent orbits. Until the inevitable day when they collide and everything changes."

"You're out of your mind."

"Everything I'm saying is quite lucid," Livermore said, and in that moment I saw a flash of something in his eyes. Something between impatience and outright anger. "Lucid and accurate. Our connection is real, Alex. It has shape, it has substance. A past and a future. You just haven't seen it yet."

"The only thing I see," I said, remembering what Halliday had told me on the plane, "is a lunatic who kills women and has sex with their dead bodies."

"I knew you'd say something like that. Eventually."

"You don't know a goddamned thing about me, Livermore."

I felt Halliday's hand on my back. I ignored it.

Livermore leaned forward and smiled at me.

"Four years in the minor leagues," he said. "Never made it to the show. Your strikeouts-to-walks ratio was never good enough. A classic case of overprotecting the plate, which I suppose says something about your personality. Your best batting average was .249."

That's when the room started to tilt. I could feel the other three men watching me. Agent Halliday, the two detention officers, measuring those words, watching for my reaction. A batting average is a hard number. It's right or it's wrong.

Livermore had it right.

"Eight years as a police officer in Detroit," he went on. "You and your partner answered a call one night. An emotionally disturbed individual, who ended up shooting both of you. Your partner died. You survived. They took out two slugs, left one in your chest."

He kept watching me, studying me like I was an open book to him, like he could see everything I'd ever done.

"You've been living with that night ever since," he said. "A cop's greatest failure, letting his partner get killed. Unfortunately for young Officer Franklin and his family, you couldn't protect your partner as well as you protected the plate."

I tightened my grip on the edge of the table. My partner's name on this man's lips... It was an obscenity.

"All right," Halliday said, "that's enough."

"You were married for nine years," Livermore said, ignoring him. "Your wife left you after you were shot. You ran away from what was left of your life, and you've been hiding in a little cabin on the edge of the world."

I came two thousand miles, I thought, *to have my whole life laid out on this table.*

By this psychopath I've never met before.

"You hunt bail jumpers now. You pretend that this matters, even though you're no better than a janitor, collecting human refuse. Tracking down petty drug dealers who'll be replaced the next day. It's such a pale imitation of what you once were, Alex. Being a police officer may not be much, but at least you were *something* then. You were a man who could actually change things in the world."

I didn't move. I kept staring into his eyes.

"Look at your hands, Alex. You chop wood, and you shovel snow. You have no other purpose now. And a man with no purpose is hardly a man at all."

He waited for me to look down at my hands. I didn't move my eyes.

"You should be thanking me," he said. "I am giving you a great gift today."

He's trying to get under my skin, I thought. *I'm not going to let that happen.*

"As much as you might deny it," he said, "there is some essential part of you that is *excited* to be here with me."

"We brought him here like you asked," Halliday said. "Now tell us where Stephanie Hyatt is."

Livermore's eyes flashed again, like he was annoyed by the interruption to his little soliloquy about my worthless life. But then a half second later, his composure had returned.

"I was clear on this point," he said. "I will take Alex to her."

"You're not taking him anywhere," Halliday said. "You're dealing with me now."

"As of this moment, she has been tied up for seventy-two hours. I was careful not to constrict her circulation, but after so many hours in one position, it becomes unavoidable. The pain at this point must be unimaginable."

The words hung in the air. I could sense the tension building in Agent Halliday's body. Even the two guards were looking down on the back of Livermore's head like they wouldn't mind choking him right here in the interview room.

"She's out of water by now," Livermore went on. "I left her one container, with a straw. That means she's already gone through several stages of extreme thirst. Her muscles are cramping, which adds to the pain. Her tongue is swelling. If she tries to cry out for help, she'll barely make a sound."

He paused for a moment, gauging my reaction. I stared back at him without giving him anything at all.

"She'll soon have a severe headache," Livermore said, "as her brain literally begins to shrink inside her head. She'll have hallucinations. Then seizures. Her vital organs will shut down, one by one."

He regarded everyone in the room, even the guards behind him, with an imperious look on his face, like a military officer reviewing his troops and finding them lacking. Finally, he settled on Halliday.

"She is alone, Agent Halliday. Alone and scared. She knows she's been abandoned, and that she will soon die. And the saddest part of all . . ."

His eyes left Halliday and came back to me.

"She can't even cry about it," he said. "Because there is no water left in her body to make tears."

In that moment, I wanted nothing more than to go over the table. I would have done anything to him, would have waterboarded him, would have driven nails into his hands, whatever it took to make him tell us where this woman was.

"There is still hope for her," Livermore said to me. "These men all want to find her, but they have no idea how. You are the key."

"What do you think's going to happen here?" Halliday said. "We're going to open up the front door and let you out?"

"I understand you'll need to have a number of men involved," Livermore said. "As long as Alex is one of them."

"How many more men would you need?" I asked Halliday.

"Alex, we have to talk about this."

"How many?"

"My partner and I," he said. "The jail will want two men, three if you include a driver. The state police..."

"You already have a plan," I said. "In case you decided this was real."

He hesitated. "Yes."

But something still didn't feel right to me. I would have gotten my gold shield if I had stayed on the force, and if I had, my instincts would have guided me for the rest of my career. Serial killer, psychopath, it wouldn't have mattered. It all would have come down to one question.

Is he telling the truth?

I leaned forward across the table, so close it startled the guards behind him. He kept looking me in the eye, without moving a muscle.

"I don't think this woman is alive," I said.

He smiled. "Are you willing to take that chance?"

Halliday stood up and tried to grab me by the shoulder. I pushed him away. It was becoming a bad habit, physically resisting a federal agent, but at that point I didn't care anymore.

"Livermore," I said, "what the hell do I have to do with any of this?"

"I know I'm not answering your questions," Livermore said to me. "But that's not why I brought you here. You just have to play your part, Alex. You don't have to know how it ends."

"It ends with you strapped to a table," I said. "You know that, right?"

"I think we're done," he said with another smile. "For now."

He startled the guards again when he stood up. Each man

grabbed one of his arms. A pained look crossed Livermore's face, like this was just one more annoyance. He looked nothing like a man who'd have to start accepting treatment like this for the rest of his life. As the guards pushed him toward the door, he stopped just long enough to meet my eyes one more time.

He nodded to me, gave me one last half smile. Then he walked out the door.

CHAPTER FIVE

WE NEED TO BE ready for anything," Agent Halliday said. "I don't want any surprises."

"What the hell's he going to do?" Agent Cook said. "His arms and legs will be chained. With seven armed men watching him."

He had left me out of the equation, the eighth man along for the ride, but I wasn't going to say anything about it. One hour had passed since the jailhouse interview. One hour of me replaying everything Livermore had said to me, trying to make it all add up into some kind of sense. But it still wasn't coming together.

I shouldn't be here, I said to myself. *I should be back home in Paradise, plowing snow.*

But if there really is a woman out there somewhere…

We were all in the FBI sedan, with me in the backseat again. Cook was driving, Halliday was riding shotgun. We'd been up for almost thirty hours straight by now. I could see it weighing heavy on Halliday as he turned to look at me.

"Alex," he said, "I want you to be ready for an audible."

"What are you talking about?"

"You're the X factor here," he said. "These other men don't know you."

You don't know me, either, I thought. But I let it go. If I were in their shoes, I'd be just as mystified by this stranger from Michigan, who didn't seem to know anything about Livermore, even though he could sit there and recite my batting average.

But still, what would the plan be? Cook was right—with Livermore's hands cuffed and chained to his belt . . . In their wildest imagination, how did they think one stranger could change that equation?

"Everything's covered," Cook said to his partner. "He'll be tied up like a Christmas turkey."

Halliday shook his head and looked out the passenger's-side window as the city of Phoenix passed by. I could feel the nervous energy coming off of him in waves, even if his partner didn't share it. I knew the feeling, despite every reason not to, because I had it myself. Something about this whole setup didn't feel right to me, and the feeling got stronger with each passing mile.

"Where are we going?" I finally said. "Unless that's classified information . . ."

"Little mining town called Bagdad," Halliday said. "Up in Yavapai County, about two and a half hours away. DPS is going to run the first vehicle, then Livermore will be in a prison van behind that, with two guards. We'll follow behind."

"Who's DPS?"

"Department of Public Safety. That's the state police here."

I nodded and sat back in my seat. We seemed to be alone on

the road, but I knew the other vehicles were probably up ahead somewhere.

"There's only one road up here," Halliday said a few minutes later. "US 93. That's got everybody a little nervous."

"Livermore's a loner," Cook said. "Can you really see him with a crew of men up here waiting to ambush us?"

"No," Halliday said. "I can't see that."

It looked like he wanted to say more, but he kept it to himself.

"There they are," Cook said as the prison van came into view. Ahead of that, I saw the state police car with its lights flashing. We settled in at the tail end of the parade just as we were leaving Phoenix, heading through Glendale, Surprise, and Sun City West. Heading northwest, out into the great nothingness of central Arizona. The road itself was a straight line drawn on a flat plain, with railroad tracks to the right and telephone wires to the left. Beyond those, as far as I could see in any direction, it was nothing but brown earth covered by a thin layer of green and gray vegetation. Low mountains in the far distance and a bright blue sky above us. The view didn't change for an hour.

By the end of the second hour, the vegetation was growing thicker, the mountains coming closer with each passing mile. We were in a valley between the Poachie Range to the west and the Santa Marias to the east. There were great piles of red rocks on either side of the road. A voice broke through on the radio.

"Lead to Halliday and Cook. Are we sure this road is secure?"

Halliday looked over at his partner for a moment, then picked up the mic and keyed it.

"We had an advance team sweep through here a few minutes ago," he said, looking out the window. "Nothing up there but rocks."

But as he put the mic back, I could see him staring out the window, like we'd suddenly been transported to Afghanistan. Even Agent Cook, the man who'd been playing it cool all the way up here, hunched forward at the wheel to look out at the road.

All because of one man riding in that van ahead of us, I thought, *sitting between two guards and tied up, as Agent Cook had said, like a Christmas turkey.*

A few minutes later, just as we got to the turnoff for Bagdad, the same voice broke over the radio.

"Stopping ahead. Pull in behind us."

We made the turn and saw the other two vehicles pulled over to the side of the road. Cook stopped behind them and got out. The two state troopers from the lead car were standing behind the prison van, next to the van driver, and now Cook joined the conference and they stood around talking about something for a few minutes, before Cook finally gave me a wave to get out.

Halliday got out with me. It was coming up on noon now, the morning sun warming up the day, well into the eighties. I held up a hand against the glare. As I came closer to the party, I could feel the two troopers watching me carefully, measuring everything about me.

Halliday told me to wait a few yards away while he went to confer with the others. Every single man kept looking back at me until Halliday shook his head and came back to give me the news:

"They want you in the van."

"You're kidding me, right?"

"As of now, it's not our show anymore. The state guys, the jail guys, they all want you to be safe as we get close."

"*Safe*," I said, "as in locked up like a criminal."

This is the "audible" he was talking about, I thought. But before he could say anything else, I left him there and approached the rest of the party.

"Go ahead," I said. "Put me in the van if that's what you need to do."

"Those are the orders," the van driver said.

When he opened the back door, I could see Livermore through the wire mesh. He was sitting on one of the side benches, with the same two guards who had stood behind him in the interview room early this morning. His own personal attachment.

"Got some company," the van driver said as he unlocked the inner door.

The two troopers stepped up to me then. First they asked for my cell phone, promising to give it back when this whole thing was over. I took it out and handed it to them. Then they asked me to put my hands on the side of the van before going inside.

"This gets better and better," I said, but it was clear we'd all just stand out there in the sun until I let them frisk me.

It's not enough they drag me all the way out here and treat me like a goddamned suspect every step of the way...

"For all we know," one of the officers said, "you could be working with this guy."

"Doing what?" I said. "What the hell could I do?"

The officer didn't say another word. He waited for me to assume the position, and then he gave me a thorough pat-down. He nodded to the van driver, and I was allowed the courtesy of climbing up into the van.

When I sat down across from Livermore, he looked at me

and smiled. He was in the same jailhouse orange, with the same cuffs, chains, and shackles.

"This is an unexpected pleasure," he said.

"Just shut up," one of the guards said. They were both unarmed. Standard protocol. You didn't want any weapon inside the van that could be taken away and used against you.

The van started moving again. I could hear the voice of the van driver through the metal partition as he communicated with the rest of the convoy. Livermore kept watching me, that same smile on his face. I stared right back at him. I wasn't about to look away.

"We'll take a right turn soon," Livermore said without taking his eyes away from mine.

The van driver relayed this to the other vehicles. A few minutes later, we came to a brief stop, then we made a slow turn and started going downward. There were no windows to see out of, but I could tell from the rough ride that we were on a dirt road.

"Where the hell are we going?" I heard the van driver say into his radio.

Halliday's voice came back. *"Keep going. Nice and slow."*

Livermore kept watching me. "The Japanese have a saying," he said. *"Ame futte chi katamaru.* Literally, it means, 'After the rain, the earth hardens.'"

"I told you to shut up," the guard said.

"What it really means," Livermore said, "is that you and I are both going to find out just how *hardened* you really are."

"We're in the goddamned desert," I said. "I don't think it's going to rain today."

"Alex..." he said, and then he paused before saying the five words that would become burned into my mind. "You think this ends *today*?"

The guard to Livermore's left leaned forward and looked at both of us. "Everybody," he said, *"shut the fuck up right now."*

Livermore stopped talking, but he kept smiling at me, and the vague feeling I'd had all morning started to take on its own color and shape. *This man is running the whole show,* I said to myself. *Even though he's locked up tight, guarded by seven men...*

Livermore is calling every shot.

The van came to a stop. A few seconds later, the back door opened. I was told to get out first. As I did, I saw that all three vehicles were parked where the road ended in a cul-de-sac, and a few yards beyond that there was an old mining shed that looked like it had been left for decades and forgotten about. More red rock was piled high all around us. The sun was almost directly overhead now. It beat down on us in that dead-end bowl, as the dust from the vehicles' braking hung in the air.

When the guards finally led out Livermore, he stood there blinking in the sunlight. The whole thing should have looked ridiculous to me—the two state guys with their tactical vests and their shotguns, the three guards from the jail and the two agents from the FBI. All to watch over this one man in orange with his hands cuffed to his belt.

But no matter how chained-up Livermore looked... no matter how many men were surrounding him . . . no matter how many guns...

"Where is the air support?" Livermore said as if reading my mind. "You only have eight men here. Surely you need a helicopter..."

"Where's the woman?" Halliday said. "In that shed?"

"Down this trail," Livermore said. "She's not far."

"This is not believable," Halliday said to him. "You drove her all the way down this dead-end road and then what, you made her walk down the trail with you?"

"She was tied up, Agent Halliday. I carried her."

"How far can you carry an adult woman, Livermore?"

Livermore looked at him with that little half smile. I'm sure Halliday hated it by now, maybe even as much as I did.

"I'm stronger than you think," he said.

Agent Cook came up close to him. "Just show us where you took her, you sick fuck."

"That's why we're here."

He led us toward the shed. As we got closer, a narrow trail appeared, leading through a break in the red rock.

I took Halliday aside. It was time to say something to the one man who I knew would listen to me.

"I've got a bad feeling about this," I said. "I think you do, too."

"What do you think's going to happen?"

"I don't know," I said, looking down the narrow path. "But you're doing everything according to his playbook. He got you to fly me all the way across the country. Now he's got all of us stumbling around out here in the middle of the desert…"

"So what do you want us to do? Just leave her out here?"

"There's nobody here to find," I said. "Think about it. What's he getting out of this? Did you take the death penalty off the table? Promise him he wouldn't go into general population?"

"I don't know what's driving him. Maybe he's just *that fucking crazy*, Alex. But if there's *any* chance she's out here…"

He looked over at Livermore. This one man in orange, his legs so hobbled he could barely walk.

"What if this was your daughter?" Halliday said. "Or your wife?"

I knew there was no answer that would satisfy him. That was the ultimate trump card. Then Halliday took out his semi-automatic, as if that alone would be enough to convince me I had nothing to worry about.

"Let's go find out," he said.

I shook my head and followed him. The path squeezed through the break in the rocks, then opened up just enough to give us all a little more room to breathe. But the ground still rose on either side of the trail, more naked rock with that same scrubby green and gray vegetation, the great saguaro cactuses all lined up on the very tops of the ridges, like they were spectators looking down at us.

Or waving their arms to warn us.

We walked in silence for several minutes, making our way over the rough ground. Besides the shackles, Livermore was wearing his standard jailhouse shoes with no laces and struggling even harder than the rest of us to find his footing on the trail.

The sun was beating down on us, and I was already getting thirsty. One of the state men had a backpack, and he stopped to pass out bottles of water. I drained half of mine at once.

"Are you going to let me die of thirst?" Livermore said.

It made me remember everything he had said about what the thirst was doing to that woman's body.

"You'll get water after she does," the officer said. Then he closed up his pack and we were on our way again. The sun got hotter, and my head started to hurt again. But we kept moving forward, as the trail started rising and winding its way between taller hills with more cactuses looking down on us.

"You did *not* come this far," Halliday said. "Not in the dark."

"She's here," Livermore said, raising his head into the air as if he could smell her. "A hundred yards away."

Halliday hesitated. I could tell he was thinking hard about it. Finally, he nodded, and the line of men continued around a bend in the trail, until we found ourselves at the entrance to a small side canyon, the walls rising straight up on both sides, thirty feet high.

"She's in this canyon," Livermore said. "There's a small shelter at the end. Go ahead and look."

"You first," the van driver said, pushing Livermore ahead of him. "Move."

We followed them, each man looking up at the walls that seemed to close in on top of us. The two FBI agents were at the end of the line with me between them.

I didn't have a gun. That was the difference. I didn't have that simple, deadly arrogance I'd seen so many times before, the belief that a gun in your hand is enough to control everything around you.

The van driver took the radio from his belt and looked at it. When he turned up the volume, the white noise reverberated through the canyon. "What the fuck," the man said. "The radios are..."

He didn't finish the thought. Every man in the canyon stopped, and as Livermore turned, he caught my eye and smiled.

The next three seconds filled an eternity. With that one simple act, Livermore had shifted all of the attention to me.

Every other man was watching me now, waiting for whatever came next.

"It's time, Alex!"

Livermore's words hung in the still air of the canyon as seven different brains raced to process their meaning. I reached my own conclusion just as quickly, but it was too late.

"Wait . . ." I said, already feeling two hands grabbing my shoulders from behind. I had no chance to react as everything tilted, and I felt myself being brought down to the ground. A man's knee grinding into my back, a classic cop takedown, driving the air from my lungs as everything else in the world came apart at once.

The first explosion shook the walls around us, a sound so loud it was a piercing physical impact against my ears. As I looked up I saw the men going down in front of me, saw blood sprayed against both sides of the canyon. If there were screams, I did not hear them. The second explosion was a wave of heat and concussion. The weight shifted on my back, moving backward, as I started to push myself up, just in time for one more blinding, noiseless flash and a sudden sting in my left knee and across my left biceps. The man who had been standing in front of me seemed to turn in the air in an oddly graceful pirouette, so that I could see how his upper body had been turned into a tangled mass of blood and fabric. He hung there for a moment, a marionette held up by invisible strings. Then he fell to the ground, his lifeless face inches from mine.

Everything was still. Another eternal three seconds until I saw a figure slowly raising himself to a standing position, twenty feet ahead of me.

Livermore.

He shuffled toward me, his ankles still shackled together, until he came to an officer who was still moving on the ground. I saw the shotgun barrel being raised and pointed at Livermore, then Livermore calmly taking the gun away. He had just enough play in the handcuffs attached to his waist to get the index finger of his right hand onto the trigger. He pointed the gun back down at the man, and then there was a flash from the barrel and a dull sound like the dial tone on an old phone as the man's head was blown apart against the ground.

Livermore came to the next man, looked down at him and, seemingly satisfied with the body's condition, kept moving until he came to the next man.

You need to get up, I told myself. *You need to get out of here.*

But I couldn't move yet. I stayed there, feeling everything spin around me, until another dial tone hit my ears a fraction of a second before I felt the spray of blood on my face.

I'm next. He's going to do the same thing to me.

When I looked up, he was close to me. His eyes were locked on mine as he stopped three feet in front of me.

This is it. His will be the last face I see.

I looked him in the eye and wondered if I'd even be able to hear the gun go off. There was another flash from the barrel, another dull sound that barely registered in my ears. I let out a breath, waiting for my body to react to the gunshot. For the pain to reach my brain.

It never came.

He stood there looking down at me. Then his lips moved like he was saying something to me, but there was no sound left in the world. Then with a sudden painful pop, my ears cleared, just enough to hear what he was saying.

"I told you," he said. "This does not end today. Not for us."

I clawed my way up to my hands and knees and reached for him, but he took one step backward and my head was spinning again. I tried to breathe. When I looked back up, he had already gone down the line of dead men, taking a weapon from each. A shotgun from the other trooper. A sidearm from the van driver. I felt around for something to hit him with. A rock, a stick, anything. It was the only thought I could form in my head.

Stop him. Don't let him get away.

I reached behind me and felt something warm.

Blood. A body.

I turned and looked. It was Agent Cook. He was lying against the rock wall. His chest was soaked. I saw the blood coming in a steady stream from the hole in his neck.

When Livermore had raised that shotgun . . . When I was waiting to die . . .

He had shot Cook instead.

The agent's windbreaker was still tied around his waist. I took that off, wadded it up, and pressed it against his wound. But it was already too late. He kept looking at me, and then the light went out behind his eyes.

When I finally gave up, I turned around and saw Livermore at the far end of the canyon. He lingered there for a moment, a dark figure against the bright sunlight that gleamed from the other side.

He nodded to me, one more time.

Then he turned and disappeared.

CHAPTER SIX

I WAS SURROUNDED by death. Surrounded by blood. The sun had moved to a new angle, making the red streaks on the rocks all around me glow in the light. I tried to stand up, felt everything spinning around me, and I went down hard on my knees. I stayed there for a long time, taking one breath at a time, waiting for everything to stop turning.

The explosions were still pounding in my ears as I stared down at the dirt on the canyon floor.

Breathe in.

Breathe out.

When the spinning walls finally slowed down, then settled back into place, I looked up at the far end of the canyon, the last spot Livermore had stood before turning to leave. I put one foot on the ground to push myself up, feeling a sudden pain rip through my left knee. Blood had soaked through my pants, and I saw a half dozen small round holes in the fabric. There were three more holes in my left shirtsleeve, more blood soaking through. Whatever had been in those explosives, I'd been grazed on the left side, and somehow nowhere else.

I tried to stand up again, starting with the right leg this time. When I was finally upright, I leaned against the canyon wall for a while, testing out my left leg, slowly putting weight on it until I was sure I could walk without going back down again.

I knew Cook was dead. I checked on the other men in front of me, one by one. Livermore had destroyed them, every single man, ripped apart their bodies with the shotgun.

Right here, I thought as I came to a hole in the canyon wall. There was a metal pipe set into the rock, four inches in diameter. About five feet above the ground, the perfect height for a head-and-neck shot. The metal was blackened now and still smoking. If you set the right kind of charge in here, it would blow horizontally. And if you knew to hit the ground in time, and cover your ears...

How much time did he spend setting all of this up? How many days did it take for him to put this all together, before he was captured?

The ultimate escape plan.

I picked up the radio the van driver had dropped. It still had power, but I heard nothing but static. I went back to the trooper who had taken my cell phone, pulled it out of his pocket and checked the signal. It was just as useless.

He planned this so carefully, I thought, *not only does he trip-wire enough explosives to kill seven men, he also triggers some sort of battery-operated radio jammer.*

I stood against the wall for another minute, looking up and down the canyon, trying to see it from his point of view, trying to imagine how any man could see this place and come up with such a plan. And then pull it off so flawlessly.

Until he got to you, I said to myself. *He had that shotgun pointed right at you. All he had to do was pull the trigger.*

That was when it hit me.

Wait a minute…

I did a quick count of the dead bodies I had checked.

Where's Halliday?

I remembered him being at the back end of the line. I backtracked through the canyon to the point where it broke into a slight curve.

Halliday.

He was sitting with his back against the wall, looking at me. There was a great streak of blood across his face, more blood on his chest from injuries I could only guess at. As he raised one hand, I could see that he was missing the last two fingers.

I went down on my right knee beside him, tried the radio again. Tried my cell phone. Still nothing. The road was half an hour away.

"We have to get you out of here," I said.

He shook his head, but I wasn't going to leave him there. I went back and found another man's jacket, or what was left of it, came back and wrapped it around his hand, tying it as tight as I could. Then I went back and opened the state man's pack and looked inside. The explosives had ripped right through the bottles. I found one that had an inch of water left, came back and made Halliday drink it. I put one arm around him, holding myself steady with my other hand against the wall.

"Come on," I said. "You have to get up."

He cried out in pain as I half pulled, half pushed his body

into a standing position. He slumped forward against me and took what sounded like a man's last breath. Then he seemed to gather some kind of strength from God-knows-where, and he looked in my eyes as he leaned his head back against the wall.

"Can you walk?"

He didn't respond. But it was time to try. I guided him away from the wall, watching him take one slow step, then another. It took us a full minute to get out of the canyon, back into the sunlight. I felt it burning on the back of my neck.

We took another step. Then another. The blood dripped from his ruined hand. I lifted up his shirt for one moment, saw a hundred small holes spread across his chest and abdomen. Like mine, each hole was bleeding. But he had a hell of a lot more of them. There was no way I could stop them all.

"We're going to make it," I told him. "The road's not far."

We both knew that was a lie. But we kept going.

"Just had a grandson," he said to me. His breathing was ragged and shallow.

"Don't talk. Tell me later."

"No." He leaned against me, so hard he almost pushed us both over. "You have to tell him . . . And my daughter . . . Tell them I'm sorry. Tell them I love them."

We made it another twenty yards. Then he slid to the ground. I tried to pull him up again. He shook his head.

"You tell them," he said. He coughed up blood, and it fell from his chin, onto his neck. "Promise me."

"I will," I said to him. "I promise."

I moved over so that my body was sheltering his face from the sun. I held his wounded hand tight, trying to stop the bleeding. But his shirt was soaked with more fresh blood now. Every movement he made, it made his heart pump more blood from his body. He was struggling to breathe.

I sat with him like that for another minute. Maybe two. He looked up at me one more time and gave me something almost like a smile.

Then he died.

I laid him back on the ground and closed his eyes. I stayed there with him for a few more minutes. Then I finally got to my feet.

I made it about five steps before I had to stop and throw up in the dirt. I emptied myself until there was nothing more than a dry convulsion coiling through my body. I stood up, wiped off my mouth, and kept walking.

My head was pounding, making me dizzy enough to wonder if I was even going in the right direction. It was all rocks and dirt and scrubby little cactuses and nothing else.

I could get lost here. Make it out of that canyon alive, but then die trying to get back out to the road.

I found what I thought was the trail, but now my left knee was radiating with pain. I didn't want to lift up my pants or take off my shirt. I knew it would be just a minor version of what the explosion had done to Halliday's chest.

The sun had already started to grind me down again and turn my throat to dust. I wondered where Livermore was at that moment. Somewhere on the other side of the canyon. If he was smart enough to set up that ambush, then he was smart enough to leave himself a cache of water for his way out. Some new clothes so he could ditch the orange. Money. A cell phone with a separate battery to recharge it if it was dead. It would be so easy to hide just about anything in these rock piles. He might even have a vehicle hidden nearby, within walking distance. That was how empty it was out here.

The sun kept beating down on me with every step, making me more thirsty than I'd ever been in my life. My knee kept throbbing, and I started to get dizzy again. But I kept moving. I heard nothing but the silence of the desert and my own footsteps.

And the explosions. Still roaring in my ears.

The road finally came into view, waves of heat rising from the vehicles that were still parked there, exactly where we had left them. I went to the agents' car and tried the doors. They were locked. The van was locked. The state car was locked.

I went and found a rock the size of a softball, went back to the agents' car, and hit the driver's-side window, right in the center. It exploded into a thousand glass pebbles. I reached inside and hit the door lock, opened the door, and sat down behind the wheel. I grabbed the radio receiver and hit the transmit button.

"Code thirty, code thirty," I said, bringing back from my memory the one code you never wanted to hear on a Detroit police radio. "Seven officers down."

I let up the button and waited for an answer. The airwaves crackled.

"Please respond," I said, hitting the button one more time. "I repeat. Seven officers down."

CHAPTER SEVEN

THE RECOIL FROM the shotgun was still tingling in his hands as Livermore walked from the canyon. He could still see McKnight's face, could still feel the moment, that shotgun pointed at his chest. The power he'd felt, knowing he could end his life with one slight movement of his finger.

But of course he hadn't. It wasn't time for that yet.

Not for McKnight.

He found his pack where he had hidden it behind a thick juniper bush. The fabric was the exact color of the brown-red rocks around it. You could stand five feet away and not see it. Livermore pushed his way through the bush and pulled it out, zipped it open and took out the hacksaw that was inside. Priority number one, cut his hands free. That took a minute. Priority number two, cut the shackles on his legs, increase his mobility. Another minute. Then he was on the move. He ducked into another side canyon and took off the orange jumpsuit. Priority number three. He put on the hiking clothes—the shorts, the shirt, the boots. He put on the baseball cap and stuffed the orange jumpsuit in a plastic bag, left that behind as he looped the pack around his back and kept walking. Five minutes out of the canyon and he already looked like just another hiker, out on the trail on a perfect February day in Arizona.

Priority number four, he took out the metal bottle of water from the pack and drained it. It was warm, but his body needed hydration. He'd get fresh water soon enough.

That left priority number five.

He walked up the hill through the barren red rocks, taking a quick look behind him now and then, just to make sure McKnight wasn't following him. He saw a thin haze of smoke still rising from the canyon, this place he had taken so much care to choose, a couple miles down the trail from the end of the abandoned road, next to a mine that hadn't been used in years. He had known the explosives would still be intact, even after several days. The weather was dry, and he'd packed them just right. He had known the angles would be correct, and that he would have enough time to get himself safely onto the ground. Above all, he had known that the wiring would perform exactly as designed, and that the battery-powered jammer would activate in time to transmit on a broad spectrum of radio frequencies, temporarily overwhelming the service on any two-way radios nearby. And of course on any cell phone, because a cell phone is nothing but another kind of radio.

He kept walking. When he got to the road, he took it northeast, walking a little over a mile and a half to the old junkyard just outside of Bagdad. It was a graveyard of old vehicles, all stored out here in the dry weather for parts. He picked his way through the ancient Fords and Chevys, and the occasional piece of copper-mining equipment, until he came to the SUV on the far edge of the yard. It was pulled in between two panel trucks, so you had to know exactly where to find it. And even if you did, you'd see that it was covered with decades' worth of dust and sand. You'd walk right by and probably never give this vehicle another thought.

But Livermore found the key in the tailpipe, opened up the back hatch, and pulled out the broom. He climbed onto the top and started brushing off the sand he had poured on the vehicle himself. Then he opened the driver's-side door. It didn't look like an old vehicle once you got inside, because of course it wasn't. The thing barely had thirty thousand miles on it. A Nissan Pathfinder, from Japan, of course—a land where the designers knew enough to let robotic arms, machines that Livermore himself had helped design, build their vehicles with a care and a precision that no human being could ever match. Bought with cash, never registered, the Pathfinder had a pair of stolen Arizona plates from a vehicle that was up on blocks behind a barn, the registration tab still current, but the plates unlikely to be noticed missing anytime soon.

Livermore popped the hood, reconnected the battery, and started it up. Then he cranked the wipers to push off the last of the sand on the windshield, put the vehicle in gear, and drove out of the yard.

When he hit the road, he went south for a few miles. At that point, he could have turned west and driven to Las Vegas. That would have been three and a half hours. An obvious choice. *Too* obvious, because everybody runs to Vegas. The lights call to you from the desert. *Come and get lost here.* Anyone looking at a map would choose that as the first place to look for him—and there was really only one road to Vegas, US 93 all the way. They'd be all over it.

Flagstaff, on the other hand, was about the same distance to the east, with three different ways to get there. The superior choice for a superior mind.

So of course he wasn't going there, either.

When you have a mind that is beyond superior, you go in the last direction anyone would expect. That was why he was driving directly back toward Phoenix, but not before looping around to the east so he could come in from a new direction.

He settled in for the drive, already thinking about where he'd eat that night. Real food, after all of those hours spent in the Fourth Avenue Jail, his first and only experience having a metal tray slid through an opening in cell bars.

Livermore's pack was on the passenger's seat next to him. Inside was ten thousand dollars in cash, another change of clothes, his laptop, his cell phone with a charger, a set of ropes, and his Walther PPS semiautomatic with a box of nine-millimeter shells.

There were more supplies in the back of the vehicle, the things he'd packed several days ago. More ammunition for the pistol. More clothes. Two five-gallon cans of gasoline, sealed tight to prevent any fumes. A large plastic box filled with electronic components. Another plastic box filled with explosive material.

Because he needed to be ready for anything.

He turned on the AM radio, started scanning the dial for the news reports. An escaped fugitive is on the run, six foot two, with long, light brown hair. Armed and dangerous. A two-million-dollar reward for anyone who provides information leading to his capture.

Free less than an hour, Livermore thought, *and I'm already worth two million dollars.*

As he drove, he kept his mind busy by working through the odds. After another day, then another week of being free, of doing whatever he wanted to whomever he wanted to do it to, how high could that number go?

Finally, his mind settled on the last part of his plan. Almost an afterthought, the diversion he had set up to make sure the FBI and everyone else would stay busy looking in exactly the wrong direction.

They'd all be off chasing a ghost, leaving him alone with Alex McKnight.

CHAPTER EIGHT

As I WAITED, I kept replaying the scene in my mind. Watching those men die. Watching the blood fly against the canyon walls.

A squad car responded to my radio call, followed by more squad cars, ambulances, fire trucks, pretty much every official vehicle in central Arizona, until there wasn't room to maneuver on that road anymore. When the two FBI agents showed up, they took me from the ambulance, where someone had cut away my left pant leg and wrapped my knee, then cut away my left sleeve to do the same for my arm. The agents put me in the back of their sedan and drove me all the way back to Phoenix, that same two and a half hours down that same lonely road, never saying a word to me. Not that I felt like talking.

They took me to a hospital just off the expressway and checked me in to the emergency room. I sat there for another hour until a doctor and a nurse finally came in and looked me over. The nurse took my vitals while the doctor asked me about my ears and how much water I'd had in the past few hours. Then he unwrapped my knee and got to work on the shrapnel, taking out little round hunks of metal with a long set of tweezers and dropping them with a loud clang into a metal bowl.

He did my arm next. Three more clangs in the metal bowl. When both injuries were wrapped up with fresh bandages, they left me sitting there for another half hour, until I'd finally had enough of the place. I got up and limped out. I was expecting to see the agents in the waiting room, but they weren't there. All I saw was the usual assortment of the city's underclass, something I'd seen on a thousand different occasions back in Detroit. They came here because it was the one place that wouldn't turn them away.

When the agents finally caught up to me, I was standing in the parking lot, replaying the whole thing in my head and trying to find some way I could have made it come out different in the end. I noticed that my hands were shaking, and I almost wished I was a smoker then, so I could have a familiar ritual to calm myself down. The agents came out and found me, and one of them made the mistake of grabbing me by my wrapped-up arm, like I was some kind of fugitive trying to escape.

"I've had a bad enough day," I said to the man. "You grab me again, you'll have to shoot me."

He let go of me, but he didn't apologize. They put me in their vehicle and took me over to the FBI building on Deer Valley Road, parked me in an empty conference room, where I waited some more, until Agent Madison came in and sat across from me. He was another old-timer, same vintage as Halliday. Gray hair, dark suit, all business. He looked at me, took a long breath, then he went right to the question of the day.

"Why are you alive?"

I replayed those few seconds in my head one more time, right before the first explosion ripped through the canyon. How Livermore had stopped and turned, how he had called out to me... And then how someone had taken me to the ground.

Agent Cook. He'd been acting purely by instinct, neutralizing a perceived threat when Livermore had turned all of the attention to me.

"It was Agent Cook," I said. "He saved my life."

And then the next thought, which hit me even harder. *Livermore knew someone would take me down. All he had to do was wait for it, then go down himself.*

That was part of his plan, from the beginning. He wanted me to survive.

"Take me through it," Madison said. "Everything that happened."

I went over it as well as I could remember. Every detail, from the drive to the canyon to Livermore standing over me with the shotgun. Then leaving me there, with Halliday. Until Holliday couldn't go any farther.

"We're losing valuable time," Madison said. "He could be three hundred miles away right now, in any direction."

Basic fugitive-hunting, I thought. *Time equals distance. Keep the time line as short as possible, or you'll never catch him.*

"You have no idea where he is right now," Madison said.

"No."

"Or what he may be planning next."

"How the hell would I know that?" I said. "Why are you asking me this?"

He put both of his hands on the table. "You still can't tell us how you're connected to—"

"No," I said, doing my absolute goddamned best to stay calm. "If I had an answer, don't you think I'd give it to you?"

He sat there across the table and looked at me for a long time without saying anything.

"Agent Cook's got a couple of kids," he finally said. "Twelve and thirteen years old. He just recently transferred here. Roger, I knew a lot longer. We came up together. He and Louise…"

He stopped to clear his throat.

"Their daughter just had their first grandchild. I mean, literally, he was just born a few days ago."

"I know," I said. "He told me."

Madison took a moment to let that sink in. At some point, I'd want to deliver that message to his daughter and grandson, as I had promised. But today probably wasn't the day.

"You're staying in Phoenix for a while," Madison said. "We'll keep you at the same hotel, and I'll introduce you to the whole team, as soon as we have it together."

"How long will I be here?"

"I can't answer that right now. It's not totally up to me, anyway. There are other parties waiting to talk to you. Starting with the state police."

That wasn't a surprise. I knew I'd be answering the same questions, again and again.

"I know you were once a cop," he said, "so you know this is the worst day ever."

"Been there, yes."

My mind flashed to the funeral of my own partner, a million

years ago. I only saw photographs in the newspaper, because at the time I was still in a hospital bed.

"Along with the grief, there's a lot of anger."

I nodded.

"DPS lost two men. They want somebody to be accountable for that. The jail lost three men. Same feeling. Everybody's looking at each other right now."

"Looking for somebody to blame. I get it. And I'm right in the middle of everything."

"Yes," he said. "You are."

"So tell me everything you know about this guy. Show me his file. If there *is* a connection with me, that's the only way I'm going to see it."

"I told you, there are other people waiting to talk to you…"

"By the end of the day, he could be another three hundred miles away. Show me the file."

He thought about it for another few seconds. Then he got up and left the room. He came back carrying a box.

"Most recent first," he said, pulling out one file. "Not counting Stephanie Hyatt, who at this point is still missing."

I started paging through the reports for Carolyn Kline, the woman who had been taken to the house in Scottsdale. They were all from different local police departments, all written in that same bloodless cop language that never seemed to change, no matter who was writing it.

Victim is a twenty-five-year-old female, five foot five, one hundred and thirty pounds. Last seen around 2300 hrs. on 11-07-2017 in vicinity of Skyline Tavern, 2200 N. Central Ave., Phoenix. Abducted at her home by persons unknown.

Everything the writer of the report could think of saying—

but in the end just a collection of details, with no ultimate answers. Then the ME's report, which used a more obscure kind of detached language to describe this woman's last few hours on earth. The trauma, the violation, the rope ligatures.

Using every word except the one word that would have fit best.

Torture.

"It says here there's a video," I said, moving on to the Scottsdale PD report. "I want to see it."

He hesitated. "It's not an easy thing to see."

"Show it to me."

He took out his laptop and opened it. A few seconds later, I was watching the silent video of Martin T. Livermore and a dead woman in a Scottsdale bedroom.

Approaching her body on the bed.

Taking off his clothes.

Reaching out with one hand to touch her skin.

Climbing onto the bed to lie next to her.

There was an unreality to everything I was seeing, and the fact that there was no audio made it even worse. The silence should have given the images a certain distance, but somehow it did exactly the opposite. I knew I'd be seeing this, running in a continuous loop in my mind, for the rest of my life.

When it was done, Madison closed the lid on his laptop. Before he could say another word, I got to my feet, feeling stiff and uneasy. My left knee was throbbing again, but I barely noticed it. I had to leave the building, had to breathe clean air.

As soon as I was outside, as soon as I had taken three deep breaths and made myself stand still, I looked across the road at the empty desert.

I remembered everything Livermore had said to me in that interview room. How he had taken my life apart, piece by piece. Showing me every failure, every reason to believe it accounted for nothing. I had resisted the thought at the time, but I knew when I finally closed my eyes that night, I'd lie awake and wonder if there was some small grain of truth in what he was telling me.

There's one thing I can do, I said to him. *One act that will balance out everything else in my life.*

I'm going to find you, wherever you are, no matter how far away, no matter how long it takes...

And I'm going to kill you.

CHAPTER NINE

LIVERMORE STARED at the stranger's face in the mirror.

He'd already stopped at a drugstore in Anthem, a few miles north of Phoenix. One more advantage of coming back down this way, he could be off the road a lot sooner. Spend a few hours here, let them start fanning out. Take his time and then follow behind them.

After the drugstore, he had checked into a motel, paid his ninety bucks for the room, and got to work in the bathroom. He stood in front of the mirror and ran the electric razor over his head, watching the light brown hair collect in the sink. He made a point of putting it in a bag so he could get rid of it when he left. When he had all of his hair trimmed down close, he mixed up the dye and slathered it on his head. It didn't take much, because he didn't have much hair left. He waited the twenty minutes suggested on the package, then five minutes more. Then he rinsed it out and looked at himself. His whiskers were starting to come in, now that he had stopped shaving for a couple of days. He got out the eyebrow pencil and darkened in his eyebrows, then his mustache. He took the pair of low-strength reading glasses he'd bought and put them on.

He spent a long time looking at himself, studying himself from every angle. He tried to imagine what other people would think when they saw his face, what assumptions they would make and how Livermore could use those assumptions to his advantage.

He still looked good. The same smooth skin, the strong jaw-line. The piercing eyes. And, with or without the glasses, the in-telligence still burning in his eyes. A light that he could never dim, even if he wanted to. But with his hair shorter and darker... Yes, he looked younger now. That could be useful. The older man with the long hair, the man whose description was already on the radio, the face that would soon be broadcast around the country...

That man was gone.

Now it was time to leave this place. Too risky to stay the night, not with a drugstore cashier who had seen the old version of Livermore buying his supplies just down the street, and a motel clerk who had taken his money and given him the key. As he repacked his bag, he noticed the antiseptic smell that every motel room in the country seemed to share. It took him back to another day, the last time he'd stayed in a motel, and everything that had happened afterward. Everything about Liana and how that had led to him standing here, six months later.

HE'D BEEN ON HIS WAY back to Phoenix, after taking Sandra to be with the others. He came back through Flagstaff, after so many hours driving, stopping at a restaurant for dinner, in no rush to go those last two hours down to his apartment. It was a Monday night, he remembered, two restaurants closed before he finally found the little steakhouse. He went in and ordered a drink, watched the woman bring it to him. Some men might not have liked the little bump in her nose or the way her eyebrows came a fraction of an inch too close together. But there was something about her that appealed to him.

Not yet, he told himself. *It is too soon.*

But he kept watching her and the surprising way she moved like a dancer around the tables, her hair pinned up, a white dress shirt and black skirt showing off her body. She smiled at him when she brought the drink over, and he smiled back. The way he'd taught himself. The science of robotics is, after all, a science of imitating human movement. Even, if you take that idea to the next step, human behavior. Which meant Martin T. Livermore was a trained expert in watching humans, observing what they did well and what they did not. Designing a machine to do things better.

I can be a machine myself, he had realized. It was an insight that came to him after spending so much time in Japan, where *kaizen,* the continuous pursuit of improvement, was such an important part of the culture. *I can design myself the same way I design a robotic arm to assemble an automobile, can fine-tune my own programming in the same way, to be even more effective today than I was yesterday.*

He started going to bars. Not to try to pick up women. Not yet. He went there to observe, to listen, to study. To learn what worked and what didn't.

Then he started to develop his own style, using what he had

learned, adding his own touches, turning up the shining light of his own raw intelligence just the right amount, confident but not arrogant. He was surprised at how well women responded to his hair, especially when he wore it loose.

"What do you really do?" he said to her. "No way this is your true calling."

Picking his words carefully, using the exact phrases that had worked in the past. *Your true calling*. Women loved that. They loved it even more when you listened to the answer like it was the most important information you'd hear all day.

"I'm a guide at the Grand Canyon on weekends," she said.

He leaned forward and watched her carefully, watching her eyes, watching her mouth.

"I love the Grand Canyon," he said. "That must be fascinating."

She smiled again. Responding to him, just as he knew she would.

"I get a little tired of saying the same thing over and over," she said. *"The canyon is two hundred and seventy-seven miles long. At its widest point, eighteen miles across. Most of it more than a mile deep. There are two billion years' worth of rock exposed . . . Unless you're one of those nutcases who thinks this whole thing was made in a flood six thousand years ago."*

He laughed at that and asked her how many tours she typically did in one weekend.

"Seven or eight," she said. "We fly down to the floor in a helicopter. Which is what I really want to do."

He opened his eyes wide in surprise. "Fly helicopters? *Really?*"

"This job is just to pay for flight lessons."

"I've always wondered…" he said. "Do you have to learn to fly a plane first? Or can you go right to helicopters?"

She got called away to another table before she could answer. But he knew he had her hooked. He took his time over dinner and ended up sitting at the bar until closing. She came over and sat next to him when she was done with her shift, finally able to answer his question.

"Yes, you can go right to helicopters," she said as soon as she sat down. "But most people don't. I'd love to fly planes, too, so why not learn it all?"

He raised a toast to her plans, then answered some questions about what he did. Robotics engineering, and the time he'd spent in Japan. He knew that would work. A man who travels the world, who can make his way in a foreign country for years at a time…

"I worked for Seiko Epson," he said. "At the Nagano robotics center."

"Wow, you must be really smart."

"I helped design a new robotic arm. With a six-axis range of motion, instead of four. But you don't want to hear about that."

"I bet that was amazing," she said, moving a little closer. "But why Japan?"

"There were seven hundred thousand industrial robots in the world then. Five hundred thousand of them were in Japan."

He saw her eyes wander, just for a moment.

Don't talk about numbers, he reminded himself. *Women do not care about numbers.*

"But it was the culture that really turned me on," he said.

"The Japanese people seem so . . . restrained. And yet under-neath, there's this amazing sensuality . . ."

Yes, she's reengaged.

"Why did you come back?" she said.

"I missed American steakhouses."

She laughed and moved even closer. He took out his wallet to pay the bill, the wallet with the American Express Platinum Card displayed prominently. Left a hundred-dollar bill with clearly no expectation of getting any change back. Another move that never failed.

He finally got her name. Liana. He told her it was the loveli-est name he'd ever heard.

"I know you'll be closing soon," he said to her after another beat. "Where else can a man get a drink in this town?"

"There's a place down the street. They make the best martini in town . . ."

He looked at her and smiled. "I'll drive."

He followed her outside, opened the passenger's-side door to his Mercedes, made sure she was safely inside and buckled up before closing the door and going around to the driver's side.

"I don't usually get in cars with men I don't know," she said when he was behind the wheel.

"This time," he said, "I'm glad you did."

They lingered over the martinis and another hour of conver-sation, Livermore remembering to make it all about her with-out seeming obsessive about it, slipping in little references to himself when he felt the timing was right. A little bit more about his time in Japan, how tiresome it was to travel around the world so often, how hard it was to have a relationship with such a busy life, how he was finally ready to settle down and find something *real*.

Another thing women loved. *Something real.*

They went back to her apartment, just outside of town.

"This place must have a great view in the morning," he said to her. Presumptuous, and yet he knew it was time to make that move. To push without really pushing. He could see from her shy smile that it was working.

They went inside and had another drink, listened to some music. Some "good old Motown," as she called it, and of course he was quick to say that was his favorite music ever—even though the truth was he found the subtle bass note hum inside his own head preferable to any music he'd ever heard. He waited for her to move closer, then finally kissed her, making her wait for it. Even when they went to bed, he made sure to do everything right. Focusing on her pleasure first, making her feel like she was the most beautiful, most desirable woman on the planet.

It was good. Livermore was almost surprised by it. That certain *something* he had seen in her ... How she had reminded him of the one woman who had set the standard so long ago. And how she was still living up to everything that *something* had promised. Even when, toward the end, he had taken her wrists, had drawn them together over her head and held them down tight... How he felt her responding to this, how he could feel it rippling all the way through her body. This hunger inside her, something almost like desperation.

Yes, he said to himself as he lay next to her. *This could finally be the one.*

Then she lit up a cigarette.

In her own bedroom, with Livermore right there in the bed next to her, this woman *lit up a cigarette.*

"That's a nasty habit," he said to her, keeping his voice even.

"I know," she said, taking another long drag and looking at the cigarette. "I'm trying to quit."

He got out of the bed and put his pants on.

"Hey, come on, where are you going?" she said.

He kept getting dressed. His shirt, then his belt.

"To get a breath of fresh air," he said.

"Okay, look," she said, stubbing out the cigarette in a coffee mug next to the bed. "No more smoking. I didn't know it would bother you."

He stopped and looked down at her. At this woman who smoked in her own bed and put out her cigarettes in the same coffee mug she'd be drinking out of the next day. Somewhere in his mind a single green light flickered, then went off. After a moment of darkness, another light came on in its place.

This light was red.

Livermore smiled at her.

"Don't worry," he said. "I'll be right back."

She kept watching him as he left the room. When he was in the living room again, alone, he took a long look at the place. There were details that he hadn't noticed until that moment, indicators that marked this woman's life. From the dirty dishes in her sink to the pile of junk mail left on the table. A disorganized mind. Even for a woman.

He went to the bookshelf and turned his head sideways to read the titles. He stopped when he came to the erotic novels, or at least what certain people would consider to be erotic. White-washed and Americanized, huge bestsellers—but the kind of trash that would be laughed out of any Japanese bookstore.

You should have seen these signs, he told himself, *before you let yourself get involved with her. She used the human part of you to make you believe she was different.*

She tricked you.

He left the apartment and went out to his Mercedes, came back to the door with his leather bag. Liana was standing in the hallway when he came back inside the apartment. She had put on a thin black robe, decorated with blood-red flowers.

She looked uncertain when she saw Livermore coming toward her. "What's in the bag?"

He didn't answer her. He put the bag on the floor and opened it. Then he reached inside and took out one of his ropes.

He had them in different lengths, from four meters to fifty, but each one was exactly six millimeters thick, and each one was a fine three-stranded jute that he had boiled himself, then dried for several days before finishing with a thin coat of mineral oil.

Her eyes went wide when she saw it.

"What are you going to do with that?"

She kept looking at the rope, mesmerized, as he slowly wound it into a tight coil.

He stayed silent as he finished making the coil. It was part of the process. The way you quiet your mind as you prepare for what comes next.

"I've heard about this," she said. "What's it called, *shibari*?"

"*Kinbaku,*" he said. "Only Americans call it *shibari.*"

"I don't know," she said, taking a small step backward. "I've never done this."

Her eyes stayed fixed on the rope as he came closer to her. He reached out and touched the coil to her face, gently brushing her skin.

Her face flushed. "Are you going to punish me?"

"Turn around," he said.

She hesitated for a moment, then obeyed. He gave her a slight push, and she went to the center of the room. Her face was still turned away from him.

"Take off your robe," he said.

"Yes." Her voice was low, and she was already breathing hard. She closed her eyes. Then she opened her robe and let it fall to the floor.

He felt himself stirring again, willed himself back into the quiet darkness inside his head, where only the single red light burned.

"Put your wrists together," he said. "Behind you."

When she did, he tied them, then he looped the rope around her body, twice beneath her breasts, twice above. He joined these loops to her wrists. Then he kept weaving the ropes around her, forming an intricate pattern.

The *kikkou*. The tortoise shell.

Around and around her body, reversing the ropes behind and in front, until she was wearing the rope like the tightest, most intimate clothing ever made.

"It feels nice," she whispered. "These ropes are soft."

He didn't answer her. There was no more need to talk now that she was tied. When she tried to speak again, he quickly looped the rope across her open mouth. He knew this would work better than any gag. She shook her head against it, her whole body suddenly going tense. Her eyes were wide open now, her mouth working against the gag. A muffled sound came out.

He looked in her eyes, still silent. His smile was gone.

She kept shaking her head, kept trying to speak. When she tried to step away from him, she nearly fell over, because the ropes had been tied all the way down her thighs, to her knees. Livermore caught her and held her upright. When her eyes locked on his again, that was the exact moment.

The moment she knew.

The moment she could see it in his face. See the man he really was.

See what was about to happen to her.

"Only dirty whores smoke in bed," he said, and then with one push he sent her to the floor.

She tried to scream. Another muffled sound that would go no farther than this room. She kept fighting against the ropes, writhing across the carpet. He stopped her and tied her ankles together. Then he looped the rope around her neck.

Once.

Twice.

He tied these ropes to her ankles, drawing her whole body back into an arch, as if he were stringing a bow. Her face was already turning a deeper shade of red. Tears streamed down her face.

Livermore stood up and watched her for a long time, watched her struggling against the basic horrible truth of her situation, as the slightest movement of her body drew the ropes even tighter. She had to actively work against it, to keep her back arched and her ankles raised as high as they could go. To relax would mean strangling herself.

He knelt down on the floor next to her, watching the color in her face change from red to purple. Her eyelids fluttered as her body began to go slack.

When he loosened the knot linking her ankles to her neck, the color in her face lightened and she opened her eyes again. He kept watching her, watching the life come back to her, then leaving again, then coming back.

Until it didn't.

That was when he got undressed.

WHEN HE WAS DONE with her, he sat with his back against the couch. He took the laptop from his bag and checked his email.

She told me she lived here alone, he said to himself. But he knew that didn't make this a safe place. Not for long. A friend could come over, or a nosy neighbor, or even a boyfriend she had neglected to tell him about. He would have to find another place to move her to.

It was a familiar routine to him by now. A ritual.

And yet another part of the ritual, he finished with his email and went out onto the Internet. Looking up traces from another part of his life, from a memory that would come back to him whenever he spent a night like this one. It had been amazing to him how much social media had exploded in America while he'd been in Japan, how a person could splash their entire life all over the Internet for anyone in the world to see. But not everyone did that, as Livermore soon learned. He would never do it himself, so he understood. But this time, as he once again went through every website he could think of…

He found something.

One image, a single flash in time from how many years ago, and yet here it was recollected in the pixels that glowed on his laptop screen. He scanned one face, then another, then another. Until he settled on the face of a man. Composed, self-assured, athletic.

This man.

He felt a surge of electricity flowing through his body, a wave of heat and energy that he could barely contain.

What am I going to do about this man?

He worked it over in his head for an hour, coming back to the same face, over and over again.

That was when the idea finally came to him. How he would test himself against this man. How he could prove himself.

He thought about it for a second hour, working out every detail in his mind. Until it was finally time to wrap up Liana in a sheet and, after checking to make sure nobody was in the parking lot, take her to his vehicle.

All of the preparations, the designs, the planning... It would all come together on this night, every star in the universe collecting around this one perfect idea, and all of it leading to this one man. This ex-cop living in a little town called Paradise.

Six months after the night the idea was born, everything was in motion now.

For Martin T. Livermore.

For Alex McKnight.

And it had only just begun.

CHAPTER TEN

THIS IS ALEX MCKNIGHT," Agent Madison said to a roomful of men and women who all were staring a hole right through me. It was the next morning, after a sleepless night. "He is the lone survivor from yesterday's events."

A hell of a way to put it, I thought. We were in the same conference room where Madison had originally questioned me, but now there were a dozen other agents all sitting around the table. Ten men and two women, all dressed in dark suits. There was a special phone for conference calls on the table. I had no idea how many more people were listening in on that.

"Mr. McKnight was a police officer in Detroit. He's been retired for a number of years."

"What is his connection to Livermore?" one of the agents in the back of the room asked. Because five minutes had passed without someone asking that question.

"At this point, we don't know."

I could sense everyone in the room exchanging looks with one another, then returning their focus to me.

"Mr. McKnight has been a person of interest in this case since Livermore first mentioned his name," Madison said. "He will continue to cooperate with us."

That didn't seem to satisfy anyone in the room. Not that I could blame them. Two agents they had worked with every day were dead. I was alive.

Madison moved on to credit cards, bank accounts, vehicle information—anything a person could use that would leave a trail. All of the markers that someone would leave if they were actively moving, because a person who's moving needs to sleep somewhere, needs to eat, needs to refuel his vehicle. Or whatever Livermore was now driving, anyway. His vehicle of record was the black Mercedes found in the parking lot at the Sonoran Preserve the night he was arrested.

Ten thousand dollars in cash had been taken out of his account a week before, but no further activity had been seen since then. This man had apparently designed this part of his plan just as well as the escape itself. He was staying completely off the grid.

He's invisible, I thought. *But as every fugitive hunter knows, a man can't stay invisible forever.*

Madison then led the team through everything else that had happened in the past eighteen hours, from the coordination with every local police department, as well as the state police in every neighboring state, to the interface with the media. He put up the FBI website on the screen. Somewhere out there was a man named Jason Derek Brown, who was wanted for first-degree murder, armed robbery, and unlawful flight to avoid prosecution. He'd been number one on the FBI's Ten Most Wanted list the week before, with a five-hundred-thousand-dollar reward for information leading to his arrest. Now Brown was number two behind Martin T. Livermore, a man whose capture was worth an even two million dollars.

Madison's words faded into the background as I stared at Livermore's face on the screen. It burned in my mind, even as the image was replaced by a map of the United States. Madison ran through Livermore's background, highlighting each location on the map. Born and raised in Columbus, Ohio. Attended Ohio State University, then Rensselaer Polytechnic Institute in Upstate New York. Worked for three different companies in the Northeast before he took a job with Seiko Epson in Long Beach, California. Transferred to the robotics center in Nagano, Japan. Lived there for nine years. Back in the States for three years.

Long enough to kill six women. Possibly seven.

Madison highlighted the two cities in California where his victims had last been seen. Then the cities in Utah and Nevada. Finally the two cities in Arizona: Flagstaff. Phoenix.

"What were his movements in Japan?" one of the agents said. A woman, sitting close to me. "If he never killed anyone until he came back…"

"We're in contact with the NPA offices in Nagano," Madison said. "So far his time there is one big blank. He went to work every day. Otherwise kept to himself."

"Does he have any family?"

"No brothers or sisters. Father died when Livermore was seventeen years old. Mother two years ago. She lived in Columbus, in the same house Martin grew up in, although we don't believe he's been back there for several years. The house has been empty since the mother died. We're processing it today, just in case."

"What about his current residence?"

"His address of record is a single-bedroom apartment on Buckeye Road," Madison said, "but we have reason to believe he used that only as a mail drop. The apartment is completely empty right now. There's not even a bed."

"Are you saying that—"

"I'm saying that nobody in that building has ever seen him before. So finding his real primary residence is one of our first priorities today."

He was about to continue when another agent entered the room and waved Madison over. He excused himself and went out to the hallway to talk to him. I could feel every eye in the room on me again as we all waited.

When Madison came back in, he asked me if I would excuse myself.

"Are you going to tell me why?" I said.

"We need to discuss some sensitive information. If you go with Agent Larkin, he'll take care of you until we're done."

So much for being part of the team, I thought. I got up and left the room with the young agent right behind me.

"We'll go to my office," Larkin said. He was built solid, like an athlete, with a military buzz cut. "I have the case files if you want to look through them again."

I didn't answer him.

End of the day, I told myself. *As long as I can get something useful out of these guys, I'll stick around. But then I'm on my own.*

Because I am going to find Livermore, one way or the other.

I saw the agent's full name on his office door. Matt Larkin. He didn't look like he'd seen his thirtieth birthday yet, and I knew he wasn't the man I needed to be pissed off at. I tried to cool myself down a notch as I sat in his guest chair.

End of the day.

I spent the next hour going through the case files again, one by one, trying to put everything else out of my head. At one point, I took out the photographs of the six women Livermore had killed and put them in a line across the table. The same photos that Halliday and Cook had shown me on the flight out here.

I looked at the faces, carefully moving from one to the next. The hair color went from blond to brunette to black to redhead, back to brunette, back to blond. Two of the women might have been a little overweight. Two wore glasses.

"As far as we know," Larkin said, "these women have nothing in common. No connections from school or from work. His victim selection appears to be completely random."

I knew that was an important term in the Bureau. His *victim selection*. But there was something here that didn't look quite random to me. I *knew* there was something here. I just couldn't see it yet.

"How long would it have taken you guys to catch him?" I said. "If he hadn't given himself away with that video?"

"I can't answer that."

"I'm sure there was a profile."

"You're right, but—"

"But profiles are bullshit."

He looked at me. "I wouldn't say that."

"What was the profile for the Beltway Sniper?" I said. "A white loner."

"At first..."

"Until you caught him. Turned out to be a black man riding around with a kid. How many roadblocks did they slip through?"

He didn't bother answering.

"Then the Unabomber," I said. "I read you had two profiles at one point. One guy says he's an academic, which turned out to be right, while the other guy says he's an airplane mechanic. How many years was that case open?"

Larkin shifted in his chair. "Seventeen."

"Biggest manhunt in history," I said. "Every agency in the country. How many agents did they have working that case, full-time? And then how did they finally catch him?"

"His brother."

"One person," I said. "One connection. That's what it takes."

"So for Livermore, that connection is apparently you."

He's got me on that one, I said to myself. *If I only knew what that connection was.*

I'd been keeping a lid on it all that morning, the raw anger that came up every time I thought about Livermore, every time I replayed any single moment from the past twenty-four hours.

He's out there right now, I thought. *Somewhere. Wearing that same smile.*

"So what are they talking about in there?" I said, nodding toward the conference room.

"Even if I knew..." Larkin said, leaving the thought hanging. "But when they're done with the meeting—"

"We'll be gone," I said. "Let's get out of here."

"And go where?"

"Take me to the most recent crime scenes," I said. "I want to see every place he's been."

"You know I can't do that."

"I'm pretty sure you can."

He looked at his doorway as if hoping for some help.

"Look," I said. "Either I'm under arrest or I'm free to leave at any time. I just read the addresses of those crime scenes. Now I'm going to go out and look at them."

When I stood up and walked out, the only question was whether I'd hear his footsteps behind me.

IT WAS SOMETHING I'd learned as a cop in Detroit. You can't capture a crime scene with words on paper, can't capture it with photographs. You need to go there, stand in the middle of it. *Feel* the place, use all your senses at once. That's your only chance of finding something that someone else might have missed.

The first place Larkin took me was a little house over on the north side of town. This was the home of Carolyn Kline, the woman from the video. It was a small one-story house on a lot decorated with gravel and cactuses. I told Larkin to park on the street for a few minutes so I could watch the place. It was a busy street. In the middle of the day there was a steady stream of traffic.

"We believe he walked in through the front door," Larkin said. "There was no forced entry."

I nodded, trying to imagine it. Trying to put myself in his place, watching this house, waiting for the right moment. I wasn't trying to figure out *who, where,* or *when* at that point. Those questions had already been answered before I got there. I was more interested in the *how*, and even the *why* if I could get to it.

The *why* would put me closer to the mind of the man himself. Which would maybe help me understand why I was here in Phoenix, with bandages on my arm and knee, with the sounds of explosions still ringing in my ears.

"Let's go inside," I said.

We got out and went to the front door. There was no crime scene tape, but a sign posted on the locked door warned against entry by anyone but authorized law enforcement. Larkin had brought along a key. He opened up the door and let me inside. I stopped dead in the front room and looked at a section of the floor that had been marked with red tape.

"They found trace evidence right here," Larkin said. "Hair. No semen this time."

That didn't make sense to me. In all of the other cases, he'd had sexual contact with the body at the kill site, then again at the second location.

"What about the rope fibers?" I said.

"A few fibers, yes. But we found nothing in the bedroom."

I looked out the window at the busy street. Easy enough to close the curtains, but why not go to the quieter room?

Because it wasn't about physical gratification at all. Not this time.

I bent down to look at a photograph of Carolyn Kline, making sure not to touch it. Even though the crime scene had already been processed, it just wouldn't have felt right to me.

I recognized the face from the file back at the FBI office, but here she was out in a boat, with sunglasses and a big smile. An older man was sitting next to her.

Her father.

A man who had to receive a visit from two police officers, just a few days ago. Because as a cop you always want your partner with you when you go deliver the news that will destroy a family.

I took a quick look through the rest of the house. There was nothing else to see, except a back door that led to a small backyard. There were neighbors on both sides, another in back, but if you left this place at night...

"He pulls up his car and takes her out this door," I said. "Then he takes her to the house in Scottsdale."

Where he suddenly remembers why he kills these women in the first place...

It doesn't fit.

I didn't want to see the Thompson house yet. I'd seen the video and already knew what had happened there. Standing in the same room would make it even more real. Take me even farther into the man's mind. Farther than I was prepared to go.

"Take me to Stephanie Hyatt's place first," I said. As we drove through the midday Phoenix traffic, I tried to stop the endless loop that was running in my head, what Livermore had done in that bedroom, until we finally crossed over into the town of Mesa and came to a trailer park. A long line of metal boxes, baking in the sun.

"Taken just before Livermore was arrested," Larkin said, driving to the trailer on the farther end of the road. "The case is still being developed."

This trailer looked out of place to me. Once again, I tried to imagine Livermore sitting here on this road, watching the woman who lived here.

Why the hell would he come here?

We got out. Another front door with another sign. We went inside, to a small, cluttered trailer that was at least one hundred degrees. The smell was a mixture of cigarette smoke and cheap fast food, with a certain unmistakable top note, the sweet tang of marijuana.

"You found no trace evidence here," I said. "Or if you did, there was so little you might have missed it if you didn't know he was involved."

Larkin looked at me. "Yes."

I pictured Livermore standing in this room, in this exact spot, by the pile of dishes on the counter and the beer cans on the little dining room table. In that same first interview with Halliday, Livermore had told him that all of his first five victims were together somewhere. *In a special place.*

"Wherever those other victims are," I said, "this one won't be with them. Stephanie Hyatt was the throwaway."

I felt bad standing in her trailer, calling her that. Like I was diminishing her value, even in death. But I knew it was the truth. I knew that's how Livermore would have seen her.

"He never abducted two women so close together before," I said.

"True."

"And he could only be with one at a time."

Larkin nodded.

"Carolyn Kline was just for the cameras," I said. "And this one..."

I looked around the place, trying to find another way to say it. "This one was just the bait to set the trap. Nothing more."

"So where is she?" Larkin said. "Obviously not in that canyon."

I shook my head. *She's wherever you put things you don't need anymore,* I thought as I looked at another photograph. This one mounted on the wall, on one of those cheap pieces of stained wood with the clear sheet of Plexiglas. Stephanie Hyatt with another young woman on either side of her. They all had the same hairstyle. All came from the same place. Sisters.

Another family that had to answer the door and see two cops standing on the other side, their hats in their hands.

At this point, I had more of the *how*, but still wasn't close to the *why*. Still wasn't close to whatever it was that drove him.

"There's one more crime scene in town," Larkin said to me. "His fifth victim, Liana Massey, she lived up in Flagstaff, but after he killed her he brought her down here and kept her in a condo out in Fountain Hills."

"Liana Massey," I said, remembering the file. Remembering the face. "Six months ago."

A half hour later, we were on the eastern side of town, fighting our way through the seasonal traffic, with seemingly a million identical brown stucco buildings all around us, each one divided into eight or ten different condo units. It was February, so the part-time residents had left every cold-weather state in the country to come fight the same traffic and live in these cheap plaster boxes, where they could swear at the traffic instead of the snow.

"He kept her in their bed," Larkin said when we pulled up to the place. The unit in question was close to the end of the street, as secluded as you could get in a place like this, especially if you broke in during the summer.

"This place makes sense," I said as I got out of the car and looked up and down the street. I could picture Livermore parked here, watching the place, choosing the one perfect unit. The construction was so cheap, he could have gotten through any of the windows.

You're pretty smart, I thought, *when you don't want to get caught.*

"The wife didn't even realize someone had been there until she got in bed that first night. There were dried fluids from the victim's body. Some hair. Some skin that had sloughed off the body. They eventually found the victim's clothing under the bed."

We were about to head inside the building when Larkin was interrupted by his cell phone. He answered the call and listened for a moment, then he looked over at me.

"Mr. McKnight left the building," he said. "There was no way to stop him."

He closed his eyes as he listened to a few more words from whoever was on the other end. Probably Madison, and he probably wasn't happy.

"Yes, sir," Larkin said. "Right away."

"I take it we're going back to the office," I said.

He didn't answer me. He got back behind the wheel and waited for me to get in beside him. It was a long, silent ride back to Deer Valley Road. Agent Madison was standing outside the front door, blinking in the sun, as we pulled up.

"This is on me," I said to him as I got out. "Don't blame Agent Larkin."

"Mr. McKnight, you were not supposed to leave this facility."

"I'll ask you the same question I asked him," I said. "Am I under arrest or am I—"

"You're a person of interest, you know that."

"That means nothing to me. Other than getting thrown out of meetings as soon as they get interesting."

"I told you at the time, the information we needed to discuss was classified."

"You found the bodies," I said, watching him carefully. "Why wouldn't I be able to hear that?"

I didn't see anything change in his face. I thought about what else could have come to light today, what other piece of information was missing...

"You found his home," I said. "Where he really lives."

This time I could tell I was right.

"So what did you find?" I said. "Something connected to me?"

"No," he said. "It has nothing to do with you."

"Then why are you shutting me out? If you really want me to help you—"

"That was my call at the time," he said. "You can trust me or not. I don't care."

I shook my head and looked over at Larkin. He was doing a professional job of trying not to be noticed by his boss.

"That's the thing about FBI vehicles," I said, nodding to the dozen black sedans in the lot. "I can go rent a car, wait outside here and just follow the next one that leaves. Or hell, I bet if I just drive around town, I'll see them all parked somewhere."

"Don't even bother," he said, looking me in the eye. "I've made my decision. I'm taking you there right now."

CHAPTER ELEVEN

LIVERMORE LINED UP the crosshairs on Alex Mc-Knight's face.

"Stop moving," he whispered to him, from a hundred feet away. "Just stand still."

He waited for McKnight to obey him. A few seconds later, McKnight stood up straight and tall. Livermore had the shot he wanted.

He pushed the button, and the camera's shutter snapped open and closed. He pressed it a few more times, because even though he was sure the first shot was perfect, an engineer knows it's good to have redundancy.

He'd been following Alex all day, from the moment he had walked out of that hotel right down the street from the FBI offices, the place that should have had a sign reading FBI GUESTHOUSE. While he had watched Alex getting into the young agent's car, he'd sensed a police car pulling up next to him in the hotel parking lot. Phoenix PD, one uniform behind the wheel.

The officer glanced over at Livermore for a moment. Looked right at him.

Livermore smiled. *Believe in the disguise,* he told himself as the cop nodded to him and drove away. The short dark hair, the mustache that would grow in better with each passing day. The glasses. *Have absolute trust in yourself and reflect that trust to the rest of the world.*

He waited down the street from the office, picked up Alex again when he went out with the young agent, making stops all over town. The house in Mesa, then the trailer park, now here in Fountain Hills. Livermore was parked down the street in his Japanese SUV, holding the new Japanese digital camera he had bought, a Nikon with a seventy-to-three-hundred-millimeter zoom lens.

He watched Alex get out of the car, take a few steps down the street, and look up at the condo's bedroom window.

You can see why I chose this place...

HE HAD BEEN two hours from Flagstaff, driving in the dead middle of the night, with Liana's body in the backseat. He'd kept to the speed limit. Used his turn signals. Everything straight and correct, still seeing that face from the laptop screen. Still working through the new plan in his head.

He'd brought her to this empty condo, already chosen. Close to the end of the street, with one window on the back that could not be seen from any of the neighboring units. A quiet street during the summer, but not so quiet that his vehicle would be suspicious. Far enough away from his own apartment on the west side of town, but not so far as to make it inconvenient.

He went through the window and unlocked the front door, then spent another hour back on the street, watching the place to make sure he hadn't tripped any silent alarms. When he was satisfied, he brought her out, still wrapped in the sheet and slung over his shoulder, took her inside through the front door, and then arranged her carefully on the queen-sized bed in the master suite. Where he would keep her for exactly eight days.

This was the ritual. Eight days, coming back every night to be with her. To watch how she changed. Her fingernails turning black. Her skin changing color.

From pink.

To purple.

To gray.

It still amazed him how quickly it happened, how he could almost imagine the color changing right before his eyes. Like in the bamboo forests he'd seen in Japan, how they had told him that if you stood still enough, you could actually watch the plant growing. It was the same thing. Only it was the timeless changes of death he was watching, not of life.

It aroused him.

It was a simple fact, something he had learned about himself from the very first time, had observed in himself with the same clinical precision he brought to everything else in his life. He was a man, after all. He was flesh and blood, born with a hard wiring every bit as well defined as the wiring in a robotic arm.

He'd been aroused when he'd taken that first woman's life from her, more aroused an hour later when her body was still warm. Even more aroused the next day when her body was cold. Part of it was the all-consuming sense of power he felt over her. Another part of it was the sense of uniqueness: *This is something that most men do not experience.* Cannot *experience. It is something left only to the rare few. To the superior beings who walk this earth once in a millennium.*

And yet a final part of it was just a mystery to him.

I don't know why I respond this way. I just do.

Therefore it is right.

After eight days of being with her, of watching her, touching her, allowing her to give him pleasure even after her death, Livermore had taken Liana home. Not back to the empty apartment where he slept. He had taken her *home*, where he could keep her with the others.

With Arlene, Theresa, Claire, and Sandra.

All five of them together, even now.

They had all taken advantage of that one human part of him. They had fooled him into believing, for one moment, that they could live up to the standard that another woman had set.

That they could somehow take her place.

And they had all paid for this mistake.

CHAPTER TWELVE

TWENTY-FOUR HOURS after watching Livermore kill seven men, I was standing at his doorstep.

The apartment they had found was on the north side of town, in one of a dozen tall, gleaming buildings that rose thirty stories above the street. His was two blocks from the ramp to I-17. The perfect place for a man to stay anonymously comfortable, with a quick escape if he needed it.

Madison badged the security guard at the welcome desk, taking the passcard from him and leading Larkin and me to the elevator. He slid the card into the slot, and we rode up to the top floor. When the door opened, I saw a private vestibule, with access to only one apartment.

Martin T. Livermore lived in the goddamned penthouse suite.

The door was propped open, and I saw half a dozen agents already moving around inside. They were all wearing crime scene gloves and shoe covers. Madison grabbed a pair of each from the cardboard box outside the door and gave them to me, then to Larkin. The two men slipped theirs on quickly and waited for me to do the same. Then we stepped inside.

"We're just starting our work here," Madison said to me. "I'm sure I don't have to tell you not to disturb anything."

There were two agents setting up a floor grid, long white strings that would run parallel across the hardwood floor, with another set of strings running perpendicular. The result would be a perfect set of one-foot-by-one-foot squares covering the entire apartment. They would use this to catalog any trace materials found on the floor.

As Madison and Larkin went to talk to one of the other agents, I looked the rest of the place over. Everything was sleek and modern, with an open plan that provided a sight line all the way through the kitchen. There were granite countertops with brushed-steel side plates. White cabinets with European-style handles. The living room was bigger than my entire cabin back in Paradise, with black leather furniture on chrome frames. There were two huge Japanese prints on the walls, a crane standing in a pond, and a twisted tree in fog with a pagoda in the distance. No human figures anywhere. No television.

Another agent was busy setting up a series of numbered yellow evidence tags, small tents that would be placed next to anything of possible interest. He'd already put one next to a neat stack of mail on the dining room table, and another tag next to the newspaper, carefully folded next to the mail. I went to the big picture window and looked out over the city of Phoenix. The Superstition Mountains rose in the eastern distance.

As I went into the living room, I scanned the bookshelf. There were thirty or forty engineering reference books, a few books on Japan. Nothing else.

I stepped around another agent who was putting an evidence tag next to a slight indentation in the hardwood floor. Probably just an old dent in the wood, but I knew they'd run DNA tests on everything they could find, trying to determine if anyone else had been here. They'd also dust for prints, and they'd spray luminol under a black light to test for blood.

My gut told me they'd find nothing. As luxurious as this place was, there was something oddly sterile about it. Something almost impersonal.

This is where he lives, I said to myself, *but he doesn't really* live *here.*

When I went down the hallway, I saw that the first door was closed. I could hear voices coming from behind it. I continued down to the bedroom, to the bathroom, back to the kitchen. Everything was just as immaculate. Just as sterile.

"McKnight," Agent Madison said. I turned to see him standing before the first door, which was now open. "In here."

I followed him into the room. It was Livermore's home office. Filing cabinets, a computer station, and a separate writing desk stacked with papers.

"Give us one moment," Madison said to Larkin and the other two agents in the room. His voice was all business.

The three men left the room. I stepped closer to the desk and looked at the papers. It took me a while to process what I was seeing. On top was a large map of San Francisco, then beneath that a set of blueprints with neatly drawn red arrows pointing to several different parts of the building.

"This is the classified information you were talking about at the meeting," I said. "I don't understand why I couldn't—"

"This is national security, McKnight."

I looked up at him. "Are you kidding me?"

As I carefully lifted the blueprints, I saw another map below it, this one of the larger Bay Area, and beneath that I saw the corner of a brochure, with a list of times and what looked to be names of events. *Welcome Cocktail Party. Opening Ceremony.*

I put everything back in its original place. "You don't believe this bullshit, do you?"

"Give me a reason not to."

"What's he going to do?" I said, reading the text on the blueprints. "You think he's really going to blow up the Moscone Center?"

"This evidence points that way. We have to take this seriously."

"He's a killer," I said. "He's not a terrorist."

"You don't know *what* he is, McKnight. You don't even know why he brought you here, remember?"

"Look at this apartment," I said. "Think about the man who lives here. Everything you know about him so far. Would he really leave all his master plans out here for you to see? Unless he *wanted* you to?"

"So what are we supposed to do? Ignore this?"

"Yes, you're supposed to ignore it. You know why? Because you're too smart to fall for this. You're supposed to go back out there and find him."

"We'll find him. I promise you."

"Not in San Francisco you won't."

He took a beat, then nodded to the wall behind me. "Look at that time line."

I turned and looked at it. Several sheets of paper neatly stapled to the wall, with carefully drawn lines in a dozen different colors, each labeled with the name of a convention event. Another line read *Travel time, Moscone to San Mateo*. Another, *Enter and exit building*.

"The only thing missing is 'Dear FBI,'" I said.

"In five days, there'll be twenty thousand people there. How many—"

"But not Livermore."

"*Listen to me*. Twenty thousand people. God knows how many more in San Mateo. All in the same weekend. He can hit both venues within five hours."

"No," I said. "That's the diversion. You'll be in San Francisco while he's off killing ten more people somewhere else."

"If this is all fake, why did he keep this place a secret?"

"He didn't," I said. "Come on. He *knew* you'd find this place."

"I don't know about that. He kept his computer pretty damned secure. We took a heavily encrypted hard drive out of his computer, and as soon as we crack it—"

"Don't you understand what's going on here? He'll tie up your computer people for a week. Along with every agent you've got. You're going to spend all this time, all this manpower... On what? On an *illusion*."

"Maybe," he said, looking me in the eye. "But I'm not going to have fifty thousand deaths on my hands. This is the same man who killed seven cops yesterday."

"I know," I said, "I was there, remember?"

"We have no idea what he's capable of, McKnight. We have an obligation to—"

"You have an obligation to catch him," I said. "Nothing else matters. How many more people does he have to kill before you realize that?"

"We're going to catch him," Madison said, after taking a beat. "But this isn't just a manhunt anymore. It's a potential *massive casualty disaster*."

I took a beat of my own, looking down at the pile of papers on the desk.

You're not going to win this argument, I said to myself. *They're going down the wrong road, but you can't stop them. They're going to throw everything they've got at this, because after 9/11 you can't be the one person who didn't take a threat seriously.*

Which is exactly what Livermore is counting on.

"So just tell me one thing," I said, looking him in the eye again. "What does he get out of this?"

"Whatever a psychopath gets out of anything. Revenge. Fame."

"No," I said. "That's not the man I sat across the table from. He doesn't need any of that."

"Then what *does* he need?"

I took a moment to think about it. "I don't know yet," I finally said, looking around the rest of the room. "But none of this is real. He's not here."

"So where is he?"

"Somewhere else," I said. "Somewhere he doesn't want us to see."

"Well, until you figure that out, we're going to follow the evidence we actually have. Agent Larkin will take you back to the office."

"No, thanks," I said.

"McKnight—"

"You can go chase your terrorist if you want," I said, taking off the gloves and handing them to him on my way out of the room. "But I'm going to go find Livermore."

A few minutes later, Larkin and I were alone in the car. His face was red, and he was gripping the steering wheel like he was about to tear it right off its column.

"If you were him," I said, "where would you go to be alone?"

Larkin didn't look over at me. He kept driving.

"You need to be able to work. Maybe make some noise. Someplace *clean*. That's important to him."

Still nothing.

"A storage unit," I said. "Think about it. Metal walls, concrete floor. Electrical outlets. Plenty of privacy. And best of all, you can pay for the place with cash."

"We're going back to the office," he said, keeping his eyes straight ahead.

"Take me somewhere I can rent a car," I said. "I'll do this on my own."

He shook his head.

"Or you can come with me. Actually help me find this guy."

"Mr. McKnight, I'm already—"

"Call me Alex. I'm not that old."

"Alex…"

"It's time to decide," I said.

He let out a breath and shook his head again.

"You either tell them I walked away," I said, "or you tell them you helped me find out where this guy really *lives*. It's up to you."

CHAPTER THIRTEEN

I T WAS LIVERMORE'S personal conception of hell.

He was standing in line, in this forgotten little run-down gas station that smelled like the bottom of an old oil drum, after being on the road for seven hours straight. He was somewhere in the middle of New Mexico, trapped in this place, looking it up and down and seeing one horror after another, from the broken linoleum floor to the dust-covered vents on the stand-up cooler to the sagging yellow ceiling tiles. He had passed the bathroom door on the way in, locked up tight. You probably had to ask for the key, and when they handed it to you it would be chained to a urine-stained block of wood. Livermore would go outside and piss against the wall before he did that.

The man behind the register looked like he was eighty years old, an obsolete machine that should have been left out in a field years ago. Livermore had already waited for the man to verify that his hundred-dollar bill was the real thing, taking out his currency pen, drawing a line across the face, then holding it up to the light, the whole operation taking as much time as a U.S. Treasury agent breaking up an international counterfeiting ring. Now he was slowly counting out the change, one crumpled bill at a time, with his old, stained fingers. Livermore's mind drifted to different ways he could persuade the man to move a little faster, maybe starting with the box cutter hanging in its plastic container on the dusty wall behind him. Start with one ear, see if that motivated the man. Then move to the other. The man was probably already mostly deaf, anyway.

"The reward's up to two million dollars," another man said from behind him. "Wouldn't mind running into him, no matter how dangerous they say he is."

Livermore came out of his reverie and listened to what the man was saying.

"I'd knock him right out," the man said, speaking to whoever was standing in line behind him. "Throw him in the back of my truck like a goddamned buck. Go collect my reward."

Livermore turned around and looked at him, another old man, a foot shorter and starved down to skin, bones, ligaments, and an Adam's apple that bobbed up and down as he rambled on.

"Better believe I'd give him a taste of his own medicine. Get out my tire iron, you know what I'm saying? Give him a once-over. Make him suffer, like he done to those poor women."

As Livermore took his change and left, he overheard the same man prepaying on pump number seven.

A minute later, the man came back out to his truck and opened up the front door just long enough for Livermore to pop the gas cap. When he shut the door and turned around, he nearly jumped out of his skin. Livermore was standing right in front of him.

"Let me help you out there, sir," Livermore said, taking the nozzle from the pump.

The man raised a hand to stop him, but Livermore was already squeezing the handle to start the flow of gasoline.

"I overheard what you were saying in there," Livermore said.

The man just stood there, still confused.

"You really think you could do that?" Livermore said as the numbers on the ancient pump clicked by slowly. "You think you're capable?"

"Look here," the man said, "I don't need you to pump my gas..."

"This man you were talking about..." Livermore said. "This man who knows all about pain . . . Who spent his whole life studying it... Maybe even turning it into an art form. I'm not sure how impressed he'd be by your little 'once-over' with the tire iron."

The man was shifting his weight back and forth from one foot to the other, scanning the other vehicles at the pumps, as if hoping for a friendly face. Someone who might come to his rescue.

"You think it would be your cold metal against his flesh and bones," Livermore said. "That you'd be the one in control. But you're wrong. You'd have to meet this man where he lives. To beat him, *you'd have to become just like him.*"

Another man walked by then. Livermore smiled to him and gave him a friendly nod.

"I see you work in a shop," Livermore said, reading the lettering on the side of the truck's door. "So I'm sure you know the value of picking the right tool for the job. Let's say you used your acetylene torch . . . Can you even imagine what that would be like? Watching parts of your own body being melted away?"

"Listen, buddy . . ." The man was licking his lips and wavering on his feet like he might get sick. His eyes kept darting to the numbers on the pump, as if willing the gas to flow faster into the tank.

"But be careful," Livermore said as the nozzle finally hit the automatic shutoff point. "By the time you're done, you'll be a different man. You might even find you have a real taste for it. Then maybe it'll be *you* with the two-million-dollar reward on your head."

The man kept standing next to his truck as Livermore returned the nozzle to its place beside the pump. The entire exchange would have been a foolish move for most men. Pure insanity to draw attention to himself, to make this man remember him, here at this gas station in the middle of New Mexico. How easy it would be for him to remember Livermore, to recount all of the things that he'd said and to sit with the sketch artist and re-create the face that had become burned into his mind.

How easy, assuming that the man lived to see the end of this day.

"You have a good afternoon," Livermore said, taking another look at the name of the business on the door. "Mr. Henderson of Edgewood, New Mexico."

Livermore watched the man get behind the wheel of his truck and quickly slam the door shut. He gave a long look over his shoulder as he cranked the truck to life and put it in gear.

If you're going in my direction, Livermore thought, *then maybe I'll make a stop in Edgewood so we can finish your education.*

He got in his own vehicle and watched the truck go back to the expressway. It turned west. Livermore was going east. He put the man out of his mind and kept driving.

CHAPTER FOURTEEN

AGENT LARKIN made his choice. He was coming with me.

We came up empty on the first two storage facilities. As soon as I saw the third facility, I knew we had a shot.

It was at the end of the street, set back a good hundred yards once you made your way through the gate and down to the main building. I could see the large doors on the units as soon as we got close, and beyond the back fence there was nothing but the desert and the Salt River in the distance.

We walked into the office and had to wait a few minutes, until the manager peeked around the little partition and looked surprised to see us standing there.

"Help you?"

Agent Larkin showed him his badge and told him he was looking for a unit that might have been rented by a man named Livermore. The manager shook his head at the name until

Larkin pulled out the photograph and showed it to him. Then the color drained from his face.

"I take it he was here," Larkin said.

"Yes," the man said, "but he didn't call himself Livermore."

The manager went through a little box of index cards, until he finally found the one he was looking for.

"Gene Lamont," he said. "Yeah, that's it."

"Wait a minute," I said. "What was the name? How did he spell that?"

He showed me the card.

Gene Lamont.

"That mean something to you?" Larkin said.

"He's a bench coach for the Tigers," I said. "Managed a couple teams, too."

Larkin just looked at me and waited for more.

"We were teammates in Toledo," I said. "Both catchers. My last year there, Gene got the September call-up, and I didn't."

"That's either a hell of a coincidence—"

"Or he was already messing with my head when he rented this place months ago."

"Any chance we could get into that unit?" Larkin asked the manager.

"If you want to," he said. "But it's empty now. I made him pack up and leave."

"Why is that?"

"Strict rule," the man said. "You can run power tools, anything you want, but no open flames."

"Open flames?" I said. "What the hell was he doing?"

"He had this whole grill thing set up, with a huge pot of water. First I thought he was cooking meth or something. I mean, what do *I* know, right? Wouldn't be the first time. But turns out he was just boiling water."

"For what?"

The manager shrugged. "Hell if I know. He'd just moved everything in, all these crates and boxes, and then I notice he's got this big pot of water going. I told him he can't do that and he, um…"

The man stopped talking and looked away from us.

"What happened?" Larkin said.

"Nothing," the man said a little too loudly, like he was trying to convince himself. "He just said some things and he left."

"What did he say?"

"Something about rules being made for men with small minds, then something about the Air Force, how it was obviously the right place for me. Not sure how he even knew I was a veteran, let alone an airman."

Larkin shot me a quick look. This sounded like the Livermore I had met in that interview room, a man who somehow knew your whole life story.

"Then he said something else…"

We both waited for him to take a moment, clear his throat, and continue.

"He said he'd read about a man who got trapped in a storage unit for nine weeks straight. Guy was lucky, he said, because he had some food and water in there. But he was still almost dead when they found him."

The man paused for a moment, bringing it all back.

"He said, even though he was alive when they got him out of there, he never really came back from it. The heat, the darkness, the isolation… The man's mind just snapped. And of course, he said, this happened in New York, so just imagine if it was Arizona, how hot it would get. That man would have been cooked alive."

He paused again, swallowing hard.

"I told him to get the hell out of here," he said, "but he just stood there, right where you're standing now, and he told me that man was locked in accidentally. Because who would do something like that on purpose? And the way he kept looking at me as he drove off... I still think about it. Like I wouldn't be surprised at all if he came back someday."

"I'm going to give you this," Larkin said, taking a card out of his wallet and putting it down on the counter. "Just in case you do ever see him again. You call me right away."

If you're alive to make the call, I thought. *This may be the last man on this earth you'd ever want to piss off.*

"What was the exact date?" Larkin said. "The day this all happened?"

"Let's see," he said, looking at the file card again. "It had to be, what, October thirteenth? Fourteenth, maybe?"

"If he couldn't work here," Larkin said, looking back at me, "he must have gone somewhere else."

"Pretty sure most places have the same rules," the manager said. "But why are you looking for him, anyway? Should I be worried?"

Larkin thought about his answer. "If you watch the news on television," he finally said, "you may see his face. But he's probably long gone by now, so don't worry. You just keep that card by your phone and call me if you need to. There's a reward for information leading to his capture, too."

The manager still didn't look like a man who'd be sleeping

well that night. But we thanked him and left. When we were back outside, I saw an old Lincoln Continental parked beside the building, the dark blue paint peeling in the harsh sunlight. I looked it over until I finally spotted the sticker in the corner of the windshield. Faded by the same sunlight, the faint outline of the Air Force symbol, the star with two wings.

I never would have noticed this if I wasn't looking for it, I thought. *But Livermore does this automatically. He looks for information about everyone he meets, then uses it to his advantage. Even if his only goal is to unnerve you.*

"I don't understand," Larkin said. "What does boiling water have to do with making explosives?"

"Whatever he was doing, he took it somewhere else. Middle of October. We could keep checking other storage units…"

"You heard the guy."

"Or we could look somewhere else," I said. "What would be his next choice?"

"Something private. Someplace he could do whatever he wanted."

"If you're him," I said, "where do you find that?"

A few minutes later, we were sitting in a coffee shop. Larkin had his laptop open and was using the Internet archives to go through the Craigslist ads for October. He wrote down the contact information for half a dozen people who had advertised space for rent.

"This one looks interesting," I said. "Five hundred square feet of workspace on a secluded road, metal building with good ventilation…"

"It's miles out of town. Almost in Maricopa."

"Call the number. See if the space got rented."

Larkin took out his cell phone and dialed the number. He asked whoever answered the phone if the space had been rented. He looked at me and nodded. He wasn't even halfway into his next question when the call ended.

"Doesn't want to talk about it," he said.

I nodded. "Sounds like somebody we need to go see."

CHAPTER FIFTEEN

THE SUN WAS SETTING behind him when Livermore hit the Texas panhandle. He found an electronics store in Amarillo and went to the photography counter, gave the woman the flash card from his camera, asked for eight-by-ten prints in the best quality she had. While he waited, he went through the rest of the store until he found the GPS trackers.

He settled on a SilverCloud Sync GPS with a magnetic mount. Two inches square, it would fit in any vehicle's wheel well and operate for days at a time, at temperatures as low as twenty below zero.

When he took the tracker to the counter, the woman was looking at the prints she had made. The half dozen shots of Alex McKnight, walking out of the hotel lobby.

"Are these… surveillance pictures?"

She was smiling as she said it. It was obviously the most interesting thing that had happened to her all day.

Livermore put a smile on his own face to mirror hers.

"Yes," he said. "They are."

She was in her late twenties, maybe thirty years old. Her hair was dyed a shade of beet red that didn't look quite natural. A shade she probably should have left behind in her teenage years, Livermore thought. She wore a lot of makeup around her eyes, and her fingernails were painted the same shade of red as her hair.

She thinks this makes her interesting, Livermore said to himself. *Painting her hair, painting her nails…*

"Why were you watching him?" she asked as she paged through them again, one after another. "Is he wanted for something?"

He took the photos from her gently, noting the fingerprints she was leaving on the glossy surface of the paper. He would have to clean them now.

"I can't talk about it here," he said.

"I get it. Top secret stuff." She pantomimed zipping her lips shut and throwing away the key.

"You could say that."

"So are you a cop? No, wait, let me guess."

She backed up a step, looking him up and down. Livermore waited patiently. He took a quick glance toward the front of the store, then the back.

The place was empty. They were alone.

"I don't think you're local," she said. "You sure don't *sound* like you live around here."

She has a good eye for detail, he thought. *And a good ear.*

"So I'm thinking you're something federal. FBI, maybe, or a marshal."

She'll remember everything about me. And she'll remember these photographs.

"I'm going to say a U.S. marshal. That's my guess."

He smiled again. "What's your name?"

"Irene."

He nodded. "So, Irene, let me guess what *your* job is."

"No, see, this is just until my—"

"Until your band hits it big," Livermore said. "And you can stop driving around in your little Hyundai."

She looked at him with surprise. "How did you—"

He nodded to the set of keys resting on the stool behind her, next to her purse. There was a guitar pick with a hole drilled through it attached to the ring, and the Hyundai symbol was prominent on the biggest key.

"In the meantime," he said, "you sell electronics to people who don't understand how they work. And you develop photographs."

Her smiled faded slightly. "Yes..."

"And when you develop those photographs," he said, taking a half step closer to the counter, "sometimes you break up the monotony by looking at them, by trying to imagine the story behind them."

"I didn't mean to do anything like that. I was just—"

"You do this with all of the photographs you develop. To pass the time."

She looked down and cleared her throat. "No. Not really."

"Someday a man will walk in here with some pictures," he said. "Pictures you aren't supposed to see."

She looked toward the front of the store, like she was hoping someone else would come in. But there was nothing but the darkness outside.

"You won't try to imagine the story behind those photographs. You'll try to forget them. Wish you never saw them. But he'll know."

"Okay," she said, clearing her throat again. "Can I get you anything else?"

"You need to be careful with a man like that. The fact that he's bringing his photographs here... It means he has an appreciation for the finished product. He wants a good-quality print. But it also shows a lack of self-control. He's taking a risk by letting them pass through your hands. A risk he's prepared to deal with if he has to."

She looked back at him without saying a word. The entire store was silent.

"You don't want a man like that walking into this store," Livermore said. "Not if you're here all by yourself."

She looked down at the phone, then at the front of the store again. Then back to Livermore. "The manager is usually in the back."

"Usually. But not right now."

She didn't answer. She put her hands together to stop them from shaking.

Livermore checked his watch. Then he smiled at her one more time.

"You'll be closing the store soon," he said. "Looks like you'll be safe for tonight."

Like the man in the gas station back in New Mexico, she would remember him. She would be able to describe him exactly, re-create his face, transcribe virtually every word he had said to her. Once again, a foolish move for any other man. A tightrope act that Livermore would not trust to anyone else.

He put the GPS tracker on the counter, next to the envelope containing the prints, and paid for it all with cash. She rang up the transaction quickly, and her hands were still shaking as she put everything in a bag.

"Enjoy the rest of your evening," he said.

Then he went out to his car to wait for her.

CHAPTER SIXTEEN

THIS LOOKS LIKE something out of a Mad Max movie," Larkin said as we got out of the car.

We had driven south, past the edge of the city. No more water, no more attempts to claim land from the desert. The Sierra Estrellas loomed to the west as we went twenty more miles, until we came to a huge sand-and-gravel pit. Then another mile to a turnoff, leading down a long dusty road that seemed to go nowhere. Until we finally came to a homestead and a small cluster of buildings, all glowing in the last light of the day.

We went to the front door and knocked. I looked around the place, at the old tractors and tools and a million other scraps of metal. An older man answered, a man wearing work pants and a filthy undershirt, with skin slightly less sun-worn than an Egyptian mummy. Larkin had his badge out as soon as the door opened.

"Who rented the space on your property?" I said.

"My daughter did the ad," he said. "A man answered it."

"That doesn't answer the question."

"He paid cash. He said he'd give me extra if I made sure nobody ever went inside."

"Name."

The old man had to think about it. I was expecting him to say *Gene Lamont* again. But he didn't.

"Tim Hosley."

Another old teammate of mine, from that same team in Toledo. Another young player who got a September call-up.

It's like he knew I'd be standing right here, I thought. *Right here in this spot. Asking this exact question.*

"We're going to have to see inside that building," Larkin said.

"It's got a padlock on it. Don't have the key."

"That's what bolt cutters are for," I said. "I'm sure you have a pair."

The man didn't bother to lie. He closed the door for a moment, came back with a huge pair of bolt cutters, and we followed him down a long driveway that passed by other buildings, a few old cars, another tractor, another few million scraps of junk metal, until we got to the end.

Gene Lamont, I thought. *Tim Hosley.*

I'd been keeping myself focused on the job at hand, hunting down the leads, from one location to the next... But now that I was here, I could feel myself getting closer to him, to the place where the real Livermore lived. Those names from my past, they just fed the flames, made me want to find him even more.

It felt like he was watching us. At that very moment, as we walked down that last dusty road to the place that held his secrets.

It felt like he was laughing at us.

"Alex," Larkin said. "We should call the office first."

"We're here," I said. "Let's see what's inside."

The building was made of tin, every wall visibly warped from the heat. It was about five hundred square feet, as advertised, but with no windows. It looked a hundred years old, the kind of ramshackle shack that would have been claimed by rust a long time ago if it wasn't in the middle of a desert. There was a round circulating fan positioned on the corrugated roof, but it wasn't spinning. A horrible place to do anything in, I was sure, but I could imagine Livermore seeing this godforsaken shack on the end of a forgotten desert road and knowing he'd found the perfect home.

We watched the man line up the bolt cutters and squeeze the handles together. When the shank was cut clean through, he pulled off the lock and yanked open the door. I had a sudden thought, a moment too late, that the man who knew I'd probably be standing here, waiting for this door to open, was the same man who could set up a remote ambush in a canyon to kill seven men.

But when the door swung open, there was no explosion—just a wave of trapped heat coming out at us. I let out my breath as we both looked inside.

The first things we saw were the ropes. Dozens of them, hanging from the rafters in two parallel rows and creating a sort of hallway that led into the room.

"What the hell," the man said.

I walked between the rows, the ropes so close that they brushed against my shoulders as I passed through. Some of them were just a few feet long. Some of them were so long they had to be looped several times from the floor to the ceiling. In the dense heat, there was a strange, earthy smell to them.

The back of the building was obscured in the darkness. That was when the man turned the overhead light on.

"I don't know nothing about anything that went on in here," he said. "So whatever you find..."

"Don't touch anything else," Agent Larkin said to him. "Just step back."

The light was filtered through the ropes, casting a hundred thin shadows on either side of the room. It was really more like two separate rooms, divided by the hallway. I chose the right side first, pushing myself through the ropes, into what was clearly Livermore's laboratory. There was a metal worktable running along the wall. On top of that was a large tabletop grill, with a single iron pot that could have held twenty gallons of water. Beside that was a large bottle of mineral oil.

Agent Larkin pushed through the ropes to stand next to me. He'd already pulled out his cell phone and started dialing.

There were semi-clear boxes of wires stacked neatly on the workbench. Other boxes contained circuits, relays, connectors, other electrical parts too obscure for me to recognize.

"This is where he made his explosives," Larkin said, nodding toward the other side of the workbench, past the grill and the big iron pot. There was a set of glass beakers there, a rack of tubes, and a Bunsen burner. And several unmarked plastic containers of powders and liquids.

I moved to the metal utility shelves that sat next to the table. On one shelf there was a large collection of iron pipes, of all different sizes. On another shelf a half dozen pressure cookers.

"He was experimenting," Larkin said. "Pipe bombs, pressure cookers..."

I was already feeling numb, already overwhelmed by the scope of what this man had done here. All of the time and effort that had gone into these instruments of murder.

There was a box of fuses among the pipes. Slow burn, fast burn . . . Other fuses I couldn't identify, all homemade from matches or black gunpowder, even a few from Christmas tree lights.

This is what he did every day. This was his hobby, finding new ways to kill people.

"Just like the Boston Marathon," Larkin said. "You still think he—"

"No," I said. "This doesn't make him a terrorist. All this stuff, it still feels... too personal."

But then I looked at everything in front of me again, all of these lethal tools spread out on these tables. And I started doubting every gut instinct I'd ever had about this man.

Maybe Larkin is right, I thought. *Maybe we really don't know what this man is capable of.*

I moved down to another shelf, where several clear jars sat in a neat line, all filled with a pale yellow jelly. Larkin bent down to look closely at the jars without touching them.

"This is... napalm."

I looked at him. "Are you kidding me?"

"He could have used this in the canyon instead, but he was probably worried about leaving it in the heat."

"So he blew us apart with shrapnel," I said, looking at another shelf filled with boxes of lead shot, everything from tiny birdshot to ball bearings a good inch in diameter.

Leaning against the shelves was a large industrial drill.

"That's a core drill," I said. "With a diamond-tipped bit, he could have cut right through the rock in the canyon. Set those pipes in, like little howitzers."

I kept moving, to the far corner of the room. There was a full-sized refrigerator standing there. It was humming, and there was a rusty metal latch bolted onto the door to keep it closed.

"That's for the ammonium nitrate," Larkin said. "You freeze it before you filter it. I can smell a little ammonia, can't you?"

I could only smell the ropes, but I took his word for it. I was looking at the latch, wondering why it was necessary...

"They track that stuff now," Larkin said. "Livermore went to a lot of trouble here, to stay off the grid. Or maybe he just liked making all of this stuff himself."

As I happened to look down at the floor in front of the refrigerator, I saw a constellation of red dots.

Drops of blood.

I picked up a neatly folded kitchen towel, used that to undo the latch, then grab the handle of the refrigerator and pull it open.

"Alex," Larkin said, "don't open that."

But it was too late. The door swung open, and the cold air hit us in the face.

Then we saw the body.

It was a woman, curled up on the floor of the refrigerator, like she had been trying to keep herself warm. She was naked except for a pair of blue panties. There was a butterfly tattoo on her left shoulder blade.

There were gouges all along the walls. From her fingernails.

"That's her," Larkin said. "Stephanie Hyatt."

He pushed the door closed and got back on his cell phone. I just stood there for a while, thinking about what could possibly come next.

Six women wasn't enough, I thought. *You had to lock up number seven in a fucking refrigerator.*

I wanted to pick up the drill and start swinging it, knock over every box, every jar, break everything I could find.

"Easy, Alex." Larkin stood next to me, waiting for his call to go through.

I walked away from him, through the rope hallway, pushing my way to the other side. Where there was the worktable and all of the supplies on the first side, here the back wall was dominated by three large hanging tapestries. All Japanese art, but not like the prints in Livermore's apartment. These depicted something else entirely: in one, a naked woman was blindfolded and tied to a chair, in another a man in an ornate robe dripped hot wax from a candle onto a woman's chest.

No, not wax. It's burning right through her skin. It's hot metal.

On the second tapestry, a man was tied up and hanging upside down with what looked like a great iron wagon wheel around his neck. The third might have been the most disturbing of all, a man suspended over several bamboo stakes with the pointed tips piercing his body. As if to bring that image to life, there was a glass case beneath the image with a grow light shining down on a dozen short stalks of bamboo.

I went closer to the case and looked inside, then moved to the desk next to it, where parchment paper was kept rolled up in several bins. One paper was laid out flat, with a pen and ink nearby. There were Japanese symbols drawn on the paper, which of course meant nothing to me. But I would have bet any-thing the meaning of the symbols was as dark as the artwork hanging on the walls.

I felt like I had just walked from one half of Livermore's brain to the other, from the logical, analytical side to whatever the hell you'd even call the rest of it. The creative, the intuitive... I didn't know if you could even use words like those to describe the inside of this man's head.

Next to the desk was another glass case, this one containing an elaborate metal birdcage—except that the bottom of the cage was open and there were leather straps attached to it, as if you'd actually have a reason to strap a cage to someone's body. I didn't have to know anything else to know that this was something evil.

"Alex!"

Larkin's voice came to me from the other side of the ropes. I went to the last corner of the room, where a bookshelf stood. I looked at the spines. More Japanese symbols. There were larger books on the lower shelf. I still had the kitchen towel in my hand, and I used that to pull out a book and open it.

In the dim light I could make out the elaborate ink draw-ings, some with text, others spread across two facing pages. A man in an ornate robe tying a woman's wrists together. Then wrapping ropes around her body, above and below her breasts. I went through the pages quickly, each one more and more elab-orate, a woman tied up and hanging in the air, then another with her legs doubled back into a painful hogtie. Yet another hanging from one leg, the other leg folded together and tied tightly, her arms trussed behind her back.

The ropes, I thought. *The ligatures found on the victim in Scottsdale, the fibers at the other kill sites...*

This is what he does to them.

This is why he needs all of these ropes.

I put that book back and took out another. Another set of drawings to see, these even more sickening. This book was more general, with no artistic rope designs, just basic human suffering inflicted by every means I could ever imagine. Men and women spread out on racks, violated with instruments, pierced with needles and stakes and barbs.

"Alex, what are you doing?"

I took a breath and kept paging through the book. A man's body slowly crushed by an elephant's massive foot. A man with a cage tied to his stomach...

I looked back at the cage in the glass case.

You tie this to your victim. Open the little door and put the rats inside.

It washed over me in a hot, sick wave.

This is Livermore.

This is what he dreams about.

I closed the book and put it back in its place. I was glad to be holding it with the kitchen towel. Never mind the crime scene, or the handling of evidence. I just didn't want any of this to touch my skin.

Before I stood up, I saw one more book on the bottom shelf. It was the only book without Japanese symbols. As I pulled it out, I saw that it was a scrapbook.

I took it over to the desk so I could see it in better light. As I put it down, I heard Agent Larkin behind me. He had pushed his way through the ropes to join me on this side. He stood in the same spot I had, looking up at the images on the wall.

"Holy fuck," he said.

Still holding the scrapbook with the towel, I opened it to the first page.

"I've got agents on the way," Larkin said. "We'll wait for them outside."

I saw a face.

My face.

It was a photograph of me from my high school yearbook. I flipped the page, not even bothering to be careful now. One page after another, it was all here.

My whole life.

There were old photographs from the *Detroit News* and the *Detroit Free Press*, some of them reprints done on modern paper, some of them originals on yellowing newspaper stock. My entire career as a high school baseball player—high school tournaments, all-star teams, year-end awards. On the next page, my minor league career began. More pictures. Team statistics. Even box scores. This was where he got my .249 average at Toledo. This was where he got Gene Lamont's name. And Tim Hosley's.

I kept going, feeling another stream of ice water run down my back with every turn of the page. After baseball, my time in college. My official portrait from the Henry Ford College yearbook. No surprise, he'd actually gotten his hands on a copy of my college yearbook, too—just to cut out my picture and paste it into this book.

Another page and I was looking at the coverage of my engagement in the newspapers. Then my wedding. This was back in the day when the papers would actually send a photographer to take pictures at weddings, especially if the groom was a semi-famous local athlete. All of those clippings were here.

Then my career as a cop. My graduation picture from the police academy. And finally, what I knew was coming next...

The front pages of both local papers, showing my partner's picture next to the grainy image of me being carried on a stretcher into the ambulance.

TWO OFFICERS SHOT
One Dead, One in Critical Condition

I felt Larkin grabbing my arm, trying to pull me away from the scrapbook. But I didn't want to leave. I didn't want to go outside, into the light, into the fresh air. I didn't want to move until somebody explained to me why this was happening.

"Who are you, you crazy piece of shit?" I said. Because there was no explanation coming. No answers. Not yet.

"Who are you?"

CHAPTER SEVENTEEN

CREEPIEST CUSTOMER EVER.

Irene Murphy texted these three words to her best friend, Sarah. Still trying to laugh it off, but her hands were shaking as she keyed in each letter. She kept looking out at the darkness just beyond the windows, wondering if he'd come back, this man who had seemed kind of interesting and mysterious at first, until she had looked into his green eyes one time too many and had seen something else there. Something that scared her. Something that made her keep the phone in her hand while she counted down the last few minutes.

But he never came back.

She texted Sarah again, asking her about the next practice for their band. Still no response. She pictured her standing behind the bar, mixing a half dozen drinks at once, the phone buzzing away on the bar top, drowned out by the noise.

When the clock hit nine, she went to the front of the store

and flipped the sign to CLOSED. Then she locked the door and spent the next half hour running the receipts. She activated the alarm, turned out the lights, then opened the door again, just long enough to step outside. She locked the door behind her and walked through the parking lot. There were a dozen cars in the lot, but that wasn't unusual. Not when your store was next to a restaurant that stayed open until midnight. Still, she made a point of looking through every windshield as she walked by. Her car was parked on the far side of the lot, beneath the last light.

She hurried to get in the car and lock her door. Letting out a breath, almost laughing to herself. It felt like when she was a kid, and she'd run up the stairs from the basement after she'd turned off the lights, trying to outrun the tentacles that were coming up after her.

She drove home to her apartment on the other side of Amarillo. Not much of a place, but she'd be able to move soon, maybe, if the band ever got some gigs. Or if she just found a better job, the kind where she didn't have to deal with creepy customers.

At one point, she saw a pair of headlights behind her. They were still there when she made one turn, then another. For a moment, she thought about driving right over to Sarah's bar. Running inside and telling her to call the police. Then she made another turn, and the car behind her kept going.

She let out another long breath.

When she got to her apartment building, she heard her phone beep. She picked it up, saw the text back from Sarah, finally.

are you okay? come to the bar!

She texted back, *Home now, call me when you get off.* Then

she got out of her car and went inside. She went up the stairs to the third floor. Her apartment was the first one on the left. She took her key out and put it in the lock, just as she heard something behind her.

Before she could even turn, she felt a hand closing around her right wrist. The scream had barely formed in her throat when another hand came across her mouth. She tried to kick at the man's legs, but he was already pushing her inside her apartment. Her arm was twisted painfully behind her back, until she tried to scream again, biting at the hand on her mouth and tasting blood. As he cursed and let go of her, she spun and tried to rake his face with her keys. A self-defense lesson she had practiced in her head a thousand times, walking through that empty parking lot. But he caught her wrist, and his other hand shot forward, fast as a snake striking, to latch around her throat. He stood with his face close to hers.

It's him. The man from the store.

He still had the same dead-calm expression with the strange half smile, even as he tightened his grip on her neck. She tried to suck in air, to fill her lungs with just enough to scream one more time, but he slammed her against the wall. She felt the impact on the back of her head and then everything went out of focus.

"Please," she said with her last breath. "Don't."

"You brought this on yourself."

The voice echoed in her head as she felt the grip tighten around her neck again. She clawed at the hand with her fingernails until she started to feel herself sliding down the wall. Lower and lower.

Until she had fallen all the way into nothing.

———

She opened her eyes again. It took her a moment to realize where she was. Lying on her stomach, but somehow raised above the ground, looking down at the carpet. She tried to speak, but her mouth wouldn't open. As she moved her arms, she felt a sharp pain in her shoulders. Her wrists were bound together, behind her back. Her feet were bound, too. She couldn't lift her head more than a few inches. She turned as far as she could, to see what he had done to her.

I'm on the coffee table, she said to herself. *He's tied me down. No, he's* taped *me down.*

The tape was looped across her mouth, then wrapped several times around her neck. She felt it against her back, against her legs and her ankles. From one end of her body to the other, the loops disappearing under the table. She even saw the empty roll, discarded a few feet away. As she strained to see the rest of her apartment, she didn't spot him anywhere. A full minute passed. She fought down the panic, made herself be still. Another minute.

He's gone, she thought. *He left me here. I have to get free.*

She worked against the tape, rocking back and forth and nearly turning the table over. She screamed inside her head, losing the battle against the panic, fighting and fighting until she had used up the last of her strength. She made herself be still again, made herself breathe.

Then the door opened, and the man came back inside. He was carrying a large shopping bag.

"Don't make this worse for yourself," he said, coming close and setting down the bag.

You don't have to kill me, she thought, willing the words to life, trying to transmit them through the air to him. *You can do anything you want. Just don't kill me.*

"You will not scream," he said as he bent down even closer and started to pull the tape from her mouth. "You will say exactly what I tell you to say. Do you understand?"

When her mouth was free, she gathered in her breath, but the scream died in her throat as he pulled her arms away from her back, igniting the dull ache in her shoulders into a white-hot blast of heat.

"That's approximately ten pounds of force," he said to her. "From this angle, it would take twenty to dislocate the shoulder. Do you want to know what thirty pounds feels like?"

She shook her head frantically. He repeated the words he wanted her to say, then he pointed the phone at her face and told her to start speaking. She strained to hear them, to remember them. Then she said the words, one by one, not even knowing what she was saying. None of it made sense. But she didn't want to feel that pain again.

When she was done, she closed her eyes and started to cry.

This is really happening, she said to herself.

I am going to die.

He said some words of his own into the phone, more words that made no sense to her.

I am going to die.

He put the phone in his pocket. Then he bent down to the shopping bag and took out a small combination safe. He set the safe on the floor, directly in front of her. She could see that the door was slightly open, but she couldn't see what was inside.

I am going to die.

She had already given up when he reached into the bag one last time.

I am going to die.

I am going to die.

CHAPTER EIGHTEEN

I HAD BEEN A SPLIT SECOND too late to save my partner, back on that hot summer night in Detroit. Now I
was God knows how many *days* too late to save this
woman in the refrigerator. I stood there trying to imagine what
she must have gone through in her last hours as I watched them
take her out in a body bag, along with everything else from that
metal shed at the end of that desert road.

They took down over a hundred ropes. *Why had he boiled so
many of them?* Maybe it had become a ritual for him. What was
more interesting to the techs was the chemistry set, the electronics, everything he had used to build his explosives.

They took the torture books, bringing each one of them out
into the daylight. Some of them looked old. Rare, probably
worth a lot of money to a collector, if there were such people in
the world. Which I was sure there were.

They took down the wall hangings, brought out the glass

cases with the bamboo and the rat cage. All of the parchment, every last piece of Livermore's life.

And then, in the midst of all this madness, for reasons I still didn't understand...

My life.

They took the Alex McKnight scrapbook to the FBI offices to be held and processed as evidence. I spent an hour in the lab, watching them go through every page. When they got to the end and I had to see the clipping from the Detroit newspaper again—from the night I watched my partner die—that was when I'd had enough.

I left the place without bothering to tell anyone, went outside, and walked down the street. The sun was down, the air cooler. It was the first time I'd been truly alone since I'd arrived in Arizona, and somebody was probably already looking for me, but I didn't care anymore.

The FBI office was right next to the little regional airport on the north side of town, so I went into the rental car office and drove off the lot in the car I'd been threatening to rent all day. I made my way across town for a while, not even sure where I was going. Until I saw the gun shop.

It was lit up bright and cheery and it occupied half a city block, as only an Arizona gun shop could. There were full-color pictures of guns showcased in the windows as if they were fine pieces of jewelry, everything from handguns to assault rifles. I went inside and saw enough firepower to arm a small country, in glass cases that ran along three sides of the store, with more guns hanging on the walls.

I had carried a gun for eight years as a cop, only tried to fire it once—and that was the night I took it out a beat too slow. I had bought another gun when I got my PI license, but ended up throwing that into Lake Superior. I had sworn that day I'd never hold a gun again.

But now, as I picked up a Glock 22, the last weapon I had carried in Detroit, I sighted down the barrel and imagined Martin T. Livermore standing on the other end of it.

I would kill you right now if I could. I would pull this trigger without a second thought.

I was about to fill out my ATF form 4473 and wait for the shop owner to run me through the NICS database, but when he asked me for my state of residence, I had to tell him Michigan.

"Gotta be an Arizona resident to purchase a handgun here," he said. I told him I was an ex-cop. He still couldn't sell me the gun, but he did direct me to a local gun owner a mile down the road who could help me out. A half hour later, I had a similar model Glock and a box of .40 caliber ammunition.

I bought some clothes and a bag to carry everything in, put it all in the trunk of the rental car, and drove back to the FBI office. Larkin seemed to be the only agent who'd even noticed that I had left. He didn't ask where I had gone.

He had a copy of the scrapbook pages to give me, and I spent the next couple of hours going through them. Every photograph, every article. If my own mother had lived past my eighth birthday, she couldn't have kept a more complete record of my life.

But why?

I was still no closer to the answer.

AFTER I DROVE BACK to my hotel room, I took apart the gun, cleaned and oiled it, put it back together again. Then I loaded it.

An old ritual from another lifetime, but it made me feel better just having it in my hand.

His words came back to me, what he'd said to me in that van...

Do you think this ends today?

No, I thought as I sat there in a hotel room with a freshly loaded Glock in my right hand. *It's not over.*

I put the gun in the bedside table drawer, next to the Gideon Bible. Then I spread the scrapbook pages out on the bed and looked at them again. I might have slept for a while. If I did, it was a shallow sleep that didn't begin to ease my exhaustion. Then at some point in the middle of the night, I felt my phone vibrate. I turned on the light and looked at it. I had a new email message.

I shook myself fully awake and opened the email. It was from an address I didn't recognize—in fact, it looked like nothing more than a random string of letters and numbers. I opened the video that was attached to the email. It was hard to make out what I was seeing at first. Just a blurry, cheap video taken on somebody's cell phone, but then the image stabilized and I saw a woman's face. Young, maybe late twenties, with a nose ring, and even with the washed color on the video I could see that her hair had been dyed a bright shade of red. She was lying down on something...

A table. Something about her arms didn't look right. Like they were twisted behind her. I stayed right there on the edge of the bed as I watched her, my heart pounding.

"Say it," a voice said. A man's voice. A voice I knew.

Livermore.

"Say exactly what I told you to say."

The woman started crying. A shudder ran through her body. I could only imagine what was going through her mind. The fear, the pain, all of it at once.

"Alex," she said, choking back sobs. "Alex McKnight. You have to come save me. Please. It's all up to you. Please hurry. Please…"

She started crying again. Then her eyes went wide as duct tape was pulled tight across her mouth. The video stayed focused on the woman's face, but it was Livermore who spoke next. "Come alone," he said. "If I see anyone else… *anyone*… she dies."

"Where are you?" I said to the video. *"Where the fuck are you?"*

"This is between you and me," he went on. "If you tell anyone else, I'll know. And she will suffer more than you can imagine."

I kept watching and waiting, holding the phone tight in my hand.

"Start driving to Albuquerque," he said. "Right now."

Then the video ended.

I WAS DRESSED within two minutes, in my rental car and on the road within three. It was just past four in the morning, the roads almost empty. I headed north, trying not to drive recklessly, trying to keep myself steady. It was a long way to Albuquerque.

He sends everyone else to San Francisco, I thought. *Then he brings me east. I shouldn't be surprised.*

It really was a diversion all along.

As I drove up through northern Arizona, into the higher elevation, the air got colder and condensed against my windshield. I started to see traces of snow. By the time I hit Flagstaff, there were piles of it on either side of the road. I stopped and got some gas, breathing in the cold air. The sun was coming up, casting a thin light that didn't even begin to warm me.

You have to stay alive, I said to the woman in the video. *Whoever you are, you have to stay alive.*

I hadn't heard from Livermore again. I just had to keep going. It was the only thing I could even think of doing. For hours.

And hours.

I was in New Mexico, driving east, pushing the rental car hard, doing ninety in the left lane. As I got close to Albuquerque, my phone vibrated and I pulled over to see what had landed in my email.

It was another video. The same woman on the same table. She was looking up at me, her eyes glazed. Livermore's voice came from off camera again.

"Did I say Albuquerque? My mistake. I meant Amarillo."

The video ended.

I got back on the road, kept driving around the city, more hours until I was in the flat red dirt lands that told me I was getting close to Texas.

It's been eight hours, I told myself. *Eight hours taped up like that. No human being could endure it.*

But I kept going. Fighting through my own exhaustion, the road starting to go double in my eyes as I crossed the Texas border. It was just after noon now, the low February sun making my head hurt. I felt the phone vibrate in my pocket again, almost drove off the road trying to get to it. I pulled over and opened up the next email.

The woman's eyes were open, but she didn't move. I wasn't even sure if she was still breathing, but then she blinked.

"I hope you're not too late, Alex." Livermore's voice. I had a sudden vision of my hands around his throat, of me choking the life out of him so that nobody would ever have to hear that voice again.

"Here is the address," Livermore said. He said a number, a street, and an apartment number. I grabbed a pen from my bag and wrote it down on the back of my rental receipt. Then I plugged the address into my phone. I was still twenty miles away.

I left the expressway and made my way through town, second-guessing myself the whole way. Maybe I should have called somebody, even though I didn't have an address until just now. But the police could have been out searching for her. Or now that I *do* have the address... I should call them *now*.

I kept up the argument with myself until I was close enough to the address to put it aside. *Time to think,* I said to myself. *Time to be sharp.*

You're here.

I parked next to the building, took the gun out of the glove compartment, and went inside. It was three stories high, maybe seven or eight apartments per floor. There was no way to look through a window. I went up the stairs and found apartment 301, stood outside the door for a moment.

Now what?

I pictured him on the other side of the door, waiting for me. *If I open it, I'm walking right into a trap.*

No, it's your only chance to surprise him.

I tried to put myself in his place, imagine what I'd do…

I put my hand on the doorknob and turned it slowly. It was unlocked.

No, you can't do it this way.

I took my hand away from the door, waited another few seconds. Listening. Then I knocked.

"Livermore!" I said. "I'm here!"

I moved back to the stairwell, put my back against the wall, and watched the door.

Nothing happened.

I moved back slowly, careful not to make any noise. This time I put my ear against the door. I heard a sound on the other side. It was faint. Muffled.

She's still alive.

Her face flashed through my mind, the face of that woman, taped down to the table. *Open the door,* I thought. *But then step back, wait for him to move, or shoot, or whatever the hell he's going to do.*

I took a breath, lined myself up, and then kicked the door, just above the knob. It was cheap wood, both the frame and the door itself, so it flew open as I fell backward. I came back up with the gun drawn, just long enough to smell the gasoline. *No, not gasoline, something else.* There was a loud whoosh, and then a great wave of heat blew me back to the floor. From one second to the next, the doorway had turned into an inferno, the black smoke already billowing out into the hallway. I tried to wave it away, tried to take a step into the apartment, but I felt the flames on my shoes and on my pants and in another instant it felt like I was on fire myself. Then a strong pair of hands was grabbing me from behind and pulling me away from the door, just as I heard the scream coming from inside. It lasted for only a second, but it was a scream I'd hear for the rest of my life, as the hands pulled me back down the hallway with the fire trailing after me, as if chasing me.

I pushed the man away and tried to go back, but another blast of heat hit me square in the face, singeing my hair as the flames kept burning on the floor below me.

"Alex," a voice said. "You're on fire!"

I turned and saw Agent Larkin's face, didn't even have time to think about what he was doing here as he tackled me and put his jacket over my legs. The jacket caught on fire and he threw it away, then he grabbed me by the shoulders again and dragged me to the stairwell.

"It's too late!" he said, just as the sprinklers came on above us and the fire alarm started to ring. Other doors opened, up and down the hallway, as Larkin half dragged, half threw me down the stairs.

I knew he was right. I knew it was too late. And I knew something else, something that would stay with me forever. One terrible fact that I'd never be able to erase or explain away.

Whoever that woman was, Livermore had just made me burn her alive.

CHAPTER NINETEEN

As Livermore watched Alex go into the building, he felt something that no drug could ever give him. Something like the way tying a perfect knot against white skin would feel, or drawing a perfect *kanji* on white parchment. The perfect execution of a perfect idea. He could see the compound symbol for *kanpeki* in his mind, meaning something so much more profound than any English word could capture. The symbol for *complete* above the symbol for *jade*.

A perfect jewel.

That's what this moment was.

He pictured Alex going up the stairs. Going to the door marked 301. The hesitation he must have felt at that moment, wondering what to do next. Livermore wished he could see it. Alex weighing his options, not even knowing that no matter what he did, it would be wrong.

He had taken five gallon jars of the napalm he'd made in his laboratory. Styrofoam dissolved into gasoline, stirred with great patience until it turned into jelly. When lit, napalm is virtually inextinguishable. It is liquid fire, clinging to whatever it touches. Spread across the floor of that woman's apartment, with a simple electronic igniter wired to the door. A Christmas tree bulb with the tip removed, a small amount of the napalm put inside, to come in contact with the filament. Two nine-volt batteries. Such a simple device, not nearly as complicated as his explosives in the canyon. But safe, stable, foolproof. There was no danger of the napalm igniting until the exact moment when the door was pushed open.

Now as he waited for the second half of the show, Livermore got out of his vehicle and took a red metal canister with him to the side of the building. Straight gasoline this time. He found a good spot on the grass and carefully drew his design. The grass was already brown in the Texas winter, but he knew there'd be no misreading the char pattern. When he was done, he struck a match and watched the flames come to life.

He set down the gasoline container and went back to his vehicle. He didn't bother wiping down the fingerprints. He was past that now.

There was nothing to hide anymore. They would all know that Martin T. Livermore had been here.

A black sedan pulled up to the building, just as Livermore was about to turn the corner. He stayed on the other side of the building and watched the man get out and run inside. It was the young agent he had seen in Phoenix.

I told you to come alone, Alex. I set up everything so carefully, created my little sleight-of-hand diversion just to make sure everyone else was looking in another direction...

Just to keep this between us, Alex. Like the great samurai Musashi's duel with Sasaki on the island of Funajima, how Musashi waited until everything had turned in his favor—the tides, the angle of the sun, even the rising impatience of Sasaki and how that drained his energy—until the moment came for Musashi to face him.

That moment is coming, Alex.

It is coming.

Livermore waited another beat, then he went around the building to McKnight's car and slipped the magnetic case containing the GPS tracker above the right rear wheel well. He didn't even have to stop, just a quick movement of the hand as he walked by, feeling the magnet come in contact with the metal, even as the first person came running out of the building, then the second, then a great tidal wave as every resident streamed out of every door. Nobody noticed the stranger walking back to his vehicle.

He watched the first fire truck arrive. The first police car. Then finally Alex McKnight himself, being pulled from the building by the young agent. Livermore took out his Nikon binoculars from the black case and focused in on Alex. The young agent was holding him by both arms, talking to him. As Alex broke away from him, the look of anguish on his face was another moment of *kanpeki*.

Livermore tilted the binoculars down to see the burnt material on Alex's pant legs, where the napalm had stuck to him. His shoes were still smoking.

The agent approached him again as Alex stood half bent over, like he was about to throw up. Larkin put a hand on his back, and Alex straightened and then walked away. That was how he ended up at the other side of the building.

One of the apartment windows blew out, and the smoke billowed out into the sky, as black as death. Firemen dragged one hose into the building while another hose was trained at the window from outside.

But Livermore saw none of it. He kept his eyes on Alex McKnight, even as he put his vehicle in gear and started to drive away. One last moment of *kanpeki* as he watched Alex standing over the message he had left for him, *just for him,* burned into the dead grass.

CHAPTER TWENTY

WHATEVER MADNESS had driven Livermore to coat that apartment, *to coat the woman herself,* with *napalm* ... it was the same madness that had driven him to create this line in the grass, ten feet long, with two shorter lines joining it at the point.

An arrow.

Drawn with great care, the lines smooth and even and straight. Lines drawn by an engineer.

Lines drawn for me.

I could still feel the heat on my legs, where the napalm had stuck to my pants and to my shoes. I could still hear that woman's scream in my head as I played it back, over and over, trying to make it come out differently. If I had known somehow, if I had been more careful, or quicker, or slower, or God knows what. In the background, there were windows blowing out, firemen yelling at one another and running hoses inside and out of the building. But I didn't hear any of it.

I heard only that one last scream.

As I looked back down at the arrow, I followed its line across the street that ran behind the apartment building, directly to an office building. Even now the building was being cleared out by the FBI, working with Amarillo PD and the Texas DPS, and they were searching it from top to bottom.

My gut told me they would find nothing. This arrow was pointing at something else, beyond the building.

But what?

Maybe he was pointing it at himself somehow, wherever he would be next, and that was the only thought I could hold on to at that moment.

Tell me exactly where to go, you sick fuck. Bring me right to you. I don't care if you kill me. As long as you go down with me.

"You all right?"

I turned to see Agent Larkin standing behind me.

"What are you doing here?" I said.

"You shouldn't have come here alone, Alex."

"What do you want?"

He looked down at the plastic evidence bag he was holding. "You need to see this."

He came closer and showed it to me. It was an eight-by-ten photograph.

Of me.

"There was a fireproof safe in the apartment," he said. "This was inside. Looks like it was taken yesterday. That's the roof of my car."

I looked at the tired face in the photograph. The condos be-hind me, just as I was about to get back into the car with

Larkin. He was right, it was from yesterday, when we were out retracing Livermore's crime scenes.

It didn't surprise me that he would have followed us, that he would have taken this photograph. That he would bring it with him and leave it here next to the woman.

I was beyond surprise by now.

I turned it over and looked at the back. Livermore had drawn an elaborate Japanese symbol, like the symbols I had seen in that storage shed.

"What does this mean?" I said.

"We don't know yet. I'm taking it to the Amarillo FBI unit."

I nodded and handed it back to him. This young agent who must have stayed up all night, keeping watch at the hotel in Phoenix, then driving all day to follow me here. To a burning doorway. Where he had probably saved my life.

"I'm taking you, too."

I SPENT ANOTHER two hours sitting in another interview room. This one was a lot smaller, with no windows. I felt the walls closing in on me as yet another FBI special agent in another dark suit asked me the same questions and I gave him the same answers.

I have no connection to this woman.

I have no connection to Martin T. Livermore.

I have no idea where he'll go next.

"They've got the state police on every road leading out of town," Larkin said to me when the interview was over. "They're knocking on every door in the neighborhood, looking for a witness. If we can get a description of his vehicle, at least..."

"Let me see a map," I said.

He showed me a map of northern Texas. There were six major roads leading out of Amarillo, the land crisscrossed with two dozen smaller roads, heading in all directions.

"You guys still think he's on his way to San Francisco?" I said.

"We can't rule it out, Alex. Maybe that's still the real plan and *this* is the diversion."

I looked at him. "You don't believe that."

He didn't answer me. So I just got up and left the room. Larkin caught up to me in the parking lot. The sun was down, the air turning cold again.

"Where are you going?" he said.

"I don't know."

"I've been told to bring you back tomorrow. It's the only reason you're not in custody right now."

"You said you were going to help me."

"I'm trying to, Alex. But you're putting me in a tough spot."

"I need a drink."

We went into the first bar we found. We sat at the rail, and he watched me down one shot of Wild Turkey while he nursed a beer. I knew a second shot would lead to a third and a fourth. It was tempting, because I wanted to be numb. But I knew I needed to stay sharp, so I turned my glass over.

When Larkin's cell phone rang, he took it out of his pocket and looked at me while he talked to whoever was on the other end. Probably Agent Madison.

"I'm with him right now," he said. "Yes, we will. Tomorrow morning."

Someone turned on the jukebox, and he had to cover his other ear.

"It means *what?*"

He got up and went outside to finish the call. While he was gone, I sat there thinking about Livermore, wondering if he was still here in town. Maybe even taking more photographs.

Come find me, I said to him. *You want me so bad, I'm right here.*

Larkin came back inside and sat down next to me.

"The symbol on the back of the photograph," he said after a few long seconds of hesitation. "It's Japanese. It means *failure.*"

I nodded, staring down at my overturned shot glass.

"He's just trying to fuck with your head," Larkin said. "You know that."

I picked up the glass, weighing it in my hand.

"Look," Larkin said, leaning in close to my right ear. "You were a cop before I was even born, so what the fuck am I even going to say to you? That you're not responsible for that woman's death? *You already know that, too.*"

I didn't try to answer.

"You come back with me, Alex, and we all work together. We catch him. End of story."

I turned and looked at him, and that was all it took for him to shut his mouth for a while. There were two seconds of silence, then the jukebox cranked out another bad country song, even louder than the first. Someone came up behind me and leaned over the bar to order a drink.

"I know that smell," he said with a heavy Texas accent, saturated in alcohol. "You're a nozzle jockey."

I ignored him.

"Y'all must'a just rolled," he said. "Smells like the Old Testament in here."

"If you don't mind, sir," Larkin said to him. "We're not firemen."

He looked back and forth between us, and then down at my burnt shoes and pant legs. He swayed back and forth for a moment, then caught his balance by grabbing me by the shoulder.

"Hank," the bartender said to him, with an accent just as heavy, if less soaked with cheap whiskey. "Leave 'em be."

"I'm just trying to understand," he said, his hand still on my shoulder. "One of 'em's half burned up, and they say they're not firemen. So what the hell were you guys doing?"

"None of your business," I said without looking at him. "And take your hand off my shoulder."

"Alex," Larkin said, "take it easy."

"It's okay." The man lifted his hand off my shoulder and then gave it a quick flick of his fingers like he was brushing away the dirt from home plate. "You boys ain't from around here, are ya . . ."

"Do you have a problem with that?"

"Hank," the bartender said again. "Go sit down, all right?"

"I got no problem," he said, putting a hand on the bar to steady himself now. "We're a friendly bunch around here. We like everybody. Even people who got no business being here."

I closed my eyes and waited for him to say something. Just one more sentence.

"I just wanna know why I wasn't invited to the barbecue."

I came off the barstool and grabbed him with both hands, driving him backward toward the jukebox, still playing that same bad song too loud, until I put his back against the glass and the whole thing rocked for a moment and then went silent.

I felt Larkin pulling me away from him, then he and the

bartender both pushing me outside. The man trailed behind and stood in the doorway, an easy place to be brave with two other men between him and me.

"That's right," he said, "why don't you boys go back where you came from!"

I pushed the two men away from me and went to my car.

"Alex, wait."

He grabbed me from behind, just as I was opening my car door. I spun around to face him, and as I did I caught sight of the man still standing in the doorway, looking like he'd just won some sort of victory.

That's when it came to me.

The arrow.

I know what it means.

IT WAS FIVE IN THE MORNING when Larkin found me outside the motel, putting my bag in the backseat of my car.

"Going somewhere?"

"First rule of tracking a fugitive," I said. "They always go home."

"Livermore lives in Phoenix," Larkin said, his arms folded against his chest.

"Before that."

"California."

"No," I said. *"Home."*

"That arrow was pointing northeast…"

"Columbus, Ohio."

I closed the door and stood there, waiting for him to try to stop me.

"You can't go there," he said. "I told you, I have orders to—"

"I slipped out when you weren't looking. Nothing you could have done."

He looked at me. "Why would I let you do that?"

"Because you know I'm right. And because you're not an asshole."

"I'll call Columbus," he said. "We'll watch for him."

"I thought all your agents will be in San Francisco."

"I'll make this happen, Alex. Someone will be watching his house."

"Go ahead. I'll be there, too."

He stopped me before I could get into the car.

"Here's where I either put you in handcuffs," he said, "or risk my whole career and let you go after him."

"Once again," I told him, "it's time to make your choice."

A FEW MINUTES LATER, I hit the roadblock they'd set up on I-40. I waited in the line, wondering how busy it would get once the sun came up. Finally, I pulled up to the trooper standing there with a shotgun and waited for him to take a quick look inside my car. I was a male, around the right age, and traveling alone, so he checked my license. Then I was on my way again.

Livermore can beat that, I said to myself. *I know it.*

I passed through Springfield, Missouri, and then a long stretch through the middle of the state as the sun went down on another short February day. More hours of driving, after so many hours already spent chasing Livermore. There was nothing but the open road now, and exit signs leading to small towns I'd never heard of. I knew Livermore might be almost as exhausted as I was at that point, and I didn't think he'd try to make it all the way to Columbus. I tried to imagine him coming down this very same road, deciding where to stop for the night. I couldn't see him taking one of these exits yet. My gut told me he'd go all the way to St. Louis before stopping.

When I got to the city, I got off the expressway and drove down the dark empty streets, finally ending up over by Union Station, just on the edge of downtown. When I was finally out of the car, stretching my legs, the air was cold enough for me to see my own breath.

Larkin pulled in right behind me. I hadn't seen him in hours.

"What did your boss say?"

"He's not happy. I'm still on your trail. I won't go back until I find you."

"Tell him you lost me. You don't have to do this."

"I'm here," he said. "Let's get something to eat."

We checked in to our hotel, came back downstairs, and walked down Market Street. We didn't see anyone else, aside from a few homeless people stirring in a little park across the street. It was one of those cities that brought people downtown to work during the day, and then sent them home at night, leaving nothing but dark buildings and a single lamppost burning on every corner.

I kept looking around me, like I expected to see him.

We found the one sign of life down the street, a restaurant that probably relied on the hotel for all of its business. Larkin set up his laptop on a table and checked in with the office. I sat there and thought about how far I was from home. How I should have been sitting by the fire at the Glasgow Inn, having some of Jackie's beef stew.

"Amarillo developed some more information," he said. "Found out that Irene Murphy sent a text to a friend just before leaving the store last night. She was disturbed by an encounter she had with a customer."

"Livermore."

He nodded. "That picture he left in the safe, looks like he had it printed there. We can't see any other reason why he would have chosen her. Wrong place, wrong time."

There wasn't much else to say. I shook my head and looked up at the three big HD screens over the bar, each tuned to a different sport that nobody in the place seemed to be watching. Until the one screen in the middle broke into some kind of news report and suddenly Livermore's face was looking down at me.

The sound was off, but the caption read MANHUNT CONTINUES FOR SUSPECTED SERIAL KILLER.

Larkin and I both looked up at the mug shot, at the face of the man as he seemed to look back at us, with that half smile.

"He could walk in here right now," Larkin said. "Think anyone would recognize him?"

"That video he sent me," I said. "I didn't see his face, but I'm sure I'd know him in a second, no matter what he's done to himself."

Larkin nodded. There was nothing else to say. We finished eating, paid our tabs, and left.

"You got a family?" I said as we started walking back to the hotel. I kept looking around me, still expecting to see Livermore right behind us.

"Not yet. Just got engaged. You?"

I shook my head.

"Why the Bureau?" I asked him, not bothering with the

follow-up: *Why would you want to be hated by so many other cops?* I'd worked with plenty of agents back when I was a cop in Detroit, and I knew what my fellow officers thought of them. I remembered one informant who got killed because a feeb made him go back into a drug house to get a refund on some drugs that turned out to be fake. The feeb didn't want to go back and tell his boss the money was gone. It was something that had happened in another time, in another city. But I knew it was still true. You become a feeb, you set yourself apart.

"It was always hockey or the FBI," he said with a shrug. "Ever since I was a kid."

The former train station loomed high above us as we kept walking. It was something from another era, a full city block of ornate architecture, limestone with a red roof, and dominated by the clock tower at one corner. The streets seemed even emptier now. The homeless men in the park were either gone or wrapped up tight against the cold, huddled around small fires.

I said good night to him. When I was back in my room, I looked through the scrapbook pages again. I took the gun from my bag and set it on the bedside table. I imagined Livermore sleeping in another hotel room, maybe in the same city.

Or maybe he wasn't sleeping at all.

I opened up the window. The night air came into the room, mixed with the faint smell of smoke from the homeless men's fires still burning across the street.

I hadn't slept in so long. The smoke stayed with me as I finally drifted off, turning into a raging fire that burned inside my head as the woman trapped inside the flames kept calling my name.

CHAPTER TWENTY-ONE

W HEN A MAN *tries to get into your head, he leaves the door to his own open.*

The thought lingered in Livermore's mind as he sat in the line leading up to the roadblock, using the opportunity to watch the progress made by a little orange blip on his laptop.

You think you know where I'm going, he thought. *You might even try to guess where I will spend the night.*

The best part of that is, the absolute genius of that idea... is that wherever you guess...

You will be right.

When he pulled up to the officer with the shotgun, Livermore couldn't help but flash back to the canyon, taking a similar weapon off that Arizona cop and using it to shoot that agent. The feel of it in his hands, the lethal power capable of not just killing but destroying. Of *deconstructing*. He'd only fired small arms before that, but how many hours had passed since the canyon and he could still feel the almost sensual tingling of that shotgun's recoil in his fingers. He put the thought out of his mind as he rolled down his window.

I'm an airplane pilot, he told himself, *from Wayzata, Minnesota, just outside of Minneapolis. I fly 727s exclusively. This is my brother-in-law's car, which is why it has Arizona plates. He's letting me use it to drive up to the Grand Canyon. My wife is not with me because we're currently separated, but I have every hope that we'll be back together someday soon.*

It was all necessary, every detail of his story. He needed to become that other person completely, even if it was just for one minute.

"License, please," the officer said as he gave the whole vehicle a quick scan.

"What's going on?" Livermore said.

"Looking for a fugitive." He was studying the license, looking back and forth between Livermore and the photo.

Livermore waited.

"Minnesota," the officer said. "Long way from home."

"Yes."

"You have a good trip back," he said, handing Livermore the license.

"Thank you. I hope you catch your man."

Livermore pulled away from the roadblock, speeding up smoothly as he hit the open road ahead of him. He tucked the license back in his shirt pocket.

He'd used Minnesota's non-enhanced license template, one of the last few that didn't comply with the new federal standards. Editing the image, adding the barcode and the encoded magnetic strip, printing it on Teslin synthetic paper, then laminating it. Twenty dollars and maybe two hours of his time. All well spent.

He settled in for the long drive across Oklahoma and Missouri. When he got close to St. Louis, he found a hardware store that was still open and bought his supplies. He checked his laptop again. The orange GPS dot was just ahead of him. He watched as it left the expressway and made a few turns downtown. Then it stopped.

Livermore started moving again. When he pulled up on Market, he saw two men walking down the dark street. From behind, it looked like Alex and the young agent.

Let him come along for the ride, he thought. *It's all the same to me now.*

He watched them go into a bar at the end of the block, then waited until they came back out, maybe forty-five minutes later. He watched them go back to the hotel, and then started counting down in his head as soon as they walked through the front door.

Cross the lobby. Get in the elevator. Get out of the elevator and walk down the hall.

When the lights came on in two adjacent windows on the fifth floor, he waited another minute, until the curtains opened on the window to the left. He caught a quick glimpse of the young agent. That meant Alex was in the other room.

Fifth floor. Fourth room from the end.

He took his bag from the vehicle and locked it. He was about to cross the street, then stopped himself when he saw another car pull up to the front. A man and a woman got out, taking out two suitcases and putting them on the sidewalk. The man left the woman there, got back in the car, and drove away. Going off to park the car, but the woman was obviously uncomfortable standing out on the empty sidewalk in the darkness. Livermore stayed hidden behind his vehicle, watching her. He wondered why she didn't just go inside and wait there. Just because she didn't want to leave the two suitcases outside? Were the contents of those bags more valuable to her than her own life?

I could pull up next to her right now. Pretend I'm another guest checking in, give her a smile, take a quick look up and down the street...

He felt a warmth spreading through his body as he saw it in his head, every movement perfectly choreographed, as if it was written down on a script.

Push her into the backseat, drive off before she can make a sound. The man would come around the corner a minute later, wondering where his wife had gone.

But at least the suitcases would be safe.

He waited another minute, watching the woman shivering on the sidewalk, until the man came back from parking the car around the corner. The woman had something to say to the man, and they stood out there talking about it for a few seconds. The argument ended, and he hugged her. Then they went into the lobby.

Livermore crossed the street again, carrying his bag. There was one man behind the check-in desk. He was talking to the couple. Livermore put his head down and opened the door. He walked through the lobby without so much as a sideways glance. A man who belonged there. He headed right for the door marked STAIRS, opened it, stepped through, and went up the stairway.

When he got to the sixth floor, he counted down four rooms.

He knocked softly on the door, then waited a few seconds, listening carefully. Then he took a quick look down the hallway in both directions, got down on one knee, and opened up his bag. Purchase number one at the hardware store was a long, thin strip of metal, eight feet long and bent into quarters. Livermore unfolded the strip and then refolded one end into a hook, about six inches in length. Then he placed the strip against the door, noting the exact distance between the floor and the door latch. He made another fold, then another to accommodate the thickness of the door. Then finally one more hook to use as a handle.

He worked the strip under the door, careful to preserve the folds, then turned it so that the hook inside the door would be extended upward. He worked the strip sideways, moving carefully until he felt it make contact with the door latch. He maintained the tension as he pulled down... a little more... a little more...

Until he heard the lock open.

He pushed the door and stepped inside.

The door wasn't stopped by the safety latch. If it had been, he would have had to refold the strip, running it higher up the door to push the latch open first. He turned on the light to make sure the room was unoccupied. The bed was made. There were no suitcases in the room.

Perfect.

Livermore put his bag down on the bed. Then he went back out into the hallway, careful to leave the door ajar, and walked to the stairwell door, then down the stairs to the ground floor. As he looked through the little window in the door he saw that the clerk had been replaced by a young woman. Maybe the clerk was helping the couple bring their suitcases up to their room.

He didn't know. It didn't matter. He paused just long enough to put a smile on his face.

I'm the airplane pilot from Minnesota, he told himself. *Only now I'm on a layover. I fly for Southwest Airlines. I stay at a lot of hotels.*

He opened the door and went into the lobby. The woman behind the desk looked up at him and smiled right back.

"How are you tonight, sir?" She spoke with a slight Latin accent, and she looked a little heavier now that he was closer to her. But he liked the way her dark hair fell to her shoulders.

"Happy to be on the ground," he said, taking a quick look around the lobby. They were alone.

"We get a lot of pilots here," she said, nodding her head. "Must be doing something right."

He smiled again and waited a beat. She was very good at her job, Livermore could see. Very good at making someone feel like she would do anything to make sure you had a wonderful stay in her hotel.

"I hope everything's satisfactory with your room," she said. "Can I get you anything else?"

"Some extra towels would be nice. Room 604."

"Yes, of course," she said. "If you'll give me a moment, I'll bring those right up."

"No rush," he said with another smile. Then he went back to the stairwell.

"Sir," she said from behind him. "The elevator…"

He turned to look at her.

"I know it's slow," she said, shrugging her shoulders like *What are you gonna do?* "But it's coming back down now."

Livermore looked at the lighted number above the elevator, as the *3* turned into a *2*. The door would open and the other clerk would step out, the man who'd taken the suitcases up to the couple's room.

"I like the stairs," Livermore said. "Gets your blood flowing."

He smiled one more time and went through the door, just as he heard the elevator open behind him. He went back upstairs and into room 604. He had just enough time to get up onto the bed and tap the ceiling, to find where the joist ran above the plaster. He took out the cordless drill he had bought at the hardware store, and one of the two bits. After drilling the pilot hole into the ceiling, through the plaster and into the wood, he took the large metal hook and screwed that into the pilot hole. He brushed the sawdust from the bedcover. Then he took the twenty feet of grade-30 galvanized anchor chain he had bought and hung that from the hook. He pushed the bed away from the center of the room and tested the hook with his own weight.

It wouldn't be a work of art, but just like in Amarillo, he didn't want to waste his ropes here, didn't want to have to leave them behind when he left. And this chain would be much quicker, too.

He took out the last hardware store purchase from his bag. Another drill bit, this one bigger and almost comically long. It was used by electricians to drill holes all the way through thick walls, but he knew it would work here.

It would work exactly as he wanted.

He put it down on the bed, just as he heard a knock. He opened the door and saw the same woman from downstairs standing outside, holding a small pile of towels.

"Is this the right room, sir? I didn't see a record of—"

She stopped when she saw the chain hanging from the hook in the ceiling.

Another long moment passed as her eyes went from the ceiling to Livermore's face. She dropped the towels, caught in that one long moment, torn between screaming and trying to run away.

"Yes," Livermore said calmly as he grabbed her by the wrist and pulled her inside. "This is the right room."

CHAPTER TWENTY-TWO

ABELL RANG IN THE DARKNESS.

A fire alarm. An air raid siren. A sound as loud and as jarring as that first explosion in the canyon.

I opened my eyes. It was dark.

It rang again.

This time, I pushed myself up from the bed. I didn't even know where I was for a moment, until I finally put it all back together.

I'm in St. Louis. I'm in a hotel.

My curtains were closed, with only the thinnest beam of light coming into the room between them. I'd been so tired, after I don't even know how many nights of not sleeping. I had collapsed on this bed, and now...

The phone rang again. I needed to either smash it against the wall or answer it.

I answered it.

"How many more women are you going to let die, Alex?"

That voice.

"Where are you?" I said.

"Right above you."

"What are you talking about?"

The line went dead. I fumbled with the switch on the lamp, almost knocked the damned thing over, got it upright again, finally turned it on. I blinked in the sudden light, everything a blur until my eyes focused and I saw what was on the bed.

Red.

Bright red.

Against the white bedcover, a great scarlet stain, all around me. No, it was *on* me, too. On my pants, on my shirt. That familiar coppery smell...

Blood.

My first animal reaction was that the blood must be mine. *I'm shot. I'm cut. I'm bleeding.*

Then the next thought: *No, it's not my blood.*

Then the next, as I looked around the empty room, then finally up at the ceiling.

A hole.

The rim of the hole... it was red. Another drop collected and fell onto my face.

There was blood coming from this hole in the ceiling.

I grabbed the gun off the nightstand and threw open the door to my room, ran down the empty hallway to the stairwell. I went up one flight, paused for one half second as I checked the sixth-floor hallway. It was empty.

I ran to the room above mine, 604, and kicked open the

door, my gun drawn. I could barely process what I saw next, the woman wrapped up and hanging by a chain from the ceiling. She slowly turned toward me, as if to greet me, and I saw the jagged line across her throat, the two streams of blood running down either side of her face, into her hair, and then one final stream dripping down onto the floor.

I went to her and was about to put two fingers to her throat to check her pulse. Pure muscle memory in the face of madness, until I saw her lifeless eyes and realized that most of the blood from her body was either on the floor or on my bed. Or on me. I wheeled around with the gun still extended, made sure there was nobody waiting for me in the blind spot behind the door or hiding in the bathroom.

The phone rang. I picked it up.

"I'm outside, Alex."

I left the room, went down the hallway to the stairwell, and pounded my way down all six floors to the ground level. When I opened the door, the lobby was empty. I had no idea where the clerk was, until I saw the lighted panel above the elevator. He was on his way upstairs. God help the man if he walked into room 604, but I couldn't stop him now.

I stepped outside, into the cold air. The old train station loomed behind me in the darkness. I didn't see anyone, in any direction.

I pictured my cell phone, sitting up on the desk in my room, plugged in and charging. But I wasn't about to go back for it. I wasn't about to do anything except keep moving forward, keep trying to find him. I went up to Market Street and looked west. It was just one lonely streetlamp after another, as far as I could see. When I looked east, toward the river, I saw more streetlamps, more darkness, more emptiness. But then something else, in the park across the street. A movement.

It could be one of the homeless men, I thought. *Or it could be* him.

I ran across the street, into the park. It was two city blocks long, a great tree-lined rectangle, with a single pathway crossing through the middle. I could make out a number of fires spread out along the perimeter. Homeless men in small groups, huddled against the cold.

I stayed on the tree line, going from one tree to the next, looking into the interior of the park. I came upon three homeless men all wrapped up in blankets and gathered around a fire in a small metal bucket with holes poked into the sides. I scanned their faces.

"Did you see someone come this way?" I said.

"That's blood!" one of them said, and as I looked down at myself I realized my clothing was still soaked and the blood was splattered all over my arms and probably my face. I didn't have a coat on. I was stumbling around in the cold darkness, looking like I'd either been stabbed half to death or had done the stabbing myself.

The men all ran away from me, scattering in every direction. As I followed the progress of the man who'd pointed me out, I looked past him and saw, a block down, a silhouette standing under a streetlamp. Leaning against the pole, as if waiting for me. As soon as I started running, the figure vanished.

It's suicide, said a small voice in my head as I got closer to the streetlamp. *You're running into the light, and you might as well paint a target on your chest.* But I was past reason now.

Past all of the training I'd received as a cop, past any amount of common sense I'd ever had. It was only the madness now, everything I'd seen, the images coming back to me one after another as I ran. Agents blown apart in a canyon, the shotgun wound in Agent Cook's neck, the blood pumping from a hundred holes in Agent Halliday's chest, his face looking up at me as he asked me to send one last message to his daughter and grandson.

A woman taped up and left to die. Left to burn.

Another woman hung from the ceiling by a chain, bled like an animal on a killing floor.

I made it to the streetlamp, stopped in the light for a moment, and put one hand against the post to catch my breath. My wrapped-up left knee was throbbing.

"Where are you?" I yelled into the night as soon as I had my wind back.

I saw him another block down Market Street, standing under another streetlamp, this one at the base of the steps leading up to a huge courthouse. Behind him, far down the street but lit up and positioned perfectly over his head like a frame, was the Gateway Arch.

I ran down the street toward the courthouse, but by the time I got there, he was gone again, and I thought I saw him standing at the very top of the steps, between two of the great columns. I took the steps two at a time, still holding the gun in my right hand, forgetting everything I'd ever learned about trigger discipline as I tripped and almost squeezed off a shot. I pushed myself back up and kept climbing, limping now, until I was at the very top. He wasn't there. I tried pulling on the great glass doors leading into the courthouse, but they were locked tight.

I turned around and looked everywhere, at each cone of light under each streetlamp. Then I heard the crack of a gunshot and one of the glass doors behind me shattered. I ducked down behind a concrete rampart.

"I'm right here, Alex!" A voice coming from the darkness, maybe a block away. "Are you that old? Are you that slow?"

I knew the gunshot would bring the police eventually. The only smart play was to stay behind the rampart. But I saw another movement across the street and I took off down the steps. When I hit the street I saw the long concrete wall on the other side, and beyond that a parking lot. The perfect place to wait for me, safe behind the wall, another easy shot as soon as I came to a stop.

I should be dead already. He's had at least three shots at me, and the only time he fired he took out the glass behind me.

He's toying with me.

But that just made me want to kill him even more.

When I got to the wall, I stood with the gun in both hands, peering down the line in one direction, then the other. The movement I'd seen was left to right. He was moving farther down Market Street, toward the arch.

I started running again, my left knee a riot of pain with every step, my lungs screaming. There was another streetlamp, another silhouette. This time I actually stopped and leveled my gun at him, half a block away. Trying to steady my hands, trying to aim... I knew it was an impossible shot.

This is insanity, I told myself. *You can't shoot at a shadow from fifty yards away.*

"Alex!"

A different voice this time. I turned and saw Agent Larkin racing to catch up to me.

"*He's there!*" I yelled. "*That's him!*"

I pointed back toward the silhouette, just as he disappeared around another building. I kept running, one block, then another, stopping just long enough to look for him. There was another small park, just before the arch.

I saw a movement in a break in the trees, kept running until I reached it. Livermore was gone. Before I could move again, Larkin intercepted me and did everything but tackle me to the ground to stop me.

"Alex," he said, putting his face close to mine. "*What are you doing?*"

I tried to answer him. But I was gasping for air.

"The police are coming," he said. "Give me the gun."

"That woman..." I said, still fighting for air. Then there was another gunshot. I could practically feel the bullet passing over my head. As I pulled Agent Larkin down to the sidewalk, he drew his own weapon.

I pulled him away from the light, toward the line of trees. We stopped with our backs against two thick trunks, a few feet away from each other.

"Think about what you're doing," he said. "What he's *making* you do."

Breathe, I told myself. *Breathe and get ready.*

"Do you hear me?"

In the distance, the faint sound of a police siren.

Then Livermore's voice again, from behind us. Not far.

"*Alex! Where are you?*"

I turned and ran toward the voice. I didn't care if he shot me anymore. He could put a bullet right through me. It wouldn't even be the first time in my life. *Shoot me as many times as you want, you evil piece of shit, and I'll keep coming.*

I heard Agent Larkin calling my name behind me as I saw the figure moving. Then it stopped. There was one more line of trees behind him, one more square of open ground, then the last empty road and the arch glowing high in the sky. Beyond that nothing but the dark water of the river and the lights from another city on the far banks, looking so far away it might as well have been in outer space.

I've got you. There's nowhere else you can go.

I didn't have any strength left in my legs, or any air in my lungs, but I kept running, getting closer and closer, waiting for the shot.

Go ahead. Try to kill me. It's your last chance.

He was standing next to another campfire, the embers glowing at his feet. I didn't slow down. I didn't aim. I jumped over the fire and grabbed him by the shirt with my left hand, put the gun to his head with my right.

I looked the man in the eye. He stared back at me, with no understanding of what was happening to him. All he could see was a blood-soaked stranger leaping at him from the darkness. I could feel him shivering.

It wasn't Livermore.

I half doubled over, drawing the air into my lungs.

"Right here, Alex."

Livermore's voice. I turned and pointed the gun.

Right at Agent Larkin.

He was on the other side of the fire. Standing there, not

moving, both of his hands empty. It didn't make any sense for a second, until I saw the man behind him. There was a homeless man's blanket wrapped around him. It fell to the ground.

I saw that face over the agent's right shoulder. Most of the hair was gone from his head. He had whiskers and a mustache. Everything was different, and yet he was the same man.

Livermore.

"Drop your gun, Alex."

I didn't. I tried to hold it steady. I had three inches of clearance. Thirty feet away.

"Do what he says," Larkin said. I could see his face clearly in the firelight. He looked scared and embarrassed at the same time.

The sirens got louder.

I dropped the gun to the ground.

"Let him go," I said. "He's got nothing to do with this."

"I let you live in that canyon," Livermore said. "I'm going to let you live again. Remember that, Alex. Remember that when we get to the end of this."

"The end of what? I don't even know what this is."

"You haven't figured it out yet? How we're connected?"

The sirens, louder and louder. The red and blue lights, flashing through the trees.

"It's over," I said to him.

"Not even close."

Then he shot Agent Larkin in the back.

As Larkin went down in slow motion, Livermore turned and ran. I had a gun at my feet, and a young man dying in front of me. I made my choice, the only choice there was. I went to him and tried to stop the bleeding, took off my shirt and held it against the entry wound in his back, turned him over and saw the exit wound.

Matt Larkin looked up at me. *It was always hockey or the FBI.* That was what he had told me. A kid's dream that went one way instead of the other, leading up to this moment, bleeding on the ground as I yelled at him to hold on. For the second time in a week, I was about to watch a federal agent die in my arms.

"Fuck that," I said, picking him up off the ground. I staggered for a few steps, found my balance, and started moving toward the street.

"Alex..."

"I'm going to get you some help. Just stay with me."

When I finally got to the street, a police car came to a skidding stop right in front of me.

"Ambulance!" I yelled as soon as the officer came out of his door. He had his gun drawn, but he holstered it when he saw me.

"Where's the shooter?"

"That way," I said, jerking my head toward the park. But Livermore had at least a full minute's head start by now. This was a man who had escaped from seven armed men while handcuffed. Then he'd gotten out of Amarillo, driving right through the roadblocks.

I knew he'd walk away from this, too.

"The ambulance will be here in two minutes," the officer said to me. Then he picked up his radio to communicate with the other cars.

"Ten thirty-two, Fourth Street and Market," he said. He repeated the information and then gave the ambulance a ten fifty-two for the same location. I kept cradling Larkin, looking into his eyes to make sure they were still open.

"You're going to make it," I said to him. "Just hold on."

When the ambulance finally arrived, they wheeled around a gurney with collapsible wheels and took him from me. He gave out a loud groan as they laid him down and wheeled him toward the back of the unit.

"One shot through the back," I told them. I didn't have to say anything about the exit wound, because the blood had already soaked through his shirt, to his coat.

"Alex…" he said again as they lifted him into the ambulance. I jumped in behind them, waiting for someone to stop me.

"Go with him," the cop said to me. "I'll catch up to you at the hospital."

I nodded, and they closed the doors. Then I watched the two medical techs working to stabilize Larkin, compressing the exit wound, checking his vitals, starting an IV.

"What's his name?" one of them asked me. He gave me a towel to wipe the blood from my face.

"Matt Larkin. He's an FBI agent."

They kept talking to him, told him he'd be at the hospital soon. His eyelids fluttered, and I thought we were going to lose him. But then he coughed and waved me over to him.

I came closer, struggling to keep my footing as the ambulance took a tight corner.

"You have to get him," he said to me.

"I will." It was the one thing he didn't have to tell me.

"Don't talk," the tech said to him. "Just relax. We're almost there."

"No," he said, looking me in the eye. "They'll try to stop you. You have to *go*."

I sat back down on the ledge, thinking it over. He was right. As soon as we got to the hospital, I'd be detained. At least overnight, possibly longer. Hell, I could picture Agent Madison on his way to St. Louis to personally escort me back to Phoenix. In handcuffs, if necessary.

Meanwhile, Livermore was still out there. Still moving.

"I'll be okay," Larkin said. "I promise."

I put my hand on his leg and gave it a squeeze. When the ambulance pulled up next to the hospital, they threw open the back doors and wheeled him inside. I saw two police cars, just a few yards away. I didn't see any officers yet. In about ten seconds, someone would find me.

I turned and moved away as fast as my wrecked body would let me, slipping into the night.

CHAPTER TWENTY-THREE

LIVERMORE PULLED UP to the house, to the place where everything would end. He saw the man there, already waiting for him.

Livermore stayed in his vehicle for a few seconds, watching the man walk around the house. A cold wind picked up and the man turned away from it, hunched over and clutching at his coat. There were two inches of new snow on the ground.

When he got out of the vehicle, Livermore took a moment to reset himself. Then he approached the man and gave him a smile.

"You must be the inspector," he said.

The man was forty or fifty pounds overweight. He wore thick glasses, and his coat was tattered and stained with a decade's worth of coffee spills and sawdust.

"I am," the man said, taking off his glove for one moment to shake Livermore's hand. "Finally feels like February, eh?"

"I wouldn't know. I just came from Arizona."

"Lucky you," the inspector said. "You should have stayed there."

"I think I'd already overstayed my welcome."

The inspector smiled and nodded and looked up at the roof of the house. "I got started with the exterior. Doesn't look like the place gets used much these days."

"I only come back here from time to time," Livermore said. "Special occasions."

"Whose name is this place in, anyway?" the inspector said, looking at his sheet. "I was looking at the records and—"

"That wasn't necessary." This man wasn't here to ask questions like this. Somewhere in the town hall there was a piece of paper with his mother's maiden name on it, a name that had never been corrected by the barely competent small-town clerk who sent out the tax bills. Livermore paid the bills and never corrected the error, because he knew it gave this place an important layer of protection.

"I understand," the inspector said, "but if you're going to sell it..."

"I'm not selling. I just wanted to have a thorough inspection done. So please continue. You started with the exterior..."

The inspector nodded, back on track, back on familiar ground. "I've already covered some of the basics here. The grading, drainage away from the house, landscaping, walkway..."

"You have a list."

"Yes, of course." The inspector showed him the dozen pages on his clipboard. "No tree branches or crawling vines touching the house, no standing water, the downspouts direct the water in the right direction, the deck around back doesn't appear to have any termite damage..."

"So everything looks good."

"Just getting started," he said. "Paint looks decent. No cracks or peeling. But how old are those shingles?"

"At least thirty years."

"See, that might be an issue," the inspector said. "They look like they might need replacing soon."

"Sounds expensive."

The inspector shrugged, then flipped to the next page.

"Ridge lines straight and level... No bowing... Windows and doorframes square..."

He kept walking around the house, asking himself the questions and putting a tick on his paper, depending on whichever answer he seemed to settle on.

Livermore watched him carefully. He wanted to learn how this man walked around a house. How he flipped through his pages. Every nuance of every single movement.

"Drip caps on the windows," he said, turning and shaking his head. "That might be another issue. Some of these older homes..."

He kept moving down his list. Gutters, chimney, soffits, fascia. Livermore stopped him when he started talking about the building code for attic venting.

"You gotta have a one-to-one-hundred-fifty ratio," the inspector said, clearly one of those men who can talk for hours about the one thing in this world they know about. "What they call the *net free ventilation area* to the total area vented. Unless you've got the right kind of vapor barrier, in which case you can go to a one-to-three-hundred."

An arcane detail, Livermore thought. *Perfect.*

Before they went inside, Livermore fired up the generator.

"You're not hooked up to the grid?" the inspector asked.

"Afraid not."

The inspector shook his head again, making another mark on his page.

When they were finally inside, Livermore watched the inspector start in the attic, checking for stains on the underside of the roof and the depth of the insulation. Then they moved through each of the rooms, starting upstairs. Ceilings, floors, walls, windows. Lights and electrical outlets. They came downstairs and spent several minutes in the kitchen.

"You need GFCI on any outlet within six feet of the sink," the inspector said, explaining that it stood for ground-fault circuit interrupter, and then taking out his tape measure to verify the outlet was five and a half feet away. He made another check mark on his sheet.

GFCI, Livermore said to himself. *Another excellent detail.*

The inspector checked all of the plumbing in the kitchen and the downstairs bathroom. He tested the smoke detectors, then he lit a match and tested the draw in the fireplace, and recommended a carbon monoxide detector even though the local ordinances didn't require one.

"You know your way around a house," Livermore said. "Where did you get your training?"

"It's a set of courses given by ASHI. The American Society of Home Inspectors."

"How many years have you been on the job?"

"Twenty, twenty-one..."

"Do you work for the county or the state?"

"I work for the county," he said. "They do have a statewide bureau. That's a different job."

Livermore nodded. Still absorbing every word. Every gesture.

"If I mess up bad enough, the state guy will be here to have my ass in a sling. Those guys are real pricks, too. Every single one of them."

A state inspector, Livermore thought. *Bad news for everyone.*

"The basement is last," the inspector said. "Gotta warn you, that's usually where we find the most problems."

"What kind of problems?"

"Moisture, usually. The water table's fairly high here. I already noticed your basement sits pretty low. You ever have any flooding?"

"Not that I can remember."

"We'll see," the inspector said. "If you've had water, I'll be able to tell."

Livermore stopped him. "Are you suggesting I'm lying to you now?"

"No, no," the man said, putting up one hand. "I'm just saying, this house has been here a long time. Longer than you and I, probably."

"I understand," Livermore said, giving him another smile to put him at ease. "And how about dead bodies? Do you have an entry on your list for that?"

"Depends on how many," the inspector said, giving him a wink.

"How about five?"

"Five dead bodies," the inspector said, pretending to write this down on his clipboard. "See, that's even worse than the moisture."

Livermore kept smiling as the inspector waited at the door

to the basement. After a few long seconds, the man scratched the back of his head and cleared his throat.

"So can we take a look in the basement now?" he finally said.

"No," Livermore said as his smile disappeared. "I think this inspection has just ended."

CHAPTER TWENTY-FOUR

I DROVE THROUGH the rest of the night, on what I hoped would be the final leg of this journey. To the place where this monster had come from.

Columbus, Ohio.

I didn't know what I'd find when I got there. I didn't know if he would be waiting for me again, or what he would have planned for me if he was. But the sun was up by the time I got there, the light filtered through the falling snow, after six hours of hard driving across Illinois and Indiana.

I had to try to remember the address of his childhood home from the files I had seen. The name of the street was in that file I'd seen in Agent Larkin's office. I had to bring it back, because I was on my own now, with nobody to help me.

I could see the name. A Canadian province.

Ontario.

That was it. Ontario Street.

I pulled over at the next gas station and filled up, went inside and bought a map of Columbus. When I saw the reaction from the man at the counter as he looked at me, I realized I was still covered in dried blood, both from the woman in the hotel and from Agent Larkin, aside from already looking like a man who hadn't had a real night's sleep in several days. I went into the bathroom to clean myself up as well as I could, stood there and looked at my own face in the mirror for a long moment. It was the face of a man who had already seen too much.

Find your second wind, I told myself. *Or the third wind or the fourth wind or whatever the hell this is by now.*

Find something fast, because this isn't over yet.

I went back out and put on the winter coat I'd brought with me from Michigan. I sat in the car studying the map until I found Ontario Street. I took a breath, put the car in gear, and headed out onto the road.

When I got downtown, I hooked north, found Ontario Street just east of the expressway. It ran south to north across several blocks, with little one-story houses on small lots packed tight on either side, the street itself crumbling from the four seasons of hard weather. A real working-class neighborhood, in contrast to the penthouse suite in Phoenix.

I figured I'd eventually have to get out and start asking people where the old Livermore house was, until I kept going and finally saw one of the bigger houses in the neighborhood. Two stories high, standing above the little ranch homes on either side of it, with old wooden siding covered with peeling gray paint. A metal FOR SALE sign was stuck in the middle of the small front yard. The news about Martin T. Livermore had obviously already reached Columbus, and several people with rocks and spray cans remembered he had once lived here, because several of the windows were broken and the house had been tagged with graffiti. I could make out the word MUR-DERER in bright orange paint, just above the front door. It would have taken the whole day to figure out the rest of it, the messages scrawled on this house by the people who were drawn to it, people who felt the need to leave their mark on it, like some primitive totem that would keep the evil from spreading. I'd seen it before, on the houses owned by murderers in Detroit. First you tag the house, then you break in and vandalize it.

Then, at least in Detroit, you burn it down.

I parked my car on the street and got out. I saw an old man walking down the sidewalk with a little dog on a leash. He had his coat wrapped up tight around him as he walked into the cold wind.

"Excuse me," I said to him, nodding toward the house. "How long has this place been empty?"

"Mrs. Livermore's been gone, what, two years now," the old man said. "Place is such a wreck, they can't give it away. Then when the news broke about her son…"

"Did you know him?"

"Haven't seen him since he was a kid," the man said, shaking his head.

I thanked him and let him get back to his dog-walking. He went a few yards before he turned to me one more time. "I tell ya," he said, "I knew that Martin was a strange one. Even back then."

He didn't wait for anything else from me. He kept going down the street, leaving me to stand there alone. And to figure out what the hell to do next.

You drew a goddamned arrow pointing to your hometown, I said to the wind. *So here I am.*

I was about to go to the front door, but then I remembered what Agent Madison had said about the agents already processing this place, and what Agent Larkin had said about calling ahead to Columbus, in case he came back here. They had to be watching, so I stayed on the sidewalk, looking up at the house like just another curious bystander. Then I got back in my car and drove down the street. I clocked the sedan parked half a block down, the man behind the wheel looking at a newspaper, doing a professional job of not looking back at me.

I kept going, circling the block and coming to the house that was directly behind the Livermores'. I parked on that street, giving all of the cars a quick scan. I didn't see anybody else doing surveillance, so I went down the driveway and hopped over the back fence, onto the Livermores' property.

There was a detached garage, in even worse shape than the house. I looked through the window. There were no cars inside, just ratty old lawn furniture and tools and a lawn mower.

I crossed the yard to the back door, leaving my footprints in the newly fallen snow. There was a sign posted on the door, warning that any trespassing would be aggressively prosecuted. It was signed by the Columbus Division of Police and the FBI. When I peeked through the window in the door, I saw a kitchen with mid-century appliances and a tile floor with a road map of cracks running in every direction. I tried the doorknob. It didn't turn. I took a quick look around, knew I was hidden from the man parked out front, saw nothing else but empty backyards on either side of me. I hit the lowest glass panel with the heel of my hand, then reached inside, careful not to cut myself on the broken glass, and turned the knob from the inside.

Then I stepped into the childhood home of Martin T. Livermore.

There was a stale smell of mothballs and cigarette smoke, misery and insanity and God knows what else. I flipped on the light switch for a moment. A single bare bulb, hanging from an open fixture, cast a greenish light on the kitchen. Every cabinet was open and empty.

I turned off the light. Thirty seconds in this place, and I already wanted to be back outside, breathing the cold, fresh air. But I kept going.

I went into the living room, saw my own reflection in the mirror above the fireplace. There was a couch that should have been dragged out to the curb years ago, a coffee table with a half dozen scars along one edge, places where cigarettes had been left to burn. An old console television. The curtains were drawn shut, keeping everything in near darkness. I didn't want to turn on any more lights, not if they could be seen from the front of the house, but I did go close to the fireplace mantel and look at the framed photographs that were stacked on the floor, left here by whoever had been given the task of cleaning this place out. Probably throwing everything else away, but when you come to something like this, a half dozen photographs from someone else's life, it's the one thing you can't bring yourself to toss in the Dumpster.

The first was a black-and-white wedding picture. Mr. and Mrs. Livermore. A small, timid-looking woman in a white gown, a man twice her size in an Army dress uniform. One look at the unsmiling face of this man, a man now dead and buried, and I was already getting a small glimpse into the life that Martin T. Livermore had lived here in this house. An only child, with an Army father who probably domineered his wife and disciplined his son severely...

No, I told myself. *Don't even start down that road. None of this turns a man into a serial killer. You can look for a reason for the rest of your life, and it will never be enough.*

There was another photograph of the two parents with a young child in a baby carriage. The man still wasn't smiling. Then one more photograph of Martin as a three-year-old, wearing a little Army uniform, looking up at the camera and squinting in the sun.

And then nothing after that. No photographs from his teenage years. Or his adulthood. Maybe someone had taken those photographs. Or maybe Livermore's mother was trying to stop time, trying to remember her son only as a toddler, and nothing beyond that.

She died before he was ever arrested, I thought. *But had she known that her son was a monster?*

How could she not *know?*

I kept walking through the house. A bathroom with an old clawfoot tub, a master bedroom, another table scarred with cigarette burns. More closed curtains. The darkness and the silence, it was unnerving.

Show me why you brought me here. There has to be something else...

I went up the stairs, hearing them creak with each step. Whoever had cleaned out the first floor had come up these same stairs, and for whatever reason had given up on the job, leaving everything exactly as it had been on the day Livermore's mother had died. There was a sewing room with baby clothes still spread out on a table, then a baby's nursery that looked like something preserved in a museum. The room next to that was apparently Martin's. It was half the size of the nursery. Meaning what, I don't know. His mother had been either waiting for Martin's brother or sister, who never came, or hell... I didn't even want to think about it anymore. I kept the light off, but there was enough light to see the bed, neatly made up with a patchwork quilt. The desk and the dresser. The shelf hanging on the wall, with a collection of plastic models. Everything still the way it was. Cars, airplanes... Livermore's young mind already thinking like an engineer. And then the body of a man supported by a stand, his skin transparent so that all of his organs were visible. Next to that the body of a woman, with the same transparent skin.

A lot of kids had these, I knew, but here, in this room, these bodies with the clear plastic skin looked obscene.

I opened up the drawers to the dresser, found nothing but old clothes. In the desk drawer there was nothing but pens and paper clips and everything else you'd expect to find. In the closet, more clothes hanging, and leaning against one wall was a large telescope.

This room was almost as sterile and impersonal as his apartment in Phoenix. It wasn't until I'd gone out and found that metal shed he had rented... That was where I had seen the *real* Livermore...

So where's the real Livermore in this house?

The FBI had already been here. I knew that. They'd gone through every room, seen everything that I'd seen. But they didn't expect to find anything.

I did.

I knew there was something else.

When I went back out into the hallway, I saw the attic access door above my head. A rope hung from one end, with a red wooden ball on the end. I grabbed the ball and pulled down, hearing the whole thing screech like a wounded animal as the stairs were extended down to the floor.

I took a moment to recover from the shattered silence, then I climbed up the stairs and into the attic, smelling the dust and the mildew. There was barely enough room for me to stand up straight, if I kept to the center. There were two small windows, one on either end. Both were covered with curtains. I went to one end, opened the curtains and looked outside at the backyard. I saw my own footprints in the snow.

As I turned, I saw boxes and a standing clothes hamper with an old Army uniform sealed in plastic. Then at the other end of the attic, another small window. As I moved closer, I could see the car still parked across the street, the same man behind the wheel. I stood up and walked back through the attic, slowing myself down, looking at everything carefully. Someone had built out this room for storage, the rough ceiling running from the roofline down each slope until it hit a short wall on either side of the room, maybe three feet high. It made sense to cut off the tight angle, but it also left a small space behind the wall. Perfect for a young Livermore to hide things.

I pushed my way through some boxes and saw the old wooden paneling that was tacked to the short wall. I tapped on it, and it felt solid. Moving down the course of the wall, I tried to find a spot that might look or sound different, until I came to an old wooden trunk that had been pushed back against the wall. A hundred years old, and it weighed a ton as I tried to move it. There were old caster wheels on the bottom, but they had seized with age, and they made a loud scraping sound on the wood floor as I pulled the trunk away from the wall. I stopped and pushed it back a few inches, got down on my knees and looked at the grooves the old wheels were making in the floor. I saw the old tracks, from years of use, running roughly along the same line. The lines I had just made looked fresh, the wood newly gouged. That told me one thing: if someone else had been up here recently, looking for something, they hadn't moved this trunk.

I pulled the trunk away from the wall again, far enough for me to kneel down behind it. As I felt along the paneling, nothing felt different, but it was that old, cheap paneling that came in sheets, with grooves running vertically to make it look like actual boards. A perfect way to cut a door into the sheet without making it obvious. I tapped along the wall until I came to the hollow spot, then felt along the grooves.

Yes. A thin line cut here. There's something hidden behind this.

I didn't have much light to see what I was doing, and I wished I had a knife to pry open the piece of paneling. I worked along the edges with my fingers until I finally gave up and started tapping it hard on one side. It finally separated on the opposite edge. Then I pulled the little door open and looked into the darkness behind it. Another moment of apprehension as I imagined a young Livermore booby-trapping his hiding place, maybe setting some kind of spring-loaded spike that would impale the hand of anyone foolish enough to put his hand in there. *The hell with it,* I thought, and reached inside and pulled out a shoebox.

I took it back to the little window to give myself enough light to see what was I was doing. Then I opened the box.

This is it, I thought. *This is where he shows himself.*

I pulled out the first photograph, an old-fashioned film snapshot with white borders, the kind you'd pick up at the drugstore a few days after you'd dropped off the film. I didn't even recognize the figure I saw in the first photograph. I moved to the second.

Everything stopped.

My heart. The spinning of the earth. Time itself.

No, I said to myself. *No way.*

I went to the third photograph.

Then the fourth.

I took the fifth photograph out of the box, held it up close so I could see it clearly.

That face.

"This can't be right," I said, breaking the silence.

After days of chasing Martin T. Livermore across the country, wondering how I could be connected to him…

I finally had my answer.

CHAPTER TWENTY-FIVE

As LIVERMORE watched the house, his mind went to that dark and quiet place again. The single red light inside his head flickered. Then it turned green.

He'd been parked on the street for an hour, watching the workmen replacing the roof. They had already taken off all the old shingles by the time he pulled up. A hard, dirty job, made all the harder by the cold weather. There was a Dumpster sitting next to the house, and it looked like they had spent the entire morning filling it. Now they were putting on the new shingles, starting from the crown of the roof and working their way down. They had a good three-man system going—one man bringing the shingles up the ladder, the second man holding them in place while the third man worked the nail gun. If they kept a good pace, even on a short February day like this one, they would have the new roof completely installed by nightfall.

It was Livermore's job to make sure that didn't happen.

He grabbed his bag and his clipboard and walked up the driveway. He was wearing a good sturdy winter coat, work boots, a new pair of reading glasses. When he got to the house he stood there looking up at the roof, until one of the men came down the ladder for more shingles.

"What can I do for you?" the man said.

"You can stop working. Immediately."

"And you are?"

"The state building inspector."

The worker scratched his head for a moment, then he called up to the other two men on the roof. A minute later, all three of them were standing on the ground. None of them looked happy.

"I'm sure we can work this all out," the man said. He gave the other two men a look, like *This is just what we need, huh?* "Just tell me what you need so we can get back to work."

"I need to see that the vapor barrier has been properly installed," Livermore said. "As well as the flashing around the chimney. I need to see that you're using the correct grade of nails, and that your gun is set at the right pressure."

"Wait a minute…"

"And as long as you're making renovations to the roof, you need to bring everything else up to code, including the net free ventilation area."

"Just hold on," the man said, putting his hands up in surrender. "The net *what*?"

"What's going on?" a woman's voice said.

Livermore turned to look at the homeowner. She had grabbed a coat to wrap around herself, but was still shivering as she stood on the front porch.

This is why I practiced, he told himself, *to be ready for anything.* He had total confidence that his heart rate was unchanged. That the command in his voice had not diminished by one degree.

"This is a state inspector," the head worker said to her. "We were expecting our guy to stop by, but—"

Livermore put up a hand to stop him and addressed the woman directly. "Are you currently living here, ma'am?"

"No," she said. "I came up for the day."

"These men need to stop working," Livermore said. "If I go over everything, they should be able to start again tomorrow morning."

"We need to get this roof done," the man said. "We can't just leave it."

"My call."

All three men threw their hands up in exasperation, and the homeowner turned away from all of them, muttering something under her breath.

"All right," the man said. "For God's sake . . . We're gonna clean some of this stuff up first. I mean, if that's all right with you."

"By all means," Livermore said.

All three men moved away and started picking up the last of the old shingles.

"Is this really necessary?" the homeowner said.

"I'll check out the rest of the house," Livermore said, "as long as they're still here."

She shrugged her shoulders and turned to go inside. Livermore followed her.

"Knock yourself out," she said, taking off her coat. She was wearing a thick sweater underneath, because the only heat in the house came from a kerosene lantern set up in the center of the kitchen.

She saw him looking at it. "I hope this is acceptable," she said, "unless you want me to freeze to death."

"It's fine. Is there anyone else staying here with you?"

"No, just me."

He nodded. "Maybe we can start upstairs…"

She shook her head again and led Livermore up to the second floor. He went through each bedroom carefully, making check marks on his clipboard. He took a look out the window and saw the men outside, putting away their tools and covering the new shingles that were still stacked on the ground.

Livermore worked his way back down to the ground floor, taking a few minutes with the fireplace, then finally coming back into the kitchen to inspect the outlets and the plumbing. Through the window, he could see the men still finishing up outside.

"GFCI outlets within six feet," he said, making another check mark.

"Is that a good thing or a bad thing?" she said.

"Is there a full basement?"

She nodded toward the door. Her arms were folded, and she let out a long, tired breath.

"Oil burner?"

"Yes," she said. "But no oil in the tank."

"Where's the emergency shutoff?"

She let out another breath and went down the stairs. Livermore followed her. When they were at the bottom of the stairs, Livermore could hear a cell phone ringing in the kitchen.

"It's right here," she said, ignoring the phone. She showed him the red switch mounted on the wall.

"This should be at the top of the stairs."

She turned away from him, shaking her head.

"The workmen can move that for you. When they come back tomorrow."

"Sure," she said, rolling her eyes. "Why not?"

They both went back upstairs. Livermore went to the living room and looked out the window. The men were finally in their truck and backing out of the driveway.

The cell phone rang again.

"Excuse me," she said as she left the room.

Livermore took the gun from his bag and, moving quietly, followed her into the kitchen.

CHAPTER TWENTY-SIX

I HELD THE PHOTOGRAPH in my hand, trying to breathe. Trying to convince myself that it was real.

Everything that had happened to me that week, from the moment I was taken onto that plane and flown to Phoenix, the trip to the canyon where seven men died, then two more dead women as I chased this man across the country, another agent with a bullet blown right through him, his blood still on my clothes...

It all came down to this.

To this faded image hidden in a shoebox behind an attic wall in Columbus, Ohio.

A young woman standing at the shore of a lake.

Jeannie McDonald, who would someday become Jeannie McKnight.

My ex-wife.

She looked like she was maybe sixteen years old in this picture. A few years before I'd met her, but there was no mistaking that face.

The next photograph was another candid shot of Jeannie, from around the same time. She was looking up, like she was surprised by the shot.

Then another photograph of Jeannie sitting on the edge of the dock, like she didn't even know someone was looking at her. Then more like that one, distant shots of a young Jeannie, seemingly taken without her even knowing it.

I took out my cell phone and looked through the history. She had called me just before I'd started any of this. That night I was sitting in the Glasgow, listening to her voice from across the miles and the years. Something about the stuff her grandmother had left her...

A car. A house.

A house.

I stopped for a second and grabbed that first photograph again. I had only been there once, not long after we were married. A little house on an inland lake, north of Grand Rapids. I couldn't even remember where it was exactly.

But this is the house, I said to myself as I looked at the porch and the siding, and the yard that sloped down toward the lake. *This was taken at that same house when she was just a teenager.*

I went back to my phone, kept looking until I found her number. I dialed and waited for it to ring. Once, twice, three times. Then it went to voicemail.

"Jeannie," I said. "It's Alex. Call me right away. As soon as you get this."

I hung up and hit the redial button.

It rang once, twice. This time, she answered.

"Jeannie," I said. "Are you okay?"

"Alex? Is that you? What's going on? You sound like—"

"Listen to me carefully," I said. "You may be in danger. There is a man named Martin T. Livermore. You knew him when you were younger…"

"Wait, what?"

"*Martin T. Livermore.* He may be coming after you."

"Slow down," she said. "That name's familiar…"

"At your grandmother's house. On the—"

"Yes! He was that boy on the other side of the lake. That one summer I spent here…"

"What do you mean, *here*? Where are you right now?"

"At the house on the lake. I'm having some work done so I can—"

"Jeannie," I said, my gut already tightening into a knot, "who else is there right now? Are you alone?"

"No," she said, "there's a whole crew of men here. They're working on the roof."

A whole crew of men. I let out my breath. She was safe, at least for the moment.

"I mean, they *were* here," she said, "until the inspector came and stopped them. Hold on…"

I heard her footsteps over the line, the sound coming to me through the cell phone signal, over the span of three hundred miles. Then her voice came back.

"They just left," she said. "It's only the inspector now."

One man, I thought. *She's alone with one man.*

"I know it's been a long time," I said, "and you may not recognize him now…"

I flashed back to the park in St. Louis, seeing his face over Agent Larkin's shoulder, just before he shot him.

"He's about six foot two," I said. "His hair is short now. Dyed black. And he's growing in his mustache. When I saw him, he was wearing glasses…"

There was a long silence.

"Jeannie, are you there?"

"Alex," she said. "He's here."

CHAPTER TWENTY-SEVEN

JEANNIE FELT the phone being taken from her hand. She was still processing the shock from that, how a stranger in her kitchen could do that... On top of the shock she was already feeling... Alex calling her... Everything he had said to her...

Until she finally looked at the man standing in the kitchen with her.

Really *looked* at him.

She hadn't seen him in years. In decades. But he matched the description, all of the details Alex had given to her. More important, now that he had taken off his glasses, she could see his eyes, see across the years to that summer, so long ago...

It was him.

It was the boy from the other side of the lake.

"The last time I told you to come alone," she heard him say into the phone, "that agent was right behind you. If anything like that happens again, *anything*, Alex..."

He paused to look at her.

"Then she will die in a way you can't even imagine."

He ended the call and put her phone in his pocket.

"What are you . . ." She didn't even know how to finish the question. She was still trying to put everything into place, to reconcile him being here, in the kitchen. Inspecting her house...

He smiled at her as she looked down at the gun in his hand. He held it pointed toward the floor, like it was just another *thing* a man would carry around with him. A wrench, or a pencil.

"I'll put this away," he said as he lifted up his shirt and tucked it into his belt. She saw the hair on his tight stomach. The muscles and the flesh of this real man standing in front of her...

It's really him.

That was when Jeannie came back to herself, as one second passed into the next, like a hypnotist snapping his fingers in front of her face, every emotion and impulse catching up to her at once.

She bolted from the room. The door was right in front of her, close enough for her to feel the metal brush against her fingertips, but then she felt one strong hand grabbing her by the back of the arm. She was spun around to face him again.

"Jeannie," he said. "We have a lot to talk about."

As she pulled her arm free and backed away from him, she saw something change in his expression, like a storm cloud suddenly forming in the sky. She kept backing away, thinking about her next move, trying to keep her panic under control, because she knew that panic would not help her.

He stepped toward her, matching every movement she made with his own. She was back in the kitchen now. There was another door behind her. If she went for it, he'd grab her again. She needed to distract him.

"I remember you," she said. "That summer…"

His face changed again, and now it was something that scared her on such a deep, primal level, she forgot all about panic and distracting him and everything else in her head except *getting out of there right now*, as she made a break for the door and felt his hand on her arm again, and then her head pulled back as he grabbed on to her hair. She turned and swung her fists at him, kicking with both feet and screaming.

He threw her down and she slid across the kitchen floor. She saw the phone on the wall as she pulled herself up, grabbed the receiver, and tried to start dialing. But of course the rational part of her mind knew that the phone had been disconnected, and she only got to the nine anyway, one button before he was on top of her again. He grabbed the phone from her, threw it across the room, then took the base unit and ripped it from the wall. He left it swinging by a single wire as she ran back into the front room, got the door halfway open before he put one hand on it and slammed it shut.

She put a knee into his groin, heard him let out a yell of pain, and then she was running up the stairs. Nowhere to go from there, she knew that, but it was the only way to get away from him.

She went into her grandmother's bedroom, picked up the phone, and of course it was dead—why in God's name was she trying to use a phone when she *knew* it was dead, because what she really needed was to open up a window and jump out, no matter how high it was, no matter how badly she would hurt herself.

No, she told herself. *Get a hold of yourself and think.*

She went into the bathroom and pulled open every drawer, looking for some kind of weapon. She pulled out a nail file, then a little pair of nail scissors. Not nearly enough, and then she remembered her grandfather's old hunting rifle, and that one day she'd watched him load it and how he'd told her that it would be hers someday, because he didn't have a grandson to give it to. But she hadn't seen that damned thing in years. Where would it be, if it was even in the house anymore?

She heard footsteps on the stairs, grabbed the scissors, and left the bathroom. She went out into the hallway, saw the top of his head as she went down to the other bedroom. When she pushed the door open, it caught against the boxes that were stacked inside. It was just a storage room now, used by her grandmother for a lifetime of clothes and furniture and whatever else. She locked the door behind her and pushed the boxes against it. Then she grabbed everything else she could—an old bowling ball in a bag, more clothes, a box of books, so heavy she could barely lift it—and she piled it all in front of the door.

She went to the window and opened it. The cold air rushed inside as she stuck her head out and looked down at the ground. There wasn't enough snow to break her fall. She would fracture both of her ankles, but at least she would be out of this house.

And then he'd just walk right outside and grab you. You wouldn't be able to run.

"Help!" she yelled. "Help me!" Into the wind, again and again, until her voice started to break and her throat hurt. There was another house fifty yards away, through the woods, one more house another fifty yards beyond that one, but those houses and every house on the lake had been abandoned and locked up tight for the winter.

There was nobody to hear her. She was alone with this man, who even now was turning the doorknob. She looked for more heavy objects she could put on the pile, but it was useless. He would get this door open eventually.

Another weapon, she thought as she rummaged through the rest of the boxes, finding a heavy wooden picture frame with an old photograph of her great-grandparents behind thick glass.

I can use this. As soon as he puts his head through the door, I can hit him.

She put it near the door, even as she heard him throwing his weight against it from the other side.

Something better, she thought, *there must be something…*

She kicked over another box, more old photographs, movies, letters, everything from her grandparents' life, all of it useless to Jeannie right now. More clothes. A table in the corner, with more boxes.

The sound of him kicking the door now, every thump resonating through the floor, right into her bones.

She threw open another box, then another, until she'd finally made her way to the closet. She wedged open the door and worked her way inside. A foolish move, she knew that, like a child running away from danger, thinking that she could hide from it, but she couldn't stop herself from huddling in the corner, in the darkness, the tears streaming down her face now, another scream building in her throat.

No, I have to be quiet.

She folded herself into a ball, listening to the assault on the door. He was kicking and kicking and finally she heard the splinter of wood and then the sound of boxes falling away from the door.

"Jeannie," he said, his voice back to a dead calm now. "Where are you?"

Her eyes were adjusting to the dark. She pushed aside the old coats and dresses to see what else was in the closet. The old movie projector, a fold-up screen…

And a gun case.

Here it is, she said to herself. *My grandfather's rifle.*

She pulled the case over and opened it. She'd fired a pistol before, more than once. Alex had made her learn gun basics, back when they were living in Redford, just a few blocks from the Detroit city line, and there was always a gun in the house. Then a few years later she had even owned a little semiautomatic of her own before her friends talked her into getting rid of it. But she had never fired a rifle.

She smelled the gun oil as she took the rifle out of the case. It would have brought back a pleasant memory in any other circumstances, her grandfather loading it, how he'd promised her that it would be hers someday, but telling her that in the meantime she must never, *ever* touch it. She tried to think back to that day, watching how he'd loaded it. Because right now that was the only thing she needed to remember.

"You have nothing to be afraid of," the voice said from miles away.

Then the sound of another box falling away from the door. He was in the room.

It's a muzzleloader, she thought, pushing Livermore's voice out of her head, trying to focus on that day. Her grandfather's words coming back to her from across the decades. *You have to load this thing by hand, honeybunch. The way it's been done for hundreds of years.*

She willed her heart to stop pounding, so she could breathe, so she could *think* about what she was doing. There were a few steps to the process. Starting with the gunpowder. *Black powder,* he'd called it. She found the bottle of black powder, and the metal tube she had seen him pour it into. She couldn't remember how much it took, but she could hear him warning her about putting in too much. *Just enough, not too much. Just a hundred grains, no more.* Whatever the hell that meant. She opened the bottle and poured some of the powder into the tube, then tipped that into the barrel.

"Come out," the voice said. "Right now."

There was a little cup that went in next, she thought. A *shell cup,* he had called it. She rummaged through the other supplies in the case, found the plastic cup, about three inches long, just the right diameter to fit down the barrel. Had he put that in first? Before putting in the birdshot?

Yes, he did. I can remember the sound of the shot going down the barrel. But first he used the ramrod thing to push the shell cup all the way down...

She pulled the ramrod out of its holder next to the barrel, put in the shell cup, and then she tapped it down with the rod.

He used another cap to measure the shot ... Filled it up, poured that down the barrel...

She opened the bottle of number six birdshot and poured it into the second shell. When it overflowed, it made a sound as it hit the floor, a hundred little pieces of metal drumming against the hardwood.

"What are you doing in there, Jeannie?"

She poured the shot down the barrel. Then she found the little plug and put that down the barrel.

One more time with the ramrod. And then I'm ready.

She pushed the rod down the barrel, feeling the plug hit the bottom. Then she threw the ramrod aside.

"Jeannie . . ." She could hear the anger coming back into his voice.

Wait. There was one more thing.

She tried to put herself back in that day, watching her grandfather. One more thing he'd done before the gun was ready to fire.

What am I missing?

She went through the rest of the supplies, found the little metal piece, tried to think back to where that went.

She heard the boxes being moved around on the other side of the closet door, made herself ignore everything else but that one day and that last step, her grandfather opening up the breech and putting in that last piece, something about a *metal jacket* and how he put that little metal piece on the front end of the shell before closing it all up and telling her it was ready to fire.

She fumbled with the little metal jacket, dropped it on the floor and picked it up again. She slid the breech open and put it inside, closed it up, and thought about the safety and whether it was on or off or how to even work it, but it was too late now, anyway. The last box was moved, and she could hear his footsteps on the other side of the door, just inches away from her.

He wasn't talking anymore. He was standing there, waiting to open the door.

Waiting to take her.

She slowly pushed herself to her feet, the rifle across her chest, ready to swing it, ready to point it at his chest and fire.

I hope to God I did everything right. Please, God, just let me get out of here.

She took a deep breath. She waited.

Nothing happened.

She could feel the panic building inside her again, filling up her stomach, her lungs, her throat...

I can't just keep standing here. I have to do something.

One more breath, then she kicked the door open, heard it slam into him and drive him backward. In the next instant she was out and pointing the rifle at him.

"Get back," she said, a sudden resolve coming to her from somewhere inside her. "I'll kill you."

Yes, she thought. *Even if this gun doesn't work ... It doesn't need to ... As long as he believes it might...*

"Jeannie, what are you doing?"

"I'll do it," she said, inching forward, the barrel still leveled right at his chest. "Get away from me."

"You do *not* want to do this," he said, but he took another step backward.

"Sit down. Right now."

"No."

"Sit down or I'll kill you," she said. "I swear to God."

"You're not going to do that."

"Sit down!"

He held up his free hand to stop her, looked behind him to see where he would sit, then he started to bend down.

She saw him picking up the old electric coffeepot and throwing it at her, but it hit the barrel of the rifle a tenth of a second after the signal from her brain reached her trigger finger and the world erupted in a flash and a sound that obliterated everything else, the window shattering behind him as she tried to pull the trigger again but of course there was only one shot, only one chance, and she felt the rifle being pulled from her hands as she twisted away from him, tried to run, fell over a box, got up and took another step to the open door. He was right behind her. She grabbed the big wooden picture frame, turned and swung it at him, felt it connecting against his head, the glass cracking and the man going down, just long enough for her to get out into the hallway.

Down the stairs, hearing his footsteps behind her.

Throwing open the front door, letting out another scream that would be heard by nobody, nothing but the woods and empty houses all around her.

Except him, still behind her, getting closer.

She slipped in the snow as she ran to her car, touched the cold metal of the hood, turned the corner, and was about to grab for the door handle. But then the hands came around her again, catching her around the waist, pulling her backward.

She remembered the little pair of scissors she had taken from the bathroom, pulled them out of her pocket and slashed him across the face with them. He let out a yell, a sound like something from an animal, as he grabbed her hand and bent it, making the scissors fall into the snow. She tried to kick at his legs, slipped in the snow again, fell down hard and hit her face against the ground, tasted the blood in her mouth as she felt everything fading.

The last thing she remembered was being dragged along the snowy ground, back to the house.

CHAPTER TWENTY-EIGHT

I WAS THREE HUNDRED MILES away when I heard Livermore's voice coming from Jeannie's house on the lake. Three hundred miles away when he hung up her phone.

Three hundred miles away from whatever he did next.

I went out the back door at a dead run, and as I did I heard the man coming up behind me. The man who'd been sitting in the car, watching the house, not that I even cared who he was or why he was suddenly right behind me.

"Stop!" he said. "FBI!"

I went over the back fence, waiting to feel the bullet ripping through my back. The shot never came, and I ran up the driveway, almost falling in the snow, catching myself as I got to my car. I started it, put it in gear, and took off, spraying snow behind me. The man appeared in my rearview mirror as I made the turn and gunned it back down Ontario Street, toward the expressway.

I heard a siren in the distance, then another coming from another direction. I caught the lights flashing just as I made the final turn, burying the accelerator as I merged onto I-270.

You'll need a barricade to stop me. You'll have to blow out my tires and then shoot me when I come out of the car.

I saw another police car racing up behind me as I got off the expressway and hit US 23. The car blew past as I made the connection. I let out a breath and kept going, knowing that this was the fastest road to Grand Rapids, but knowing at the same time that this was a secondary highway, with slower traffic, and that more snow was starting to fall.

God damn it, I said to myself. *Why did I rent this little shitbox car, anyway?* Even though I already knew the answer: because I never thought I'd drive it all the way across the country and then have to push through yet another three hundred miles to get to Jeannie.

I'd settle in at around eighty miles an hour, until I'd feel the tires starting to slip and I'd have to back off. Then after a few minutes I'd be back to full speed. I watched a hundred miles go on the odometer, racing through the empty fields of central Ohio. Then another hundred miles until I reached I-75 and took that through Toledo. The traffic got heavier as I hit the late-afternoon hours. People on their way home from work. But I picked my way through the cars, weaving from one lane into the other.

When I hit the Michigan state line, I knew I still had a long way to go. I had to stop myself from imagining what Livermore could be doing to Jeannie at that moment. Had to shut out every other thought from my mind but keeping the car on the road and getting to her as quickly as possible.

I came up behind two trucks driving side by side, leaned on my horn and flashed my lights until one truck finally pulled ahead of the other and I was clear. A few minutes later I cut between two cars with not enough room to spare, and I actually felt my driver's-side door brushing up against the front corner of his bumper. The driver swerved and fought to keep control, and for one second I thought he was going to go right off the road, but then he got all four wheels under him again and I left him behind.

I picked up my phone and hit the redial button, hoping by some crazy chance that she'd answer. Or even Livermore. But it rang through. I threw the phone on the passenger's seat and kept going.

The snow was falling harder. Nothing by Upper Peninsula standards, but enough to make everyone around me drive even slower. I was on I-96 now, heading northwest, passing through Lansing as the sun went down.

This will be the last day, I promised myself. *Whatever happens, if you kill him or he kills you…*

Then I saw the flashing lights behind me.

I'm not stopping.

It was a Michigan State Police car, one of the new blue Dodge Chargers. I would never be able to outrun it. The car stayed behind me for a half mile, finally pulling up next to me. I could see the red face of the trooper, and as he tried to wave me over I could see exactly how the rest of the scene would play out. I can usually talk my way out of just about anything—in the state of Michigan, at least. A Detroit cop who took three bullets on the job, I can drive ninety miles an hour anywhere in the UP, and even the troopers will let me get away with it. But I was a long way from the UP, and I was sure the FBI had put me out on the wire.

I knew that as soon as I pulled over, this trooper would come out of his car with his gun drawn. A felony stop, telling me to put my hands out the window. To open the door from the outside, stay facing away from him, move backward to the sound of his voice. Then get down on my knees with my hands interlaced on my head.

You'll never talk your way out of this one, I thought. *And you can't outrun him.*

But then, as I looked ahead, I saw the exit sign about a half mile down the road. Grand Rapids. The biggest city in western Michigan, which meant a lot of streets to get lost on, as soon as I was off the expressway.

I started to slow down, watching my rearview mirror as the trooper settled in behind me, his lights still flashing. There was maybe twenty feet between us.

You need to find some ice, I told myself. *It's your only chance.*

I kept my car rolling. The trooper stayed behind me, and through his windshield I could see his face turning an even deeper shade of red. I tested my brakes, hit a little patch of ice and slid, tested them again. There was enough snow on the ground that it was hard to see just how much ice might be hidden beneath it. I hit my brakes one more time and felt the car start to go sideways. I turned into the skid, pure instinct after God knows how many winters on Upper Peninsula roads, until I finally felt the tires hitting solid ground.

That was when I hit the gas, pulling away from the trooper just as he hit the patch of ice I had left behind me. I could see his tires spinning as he used all of his car's superior power at exactly the wrong time. He went completely sideways, and his front wheels were off the road. I kept pushing it as hard as I could, being careful not to go off the road myself. Fifty yards ahead of him now. Then a hundred.

I checked the rearview mirror and saw him backing out onto the highway and finally getting himself pointed in the right direction, but by then I had hit the exit ramp.

He had already closed half the distance when I hit the cross street and took the right, practically putting my car up on two wheels.

I have to keep this separation, I thought. *Just enough to lose him for ten seconds.*

I weaved my way through the traffic, watching him in my mirror, until I came to a curve in the road and he disappeared behind me. There was a gas station on the next corner, so I pulled in behind it, making sure I was out of the sight line. A few seconds later, I heard him blasting through the same intersection, heading north. I gave him a few more beats, summoning the patience from God-knows-where to make myself wait long enough. Then I went back out and headed west.

I kept my eye out for him, or anyone else in an official vehicle, as I made my way over to US 37. It was a smaller, secondary road that eventually went down to one lane in each direction. I was back to thinking about Jeannie, now that I had lost the trooper, and I drove with a new sense of purpose. Because I knew I was getting close.

I passed one car after another, cutting over into the other lane, driving toward the oncoming traffic, then cutting back. I had more close calls than I could count, until it was finally just a blur of speed and more honking horns. The plows hadn't hit this road yet, and one icy spot nearly put me in the ditch. As I straightened the car out, I realized I had an even bigger problem:

I couldn't remember where the house was.

It was a small lake, in the middle of absolutely nothing, like any of a thousand other lakes in this state. It was right after we were married, how many goddamned years ago, that one time we drove up to this place...

Up this road, to a town with a funny name. Then west. That was all I could remember. But I didn't have time to stop and think about it. I just had to trust that I'd know the place when I came to it.

I drove through Sparta, Kent City, Casnovia... Little towns with stoplights that I blew through, barely slowing down enough to make sure I didn't hit another car. Then Bailey, Ashland, Grant, Newaygo... It felt like I'd been driving forever.

It can't be this far, I said to myself. *You missed the goddamned town.*

But then I saw the sign for White Cloud, Michigan, and it all came back to me. Driving down this road as a much younger man, with my new wife.

I slid through the stoplight and took the hard left onto the narrow county road. Over one river, past Alley Lake...

Robinson Lake was next. Just another half mile.

Jeannie's lake.

As I drove down that last stretch of road, already seeing a single light coming from one of those houses on the edge of the lake, I could only wonder if I was too late.

CHAPTER TWENTY-NINE

WHEN SHE OPENED her eyes again, Jeannie had no idea where she was.

She was staring at the ceiling. A ceiling she didn't recognize at first, until she tried to lift her head and felt everything spinning. It all started to come back to her, piece by piece. The lake house. The inspection.

Livermore.

She sat up on the couch, feeling the rough cloth against her arms. He had taken off her coat and her sweater. As she put her feet to the floor, she felt the cold wood. He had taken her shoes and socks, too. Her face was wet and numb from the snow, and she felt a raw scrape across her chin.

As she slowly got to her feet, holding the arm of the couch for balance, she felt the warmth coming from the fireplace. She looked over and saw the logs burning, then shuffled carefully over to stand in front of it. The heat radiated through her body, making her forget everything else.

Then she heard the noises from the kitchen. Chopping, water boiling on the stove.

He's still here. She looked down at the iron rack that held the fireplace tools. But the poker was gone.

The door. I have to get out of here.

"You took a bad spill out there." The voice came from behind her, strangely calm.

She turned and saw him standing in the doorway. He was holding one of the kitchen towels to his face.

"You have to be careful on that ice," he said. "Come sit down. Dinner's almost ready."

She looked back at the front door, measuring the distance, estimating her chances.

"You don't want to go outside again," he said. "You'll freeze to death."

She hesitated for a moment, then she felt herself moving toward the kitchen, almost against her will. She stopped when she saw the table. It had been set with two plates. Water glasses, silverware. Everything in its perfect place. As if they were two normal people actually about to sit down to dinner.

"Why are you doing this?" she said, her lips trembling.

"Because this is a very special occasion."

"No," she said, shaking her head and looking around the kitchen. "Please…"

She had to fight down the urge to try to run again. She knew she wouldn't make it more than halfway across the room, even if she surprised him.

And he was right. Even if she got outside, she would freeze to death. There was nowhere to go. Just empty houses in either direction. Her car keys were in her coat, and that was gone.

"I'm making your favorite," he said. "It'll be ready in a moment."

My favorite? How does he know that? How does he know anything about me?

She looked at the butcher-block knife holder on the counter, just a few feet away from him. There were a half dozen knives in the block.

If I can just get to them. That one long knife…

"I sharpened your knives," he said, turning and watching her eyes. He held up the knife he'd been using to cut tomatoes. "Any chef will tell you, dull knives are more dangerous than sharp ones."

"Where are my clothes?" She heard her own voice breaking.

"They were wet," he said. "We don't want you to be… uncomfortable."

"I'm cold." Another shiver ran through her body.

"The food will warm you up."

He went back to his chopping. She stared at his back, wondering what to do next. She wanted to go back to the fire, but she didn't know what would happen if she tried to leave the kitchen.

He turned and looked at her, still holding the knife. "Sit down, Jeannie."

Jeannie swallowed hard and sat down. She massaged her legs, trying to rub some warmth into them.

A minute passed. The only sounds came from the stove or from the settling of the logs in the fireplace. Livermore drained the pasta in the sink, visibly wincing as the steam rose and gathered around his face. As he turned to her, she could see the jagged, red gash on his cheek.

I slashed him with the scissors, she thought, *but he's not saying anything about it.*

Somehow that was the most frightening thing of all.

He shook off whatever pain he was feeling, regained his composure, and brought over the pasta in the strainer. As he got close to her again, she could smell the odd, antiseptic odor that came from him, mixed with something else. Fire... smoke...

Pure evil. The words came into her mind, lit up in neon. She had to fight down the panic again.

"I want tonight to be perfect," he said as he put the rest of the pasta on his own plate. "You have no idea what I've gone through to make this night happen."

He went back to the stove and brought over the saucepan, ladled out some sauce on her pasta, then he did the same on his own. She watched him, strangely transfixed by his movements. Wondering again how any of this could be happening.

"I always hated this lake," he said as he sat down.

His cheek twitched as a thin line of blood dripped down onto his plate.

"Until that last summer," he said. "The summer we were together."

The words washed over her. She'd been sixteen years old back then, her parents sending her up here to spend a month with her grandparents. The last thing young Jeannie had wanted to do, spend four weeks in this stuffy little house that smelled like liniment and cigarette smoke, with nobody else around less than four times older than she was, without a television even.

And then on top of that, there was the strange boy across the lake.

Watching her.

Stalking her.

Taking pictures.

"You remember . . ." he said. The same boy, grown into a man, sitting across from her now. She would have never recognized him.

Until she saw those eyes. That same unblinking stare that had sent a cold chill through her body even then, as she sat on the edge of the dock, refusing to move. Refusing to give in to this stranger.

Until she'd look up and see him again, impossibly close to her, the camera around his neck. Wondering how he'd been able to sneak up on her, wondering how long he'd been standing there. That smile he'd have on his face when their eyes met. And how she'd finally break down and go inside, just to get away from him.

I never said a word to you.

Not once.

"Jeannie . . ." His voice went lower as he put his fork down. She closed her eyes and tried to stop shivering.

"Eat your dinner."

She kept her eyes closed.

"I SAID EAT YOUR FUCKING DINNER!"

He banged both fists on the table as he yelled, rattling the plates. The shock sent her back in her chair like a slap across her face. She fumbled for the fork, held it in her hand like she couldn't even remember how to make it work.

"Martin . . ." she said. The name sounded strange on her own lips. Almost obscene.

"This is not how tonight is supposed to go!" he yelled, taking out the gun and slamming it on the table. *"You're ruining it!"*

"I'm sorry," she said, so softly she could barely hear the words herself.

"Listen," he said, fighting to control himself, measuring every word carefully. "I don't want you to be afraid of me. But you have to understand something, Jeannie. You have not made this easy for me. I think I've been more than patient."

She could see the veins standing out in his arm as he gripped his fork. She kept waiting for him to scream again. To come over the table at her. She could practically feel his hands around her throat.

"All this time, Jeannie . . . All these years. I kept thinking about you. Searching for you..."

Her whole body was going numb.

"And then I saw that picture from your wedding day," he said. "The *whole world* saw that picture. Do you have any idea how that made me feel?"

She could feel herself slipping away now, into some deep recess in her own mind. His voice sounded like it was coming from someplace else. Another room in another house. Something about a picture. And a wedding day. The last blink of recognition before she slipped away even farther. That old photo her friend Lisa had put on that Facebook page she had set up for her. *I told you not to do that, Lisa. Who's dumb enough to put a divorced woman's wedding photo on Facebook?*

"You belonged to me, Jeannie. Not to that baseball player. Not to that *cop*."

The voice driving her deeper into herself. The last remaining place where she could be safe.

"You were married to him for nine years. Over three thousand days of your life."

There was a movement, just a flickering shadow she could barely see. Then she felt the fork being taken from her hand.

"It was a mistake. But it's not too late, Jeannie. Even now, it's not too late for us."

Something touching her face now. Like a towline, bringing her back to the room. Bringing her back to her own self.

No. I don't want to be here.

"I want to believe that," he said, his voice in her ear. "I *have* to believe that."

She was back now. In this room, feeling his breath against her face, the cold tiles on her feet, the hard wooden chair against her back.

"You have no idea what will happen to you," he said, staring into her eyes, "if you can't make me believe."

She let out her breath as he took a step back. Then from one moment to the next, another kind of relief, as she let go of her bladder and the warmth spread out beneath her on the chair and then moved down her legs. She didn't care anymore. It felt strangely comforting.

"Now eat your dinner," he said. "Before it gets cold."

As the tears started coming down her cheeks, she found her voice again. "What are you going to do?"

"You'll see," he said as he returned the gun to his belt. "As soon as Alex gets here."

CHAPTER THIRTY

'M HERE, JEANNIE. PLEASE BE ALIVE.

I had driven this cheap little car from Phoenix to Michigan, chasing a monster. Now I had finally arrived at the lake, passing one house, dark and abandoned on the edge of the frozen lake, then another, just as dark and abandoned. It was February, a season that had no purpose for these houses. But there was a light coming from the next house, streaming out onto the snow. I saw two vehicles parked in the driveway. A Nissan Pathfinder and a Subaru station wagon.

This is the place, I said to myself, bringing back the memory from decades before. The house looked exactly the same, except that now the shingles had all been taken off and only half of them had been replaced.

I stopped on the street and watched the house for a few seconds. I didn't see any movement, didn't hear any sounds at all. There was no other plan in my head except walking up to the front door and knocking it down, trying to be ready for whatever happened next. But then I remembered what had happened in Amarillo, how I had opened one door and set off an apocalypse. For once in my life, it was time to think about what I was doing before I did it.

I got out and approached the house carefully, knowing that the snow would muffle my footsteps, but knowing just as well that whoever was inside would probably see me coming. I didn't go to the front door, but to the window looking out from the front room. When I put my face close to the glass, I could see furniture covered with white sheets. A box sealed up with strapping tape. Then as I moved over to get a better angle...

Jeannie.

I could barely see down the hallway, but there she was, in the kitchen. She was sitting on a chair, against the wall, her head slumped forward. It hit me right in the stomach, how long it had been since I had last seen her. And how horrible it was to be seeing her under these circumstances.

I tried to see if her eyes were open. If she was still even alive. But I couldn't quite get the right angle to see her face.

Move, Jeannie. Show me that you're alive.

I looked all around me. I hadn't seen Livermore inside the house, but I knew that meant nothing. He could have been outside at that moment, watching me from behind one of the trees, waiting for me to go in.

As I looked back in the window, I saw Jeannie stirring. Something like a shudder rolling through her body.

What did he do to you?

I had to fight the urge to break down the front door right then, finally convincing myself to move around to the back of the house. As I did, I took a quick look in each window. I didn't see Livermore.

When I got to the back door, leading into the kitchen, I could see only the side of her head. I tried the doorknob. It was unlocked.

I went inside. Jeannie turned and saw me. "Alex!"

I took one step toward her, then felt the whole world crashing down onto my head, driving me to the floor.

And then nothing.

WHEN I OPENED my eyes again, I saw a familiar face looking down at me.

"You made good time," Livermore said.

As I tried to get up, I felt the cold sting of metal against my wrists. I was lying on my back on the kitchen floor, my arms stretched out past my head. He had handcuffed me to the drainpipe under the sink. I was bleeding from a fresh cut in my forehead. The blood was running into my eyes, making it hard to see.

But there was Jeannie, still sitting on the kitchen chair. After all the years that had passed, to finally see her again, this close… She looked cold and she was somewhere beyond scared, in jeans and a tank top, with no coat, no shoes. There was a raw scrape on her chin. Livermore stood next to her, one hand on her shoulder.

"Let her go," I said to him. "This is between you and me."

"On the contrary, Alex. This has been between all three of us from the beginning."

"Jeannie," I said, "are you all right?"

"I'm sorry," she said, with a voice so weak I could barely hear her. "I'm so sorry."

I shook more blood from my eyes, rattling the cuffs against the drainpipe. As I gave it a yank, the cuffs bit deeper into my wrists.

"Look at this man," Livermore said to Jeannie. "You actually let him touch you. You shared a bed with him. Every night."

As she looked down at me, I could see her crying. I could only wonder how many tears she had already shed before I got here.

"You chose *this*," Livermore said, coming close enough to kick my left leg. "Over me."

Do that again, I thought. *Come close enough for me to reach you...*

Jeannie didn't answer him. She kept looking at my face, while tears rolled down her own.

"I'll never understand it," Livermore said, stepping back to her and putting a hand on her shoulder again. "But you have one chance to make it right."

What the hell is he talking about?

She kept looking at me, her eyes glazed over. I didn't even know if she was hearing a word he said anymore.

Wake up, I said to her in my mind. *Wake up and play along. It's your only chance to get out of this alive.*

Livermore took Jeannie's chin and tilted her face away from mine, toward his. I rattled the cuffs again as I pulled at the drainpipe.

"Don't touch her," I said.

He looked down at me and laughed, then he turned back to Jeannie.

"Stand up," he said. "Stand up for the most important moment of your life."

She kept looking back down at me as she did, swaying and then catching her balance as she got to her feet.

I nodded to her, willing her to see the only way out. The only way to at least buy some more time.

You have to go along with this, Jeannie. Whatever it is, just play along.

But then I saw Livermore take the gun from his belt.

I rattled the cuffs again, remembering how he'd stood behind Agent Larkin and shot him right in the back. Jeannie saw the gun but didn't even react. She just stared at it.

"Let me tell you what's going to happen," he said.

"Please don't kill him," she said.

"I could have killed him ten times already, if that's what I wanted."

She kept staring at the gun. Her chest rose and fell with each breath.

"No, I'm not going to shoot Alex," he said.

He handed her the gun.

"You are."

She took it from him, looking down at it like she had never seen one before. But I knew she could handle a pistol. I had taught her myself.

"Right now," he said. "This is where you prove yourself."

She looked at him, down at the gun again, then at me.

"Go ahead." He took a step backward.

She stared at the gun, finally wrapping her right hand around the handle, and then stabilizing her grip with her left. Just like I had taught her.

She wasn't looking at me anymore. She was concentrating on the gun, and in that moment I had a sudden doubt... Had she been traumatized enough that she'd actually kill me?

I can't blame her if she does, I thought. *If that's the way this has to end...*

She looked at me, raised the barrel, put her finger on the trigger.

I waited.

She looked back at him for one moment, reset her grip on the gun.

She pulled back the hammer.

Raised the barrel.

Closed one eye.

Then she turned and pointed the gun at Livermore.

He made no move to stop her. He put his hands in the air.

She squeezed the trigger.

Click.

She reracked and squeezed again. And again.

Click.

Livermore stepped forward and took the gun from her. He didn't say a word, and the silence hung in the room as he slowly tucked the gun into his waistband. I held my breath, waiting for whatever would come next. Jeannie stood motionless, looking at nothing, until her eyes finally drifted to Livermore's face.

His back was turned to me, but Jeannie saw something new in his eyes that seemed to bring her back to life. She backed away from him, and as soon as he took one step toward her, I pulled at the cuffs, ignoring the damage to my wrists.

"Livermore!" I said. "Over here! I made her do that! Take it out on me!"

But he wasn't hearing me. In that moment, he was aware of nobody else but Jeannie, as she kept backing away until the wall stopped her.

He advanced until he was close enough to reach out his left arm, to close his hand around her neck. She looked down at me, the panic spreading across her face.

"Livermore!" I yelled. "You coward! I'm right here!"

He still couldn't hear me. He had her pinned against the wall, every ounce of force pressed into her neck. Then he raised his right hand and brought it across her face.

"Livermore!"

He did it again. Then again. She would have fallen to the floor if he hadn't kept holding her up. Then he looked down at the phone unit that was still hanging from the wall by one wire, bent over just enough to let Jeannie start sliding down the wall, then pushed her back upright as he stood with the phone in his right hand. Held it like he was going to hit her in the head with it.

Think of something, I told myself. *Something to break the spell.*

"I took her from you!" I yelled at him.

He froze.

"That's right, Livermore! I took Jeannie from you. How does that feel?"

He let out a breath, and then he looked down at me, as if suddenly remembering I was there.

"She used to talk about you all the time," I said. "The boy from the lake. For years, Livermore. I knew she was still thinking about you."

He let the phone drop. It crashed against the wall, dancing on the end of the wire. Then he let go of Jeannie's neck and she slid to the floor, her eyes half open, her left cheek glowing red from where he had slapped her.

That's it. Stay focused on me.

"Every day I was married to her," I told him, "every night when I took her to bed... I laughed in your face."

Come over here, you son of a bitch. Come closer.

He was standing over me now. Then he took one step sideways so he could aim a kick at my rib cage. I tensed up as I tried to absorb it, but it hit me like a knife right in the side, knocking the wind out of me. He kicked at me again and again. It was my turn to see the unhinged fury on his face. My turn to see the evil. But it was me now and not Jeannie, and that was all that mattered.

I tried to time his motion so that I could swing my legs around and trip him. It was Jeannie's last chance to get away, if I could get him on the ground, tie him up just long enough for her to make it out the front door. She was already on her hands and knees and crawling into the living room.

When I tried to catch him, he brought his foot down hard on my sore left knee, sending a jolt all the way up my body. Then he turned and went after her. I pictured her crawling to the front door, getting to her feet and running out into the darkness. But then I heard her scream as he captured her and dragged her back into the kitchen, pulling her by her hair.

"No!" I yelled, straining at the cuffs, waiting for him to start hitting her again. To end her life right in front of me.

"Let her go," I said. "Livermore, you piece of shit, *let her go.*"

But he kept pulling Jeannie across the tile floor. He took one more look down at me. Then without another word spoken, he threw open the kitchen door and dragged her outside.

CHAPTER THIRTY-ONE

AM GOING TO DIE.

She heard those five words in her head as she felt herself being pulled from the house, out into the cold air. The snow was a sudden shock against her bare feet. And yet it was drowned out by those five simple words, echoing over and over again.

I am going to die.

"Please," she said, already shivering. "Martin..."

She went down on her hands and knees in the snow. He pulled her up and started to push her from behind, gathering her tank top in his fist and driving her forward. Through the trees, past the dark empty house next door, through more trees, past another house. All closed up for the winter. There was nobody to help her. Nobody but the man left behind in her kitchen, handcuffed to the drainpipe.

I am going to die.

She tried to resist him, tried to find some kind of leverage to pull away, but she kept slipping in the snow. Her knees and elbows were bleeding. A cold wind came off the frozen lake and sliced through her bare skin.

I am going to die.

She reached around and grabbed his wrist, tried to twist the thumb, a distant memory coming back from a self-defense class in college. His grip loosened just enough for her to break free, but then he pushed her hard from behind, and she went right out onto the ice and fell onto her back. Another sudden shock as the ice and the snow bit into her skin.

She rolled over and tried to push herself up. He stayed there on the edge, a shadow, not moving, as she kept slipping and falling back down, each time another cold shock, another scrape of her skin. In the end, she settled on her hands and knees, pulling herself into a ball, making herself as small as possible to protect herself against the wind.

This is it, she said to herself. That same calm voice from a thousand miles away. *This is the end. I'm going to die right here on this lake, and they'll find my frozen body tomorrow. Or a month from now. Or in the spring...*

He came out onto the ice and grabbed her again, dragging her back to the shore. As she stood up straight she was close enough to see his eyes reflecting the dim ambient light. He hadn't said a word since she'd pointed the gun at him, and how much more terrifying was this silent disjointed face that looked back at her. There was something fundamentally different about him now, as if some basic human quality had been left behind in that house, some essential gear in his mind stripped and spinning free.

She tried to scream again, but he slapped one open hand

against her cheek, making everything explode in a white flash of heat and pain. As he grabbed her arm, she went down to the ground, and he dragged her across the snow like a father pulling a child on a sled. The ice and the rough ground cut at her skin, until she finally managed to scramble to her feet. They continued around the lake this way, Livermore half pulling, half dragging, past more empty houses, past the part of the road that came near the lake, where Jeannie desperately hoped for one last chance, one pair of headlights coming from White Cloud. One vehicle she could wave to, could throw herself in front of.

But the road was just as dark and empty as the lake, and he kept pulling her toward the single light that loomed ahead of them. The Livermore house on the other side of the lake.

As they got closer, some primal part of her longed to be inside it, out of this cold air, sheltered from this wind. A dim light came through the back door and spilled out onto the snow. As he opened the door and pulled her inside, she blinked in the sudden glare and went down on the floor. She saw the skin on her arms, how red it was, and all the cuts and scrapes that were bleeding. She couldn't feel her feet anymore, and she was still shivering uncontrollably.

She saw drops of blood on the floor. Dried stains that had already been there for God knows how long, her own blood dripping from her face and arms to mix with it.

She didn't bother to wonder who else had bled in this room, or when. She was past caring. Past comprehending. When Livermore left the room, she looked up and made one last reach for the door. Her hands were just as numb as her feet, and she couldn't even work the knob to turn it.

"No," Livermore said as he came back into the room and threw a blanket at her. "You're not leaving."

He was talking to her again, but his voice sounded like the flat, emotionless drone of a machine. She grabbed the blanket and wrapped it around her as tight as she could, taking one breath at a time, staring at the floor, watching the snow melting and dripping from her hair, the drops of water mixing with the blood from her arms.

"There were others," he said, standing above her.

She didn't even try to move away from him.

"Women who had to pay the price."

She had nothing left. No strength, no fight.

Please stop talking, she thought. *If you're going to kill me, kill me...*

"It's time for you to meet them."

She was still trying to comprehend what those words could even mean as he pulled her back to her feet and led her down the stairs.

CHAPTER THIRTY-TWO

I KEPT CALLING Jeannie's name, long after Livermore had dragged her from the house. I wanted my voice to reach her, to let her know that I wasn't giving up hope. I couldn't let her believe that I wouldn't follow them, couldn't let her believe that she'd never see me, or anyone else, again.

But you've got nothing, I said to myself. *No chance at all. Livermore will come back eventually and finish you off.*

I rattled the handcuffs again, feeling the frustration washing over me, overwhelming me. My wrists were shredded, my arms sore from pulling against the pipe. My forehead was still bleeding, and there was no way to clear the blood that dripped into my eyes.

I'm not going to die on this floor.

One more rattle, the cuffs biting into my skin. Then I made myself stop. I made myself think.

I'm going to find a way out of this.

I have to find a way.

I pulled myself deeper under the sink, looked at everything that was around me. But it was just cleaners and sponges and a bottle of bleach. I curled up into a ball so that I could bring one foot against the side of the top drawer. I pushed the drawer out with my foot, feeling it stick as it came to the end of the track. I kicked it a few times, and the whole thing came crashing onto the floor. It was a junk drawer, old batteries, flashlights, keys, hardware. But nothing with a blade. Nothing that would be of any use to me.

I worked on the next drawer, pushed it out and heard the silverware rattling onto the floor. I kicked the drawer clear and tried to see what kind of knives I could get to.

There, a steak knife.

I worked it closer to me with my foot, but it got stuck against the lip of the under-sink cupboard I was lying in. I worked it back away from the lip until I could get one foot around each side of it. It took a few tries, but I was finally able to lift it and fling it at my own head. I was past caring if it hit me.

I pulled myself as close to the drainpipe as I could and twisted my arms around until I could get one hand on the knife. It wasn't much of a blade, but it was all I had. I twisted my arms back and tried to get an angle on the chain between the cuffs. Then I started sawing.

I had no leverage, could hardly put any force at all behind the blade. But I picked one spot and worked at it. After five minutes, stopping whenever I had to shake my head to clear the blood from my eyes, I had a small nick worn into the chain link. I took a breath and refocused. Then I kept sawing back and forth, willing the blade to cut into the metal. It wasn't working.

I was just dulling the blade more and more with each stroke, and then eventually it slipped right out of my hand and fell behind the back of the bottom drawer. I let out a yell of frustration, brought my foot up again and slid that drawer open, finally kicking it hard enough to send it sliding across the kitchen floor. Even with the drawer out, there was no way I could get to that knife.

I pictured Jeannie being dragged from the house again, could only imagine how cold she must have been feeling at that moment, wherever she was. Or what Livermore was doing to her.

I could see only one choice left.

You're going to have to find another knife. Only this time, you're going to have to cut your wrist.

You lose your left hand. You find something to stop the bleeding. You go find Jeannie.

It's the only way you're going to save her.

I cleared my eyes one more time and looked through the rest of the silverware on the kitchen floor. None of the knives looked like they could cut through anything. Not the metal chain on the cuffs. Not even my own flesh and bones—unless I was prepared to saw away at myself for the next three hours.

I yanked on the cuffs again, felt them cutting even deeper. Curling myself into a ball again, I brought my feet around and tried to set them against the back wall of the cupboard. There was a time when I would bend my legs like this a few hundred times a day, every time I put on the mask and crouched down behind the plate. Sometimes doubleheaders. Now I could barely get myself halfway into that same position. But I took a deep breath, and I forced my legs to bend... farther... farther... twisting my whole body around, the cuffs burning on my wrists...

Until *there*, I had one foot on the wall. Now the other…

You can do this, I told myself. *You have to do this. No matter what it takes.*

I kept bending, pulling against the cuffs, willing my sore left knee to bend, until I finally had my other foot braced against the wall. I was completely twisted over like a pretzel now, so tight I couldn't have gotten myself free again even if I had wanted to. I tried to grab at the drainpipe, to take some of the pressure off my wrists. My hands kept slipping.

More, you piece of shit. You need to move more.

I folded myself up the last inch, until I could get my fingers around the pipe, almost interlacing them on the other side. Just enough to keep the cuffs from cutting me any deeper.

Now I had to pull with my hands and push with my legs at the same time. I gritted my teeth and bore down on it. Straining against the pipe.

You have to explode. You're a fucking rocket ship now. Blasting out of this place.

I kept straining and finally felt the drainpipe move a quarter of an inch. I got a new grip, tried again.

One more explosion.

Move, you son of a bitch. Move!

Another breath. Another reset on the grip. I kept my eyes closed against the blood, pushed against the wall, pulled at the pipe. Pulled and pushed and pulled and I felt it give another quarter inch, and suddenly I was back in my own mind, a million years ago, seeing Jeannie walking across that campus for the first time, talking to her for the first time, kissing her for the first time, finally walking down the aisle to marry her, this woman who I'd lost and hadn't seen in how many goddamned years.

I screamed out with the pain, giving it everything I had left inside, going deep enough to find more. More than I'd ever had before.

Livermore's face. My hands around his throat.

I'm going to kill you. I'm going to kill you. I'm going to kill you.

I felt the pipe give a little more and started to time my efforts into short bursts of strength, rocking the pipe back and forth like a car stuck in the snow, give and pull, give and pull, work it, take a breath, work it, take a breath.

It gave one more time, and I heard the sound of wood cracking around the sink and I thought I had it but then it was stuck solid again. I bent over one more time, laced my fingers together, and gave out one more scream as I used every ounce of my strength, concentrating on Jeannie's face.

Come on, you piece of shit drainpipe!

Now!

I pulled one more time, felt the whole thing coming down on me, too late to stop it, too late to protect myself. The edge of the sink caught me in the head and drove me backward. I slipped under it just enough to avoid most of the weight crushing my head into the floor, but then the bowl of the sink hit me in the jaw like the biggest sucker punch that was ever thrown by any heavyweight, and I had to stay down on the floor for God knows how long, waiting for everything to come back into focus. When it finally did, I realized that my hands were free. Free from the drainpipe, at least, if not from the cuffs.

I grabbed the side of what was left of the counter, the one half that had remained attached to the wall when the sink had fallen over. I felt for my cell phone. It was gone. Then I saw the collection of knives in the butcher-block holder, took out the heavy meat cleaver and tried to line it up with the chain between the cuffs. It was almost impossible to get any force on it, holding it with one hand and trying to swing it backward, to the space between my wrists, but I raised both hands and brought everything down on the counter at once, slamming the cleaver into the chain. Raised my hands and did it again.

The chain wouldn't break.

I can't waste any more time.

I went through the other knives, pulling out the longest, sharpest knife in the block. Then I grabbed one of the flashlights that had been inside the top drawer I'd spilled on the floor, tested it, wiped my eyes with a kitchen towel, took one more breath. And went out the door.

The two cars were still parked in their spots in the driveway. I didn't know why Livermore hadn't taken one of them. Looking out at the dark road, I still didn't see any other way for him to get away from here, and as I shined the flashlight on the driveway itself, I saw no footprints in the snow.

I reversed direction, struggling to keep my balance on the slippery ground with my hands still cuffed together in front of me, and went into the backyard, finally picking up the footprints leading down to the lake.

She was barefoot, I said to myself. *Wearing a tank top. She could die out here from the exposure alone.*

When I went down closer to the lake, I saw the footprints leading along the shoreline. I followed them, keeping my flashlight trained on the ground, watching great drops of blood falling into the snow—from my face, or my wrists, or God even knows where else I was bleeding from. I flashed back to that woman in the hotel room above mine, the blood dripping through the ceiling and onto the white bedspread.

I've seen enough blood for a lifetime. I don't want to see any more, unless it's Livermore's.

The footprints eventually led right to the lake, and as I shined the flashlight I saw the dark patches out on the ice showing from where the snow had been wiped away. My heart jumped into my throat as I imagined her going down through this ice, into the water below. She wouldn't last more than a minute. But as I scanned the ice I didn't see any holes, and I finally picked up the footprints as they continued along the shoreline.

Where did he take her?

I turned off the flashlight long enough to let my eyes adjust to the dark, and to see the dim light coming from a house on the other side. The only other house on this lake that showed any signs of life.

There.

I hurried along the shoreline, seeing where the road came close and hoping that someone would come by so I could send for help. But there was nobody to help me. I would need to do this alone.

I continued to the house, saw the one light coming from the kitchen door. This was where he first saw her, I realized, a long time ago, when they were both teenagers. Not that it even mattered now. But it was an answer to my question.

I kept the flashlight off, moving in the dim light that reached across the yard. I went to the first window, looked inside and saw the empty kitchen lit by a single bulb in the ceiling, moved around to the next window, saw another empty room, this one dark. I went to the back porch, closed up for the winter. Around to the far side, another window looking in on a bedroom. Completing the circle, seeing nobody at all. There were no lights coming from the upstairs rooms, as far as I could see.

Where are they?

I got down on my hands and knees, looked through the narrow basement window that sat just a few inches off the ground. Through the cobwebs, I could make out one faint light that seemed to come from a little desk lamp. I wiped the blood from my eyes again, closed them for a long moment to give myself the best shot of night vision I could manage, and then looked through the window again.

I saw the top of Livermore's head. I didn't see Jeannie.

Standing back up, I weighed the long kitchen knife in my right hand. Still cuffed to my left, so I knew it would be hard to use the knife against him. But it was all I had.

Then I finally noticed the generator sitting next to the house. It was humming away, supplying this house with its only power. I looked it over carefully, and as I moved to the other side I saw a pair of boots first, then two legs, then the body of a man slumped against the far side. In the dim light, he seemed to be looking up at me, but as I touched his face I felt no warmth in his body. There was nothing left of his throat, just a dark frozen mass of blood and tissue that spread down onto his coat.

I don't know how long you've been out here, I thought. *You're one more victim I was too late to help.*

I just pray to God I'm not too late for Jeannie.

CHAPTER THIRTY-THREE

I DIDN'T WANT IT TO END THIS WAY."

Jeannie was huddled on the concrete floor of the basement, the blanket still wrapped tight around her. Livermore stood at the workbench, with a single light casting a pale glow that barely reached to the dark corners of the room. He had a box of shells on the bench, and as he talked to her he refilled the magazine of his semiautomatic.

"I gave you a chance," Livermore said. "You didn't take it. That was a big mistake."

Jeannie stared at the concrete floor. She had given up trying to play along.

She had given up on everything.

"This may surprise you," he said, "but I've made mistakes, too. I've let other women get close to me. Women I never should have trusted. If you think about it, it all goes back to *you*."

She didn't respond. The words were just a buzzing in her ears now.

"You were the prototype for me, Jeannie. You were the alpha. I should have known there could never be a beta."

The floor was cold against her skin. No matter how hard she clutched at the blanket, she could not stop shivering. Livermore slid the magazine back into his gun and slipped it into his belt. She heard him moving behind her, rummaging through the plastic storage boxes that were stacked against the wall. Then sliding one of the boxes across the floor.

"The first was Arlene," he said, looking back toward the other boxes against the wall. "Then Theresa."

The words started to break through. *What is he saying?*

"Then Claire, from Utah. Then Sandra, who I met in Las Vegas."

He took off the lid from the plastic box next to her. A box that anyone else in the world would use to keep Christmas decorations in.

"And this is Liana."

She still couldn't comprehend what she was hearing, because even after everything that had happened to her, there was only so much madness she could take in at once. But as he lifted the lid from the box and the *smell* came washing out over her like the hot breath from an animal, breaking right through her terror and her shock, it all came together in that single moment and turned this *thing* in front of her into a reality.

This is real.

It's a dead body.

She couldn't even scream at that point, not that anyone would have heard her, anyway. She slid away from the box, from the man who had killed this woman and had put her here. Had kept her in this box.

"She's the most recent," he said. As he tilted the box toward her, she saw an arm. Flesh still on the bone. A purplish liquid oozing from it. A black swarm, moving.

Insects.

It was all pure animal reaction now, as she tried to scream, her voice so hoarse she could barely make a sound.

"This is the price they paid," he said. "Do you understand what I'm trying to tell you? I didn't want you to have to do the same."

Before she could stop herself, she looked down one more time and saw the whole woman's body, the liquefied organs at the bottom of the box, with clumps of hair and the flesh that still clung to the bones. What was left of the woman's face, her mouth wide open as if still screaming.

He stood up and pushed the box back toward the wall. Jeannie stopped trying to make any noise. Stopped trying to think. There was no strength left in her body. If he had pushed her over, she would have stayed there and never moved again.

"Stand up," he told her.

She stayed still.

"I said, stand up."

The words didn't register. She felt the cold concrete against her hands and knees, the blanket on her back. The rest of her mind was white noise.

"You're making me angry again, Jeannie."

More words that meant nothing to her. Until she felt the smooth fibers of a rope against her neck. She reached for it, pure instinct as it tightened against her windpipe. She clawed at the rope with her fingers, but it was pulled tighter and tighter until she finally felt herself being lifted from the floor. She struggled to her knees, then to her feet, feeling the rope go slack for just an instant. But before she could slip it from her throat, her right wrist was caught in another loop of rope. Then her left. Both hands were pulled away from her body, like the wings of a bird, or of an angel, and as she looked around her she saw both ropes leading to one of the exposed ceiling joists above her head, along with the third rope still wrapped tight around her neck. All three coming together in the hands of the man standing in front of her.

He moved behind her with the ropes, and she felt the tension increase on all three at once, drawing her up onto the balls of her feet, which she could still barely feel against the cold concrete floor.

He came around to face her again, the ropes all apparently tied to something behind her now. Keeping her suspended in this position she would not be able to hold on for long. The tears started to run down her cheeks again, but she didn't say a word.

He kept watching her, his face unreadable in the dim light coming from the desk lamp behind him. She felt herself weakening, felt herself leaning back against the ropes holding her upright, felt the center rope tightening against her throat with every slightest movement.

She wanted to say something now. One more utterance while she still could. Her last words on earth. But before she could make a sound, the lights went out, and they were both left in utter darkness.

CHAPTER THIRTY-FOUR

SLIPPED INTO the dark house, ready to die if I had to. There was a knife in my right hand, a flashlight in my left, but both hands were still cuffed together.

Livermore had a gun.

And he had Jeannie.

I paused in his kitchen for a moment, waiting to hear something. The house was quiet. I took a step forward and heard the floor squeak beneath my foot. Old wooden boards, no way to avoid it. He would hear me coming, no matter how carefully I moved.

You need some kind of edge, I told myself. *Something to surprise him, to distract him, to get him away from Jeannie.*

I took another step and felt my feet slipping from under me. When I caught myself against a table, I had to take a few seconds to stand still and let my head clear.

You've lost too much blood. You don't have much time left before you pass out for good.

I covered most of the flashlight with my hand, turning it on just long enough to see the general outline of the room. I saw blood on the floor. My own, maybe Jeannie's. Maybe from the man outside. There was a door about twenty feet ahead of me. It had to lead down to the basement. When I opened it, it was too dark to see the stairs, but I could smell the basement's dampness. And something else...

It was a smell I knew, taking me right back to the first time I ever responded to a senior wellness check, in that old house in Detroit. My partner and I had found the woman on her bathroom floor, where she'd been lying for the past four days.

It was the smell of death.

I wanted to call out to Jeannie, to tell her that I was here, that I would make sure she was safe. But that would have been suicide for both of us. Instead, I crouched down at the top of the stairs and I listened. I waited. I gave my own gut instincts a chance to show me my next step.

There was nothing but silence. And darkness. And that sickening smell.

Then I heard a sharp intake of breath from somewhere below me. A muffled cry.

I took one step down the staircase, hearing the wood creaking, actually feeling the whole thing shifting under my foot.

Fuck your instincts. Fuck your training, fuck everything you ever learned about how to approach a possibly armed suspect.

Fuck Martin T. Livermore because I am not going to wait one more second.

I flipped the flashlight on for a fraction of second. Just long enough to see the stairs, to see where they started, to count how many steps I would need to take. I kept myself low and moved as fast as I could. Down the second step, to the third.

Then a flash of light and sound both exploded at once, freezing everything in that one brilliant instant, every last detail, my shoes on the stairs, Livermore with the gun raised and Jeannie standing off to the side, her eyes closed, her body stiffly upright, her arms reaching out into a letter *Y.*

Another two steps down the stairs, then another flash and another image burned into eternity. I was closer to him, but still too far away.

Two more steps and I felt the concrete beneath my feet. I turned on the flashlight to blind him, but the meager light was consumed by the third flash, and then I felt the sudden jolt in my right shoulder, my own body remembering that night so many years ago, another jolt just like this one, then the same burning sensation that came right after it as I watched my partner dying on the floor next to me. My whole right arm went numb in an instant, and the knife I was holding went sliding across the rough concrete.

A fourth flash lit up the room again, but by that time my momentum had already taken me into his chest and the gun went off right next to my ear. My shoulder was on fire but I had my hands on him, even though they were still cuffed together. After all this time, all those miles chasing him . . .

I will not let go until you're dead.

He knocked the flashlight from my other hand, but at the same time I was able to grab at the gun, using both hands together, the cold metal twisting away from his fingers and clattering to the floor as we both fell hard against the workbench behind him, tools rattling and the breath coming out of him as I drove his back into the hard wooden edge.

The flashlight was on the floor somewhere, giving the room just enough light to make out the dark outline of his body. He tried to push me away, but I redoubled my grip on his shirt. Then he sucker-punched me right in the gut and folded me in half. I felt him slipping away from me, and then he stepped aside and tried to drive my head into the workbench. I ducked down just in time to avoid the blow, came up looking for him, but he was gone.

"Jeannie," I said. "Are you all right?"

I couldn't see her now. But I remembered the image that had burned into my mind. The unnatural way she had been standing, her arms spread out wide.

"Jeannie!"

She didn't answer me. Her body was nothing but a dark shadow against the wall.

No, she's not dead. She can't be.

"JEANNIE!"

"It's too late," Livermore said, his voice strangely detached in the darkness. "For both of you."

My right arm was dead. I knew I was running out of time. As I took a step toward his voice, he picked up something from the top of a pile of plastic storage boxes that were stacked against the wall. I saw the glint of metal, but otherwise had no idea what he had just armed himself with. Something hard and heavy, something that would put me down for good if he caught me with it.

I took another step and he was gone again. He had moved deeper into the darkness of the room, choosing another corner to wait for me. I tried to quiet down my own breathing, my own mind, but as I took a step sideways he came out at me and swung the metal object right at my head. I ducked just in time, trying to move inside to tie him up, but he slipped away.

"Give up," he said. "Give up and die."

I shook the blood from my eyes, got myself low, ready to try again, ready to take my one last chance if it came.

"Come on," I said to him, wherever he was, trying to draw him out. "Don't be a fucking coward. Fight me like a man."

I heard a sound to my left, took a step, and ducked again as he swung at me.

You have to time this just right. He swings, you drive before he can slip away. You bury your head right in his chest.

I waited and listened. I heard him breathing, heard him moving from one corner of the room to another, like an animal hunting its prey. I took another step as he somehow came up from behind me, and I felt the hard metal glancing off my temple. I had no chance to go after him. He was too fast, and everything was starting to fade.

Come on, put me away. Step out and take a big swing at me.

"The minutes are working against you," he said. "You don't have many left."

I turned and moved toward the sound of his voice again, walking right into him and feeling another glancing blow against my forehead. I went down and rolled away from him. When I got back to my feet the room was spinning, and it took a long moment to determine up from down.

I took one more step backward, then another, until I sensed the stairwell right behind me, giving him his opportunity, hoping for one last chance to draw him out of the shadows.

Come on, you've got me cornered here. Finish me off.

He stepped forward, a dark silhouette against the dim glow from the flashlight.

That's right. Give me one more shot. Just one more.

He took a swing, and I felt one more blow across the top of my head. I went down to one knee again, and I knew he had me on the next swing. But then he paused. To line me up better, or to say one last thing, I didn't even know or care because it was an opening, and as I came up and put my good shoulder into his stomach, I drove him across the room until both of our bodies crashed into the stack of plastic boxes. There was a sound like many brittle sticks all breaking at once as I clasped both hands into a double fist and hit him in the face, putting everything I had left into it. He let out a cry of pain as I hit him again, then again, until he grabbed for my right shoulder and it lit me up like a fifty-thousand-volt shot from a Taser.

I felt his fingers grabbing at my face, until I tore them away with both hands and bent them back, trying to break as many as I could. He let out another cry of pain and swung with his other arm, so hard I heard it before I felt it, just under my left eye, making everything go white.

A moment later, I was on my back, looking up at the rough wooden ceiling and the cobwebs that shone in the dim light. Then I saw Livermore's face, looking down at me. He came closer, and I felt his weight on my chest.

I tried to reach for him, but he had my arms pinned down, making my right shoulder burn with a white-hot pain. He leaned more weight into it, and I felt myself losing consciousness. Then he eased back.

I spit blood in his face, tried to get free again until he put his weight back on my shoulder. As he bent down closer to my face,

I could feel his breath on me, see his eyes and that little half smile that I hated so much.

He picked up the flashlight and shined it in my face. Then he raised the weapon above his head. I still couldn't see what he was holding.

He raised his hand higher. I could see it in his eyes. This was it.

"This is how it ends, Alex."

After everything I've been through. Every mile I've chased him. This is how it ends.

But then his body stiffened. The expression on his face went from smug satisfaction to surprise, and a thin trickle of blood leaked from his mouth. Jeannie's face appeared over his shoulder, pale and streaked with tears.

As he turned to look at her, I saw the knife sticking out of his back.

"What did you do?" he said to her, and then everything froze. Jeannie stood there with her hands over her mouth. There was a rope around her neck.

"You bitch!" he said as he reached out for her, the blood running down his back. *"You stupid whore!"*

He grabbed the rope and pulled her toward him. She screamed, and as he lifted his weight from my body I rose and brought my hands up together, looping them around his head and bringing the chain between the handcuffs against his throat. I pulled back and felt him falling against me, my head hitting the concrete again, but I kept the chain against his neck, pulling as hard as I could and working the knife deeper into his back.

A strangling sound came from his open mouth as I kept pulling the chain against his throat, feeling the handcuffs shredding through the last of the skin on my wrists, but it didn't matter anymore because everything I had was focused on those few links of chain that were stretched across his throat, as he flailed his arms back at me and caught me in the face with one fist after another, but I didn't let up.

I held on as he threw his body from one side of me to the other, one last desperate chance to break free, to breathe.

I held on as he tried to hit me in the face again. The punches getting weaker and weaker.

I held on for Jeannie, for the woman hanging in the hotel room, for the woman tied up and burned alive. For the woman in the refrigerator and the woman he violated in that bedroom while a video camera recorded every second. For all of the other women he'd killed. For Agent Halliday and the other men in the canyon. For Agent Larkin. I thought about each one of them as I held on tight, feeling the convulsions rippling through Livermore's body. Even as he stopped breathing, I held on.

I'm not letting go, Livermore. Not until I can see you burning in hell.

I would have held on for another hour, just to make sure he was dead, that he was really gone, but my arms finally gave out, and my whole body went limp.

I couldn't move for a while, until I finally heard Jeannie crying softly. I looped my arms back from Livermore's head and pushed him off me. He rolled onto his back, his eyes still open. Staring back at me.

I crawled over to Jeannie, found her sitting on the blanket. I pulled the rope from her neck, saw more ropes around each wrist, took those off and let them drop to the floor. She was shivering so hard now. I tried to wrap myself around her, but I couldn't make the convulsions stop. I sat there with her, catching my breath, until the shaking in her body finally eased and I was able to stand up and pull her to her feet. I wrapped the blanket around her, and as I grabbed the flashlight from the floor, the beam settled on the contents of the box we had fallen into.

Bones.

When I moved the beam, I saw another box that had been knocked over. Another skeleton. Then another and another until I finally came to the half-decomposed body in the fifth box. I took the light away from it and had to bend over and hold my knees.

"Get me out of here," Jeannie said, the words barely audible through her trembling lips. "Please, Alex…"

"I got you," I said, putting my left arm around her. "Let's go. Right now."

We went up the stairs, taking each one carefully. I could feel fresh blood coming from my right shoulder. More blood was running from my forehead into my eyes.

When we got upstairs, I did a quick scan of the kitchen with the flashlight, saw Livermore's coat draped over one of the chairs. I checked the pockets and found my phone.

Jeannie sat down on the floor. I didn't want to stay in this house anymore, but we didn't have a choice. I wasn't going to make her walk through the snow, and I didn't think I could carry her, not all the way back to her house.

I sat down next to her and dialed 911. When the operator answered, I gave her every piece of information I could. Robinson Lake, west of White Cloud. Then I told her to have the responders work their way around from Jeannie's house, the only house with lights on. I knew they would find us eventually.

When I put the phone down, Jeannie looked at me. Really looked at me for the first time since I'd gotten there, and as I looked back I finally got the chance to see that she was still the same person I had married all those years ago. Those same eyes, the same mouth. Everything I had fallen in love with, just a few years older.

"He shot you," she said, looking down at my shoulder. "You're bleeding bad."

"I'll be fine," I said. "We'll both be fine."

I turned off the flashlight and pulled her closer. We sat there together in the darkness, leaning against each other, waiting for the rest of the world to find us.

EPILOGUE

ON OUR SECOND NIGHT in the hospital, Jeannie found me.

I was still recovering from the surgery, my right shoulder wrapped up and immobilized. They'd taken out the nine-millimeter slug from Livermore's Walther PPS. It was the same shoulder that had been hit on that summer night in Detroit. I also needed seventeen stitches to close up the cut in my forehead, another dozen or so in each wrist, and my left knee still hurt whenever I tried to put weight on it.

Jeannie had frostbite on her toes and fingers, severe scrapes and bruises on her elbows, knees, and chin. But that was the least of it. Most of the trauma she'd suffered had been inside her own head. The kind of wounds you can't sew up with stitches. The kind of wounds nobody will ever see.

And will take a lifetime to heal.

She stood in the doorway and watched me for a while. When I opened my eyes, she was there. I didn't know if her room was down the hall or on the opposite end of the hospital, but I was glad to see her. They'd even let her put on real clothes. I was still in my gown, still had an IV stuck in my arm.

"Every time I close my eyes," she said, "I see him."

I knew what she was talking about. I had seen him myself, more times than I could count. That face would wake me in the middle of the night, and I'd sit up trying to reach for him, feeling the pain ripping through my shoulder.

"Come here," I said.

She came to the bed, and I pulled her close. She collapsed against me, the dam breaking all at once. I held her while she cried, and we both ended up falling asleep together, right there in my hospital bed. When I woke up the next morning, there was a nurse in the room.

For the second time in my life, Jeannie was gone.

FIVE DAYS LATER, I was out of the hospital and sitting on an airplane. A commercial flight, back to Phoenix, in the daytime, surrounded by normal people escaping the cold weather. Agent Madison was waiting for me when I crossed over the security line.

We spent the rest of the afternoon at the FBI office on Deer Valley Road, sitting in the same conference room where he had first interviewed me.

"Agent Larkin is still recovering in St. Louis," he told me after I'd gone through everything, every detail I could remember. "He'll have to live with some of the internal damage for the rest of his life, but it could have been a lot worse."

I remembered that night, how he'd told me to walk away before the cops caught up to me. To go after Livermore on my own. I knew I'd have to find him someday, to thank him for that.

"There's someone else who would like to see you," Madison said.

I couldn't imagine who it would be, until he took me to another room and I saw a young couple with a baby fast asleep in a carrier. Madison introduced me to Agent Halliday's daughter, his son-in-law, and his new grandson.

I remembered the message he had given me. *Tell them I'm sorry. Tell them I love them.*

I wasn't sure what else I could say to them. The baby woke up and started crying. I shook the son-in-law's hand and nodded to the woman as she took the baby out of the carrier and left the room with him. She didn't seem to want anything else from me, and I couldn't blame her for wanting to leave when I was done delivering her father's message.

Madison took me back to the airport, driving in silence most of the way.

"I'm on my way to Japan tomorrow," he finally said. "NPA came back to us with three missing-persons cases. The methodology is different, but that may have evolved over time. The time frame fits on all three cases. And close enough to Nagano. Maybe it was Livermore. Maybe not."

I knew what that meant. Three families in Japan who might never get answers.

But I couldn't do anything about that.

"You call us," he said after another few minutes of silence, "we take him alive."

"I call you, Jeannie's dead. You'll never convince me otherwise."

He didn't bother to argue. He dropped me off at the airport, told me he'd be in touch if he had any more questions.

"One more thing," he said. "There was a two-million-dollar reward on Livermore's head."

"That's for information leading to his arrest," I said. "Not for killing him."

"I believe it still qualifies. And you *are* a fugitive recovery agent."

"Not anymore," I said. "If there's money coming, give it to the families of Livermore's victims."

I watched him think that one over for a few moments.

"I'm serious," I said to him. "Tell me you'll make that happen."

When he finally nodded, I got out of the car and closed the door behind me. As I walked into the airport, I heard him driving away.

JEANNIE WAS BACK HOME in Grand Rapids. She'd just started a new job as a paralegal in a law office. A long way from her major in art history, but what the hell, it probably paid a little better. I was back in Paradise, plowing out my road, getting the cabins ready for a new batch of snowmobilers. I went down to the Glasgow Inn every evening and sat by the fire. Jackie would have the Red Wings on the television over the bar as usual, the sound turned down low. Vinnie would come by after his shift at the casino and sit in the other chair by the fire.

My shoulder and my wrists were still taped up. My left knee still hurt whenever I tried to get up. They left me alone, let me drink my Canadians and stare into the flames.

My old partner Leon came by one night, just to catch up

with me. That's when I told all three men what had happened. Sat them down by the fire and gave them the whole story, from the plane ride on a cold night, all the way to the desert, to the basement of a house on a tiny downstate lake they'd never heard of. I told the story once, leaving nothing out, so I'd never have to tell it again.

Two weeks after Jeannie and I said goodbye to each other, my phone rang late at night. It was Jeannie. She asked me how I was. I told her I was fine.

She didn't believe me, and we both knew it.

"I've been talking to somebody about what we went through," she said. "You should probably do the same."

"They told me that the *first* time I got shot," I said. "Sent me to the department shrink."

"Alex…"

"I'm fine, Jeannie. But it's good to talk to you."

She didn't press me on it. I was glad I didn't have to have an argument with her, because I knew she was right. I had spent a whole year destroying my own life after getting shot and watching my partner die on the floor next to me. My own life and my marriage to this woman. She told me she was still seeing Livermore's face when she closed her eyes at night. I didn't even have to tell her I was having the same experience. Seeing the same face, and hearing his voice whenever the wind blew outside my lonely cabin in the woods.

I would still wake up in the middle of the night, reaching for him.

Trying to kill him, again and again.

The Livermore who lived inside my head would never die.

"Someone came into the office today," she said. "This woman,

Alex, I could tell as soon as I saw her. She's living in fear. Believe me, I know what that feels like now."

"Could the lawyers help her?"

"No, they couldn't."

"What is she afraid of?"

"I don't know, Alex. She wouldn't tell me."

I could hear something in her voice. And after what she'd been through, I knew it would take a hell of a lot to rattle her.

"But you know it's bad," I said.

"Yes."

"And that's why you're calling me."

"You might be able to help her," she said. "Who else am I going to call? And besides..."

"Yeah?"

"We promised to stay in touch," she said. "You haven't called me yet. A man should keep his promises."

I was sitting in my little cabin in the woods, three hundred miles away from her. But it felt good to have this woman in my life again.

"So tell me everything else you know about her," I said. Because she was right, this woman I had once promised to watch over for the rest of my life.

A man should keep his promises.

How to Dry Fruits and Vegetables at Home

AND 50 GOOD RECIPES FOR COOKING WITH THEM

By the Food Editors of FARM JOURNAL

COUNTRYSIDE PRESS
a division of Farm Journal, Inc.
Philadelphia, Pennsylvania

Distributed to the trade by Dolphin Books
Doubleday & Company, Inc. Garden City, New York

ACKNOWLEDGMENTS

"Drying Fruits and Vegetables at Home" is the title of an Extension bulletin from the University of Arizona at Tuscon, and we gratefully acknowledge the help we got from its author, Peggy H. Putnam, Extension Nutritionist. We are also indebted to Dr. George K. York, Food Technologist with the Extension Service at the University of California at Davis, for sharing his knowledge and guiding us to other good sources of information.

In preparation for this book, we reviewed Extension bulletins on drying from the Universities of Oregon, Missouri, Oklahoma, Utah, Washington, Colorado, Florida, Georgia, Nebraska, Ohio and Pennsylvania. We dried food in our *Farm Journal* Test Kitchens, and tested recipes for cooking with them. We want to thank Dr. Ruth Leverton, formerly Science Advisor for the U.S. Department of Agriculture, for reviewing the manuscript.

Book Design: Michael Durning

Cover Design: Paul Panoc

Cover Photo: William Hazzard

Drawings: Alfred Casciato

ISBN: 0-385-11357-9
Library of Congress Catalog Card Number 75-18212

Contents

CHAPTER I

Dry It Now... Enjoy It Later

If you have this book in your hand, you're at least thinking about drying some fruits, vegetables or herbs this year. Is it a good idea? Is it hard to do? Does it require special equipment?

Most important—how will the food taste months from now, when you're ready to cook it and eat it?

Our Test Kitchen experiments convince us you'll find drying an acceptable-to-excellent way to preserve many (but not all) fruits and vegetables. Months or even a year from now, you can use them in recipes. In many of the casseroles, soups, stews and desserts we tried, you'll be hard put to tell them from fresh.

Our home economists were excited about the onions they dried. Here are the comments from their Test Sheets: "Our Onion-Parsley Dip is actually better than the one made with onion soup mix. . . color is lighter, too." Oven-dried onion rings, rehydrated and cooked in casserole dishes, had "superb texture and flavor."

The convenience is another plus: When you need only a tablespoon or two of chopped onion (or green pepper, or parsley) for a meat loaf or gravy, it's handy to have a packet or jar you can open and close after you've shaken out what you want.

We made a zucchini and tomato dish using canned tomatoes and dried zucchini, which our home economists rated "as good as with fresh zucchini." The dried corn in our corn chowder was bright yellow, appetizing looking. It does not taste the same as *fresh* corn; most dried foods have their own distinctive taste. But we rated it an excellent chowder.

Fruits don't have to be dried out as much as vegetables. When drying is considered completed for most fruits, they are "pliable" or "leathery" with a moisture content as high as 15 to 25 percent. But vegetables should be "dry" or "brittle," with 5 percent or less moisture. The high sugar content in fruits makes them easier to preserve; still, the drying time is usually longer—they give up their water less easily than vegetables do.

We talked to a number of farm women who have been drying fruits—mainly apples—for years. One Pennsylvania mother told us she seldom gets enough apple slices dried and stored to make a pie. Her children love the plain dried fruit as lunch box dessert or after-school snack. Who can complain about that?

We tested our dried apples by rehydrating them and using them in some of our favorite apple dessert recipes. We were pleased with their taste and texture; the apple color was somewhat darker than if we had used fresh fruit—but it was still quite appetizing looking. We pretreated the apple slices, however, simply by steam blanching, or by dipping them in an antioxidant—ascorbic acid or lemon juice. If you want to preserve apple whiteness, our directions tell you how to pretreat the fruit with sulfur or sodium bisulfite.

We were especially pleased with the fruit leathers. . . with their good fruit taste and fine keeping qualities. From farm homemakers in Utah, we learned how to make fruit leathers in two steps, so that the drying can be done when it's more convenient, in cooler weather. To handle overripe fruit quickly—to salvage it—simply make the puree and freeze it in 2-cup containers. When you're ready to make fruit leather, thaw the puree and spread it on your drying trays.

Our thrifty Utah advisors point out that they can or freeze their most perfect fruit—and puree what's left. Sometimes they combine fruit flavors by pureeing fruits together before freezing; sometimes they thaw two or more fruit purees and mix them together at the time they're ready to dry them. Some favorite combinations are strawberry-rhubarb, apple-pear and plum-peach.

Ideally, fruit leather is packaged in plastic food wrap. Use the piece you dried it on, and roll it up tight. For long storage, overwrap it with more plastic wrap. It's a good snack to pack long on a hike, or in a lunch box. And a few of the sparkling rolls, tied with ribbon, make a welcome Christmas gift.

Drying food that your family won't eat would be poor economy, of course. But if you experiment with drying, you'll quickly discover which dried and rehydrated vegetables and fruits you and your family like. . . just as you've learned which foods you prefer to preserve by canning and which to freeze.

Certainly, one of the advantages of drying is easier, more economical storage. With water removed, food weighs one-fourth to one-tenth as much as fresh, and it takes much less space. Eighteen medium size apples, for example, weigh about 6 pounds. After slicing and drying, they'll weigh only 1 pound, and you'll be able to pack them into 6 pint containers. For best keeping quality, dried food should be stored in a cool, dry, dark place.

Try a 25-cent experiment first. It won't cost you more than a quarter to try the technique of oven drying, to see how you like the dried apples, onions or whatever you want to experiment with. Just stretch a layer of cheesecloth over your oven racks, pinning it in place.

3

This gives you a "tray" that's ventilated on the bottom, on which you can spread food pieces to dry. Then follow directions for preparing the food and drying it in the oven (See Chapters IV and V.)

If your family approves your first dried product, you can make a modest investment in time and lumber to build a few drying trays with screen or slat bottoms—they're much easier to work with than cheesecloth. And if you get interested in drying in a big way, you may want to build or buy a small dehydrator to use instead of the oven. You'll find plans and directions in this book for building a home dehydrator, heated by electric light bulbs, or by a small stove or hot plate. If you live in sunny country, look at our plans for a solar dryer. Small home dehydrators also are appearing on the commercial market.

Nature's Way

Of all the ways there are to preserve food, drying is the most natural. It's Nature's way. Look at some nuts or cereal seeds, for example—they keep almost indefinitely, preserved simply by natural removal of water. Nature, not man, dried the first raisins—and some early forager discovered how good they were. Through such observations, primitive man learned that he could preserve much of his hard-won food supply by drying it. Even though he didn't know *why* it worked, it worked.

It wasn't until 1857 that anyone knew why. That's when Pasteur demonstrated that spoilage was caused by microorganisms (bacteria, yeasts and molds) that are always present in the air, in water and in earth, and in foods.

Microorganisms multiply rapidly wherever they find good growing conditions—warmth, moisture, oxygen. The juicy surfaces of peeled, sliced fruits and vegetables make ideal culture media for them. Their rapid growth is what decomposes exposed food so quickly.

Once scientists knew what caused spoilage, they could explain why drying–and canning–worked. (The canning method was developed 60 years before Pasteur's discovery, by a French inventor named Appert.) And they could develop ever-better methods for preserving food, including our modern canning and freezing procedures.

In U.S. kitchens, canning and freezing have been the favored methods of preserving food. Not only have you become accustomed to the way this food tastes, you feel confident about the methods. Directions are precise–to the minute–for pounds of pressure and processing or blanching times. You know that if you follow them carefully, the recommended procedures will give good reliable results.

Moreover, all of this "how-to" is widely available. Both government and business have spent millions on research and experiments. Nearly one million homemakers have *Farm Journal's Freezing & Canning Cookbook* to refer to. Other information sources include government bulletins, booklets published by manufacturers of canning jars and freezers, and countless magazine articles.

With all the research excitement–and dollars–going into freezing and canning, drying was vitually ignored except in the sunny, dry states.

But every so often, in times of crisis, drying revives as an alternative way to put food by. During the Depression Thirties, people who couldn't afford canning equipment dried their garden surplus. The USDA's last bulletin on the procedure, "Farm and Home Drying of Fruits and Vegetables" was published in 1918, revised in 1933; it's now out of print.

Homemakers turned to drying again during World War II when sugar was rationed and canning jars and lids disappeared in the war effort.

In the years since, the freezing industry mushroom-
ed, and by 1975, 40 percent of all U.S. homes (94
percent of *Farm Journal* subscriber homes) had
separate home freezers. But now, with daily headlines
about the energy shortage, again many prudent families are considering drying as an alternate or addition
to freezer storage.

Camping and back-packing also have increased interest in dried foods—so much easier to pack and carry.
Commercial companies make freeze-dried food available in astonishing variety. Some religious and private
organizations advocate keeping a one-year supply of
food on hand—the Mormons, for instance, as an out-
growth of their church welfare plan during the Depression. Many of the companies distributing dehydrated
food were founded by Mormons, and much of our
knowledge about home drying comes from Utah and
California, states with large Mormon populations, also
blessed with excellent climate for drying.

You cannot duplicate, at home, the sophisticated
processing of freeze-dried food, nor its packaging in
cans that involves the vacuum removal of all oxygen
and the introduction of nitrogen under pressure. But
you can dry and store many of the foods you may have
been buying, dried, in your supermarket—such as apples, apricots, prunes, raisins, onions, herbs—at considerable saving. If you have a big garden harvest to put
by, or have access to fresh-picked produce at roadside
farm markets when supplies are plentiful, we think
you'll want to experiment with other vegetables and
fruits to see which are well-preserved by drying.

Do not expect to find drying information as precise
as the directions you get in books and bulletins on
freezing and canning. Home drying has not been as
thoroughly researched as these other more familiar
and more reliable means of food preservation. The University of Arizona Extension Bulletin on home drying
makes a statement we agree with: "There are. . . many

variations in recommendations for treatment (of foods) before drying, for methods of drying, for temperatures and length of drying time, and for conditioning prior to storage. You may have to use the 'trial and error' approach in finding out which drying technique works best for your situation."

In home drying, then "it depends"—and we suggest that you approach it in a spirit of experiment and adventure. In the chapters that follow, we'll give you our opinions based on our own Test Kitchen work, plus various drying procedures and guidelines—the best of the information now available.

CHAPTER II

How Drying Preserves Food

Drying is one of the less precise methods of preserving food. Because you have a choice—depending on your climate and situation—of pretreatments, drying methods and storage after drying, it will be most helpful if you read this chapter carefully to get an overview of what it is you're trying to accomplish. Once you understand the principle of a process, you can make better decisions.

The microorganisms (bacteria, yeasts and molds) that spoil food need moisture, warmth and air to grow. You don't have to kill these microorganisms to prevent them from spoiling food. If you dry food successfully and keep it dry, they will not be able to grow or multiply. Such food can then be stored for months without deterioration.

Drying, like refrigeration and freezing, does not sterilize foods; rather, it simply slows, or halts, growth of microorganisms. By contrast, the canning process destroys bacteria and other microorganisms in food by heating it—sterilizing it. Jars of sterilized food must be sealed to prevent more bacteria from getting in.

Food can also be treated in other ways to reduce the number of spoilage organisms or prevent their activity—such procedures include salting, smoking, pickling or the addition of various preservatives. Our modern vacuum packs, which keep out air, also make food storable—you've used that technique if you've poured melted paraffin over jelly. Primitive people used it, too: coating food with fat, as North American Indians did with pemmican. These methods are not, however, recommended because of the danger of botulism and other food poisoning agents.

We're lucky to have so many choices in preserving our food. Not only does it help to reduce food waste, it adds variety to our meals. By not being dependent on one method—freezing, for example—we're able to swing with the times. Remember 1973, when we Americans were suddenly panicked by an energy crisis? And dismayed by increases in utility rates? In response to inflation, many families planted gardens, or bigger gardens, and that led to a temporary shortage of canning jars—manufacturers hadn't anticipated such a jump in demand. Who knows what lies ahead? It seems prudent to know more than one way to take care of summer's abundance, for good eating all winter long.

Of the three major methods we use for preserving food at home—drying, canning and freezing—drying is, in most instances, third choice. But if you've got an orchard, or even a tree full of apples, and zucchini all over your garden. . . if your freezer is full-up. . . if you can't get canning lids. . . if you can't make room for more rows of jars. . . drying may be your salvation. Or if you just want to try something new.

Advantages of Drying

You can get into drying easily and inexpensively. It requires little equipment; most of that can be contrived or made at home by a reasonably handy man or woman. Dried food is easy to package and takes little storage room. One dehydration expert with whom we discussed drying techniques maintains that home drying is less risky than home canning. He worries about careless or unknowledgeable home canners who do not follow modern procedures and who may thereby risk food spoilage, including the acute food poisoning known as botulism. While there is almost no risk of botulism in dried fruits and vegetables, there are some other spoilage factors to guard against. They will be described in this chapter.

Limitations of Drying

Drying is not a complicated procedure, but it will certainly keep you in the kitchen (or wherever you set up your dehydrator) for the better part of the day—even longer for some items. While it's drying, the food needs watchful attention: the trays need to be shifted and the food stirred every half hour or so.

More important, once you start the drying process, it should continue without interruption. The reason? Molds can grow on partially dried foods at room temperature. . . and molds might produce harmful or toxic products. (If molds develop on your drying fruits or vegetables, you should discard them.)

The preparation of food to be dried is no more than you'd do if you were freezing or canning it—but no less, either. Such steps as washing, paring, slicing and blanching or other pretreatments are essential.

Drying is not the answer for all foods. Some fruits and several vegetables are better preserved another way. However, if you're willing to make freezer or refrigerator space available for storing some of your dried products, you can do more drying than used to be recommended.

An old USDA bulletin distributed during the Depression years advised against drying vegetables like asparagus, spinach, celery, green peas or green beans. These vegetables are harvested young—while they're still rapidly growing. When you dry such immature vegetables, the bulletin cautioned, "the resulting product may be satisfactory in appearance, flavor, and palatability for some time, but it gradually undergoes loss of flavor and palatability and may develop a distinctly unpleasant haylike odor."

Packaging is the problem in keeping home dried food for long periods. The vacuum packs used by commercial dehydrating companies lengthen storage life. In fact, dehydrated foods packed in cans with nitrogen under pressure will keep for years. But the best you can do at home is to pack food in airtight containers and store it in a cool, dark, dry place. For the more perishable dried vegetables mentioned earlier, refrigerator or freezer storage is recommended if you want to hold them up to six months.

Principles of Drying

Your goal in drying food is to preserve its food value and—as much as possible—its natural flavor and cooking qualities. So there's a little more to it than simply evaporating enough moisture to stop bacterial growth and spoilage.

Actually, there are two kinds of spoilage you have to do something about when you preserve food, one caused by enzyme activity, and one caused by microorganisms—bacteria, yeasts and molds.

The enzymes responsible for ripening fruits and vegetables continue to cause color and flavor changes until, inevitably, the food gets too ripe—it spoils. This ripening-spoiling action accelerates when you peel or cut the food and expose it to air—it's what makes apple slices turn brown, for example.

So when you preserve food, you must pretreat it (us-

11

ually by blanching) to halt the immediate spoilage caused by enzyme activity. Then you dry it (or can it or freeze it) to halt bacterial growth.

Food should be dried fast enough so that it doesn't spoil before it dries. You can hasten drying two ways: by raising the air temperature, and by putting the air in motion over the food to carry off evaporated moisture.

But too high a temperature causes cells in succulent fresh food to burst; the water that escapes carries off both food value and flavorings. Partially dried food will scorch.

And too much air movement, or heat and air movement, tends to dry out or harden the surface of the food, which prevents the interior from drying properly.

Because these principles are important in your understanding of how an oven or dehydrator or solar dryer works, let's tick through them again.

Success in drying depends on:
• Pretreatment of food by blanching or other means, to stop the changes that begin the minute food is cut into pieces and exposed to air.
• Drying at a temperature high enough to prevent the growth of microorganisms—yet not so high as to cause the bursting of cells and loss of juices in fresh-cut food or scorching of partially dried food.
• Continuous drying, without interruption, so that food does not spoil or mold before it dries.
• Adequate air circulation to carry off water vapor. If you are drying in a box dehydrator, it should be designed and vented so as to draw fresh air into the box, move it over the trays of drying food, and exhaust the moisture laden air.
• A good drying day or days—when weather is excessively humid, nothing will dry.

12

CHAPTER III

What You'll Need for Drying Food

The kind of equipment you need for drying will depend on the method you use. If you can depend on sunny, dry days happening when your food is ripe and ready, you can dry food the most inexpensive way: on trays in the sun. (See Chapter VI, Sun Drying.)

But if you want to dry on your time and terms, you can either use your oven for drying, or build or buy a small dehydrator. A few days of rainy weather at the wrong time may cause the loss of a large amount of food unless you've provided for indoor drying.

Since the drying idea has caught on again, there are a number of manufacturers now marketing small home dehydrators in a price range of $40 to $80. Other manufacturers are supplying bigger, more elaborate (but not commercial) dehydrators that would be expensive for single family ownership but perhaps practical for communal use by several families. One such design has forced air flow through six compartments containing three trays each; it sells for under $300.

No drying machine can do more than contain the food, keep out insects, circulate warm air over the trays of food and exhaust the moisture laden air. Engineering makes the difference in how well the dryer performs, and how much attention you will have to give it. Such devices as a thermostat to regulate heat and a small fan to move air currents, will step up the dryer's efficiency and give you closer control of the drying process.

We have sketched plans for two dehydrators which you can build. One of them is heated with light bulbs. The other is a natural draft drying cabinet which you can place over a hot plate. Before your build a dehydrator, you should think hard about how much dryer capacity you need. It would be poor judgment to build or buy an expensive dehydrator to work up a few dollars' worth of produce. But it would be impractical to try to dry the fruit from a good-sized orchard with a family size drying machine. If you have large quantities of your own apples and want to market some dried, you can afford a larger unit.

Oven Drying

If you're new to drying, experiment with oven drying first. Your oven may be all you need. If you decide you want a separate dehydrator, so as not to tie up your oven for long periods, your experience in oven drying will give you a reading on how much dryer capacity you may need.

Oven drying trays. For a trial run, make your first "trays" from cheesecloth stretched over oven racks. Use one layer of cloth; pin it to rack: the four corners first, then front and back edges. Stretch material to make it as tight as you can and pin sides around the first rung in from the edge–this allows air circulation at outer edges.

When loaded with food, these cheesecloth "trays" sag between rungs of the oven rack, which is a nuisance. Some women we've talked to, who are pretty casual about drying, say they simply spread food on cookie trays. However, you'll get more satisfactory results if your drying trays are ventilated. Until such time as you're ready to build trays with screen or slat bottoms, the cheesecloth works.

The screen trays pictured on the cover of this book are easy to make—simple butt-joint frames with screen stapled or tacked to the bottom. (See Figure 1). Tray frames should be a little smaller than the inside dimensions of your oven, so you can slide them in and out.

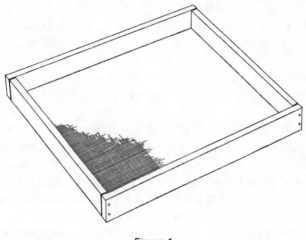

Figure 1
Oven Drying Tray

You can make frames from any scrap lumber that's clean, dry and free from pitch—do not use yellow pine. For sturdy, stackable trays, make frames from 1×2″ lumber. (Note: drying and milling reduce the nominal size of lumber; actual dimensions of 1×2″ lumber are ¾×1½″.) Trays with sides keep food from sliding off when trays are moved; they make stacking easier; they keep trays from resting on food when they're stacked; and they provide an edge to which a protective covering may be fastened if you use them for outdoor drying.

Although some foods discolor or corrode it, aluminum screen is okay for the bottoms. Stainless steel hardware cloth (⅛-inch to ¼-inch mesh) is better—especially if you want trays to hold up for years—but it's expensive, about $1 per square foot.

Do not use galvanized screen. This is important. The zinc and cadmium in galvanized screen cause dangerous reactions when they come in contact with acid foods. Also avoid fiberglass, vinyl and copper screening—they all have qualities that make them unsuitable for drying tray bottoms.

Wood slats (or dowels) make a good bottom for trays. Use thin wood lattice, ¼ inch thick, about 1½ inches wide, and nail to frames with ½-inch spaces between slats. (When drying small pieces of food, lay cheesecloth over slats, so food doesn't fall through.)

Thinking ahead. If there's a possibility you'll eventually build a dehydrator, you may want to examine dehydrator plans now, and build oven trays of a size that you will be able to use later in a dehydrator. And if you plan to pretreat fruit either by sulfuring it outdoors or dipping it in a sodium bisulfite solution (see Chapters IV and VI), trays with wood slat or stainless steel mesh bottoms are recommended. Sulfur has a corrosive reaction with other metals.

Loading the oven. You can spread from 1 to 2 pounds of fresh prepared food on each square foot of tray space. The recommended oven load is no more than 4 to 6 pounds at a time, distributed over two, three or four trays.

An oven that's 18 inches high can hold, at most, four drying trays. There should be at least 2½ inches of space between each tray, and a minimum of 3 inches free at both top and bottom of the oven.

Most ovens have only two racks which limits you to

using only two drying trays, unless you contrive some way of stacking the extra tray or trays. You could stack one tray on top of another with small wood blocks separating them. Or you could build a framework to hold all your trays and use it instead of the oven racks.

Food pieces should be spread as evenly as possible in a single layer.

Controlling oven heat. Generally speaking, the best average temperature for drying food in an oven or dehydrator is 140° F. (but see Chapters IV and V for specific temperatures for different foods). Depending on model and age, your oven may or may not have a thermostat that will maintain such a low setting. Test it with a reliable thermometer.

(Low temperatures—140° F. to 150° F.—have been on most ranges since the early or mid-Sixties. In new gas ovens, the oven "cycles"—that means it goes on and off, only the pilot remains lit. In older gas ovens, the oven does not cycle; the flame goes down but it does not cut off. Temperature settings in these older ovens do not go below 250° F. or 300° F.)

Do not use the top heating element (broiler) of an electric oven—food will burn. When you turn on a gas oven, turn just to the temperature you want. If you turn it to a higher setting, then back, you get a backlash—you never get as low a temperature as you would by turning directly to the low setting. If you have a gas oven which does not have an automatic shut-off, be especially watchful. Do not leave it unattended; do not let the flame go out unnoticed during drying.

Even if your oven thermostat has a low setting, it's advisable to use a reliable thermometer as a check on actual oven temperature. You can use an oven, candy, roasting or dairy thermometer; if using one of the last three, be sure the bulb does not touch any surface.

If you have or can borrow an extra thermometer,

place one on the top tray and one on the bottom. If you have only one thermometer, put it on the bottom tray, bulb at the back. With the oven door open, this is the hot spot in your oven. . . the spot to monitor.

Preheat the oven (see temperatures specified for individual foods in Chapters IV and V) and add the loaded trays.

Prop the oven door open for the entire drying time. This is necessary to let the moist air out; it also helps you maintain the even low temperature. Experience—and a watchful eye on the thermometer—will tell you how far open your oven door should be.

Start with a 1-inch crack for an electric oven. . . and as much as 4 to 8 inches for a gas oven.

Hold the oven door open with a folded pot holder, or prop it wider with a stick. If your oven thermostat does not have the low setting, you'll have to control oven heat yourself by adjusting the door opening. The first time you dry, check temperatures at 1-hour intervals. As you become experienced, once every 2 hours should be often enough. If oven temperature goes above 160° F., open the door wider.

Some Extension bulletins recommend directing a fan toward the open oven door during the drying process. One of the Home Economists who tested our drying procedures under home conditions has four children; she did not like the idea of a fan whirring on a stool in front of the oven. So we did all our oven drying without using a fan, and felt we got good results without it.

As food dries, it takes less heat to keep the oven at the specified temperature. . . so watch temperature carefully toward the end of the drying. At the start of the drying process there is little danger of scorching, but when nearly dry, the food may scorch easily.

Examine the food often, turning it or stirring it occasionally on the trays. Move the trays themselves every hour or half hour: rotate them top to bottom and turn them front to back, too. If you are using more than two trays, it would help you to number them—on both front and back edges—so you can keep track of your rotation pattern.

Food pieces along the edges of trays are likely to dry first—as they do, remove them to avoid scorching. When drying is almost completed, turn off the oven and open the door wide.

If you check drying charts in Chapters IV and V you'll note that in oven drying, most vegetables take from 4 to 12 hours to dry, and fruits from 6 to 20 hours. Time varies according to the kind of fruit or vegetable being dried, the size of pieces and the load on the trays.

Keep your trays clean. After use, wash them in hot sudsy water, using a stiff brush, and rinse in clear water. Air dry the trays and store where they'll stay clean and ventilated.

Portable Electric Food Dehydrator

While it will hold up to 18 pounds of fresh food for drying, this efficient home dehydrator is small enough to set up on a kitchen counter or table—it's only 18 inches wide, 24 inches high, 24 inches deep (See Figure 2). It holds five drying trays with a total drying surface of 8½ square feet and it plugs into any outlet. Heat is supplied by nine ordinary 75-watt light bulbs, and air circulation by a small household fan mounted inside the box. In Pennsylvania, in 1975, this dehydrator costs about 5¢ an hour to operate. You can get operating costs in your area by checking rates at your local utility company—it draws a little less than 1 kilowatt-hour of power each hour

Designed by Dale E. Kirk, Agricultural Engineer at Oregon State University, the dehydrator is easy to build from ½-inch plywood and 1 × 1″ wood strips. The only tools you need are a saw (hand saw, coping saw or

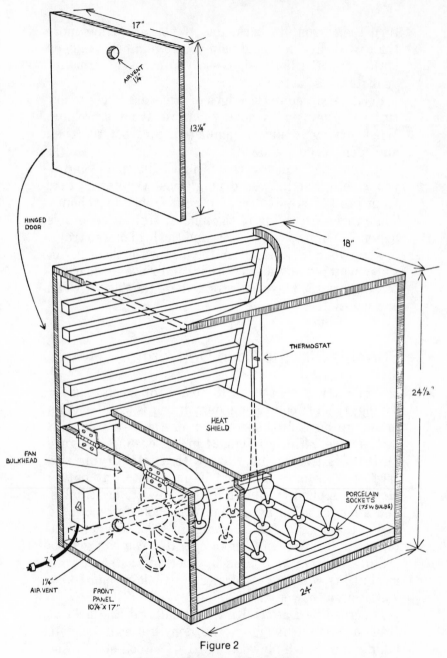

Figure 2

Portable Electric Food Dehydrator
Perspective with right side removed,
top cut away, and hinged front door removed.

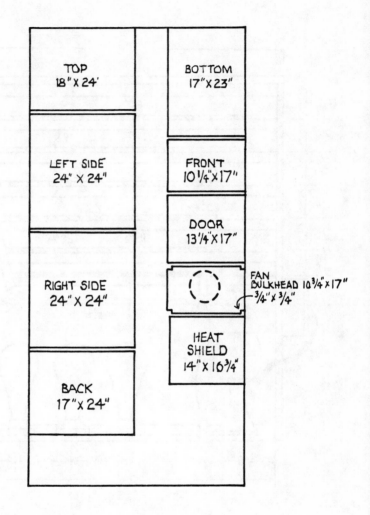

Figure 3
Portable Electric Food Dehydrator
Plywood cutting diagram.

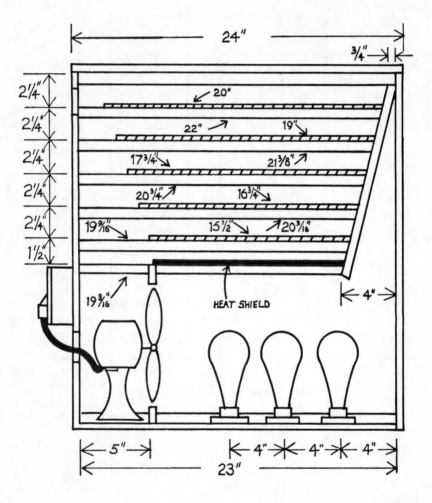

Figure 4

Portable Electric Food Dehydrator
Side view, cross-section.

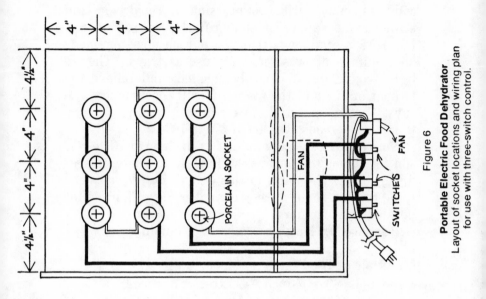

Portable Electric Food Dehydrator
Layout of socket locations and wiring plan for use with three-switch control.

Figure 6

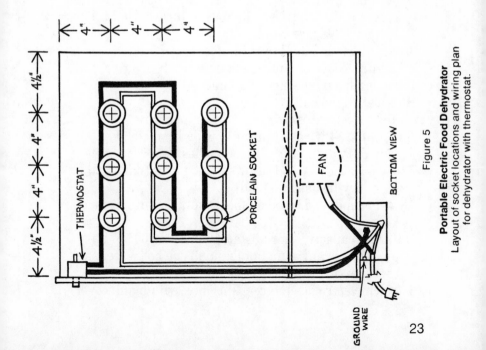

Portable Electric Food Dehydrator
Layout of socket locations and wiring plan for dehydrator with thermostat.

Figure 5

23

compass saw), drill, countersink, screwdriver and knife–and a square or steel rule for measurements. Mr. Kirk recommends that you purchase custom-made aluminum window screens for use as trays. "They're light weight, sturdy, easily cleaned, and relieve the builder of much of the more difficult construction," he says. Cost of materials in Oregon, including the custom-made screens, was about $75 in 1974.

Notice that the trays are different lengths. The reason for this is to improve the flow of air currents over drying food. The trays in this dehydrator do not need to be rotated–indeed, they cannot be (see Figure 4 for detail of tray runners).

Here are Mr. Kirk's directions for building it:

Materials needed

1 sheet (4 × 8') of ½-inch A-C exterior plywood

9 pieces 1 × 1" wood strips, each 4 feet long (actual dimensions of 1 × 1" wood are ¾ × ¾")

1 6-inch or 8-inch electric fan

5 aluminum window screens for trays, each one 16¾ inches wide; lengths as follows in inches: 20, 19, 17¾, 16¾ and 15½ (see Note)

1 pair of 2-inch metal butt hinges

1 ball-link chain or equivalent door latch

9 porcelain surface-mount sockets

9 75-watt light bulbs

15 feet of asbestos covered #14 copper wire

6 feet of #14 wire extension cord, with male plug

Heavy duty aluminum foil, 36 inches long

116 #8 flathead wood screws, 1 inch long (nails and glue may be used instead)

18 #7 roundhead wood or sheet metal screws, ⅝ inch long

1 10-amp-capacity thermostat, 100° F. to 160° F. approximate range (an immersion type hot water tank thermostat works well)

1 4-inch electrical surface utility box with blank cover

2 ½-inch utility box compression fittings
2 wire nuts
Note: You can order aluminum window screens made to measure through your local lumber, building supply or glass dealer. If you prefer to build your own drying trays, measure and cut ½×1" wood strips to make frames with outside dimensions as above. Tray bottoms can be screen or wood slats—for construction how-to, see Figure 8.

Cutting and Assembly

The cutting diagram (Figure 3) shows how to cut plywood pieces with a minimum of saw cuts. Measure from the factory-cut edges as shown. Be sure to allow for saw kerfs between pieces when measuring and marking the plywood. Cut 1×1" strips to make runners or cleats for the five trays and the heat shield. Figure 4 shows the lengths and placement of these runners—it also shows tray backstop. Attach these strips to inside surface of each side panel as shown. Position first runway 2¼ inches from top. Place remaining four runways 2¼ inches apart measuring from top of one to top of next. Place heat shield runway 1½ inches below. (Note that Figure 4 shows runner placement for left side of dehydrator. Reverse it for right side—like a mirror image.)

Next, lay out the porcelain sockets and fasten them to the base as shown in the wiring diagram, Figure 5. If you don't know anything about wiring, ask an electrician to do this part of your assembly. But before you begin wiring, fasten the left side to the base, using 1×1" wood strip to strengthen the joint (see Figure 2). Attach lower front panel, too, after you've marked position for air vent and drilled the hole (see below).

Wiring

Fasten the asbestos covered wire to the porcelain sockets. Connect the wire that goes to the yellow screws on the sockets to the thermostat, mounted near the rear on the left side panel. (The yellow screws on the sockets connect to the center pole, rather than the threaded wall of the socket.) One of the wire nuts may be used at the utility box to connect the black wire in the extension cord to one of the wires from the fan and to the wire leading to the thermostat. The other wire nut may be used to connect the white wire in the extension cord to the second fan wire and to the wire leading to the white screws on the sockets. The third wire (green) in the extension cord should be connected directly to the utility box, mounted on the front panel. Secure the wires leading in and out of the utility box by use of the two compression fittings.

If you use a household type fan with the base still attached, fasten it in place on the dehydrator base and cut the hole in the fan bulkhead to fit. If you use a duct type fan, cut the necessary size hole (approximately 8½ inches in diameter for an 8-inch fan or approximately 6½ inches in diameter for a 6-inch fan) in the bulkhead and fasten the fan mounting frame directly to the bulkhead. Now set the bulkhead in place (approximately 5 to 5½ inches from the front panel) and fasten it temporarily in position by two screws through the left side panel. Center the 1½-inch-diameter air vent hole in the front panel directly in front of the fan motor, approximately 1 inch away from the motor. This will allow cold air to enter and pass over the motor to cool it.

Final Assembly

Refer to Figure 2. Fasten the right side and top in place using 1×1″ wood strips to strengthen the joints. Attach the back. Cover the plywood heat shield with heavy duty aluminum foil and place it on bottom runway. (Aluminum foil helps protect plywood from heat; it provides a reflective surface, and if juices drip from drying trays, it's easy to clean or replace.)

Before attaching front door to front panel with

hinges, drill a 1½-inch-diameter air vent hole centered 2 inches from top of door. In addition to this hole for moisture removal, you also need some kind of adjustable latch to hold the door partly open during early stages of drying, when moisture is being removed rapidly. A ball-link chain with catch permits you to adjust the door opening as necessary.

Operation and Maintenance

Before you load your dehydrator with food, plug it in and let it run, empty, for a day. This will bake out any fumes from resins or glues in plywood that might otherwise be absorbed by drying food.

The electric fan motor is supplied by a stream of fresh air from the lower vent, positioned in front of the motor, but it will still operate at a higher temperature than in normal, open-room service. Lubricate the motor bearings with 30-weight engine oil. Lighter grade household or sewing machine oil may tend to gum and stall the fan motor after extended service.

As a check on the thermostat setting, poke the probe of a dial type or household meat thermometer through the box into free space above the trays. (Drill a hole for the probe through the side of the box at the back—behind and above the middle tray.) You can read the thermometer outside the box; it should be one that registers in the 100° F. to 160° F. range. Be sure the sensing part is in the drying part of the cabinet—not with the light bulbs.

Cover trays with a single, close layer of food to be dried; the five trays will hold up to 18 pounds of fresh, moist food, depending on what it is and how it's cut. Keep the door closed for the first 30 to 60 minutes of drying time, until dehydrator reaches desired drying temperature. Then open the door a crack at the top (about ½ inch) to let moisture laden air escape. As the moist air exhausts at the top, additional fresh air will be taken in along the sides of the partly open door.

Test to see when the first, high-moisture stage is over: Hold your hand or something metal at the opening; when moisture no longer condenses on your hand or on metal, close the door. The air exchange provided by the two 1½-inch vents should be enough to complete the drying of your food.

Wash trays with hot water and a detergent when they become soiled with dried-on juices. If you purchased the recommended aluminum window screens with an aluminum wedge strip to hold the screen in place, you can put them in an electric dishwasher without damage.

Without a thermostat

You can build the dehydrator without a thermostat. But you will have to watch it more closely, and you will certainly need the thermometer (described above) with its sensing element in the drying area to monitor the temperature in the cabinet. Wire the nine sockets to three switches instead of one, so that you can regulate heat manually by turning off three or six of the nine light bulbs. See Figure 6 for the wiring diagram. In this wiring plan, the fan is plugged into a duplex outlet instead of being wired in permanently.

All three switches and the fan should be turned on for at least the first hour or two when the dehydrator is loaded with moist food. As soon as the temperature comes up to the desired level and the extra heat is not needed to warm incoming fresh air, one or two switches may be turned off.

Natural Draft Dehydrator

The versatile drying cabinet shown in Figure 7 can be placed over a hot plate, range burner, or other central heat source. It could even be adapted for use over a small old-fashioned heating stove, if necessary—just make it taller, with the extra space at the bottom to accommodate the stove.

As shown, the dehydrator is 18 inches wide, 30 inches deep and 36 inches tall. It holds seven drying trays, enough to dry up to 14 pounds of fresh prepared food.

A sheet metal heat spreader, hung inside the box between heater and trays, helps circulate the hot air evenly; but an important part of the "natural draft" design is the staggered arrangement of the drying trays (see Figure 9). Here's how it works:

The drying trays are 6 inches shorter than the inside depth of the dryer. When you load the dryer, you place the top tray as far forward as possible and still permit the door to close. The second tray is pushed back against the rear wall; the third tray is placed forward like the first, and so on. The arrangement encourages warm air currents to flow over the surfaces of the trays as well as through them, in a zigzag pattern (see arrows diagramming air flow in Figure 9).

As the warm air moves up through the cabinet, it absorbs moisture from the food and becomes cooler. So it is inevitable that the rate of drying will be greatest at the bottom, and progressively slower at the top. While the zigzag airflow pattern helps to equalize drying through the machine, it only partly overcomes the problem. To compensate for the uneven heat, you can rotate the trays. This is no big deal, since you should examine the food every 1½ to 2 hours anyway, to see how it's doing.

Dr. George K. York, Food Technologist and dehydration expert with the Extension Service of the University of California at Davis, adapted this dryer design from one in wide use in California during World War II. This—and any dehydrator—should be built from clean, dry wood that is free from pitch. Do not use yellow pine. Plywood or other types of composition board may be used for the cabinet walls and doors. Run the dryer empty for a day to bake out fumes from

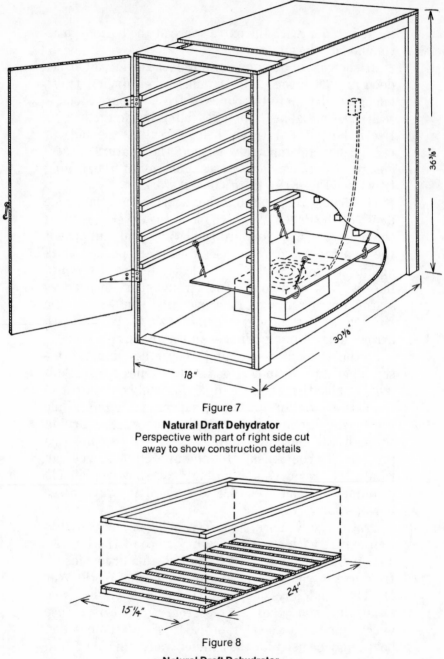

Figure 7

Natural Draft Dehydrator
Perspective with part of right side cut
away to show construction details

Figure 8

Natural Draft Dehydrator
Drying tray with wood slat bottom.

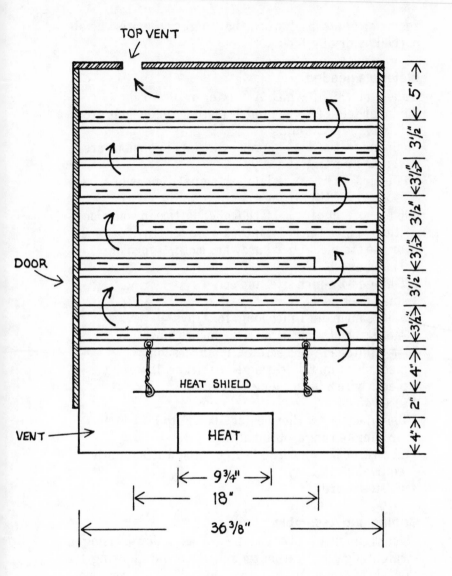

Figure 9
Natural Draft Dehydrator
Side view, cross-section.

31

resins or glues in plywood that might otherwise be absorbed by drying food.

Materials needed

1 sheet (4 × 8′) of ⅜-inch A-C exterior plywood

20 linear feet of 1 × 2″ lumber (actual dimensions are ¾ × 1½″) for framing

35 linear feet of 1 × 1″ lumber (actual dimensions are ¾ × ¾″) for tray runways

96 linear feet of ½ × 1″ lumber (actual dimensions are ½ × ¾″) for tray frames

106 linear feet of wood lath (called lattice in some localities) ¼ inch thick, 1½ inches wide for tray bottoms or use stainless steel hardware cloth, ⅛-inch or ¼-inch mesh

2 T-hinges, 2½-inch size, and screws

1 small door hook

Nails, ½ inch and 1 inch long, for trays

8 #8 flathead wood screws, 2½ inches long

16 #8 flathead wood screws, 1½ inches long

1 piece sheet metal, 16-gauge or thicker, 12 × 18″

4 pieces wire 8 inches long

4 screw eyes

1 10-amp-capacity thermostat, 100° F. to 160° F. approximate range, optional

1 electric hot plate variable up to 1100 watts (or other equivalent heater)

Asbestos board

Cutting and Assembly

Mark and cut plywood pieces as follows, using a straightedge and carpenter's square, and allowing for saw kerfs when cutting: two sides 30 × 36″; rear wall, 18 × 36″; door, 18 × 32″. Cut top in two pieces, 18 × 4″ and 18 × 23½″.

Cut framing for side panels from 1 × 2″ lumber: four pieces 36 inches long and two pieces 27 inches long. Nail and glue them flush with edges along sides and top of plywood sides. (Study Figure 7 for this and steps that follow.)

Cut fourteen tray runways from 1 × 1″ wood and attach them to inside walls with nails. Position first runway 5 inches from top. Place remaining six runways 3½ inches apart, measuring from the top of one runway to the top of the next.

Attach rear wall to sides with eight of the 1½-inch screws.

Cut two braces for front from 1 × 2″ lumber, each 15¾ inches long. Use 2½-inch screws to fasten them through side framing, lining them up flush with top and bottom.

Rout out space for hinges in framing on left side, and attach door. Door should be flush with top of dryer; the open space at the bottom provides air intake. Attach door hook.

Use remaining eight 1½-inch screws to attach the two top pieces: small piece at the front, large piece at rear, leaving a slot between about 3 inches wide, for moist air to escape.

Insert screw eyes on lower runways 8 inches from front and rear and suspend heat spreader from wire so that it hangs 2 inches above heat source.

If you use a thermostat, attach it to back wall above the position of middle tray (about 12 inches from top of dryer) and connect to heat source.

To make trays, cut ½ × 1″ wood for frames: 28 pieces 24 inches long, and 28 pieces 13¾′ inches long. For each tray, butt two pieces of each length together, to make rectangular frames measuring 15¼ × 24″ overall. (See Figure 8.)

Cut 84 slats for tray bottoms from wood lath (lattice) 15¼ inches long. Nail 12 slats to each frame leaving ½-inch space between slats. To keep food from sliding off trays, nail a second set of framing pieces on top of the slats—like a sandwich. If you make tray bottom from hardware cloth, tack it in place on tray frames.

Guard against fire. If your heat source is an open flame or unprotected electric coil, line the edges of the air intake and the interior of the cabinet near the heat with asbestos board. Place an asbestos board or a metal plate under the heat source.

Never leave a dehydrator or oven unattended during drying. If you have to leave, turn it off.

Operation and maintenance

Set the dehydrator in a well ventilated room so that water vapor will be carried away. Preheat to 160° F.

Load trays with prepared food one layer deep. If necessary, cover wood slats with cheesecloth to prevent small pieces of food from dropping through slats. Different kinds of fruits and vegetables may be dried at the same time, but odorous vegetables, such as onions, should be dried separately.

Place trays in the dehydrator following the zigzag arrangement shown in Figure 9, to channel air flow over all trays. No matter how many or how few trays you use, stagger them.

Put an accurate, easily read thermometer on the middle tray. When the loaded trays are placed in the dehydrator, the temperature will drop. Bring it up to desired temperature (140° F. for most foods) to complete drying. Even if you install a thermostat, use the thermometer as a double check.

Examine the food from time to time (every 1½ to 2 hours) and rotate the trays as necessary to get uniform drying. Also turn the food, so that it will dry evenly.

Watch temperature very closely near the end of drying. When nearly dry, vegetables are especially prone to scorch. Even slight scorching affects the flavor and may lower nutritive value.

Drying time varies according to type of food, size of pieces and the load on each tray. Approximate drying times for fruits are charted in Chapter IV, and vegetables in Chapter V.

CHAPTER IV

Drying Fruits

Fruit to be dried should be fresh, sound and tree-ripe or vine-ripe, at the peak of its goodness. If it's perfect for eating, it's right for drying.

It should be prepared for drying as soon as possible after gathering—with one exception. Some varieties of pears need to be ripened some more after picking.

If your fruit comes from your own garden or orchard, or if you can buy it fresh-picked from a farmer's market or roadside stand, you can hurry it onto your drying trays, to preserve its goodness. But it would be poor economy to spend either your money or your drying time on produce that has lost its garden-freshness while moving through a wholesale market to a supermarket to your shopping cart.

The flavor, color and keeping quality of your dried fruits will be improved if you prepare them carefully (pretreatments are recommended for several fruits), dry them properly and package them well for storage. All these steps are important.

Pretreatments are described in detail in this chapter, and the fruit chart tells which pretreatment(s) to use on which fruits. The chart also gives you some idea of how long it will take for fruit to dry, but drying times are only approximate. They depend on many factors: humidity, amount of moisture in the fruit, size of pieces, temperature and air movement in the oven or dryer.

Conditioning the dried food is explained in Chapter VII, which covers Packaging and Storing.

Preparation

• Handle fruit with care to avoid bruising
• Wash it in clean, cool water to remove dirt or spray.
• Sort and discard any fruit that shows decay, bruises or mold, or cut away the defective parts.
• Use a stainless steel knife when you pare and slice fruit, to avoid discoloring it.
• Peel, pit and cut the fruit according to directions in the chart for each fruit.
• Thin slices or small pieces will dry faster. For even drying, keep pieces all the same size.

Pretreatments

Apples, apricots, peaches, pears and nectarines begin to darken when you cut them. Without treatment, they'll get darker during drying and storage. They also lose flavor and vitamins. This darkening is oxidation: the enzymes that help fruit ripen simply don't know when to stop. Pretreating fruit is an attempt to halt or slow down enzyme activity so that fruit will "hold" until you get it dried or preserved.

Fruit dried naturally with no pretreatment is safe to eat. However, to protect color, flavor and vitamins, consider one of these protective treatments:

Ascorbic acid. Pure crystalline ascorbic acid is a good antioxidant, but it is sometimes difficult to buy. If your druggist doesn't have it, you may locate some through a pharmaceutical company or chemical supplier. Mix the ascorbic acid crystals with water. For apples, add 2½ teaspoons ascorbic acid crystals to 1 cup water. For most other fruits, 1 teaspoon ascorbic acid crystals per cup of water is enough. If you find that the variety of fruit you're cutting up darkens badly, increase the amount of ascorbic acid. One cup of the mixture should treat about 5 quarts of cut fruit. Sprinkle the mixture over the fruit, stirring and turning the fruit gently to treat each piece. Work quickly.

Ascorbic acid powders that keep fruit from darkening are sold in supermarkets also, under brand names. They're not as effective as pure ascorbic acid, but easier to find. Follow label directions for "fresh cut fruit."

Even if you plan to sulfur fruit (see below), you should treat it with the ascorbic acid solution as soon as you cut it. This helps keep it from darkening while you're loading the trays and getting them ready for the sulfuring box.

Salt water bath. Mix 2 to 3 tablespoons salt in a half gallon of water. Drop fruit into the salt water for 10 minutes. Drain on paper towels. Because fruit soaks up water, longer drying time will be required.

Sulfuring. This is the pretreatment used by commercial fruit dryers. Because sulfuring must be done outdoors, and because sulfured fruit should then be dried in the sun or open air, this treatment is more completely described in Chapter VI on Sun Drying.

Sulfuring means exposing cut fruit to the fumes of burning sulfur. Sulfuring produces better color and flavor, and for a longer period of time, than other treatments. It helps preserve Vitamins A and C in fruits. It's especially recommended for fruits to be sun dried because it helps minimize souring and insect attacks, too. Chapter VI includes directions for a sulfuring box you can contrive from a packing carton.

Sodium Sulfite Dip. If you can't sulfur outdoors, some (but not all) authorities give the alternative of dipping fruit in a solution of sodium sulfite or sodium bisulfite. (Caution: Don't confuse sodium sulf*ite* with sodium sulf*ate;* sodium sulf*ate* is a cathartic.) Sodium sulfite and sodium bisulfite are not available everywhere. We've checked and found that druggists in some states can't (or won't bother) get it for you.

To use it for pretreating fruit, mix from 1½ to 3½ tablespoons of sodium sulfite or sodium bisulfite to 1 gallon water. The amount you use depends on how you feel about darkened fruit; the weaker solution is a conservative treatment recommended by Extension specialists at the Universities of California and Utah.

Soak apricots halves 10 to 20 minutes in the solution; soak pear halves 20 to 40 minutes. Steam peaches 5 minutes, cool and soak for 15 to 30 minutes.

Obviously, the water that soaks into the fruit will have to be dried out of it later. Drain fruit and pat dry with towels before you begin drying.

Steam Blanching. If you're going to dry fruit indoors, in the oven or dehydrator, or if it's just not possible to sulfur it, you can blanch fruit by steaming (see directions on page 48). This will give you a darker color fruit than sulfuring. It may also give a slightly cooked flavor to some fruits such as apricots, peaches and pears. Blanched fruits may be soft and a little difficult to handle.

Steam blanching is also used to soften berries and to crack the skins of some fruits. Steam fruits until translucent but still firm.

Water Blanching. There's a waxlike coating on the skins of cherries, grapes, figs, plums, blueberries, huckleberries and cranberries. These fruits will dry more successfully if the coating is removed. And if the skins of these fruits are cracked lightly in many places (called checking), the fruit dries faster. A quick dip in boiling water removes the coating and cracks the skins.

Put no more than 3 quarts of fruit in a cheesecloth or mesh bag. Dunk the bag in enough boiling water to cover the fruit. Shake the bag gently, to expose all the fruit to the boiling water for 30 to 60 seconds or until skins are cracked.

Syrup Blanching. If you would like a sweetened "candied" kind of dried fruit, you can blanch it in syrup: Combine 1 cup sugar, 1 cup light corn syrup and 3 cups water; heat to boiling. Add the prepared fruit and simmer 10 minutes. Remove pan from heat and let fruit stand in the syrup for 10 minutes longer. Lift out, drain and cool.

Syrup blanching is an alternative to sulfuring—it helps hold the color in apples, apricots, figs, nectarines, peaches, pears and plums. But the fruit will take longer to dry. Also, the sweetened fruit attracts insects, so if you dry outdoors stretch a layer of nylon net over the trays.

Preparing and Drying Fruit

The fruit chart (pages 40 to 45) is based on recommendations by Peggy H. Putnam, Extension Nutritionist at the University of Arizona—a state where sun drying and controlled-heat drying are both practiced.

For each fruit listed, you'll find directions for preparing the fruit, the preferred pretreatments and the drying times and temperatures. Note that for some fruits, there's a change in temperature as drying proceeds. If you don't have that much control over your

Chart 1
Preparing & Drying Fruits

Fruit	Preparation and pretreatment
Apples *Use varieties of good cooking quality, mature, but not soft.*	Wash, peel & core. Cut into slices or rings ⅛″ to ¼″ thick, or into quarters or eighths. To prevent browning, coat with solution of 2½ tsp. pure crystalline ascorbic acid in 1 c. water. Steam blanch 10 minutes or sulfur 30 to 60 minutes depending on size of pieces.
Apricots *Use any variety. They should be fully ripened but not so soft they are easily mashed or lose shape during drying.*	Wash, cut in half & pit. Do not peel. To prevent darkening, coat with solution of 1 tsp. pure crystalline ascorbic acid in 1 c. water. Sulfur 1 to 2 hours depending on size & ripeness of fruit. (The riper the fruit, the more slowly it absorbs sulfur dioxide.) Or steam blanch halves 5 to 10 minutes. Or blanch in sugar syrup.
Berries *Firm type*	Sort, wash & leave whole. Dry without treatment, or steam ½ to 1 minute. Or crack tougher skins by dipping 15 to 30 seconds in boiling water, then in cold water. Drain.
Cherries	Sort, wash, leave whole or stem & remove pit. Dry without treatment, or check skins of whole cherries by dipping in boiling water 15 to 30 seconds, then in cold water. Drain. Or blanch in sugar syrup.

Drying procedure	Dryness test Approximate drying time
Spread slices on trays no more than two layers deep. Under controlled heat (oven or dehydrator) start at 130° F.; gradually increase to 165° F.; finish at 145° F.	Leathery, suede-like, no moisture when cut & squeezed. Takes about 6 hours in controlled heat.
Arrange in single layer on trays, pit side up. Under controlled heat, start at 130° F.; gradually increase to 150° F. Reduce to 140° F. when nearly dry. May be dried in a solar dryer.	Leathery, pliable. A handful of pieces falls apart after squeezing; no moisture in center when cut. Drying time for halves, up to 14 hours in controlled heat; 1 to 2 days in sun.
Spread on trays no more than two layers deep. Cloth on tray may help keep berries from sticking. Under controlled heat, start at 120° F.; increase to 130° F. after one hour; then to 140° F.	Dry & hard. Berries rattle when shaken on tray & do not show moisture when crushed between fingers. Takes up to 4 hours.
Spread in single layer on trays. Under controlled heat, start at 120° F.; increase gradually to about 145° F. Reduce temperature near end to avoid scorching.	Leathery, slightly sticky. Takes up to 6 hours.

41

Fruit	Preparation and pretreatment
Dates *Dates with low moisture content are desirable. Best to pick translucent fruit.*	Wipe clean with damp terry towel. Do not wash. Discard any fruit showing fungus, skin damage or souring. Dry only same type of date in any one batch. No pretreatment necessary.
Figs *Select fully ripe fruit. When not fully ripe, the sugar content is too low to produce a good dried product and fruit may sour.*	Wash or wipe clean with damp terry towel. If small or partly dried on tree, leave whole. Otherwise cut in half lengthwise. Check skins of whole figs by dipping in boiling water 15 to 45 seconds, then in cold water. Drain & blot dry. Or sulfur light colored varieties (like Kadotas) for 1 hour or more. Sulfuring is optional with others. Or, if cut, steam blanch for 20 minutes. Or blanch in sugar syrup.
Grapes *Use any seedless variety*	Wash & remove all defective fruit. Leave whole on stem; cut closely packed stems into small bunches, or remove from stems. Dry without treatment, or crack skins by dipping in boiling water 15 to 30 seconds, then in cold water. Drain.

Drying procedure	Dryness test Approximate drying time
Spread in single layer on trays. Dry in oven. Preheat to 225° F. for 5 minutes. Turn heat off; place dates in oven & leave until oven cools. Repeat process next day. Or dry in solar dryer from 2 to 8 days, depending on fruit and temperature. Pasteurize sun dried fruit in 150° F. oven for 30 minutes.	Leathery, pliable, slightly sticky. Drying time in a solar dryer is 2 to 8 days depending on fruit and temperature. Fruit temperatures above 155° F. cause caramelization of sugars with a resulting scorched flavor and a syrupy, sticky date.
Spread in single layer on trays. Under controlled heat start at 115° F.; increase to 145° F. after first hour. Reduce to about 130° F. when nearly dry. Stir or turn figs to keep them from sticking. May be sun dried.	Leathery, with flesh pliable yet slightly sticky Drying time for halves up to 5 hours in controlled heat; about 3 days in the sun.
Spread in single layer on trays. Under controlled heat, start at 120° F.; increase gradually to 150° F. Reduce temperature near end of drying, if necessary.	Leathery, pliable. Takes up to 8 hours.

Fruit	Preparation and pretreatment
Nectarines	Peel if desired. Cut in half & pit. Or cut in quarters or slices. To prevent darkening, coat with ascorbic acid solution as for apricots. Steam blanch halves 15 to 18 minutes, slices 5 minutes. Sulfur halves 2 hours, slices 1 hour. If blanched, cut sulfuring time by ½ hour.
Peaches *Use any good table variety; freestones preferred. Ripe enough for eating, but not dead ripe.*	Peel; cut in half & pit. If desired, cut in quarters or slices. To prevent darkening, coat with ascorbic acid solution as for apricots. Steam blanch halves 15 to 20 minutes, slices 5 to 7 minutes. Sulfur halves 2 hours, slices 1 hour. If blanched, cut sulfuring time by ½ hour.
Pears *The Bartlett pear is best for drying.*	Peel; cut in half lengthwise & core. Cut in quarters or eighths, or in slices. Treat with ascorbic acid solution as for apricots. Steam blanch 5 to 20 minutes depending on size of pieces. Or sulfur as for peaches. Or blanch in sugar syrup.
Prunes-Plums	Dry whole if small. Otherwise, cut in half & pit, or cut in slices. Dip whole fruit in boiling water 30 seconds or more to check skins; dip in cold water and drain. Or steam blanch halves 15 minutes, slices 5 minutes. Or sulfur whole fruit 2 hours, halves and slices 1 hour.

Drying Procedure	Dryness test Approximate drying time
Arrange in single layers on trays, pit side up to retain juices. Under controlled heat, start at 125° F.; increase gradually to 155° F. Reduce heat when nearly dry to prevent scorching. Turn over halves when visible juice disappears. May be dried in solar dryer.	Leathery, somewhat pliable Drying time for halves, up to 15 hours in controlled heat; for slices, about 6 hours.
Dry like nectarines.	Same as nectarines.
Spread in single layers on trays. Under controlled heat, start at 130° F.; increase gradually to 150° F. after first hour. Reduce to 140° F. for last hour or when almost dry.	Springy, suede-like; no moisture when cut and squeezed. Drying time for halves up to 15 hours in controlled heat; for slices, about 6 hours.
Dry like pears.	Pliable, leathery; handful of pieces will spring apart after squeezing. Drying time for whole fruit, up to 14 hours; for slices and halves, from 6 to 8 hours.

oven or dryer, try to maintain the drying temperature at 140° F.

Refer to Chapter III for detailed directions on loading trays and drying fruit in the oven or dehydrator. Sun drying is covered in Chapter VI.

Test for Dryness

You'll find a dryness test described for each fruit on the chart. Most fruits should be dried until leathery; berries should be hard; figs and dates leathery but slightly sticky.

To test for dryness, remove a piece of fruit from the tray and let it cool. (Fruits feel softer and moister while warm.) The cooled fruit should show no moisture when cut and pressed with your fingers. It will feel leathery, like suede, when you squeeze it and it will be pliable.

For directions on conditioning, packaging and storing dried fruit, turn to Chapter VII.

CHAPTER V

Drying Vegetables and Herbs

While "leathery" is the dryness test for most fruits, "brittle" is the test for most vegetables. Dried fruits are safely preserved when they still contain about 20 percent of their moisture. But vegetables must dry out to 5 percent or less moisture content to be adequately preserved for storage.

Use your common sense when you decide what vegetables to dry. Carrots, for example. Don't *buy* carrots for drying. If you have to buy them, buy them fresh as you need them. Considering energy costs, and your time, it would be hard to justify drying vegetables that are easily available all year long. If you grow them, you may want to dry some for convenience of use and storage.

Select vegetables carefully for drying. If they're not fresh and in prime condition for cooking, they are not suitable for drying. If possible, pick them early in the day and start the drying process immediately.

All vegetables contain enzymes—chemical catalysts which help food mature, and eventually, spoil. As soon as vegetables are picked, the enzymes start working faster. Their action affects the color, flavor, texture, sugar content and nutrients in vegetables.

Blanching or precooking stops enzyme action. It's an essential step in preparation of almost all vegetables. (Exceptions are peppers and pimentos, onions, parsley, mushrooms, horseradish.) Blanching saves vitamins and color, and protects flavor. It relaxes the tissues in vegetables and allows them to dry faster. Once they're dried, blanched vegetables keep better; they require less soaking before they're cooked; they have better flavor and appearance than unblanched vegetables.

Preparation

• Wash vegetables well in clean, cool water—scrub if necessary.
• Sort and discard any vegetable that shows decay, bruises or mold, or cut away the defective parts. One moldy bean may give a bad flavor to a trayful.
• Use a stainless steel knife when you pare or slice vegetables, to avoid discoloring them.
• Peel and slice vegetables according to directions in the chart for each vegetable.
• Thin slices or small pieces will dry faster. For even drying, keep all pieces the same size.
• Blanch prepared vegetables—see chart for recommended method and time.

Blanching

Blanching means to precook the food briefly in boiling water or steam—just long enough to stop enzymatic action and set the color. Steaming is the preferred method.

To blanch by steaming, you need a large kettle with a tight fitting lid to use as a steaming container, and a wire basket, colander or sieve to hold the vegetables.

The vegetables should be held above the boiling water in such a way that the steam will circulate freely around the vegetables. Water should not touch the vegetables. You may need to put a rack in the kettle to hold the basket above the water.

Pour about 2 inches of water into the kettle and bring it to a boil. Put prepared vegetables loosely into the wire basket to a depth of no more than 2 inches. Place the basket in the kettle, above the boiling water, cover tightly and let steam. Set your timer. The number of minutes to steam each kind of vegetable is shown on the chart. Let steam for half the suggested time. Check to see if steam is reaching each piece; stir if necessary and continue steaming.

Vegetables are blanched enough when they're heated through and limp or wilted. To test for doneness, cut through the vegetable; it should look translucent nearly to the center and feel soft but not cooked.

Spread blanched vegetables on paper towels to cool, and to remove excess moisture.

For water blanching, fill kettle with enough boiling water to cover vegetables. Work with small amounts of vegetables so the water doesn't stop boiling. Set your timer and watch closely; boil vegetables the shortest time possible to heat them through—see chart for timing. Reuse the water if blanching several lots of the same vegetable, adding more as necessary.

If you put prepared vegetables in a bag made of one layer of cheesecloth, shake it underwater to be sure boiling water reaches all pieces. Or, simply stir vegetables into boiling water, and scoop out with a slotted spoon or sieve.

Start timing immediately. Test for doneness same as steam blanching.

Dunk blanched vegetables in very cold water immediately, to stop the cooking and set the color. Drain at once on paper towels or cloth.

Preparing and Drying Vegetables

The vegetable chart (pages 52 to 57) comes from Dr. George K. York, Food Technologist with the Extension Service at the University of California at Davis. Although interior districts of California are ideal for sun drying, and the chart gives timing for sun drying, Dr. York recommends that vegetables be dried in dehydrator or oven, with controlled heat. . . even in California. The more rapid drying in a dehydrator means less chance of spoilage.

Once you start the drying process, it should continue without interruption. Molds can grow on partly dried foods at room temperature, and molds might produce harmful or toxic products.

For each vegetable on the chart, you'll find directions for preparing, blanching time, and drying time in the oven, in a dehydrator or in the sun.

Refer to Chapter III for detailed directions on loading trays and drying vegetables in the oven or dehydrator. Sun drying is covered in Chapter VI.

Processing mature beans and peas that you've allowed to dry on the vine is not covered in the chart. Mildred Bradsher, Food and Nutrition Specialist with the University of Missouri Extension Service, prints these directions in her bulletin on drying vegetables:

Let the beans or peas mature and dry on the vine. Pick the pods and put them in an open weave cloth or burlap bag. Tie the bag and hang it in the warm sunshine for several days; take it inside at night, safe from dew. When beans or peas are thoroughly dry they can be shelled by beating the bag with a heavy stick.

Hulls can then be lifted off and shelled beans or peas separated from the trash. Before storing, they must be treated to protect them from insect infestation. Heat them for 30 minutes in a 140° F. to 150° F. oven. Cool and seal in airtight containers.

Test for Dryness

You'll find a dryness test described for each vegetable on the chart. Most vegetables should be dried until brittle–properly dried corn, for example, will shatter if you hit it with a hammer.

To test for dryness, remove a piece of the vegetable from the tray and let it cool. (Food feels softer and moister while it's warm.)

For directions on conditioning, packaging and storing dried vegetables, turn to Chapter VII.

Drying Herbs

If you have an herb garden, you should dry your own herbs for the pure satisfaction of it. The tender young tops are best for drying; they have more aroma, are not woody, and dry more quickly.

Wash the herbs thoroughly, leaving the leaves on the stems. Shake off excess water and drain on paper towels until remaining water evaporates.

Spread herbs on drying trays no more than an inch deep and place in the oven or dehydrator at 140° F. Follow timing for parsley (see vegetable chart).

Cool a few leaves and test for dryness. When they feel crisp and dry, strip leaves from stems and crumble them, fine or coarse as you wish. Put them in clean jars, but leave the lid off. Check in 24 hours; if there's moisture on the sides of the jars, herbs must be dried longer. When thoroughly dry, cap the jars and store them in a cool, dark place.

You can dry herbs the old-fashioned way, by tying stems in clusters and hanging them upside down near the ceiling in a warm, well ventilated room or in a warm, dry attic. To protect them from dust while drying you can tie them inside brown paper bags, and hang the bags up.

Chart 2

Preparing & Drying Vegetables

Vegetable	How to prepare
Asparagus	Use tender tips only. Wash thoroughly. Cut large tips in half.
Beans, Green	Wash thoroughly. Cut in short pieces or lengthwise.
Beets	Cook as usual. Cool; peel. Cut into shoe-string strips ⅛ inch thick.
Broccoli	Trim and cut as for serving. Wash thoroughly. Quarter stalks lengthwise.
Brussels Sprouts	Cut in half, lengthwise through stem.
Cabbage	Remove outer leaves, quarter & core. Cut into strips ⅛ inch thick.
Carrots	Use only crisp, tender carrots. Wash thoroughly. Cut off roots & tops; preferably peel, cut in slices or strips ⅛ inch thick.
Cauliflower	Prepare as for serving.

Dehydrator or oven temperature: 140° F.

Hours of drying time in the sun are based on temperatures of 98-100 ° F.

†Blanching method and time (minutes)	Approximate drying time (hours)	Dryness test
Steam: 4-5 Water: 3½-4½	Dehydrator: 1-3 Oven: 3-4 Sun: 8-10	Leathery to brittle
Steam: 2-2½ Water: 2	Dehydrator: 2½-4 Oven: 3-6 Sun: 8	Very dry, brittle
No further blanching needed	Dehydrator: 2-3 Oven: 3-5 Sun: 8-10	Tough, leathery
Steam: 3-3½ *Water: 2	Dehydrator: 2½-4 Oven: 3-4½ Sun: 8-10	Brittle
Steam: 6-7 Water: 4½-5½	Dehydrator: 2-3 Oven: 4-5 Sun: 9-11	Very dry to brittle
Steam: 2½-3 or until wilted Water: 1½-2	Dehydrator: 1-2 Oven: 2-3 Sun: 6-7	Tough to brittle
Steam: 3-3½ Water: 3½	Dehydrator: 2½-4 Oven: 3½-5 Sun: 8	Tough, leathery
Steam: 4-5 *Water: 3-4	Dehydrator: 2-3 Oven: 4-6 Sun: 8-11	Tough to brittle

°Preferred method   † Blanching time will be slightly longer if you live in a high-altitude area, or if the quantity of vegetable is large.

Vegetable	How to prepare
Celery	Trim stalks. Wash stalks and leaves thoroughly. Slice stalks.
Corn on the cob	Husk, trim.
Corn, cut	Prepare in the same manner as corn on the cob, except cut kernels from cob after blanching.
Eggplant	Wash, trim, cut into ¼ inch slices.
Horseradish	Wash; remove small rootlets & stubs. Peel or scrape roots. Grate.
Mushrooms *Caution: Drying and cooking do not destroy toxins of poisonous mushrooms. Dry only edible varieties.*	Wash thoroughly. Discard tough woody stalks; cut tender stalks into short sections. Peel and slice large mushrooms.
Okra	Wash, trim & slice crosswise in ⅛-¼ inch strips.
Onions	Wash & remove outer "paper shells." Remove tops and root ends & slice ⅛-¼ inch thick.
Parsley	Wash thoroughly. Separate clusters. Discard long or tough stems.

Blanching method and time (minutes)	Approximate drying time (hours)	Dryness test
Steam: 2 Water: 2	Dehydrator: 2-3 Oven: 3-4 Sun: 8	Brittle
Steam: 5 or until milk is set. Water: 2	Dehydrator: 2-4 Oven: 4-6 Sun: 8	Dry, brittle
	Dehydrator: 1-2 Oven: 2-3 Sun: 6	
Steam: 3½ Water: 3	Dehydrator: 2½ Oven: 3½-5 Sun: 6-8	Brittle
None	Dehydrator: 1-2 Oven: 3-4 Sun: 7-10	Very dry and powdery
None	Dehydrator: 3½ Oven: 3-5 Sun: 6-8	Very dry and leathery
Steam: 4-5 Water: 3-4	Dehydrator: 2-3 Oven: 4-6 Sun: 8-11	Tough to brittle
None	Dehydrator: 1-3 Oven: 3-6 Sun: 8-11	Brittle
None	Dehydrator: 1-2 Oven: 2-4 Sun: 6-8	Brittle, flaky

Vegetable	How to prepare
Peas	Shell
Peppers & Pimentos	Wash, stem, core. Remove "partitions." Cut into ¼ inch rings or ½ inch squares.
Potatoes	Wash, peel. Cut into shoe-string strips ¼ inch in cross section, or cut in slices ⅛ inch thick.
Spinach & other greens (kale, chard, mustard)	Trim, wash very thoroughly.
Squash (Banana)	Wash, peel, slice in strips about ¼ inch thick.
(Hubbard)	Cut or break into pieces. Remove seeds & seed cavity pulp. Cut into 1 inch wide strips. Peel rind. Cut strips crosswise into pieces about ⅛ inch thick.
(Summer)	Wash, trim, cut into ¼ inch slices.
Tomatoes, for stewing	Steam or dip in boiling water to loosen skins. Chill in cold water. Peel. Cut in sections about ¾ inch wide, or slice. Cut small pear or plum tomatoes in half.

Blanching method and time (minutes)	Approximate drying time (hours)	Dryness test
Steam: 3 Water: 2	Dehydrator: 3 Oven: 3 Sun: 6-8	Crisp, wrinkled
None	Dehydrator: 3½ Oven: 2½-5 Sun: 6-8	Brittle
Steam: 6-8 Water: 5-6	Dehydrator: 2-4 Oven: 4-6 Sun: 8-11	Brittle
Steam: 2-2½ or until wilted Water: 1½	Dehydrator: 2½ Oven:2½-3½ Sun: 6-8	Brittle
Steam: 2½-3 Water: 1	Dehydrator: 2-4 Oven: 4-5 Sun: 6-8	Tough to brittle
Steam: 2½-3 Water: 1	Dehydrator: 2-4 Oven: 4-5 Sun: 6-8	Tough to brittle
Steam: 2½-3 Water: 1½	Dehydrator: 2½-3 Oven: 4-6 Sun: 6-8	Brittle
Steam: 3 Water: 1	Dehydrator: 3½-4½ Oven: 6-8 Sun: 8-10	Slightly leathery

CHAPTER VI

Sun Drying

If you live where the temperature is high, the humidity low, and the sun shines dependably and brightly just when your fruits mature, you can dry them the least expensive way—on trays in the open air. But we'll add one caution in this age of smog and air pollution: if your drying yard is close to the fallout from cars, trucks and industrial smokestacks, don't dry outdoors.

Even if your sunny days are occasionally interrupted by showers, you can still try sun drying, though you will be wise to build ahead of time some trays that will fit your oven or dehydrator. Once started, the drying process should continue with all possible speed. This is particularly critical for vegetables.

Drying vegetables in the sun is unpredictable unless temperatures are over 100° F. and the relative humidity is low. If the temperature is too low or humidity too high—or both—the food will spoil before it can be dried enough—you'll notice souring and molding. Vegetables are particularly susceptible to molding if not dried continuously and at a consistent and relatively high level of heat. This is why experts recommend that vegetables be dried under controlled heat, in an oven or dehydrator.

It is important that once vegetables (and fruits) are prepared for drying, that the drying process continue without interruption since these molds can grow on partially dried foods at room temperature. Certain types of mold growth result in the development of mycotoxins (which are poisonous products of mold in somewhat the same way that penicillin is a benevolent product of mold). Discard moldy or odorous food.

Because of their sugar content, and because they don't have to be dried as thoroughly as vegetables do, fruits are better suited to sun drying. Incidentally, if you're worrying about the discrepancy between outdoor temperatures and the 140° F. recommended for oven or dehydrator drying, you should know that the sun's ultraviolet rays have a sterilizing effect which tends to inhibit microbial growth.

Pretreatment by Sulfuring

Apples, peaches, pears, apricots and nectarines, if not pretreated, will darken during drying and continue to darken in storage. This chemical reaction, which begins the minute you cut into fruit and expose it to air, is called oxidation. It's a visible indication of rapid enzyme activity. Not only is the fruit losing color, it's losing flavor and nutrients, too.

For years, commercial fruit dryers have sulfured these fruits—that means exposing the cut fruit to the fumes of burning sulfur for a specified length of time. Sulfuring helps preserve the natural color and flavor of the fruit. It also destroys insects and many microorganisms. And it preserves Vitamins A and C (but not the B vitamin thiamin).

You can sulfur the fruit you plan to dry in the sun—it's easy enough, though it must be done outdoors in the open air. Sulfur fumes irritate eyes and nose; keep children, pets and animals safely away from the sulfuring area. If you live in a populated neighborhood, or if you plan to oven dry your fruit, you will want to use one of the other pretreatments described in Chapter IV. The odor of sulfured fruit drying in the oven will drive you out of your house!

Now, what about sulfuring—is it safe? Many people who are opposed to chemical preservation of any kind prefer to accept dark, naturally dried fruit... and they figure there are other, better sources for Vitamins A and C.

That makes it your choice, of course, but there's no evidence to date that sulfured fruit is harmful. Researchers say that the sulfurous acid that forms on the moist surfaces of the fruit is progressively lost during drying and storage; and cooking drives off most of what's left. The amount taken by the consumer is too small to have any discoverable effects.

The Sulfuring Box

Your sulfuring box can be any airtight, undamaged packing box big enough to cover a stack of trays and imprison the sulfur fumes. Ask an appliance dealer for a range or washer carton. Or build a wood frame and cover it tightly with wallboard or roofing paper. The box should be several inches higher than the stacked trays, and big enough to allow at least 1½ inches all around the sides of the trays, with 6 inches extra space on one side, where you'll set the pan of sulfur. (See Figure 11).

To burn properly, sulfur must be 99.8% pure. Ask your pharmacist, garden supply center or hardware store for flowers of sulfur or sublimed sulfur, and read the label. Garden dusting sulfur is not suitable.

Trays should be all the same size, so they can be stacked. They should be wood, with wood slat bottoms—do not use aluminum or galvanized screen. Sul-

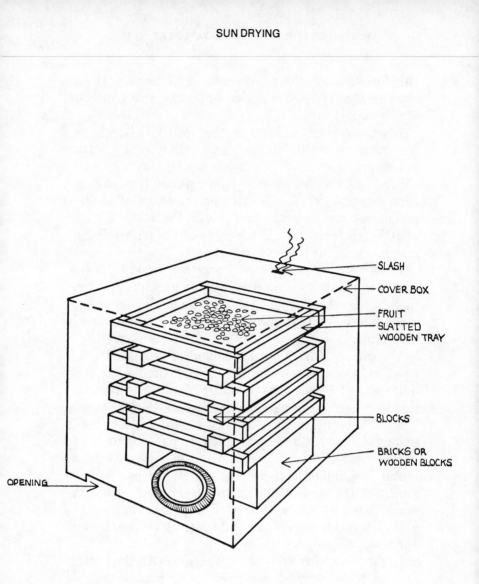

Figure 11
Sulfuring Box

fur fumes discolor and corrode most metals. (Don't even use galvanized nails to build the trays—use ordinary nails.)

Always sulfur outdoors in the open air. Locate the box so that sulfur fumes don't annoy you or your neighbors.

Line trays with cheesecloth and spread fruit of same type and size in a single layer on the trays. Place cupped pieces such as peach halves with the hollow cut side up. (Weigh fruit first. The weight of the fruit tells you how much sulfur to measure out.)

Place bottom tray on two concrete or wood blocks, so that it's at least 4 inches above the ground. Stack remaining trays on top, separating them 1½ inches with wood blocks, so that sulfur fumes can circulate freely over fruit.

Measure sulfur. For each pound of prepared fruit, use 1 to 2 teaspoons sulfur if sulfuring time is less than 3 hours; and 3 teaspoons of sulfur if sulfuring time is 3 hours or longer. (See charts in Chapter IV for specific times for each fruit.) A 2-ounce box of pure sulfur is enough to treat 16 to 18 pounds of prepared fruit.

Place sulfur (about ½ inch deep) in a clean, shallow metal container; a disposable aluminum pan will do fine. Set the pan of sulfur on the ground beside the stacked trays. Allow at least 3 inches between trays and pan, and between pan and covering carton, for sulfur to burn freely.

Light the sulfur and cover the trays with the carton. Do not leave burned matches in the container—they may keep the sulfur from burning completely. Sulfur first melts at around 240° F., becoming a brown pasty-looking substance. Then it catches fire and burns with a clear blue flame giving off sulfur dioxide gas. That is what you smell and is what protects the fruit. To provide air so the sulfur can burn, cut a little door at the bottom of the carton, in front of the sulfur pan. You will also need a tiny vent hole or slash at the upper edge of the opposite side.

The rest of the box should be airtight. The easiest way to insure this is to pack dirt all around the bottom edge, to seal it.

When sulfur has burned, close both openings tightly—you could seal them with package-wrapping tape.

Count sulfuring time when you seal the box. After sulfuring the recommended length of time, remove the trays and begin drying the fruit. Use care when moving trays so that you don't lose the rich syrup that collects in the hollows of peaches, apricots and nectarines during sulfuring.

Drying Food in the Sun

Trays of pretreated fruits (or vegetables) should be placed in direct sun and moved, if necessary, to stay in the sun's path. A slight slope toward the sun is advantageous. The sloping roof of a shed or porch with southern exposure is a perfect place for drying small amounts of food. You could even dry them inside, in a sunny window. Tilting the trays in some way will allow air circulation underneath.

Sun drying fruit in the open air takes anywhere from 1 to 2 days for apricots or apple slices, up to several days for dates. During this time, fruit should be protected from dust, birds, animals and insects. Locate the drying area as far as possible from roads, bare areas and other sources of dust and dirt. To keep out insects, lay a screen or stretch a single layer of nylon net over the trays—this cover should not touch the food. However, insects don't bother fruit that has been sulfured.

Turn the food occasionally to help it dry evenly (but don't turn cupped fruit until juices disappear from the hollows).

Except in the hottest and driest localities, it will be

necessary to shelter the trays overnight. If temperature drops more than 20 degrees, or if there's any chance of moisture—rain or dew—bring trays indoors or stack them, covered, in a sheltered area. (Let food cool before covering it.) Very slow drying may cause food to mold or sour; if the weather isn't cooperating, use your oven or dehydrator to finish the job.

Many Southwesterners who dry outdoors combine sun drying with stack drying. They expose fruit to direct sunshine for one or more days, until it loses about half its original weight. Then they stack the trays (with wood blocks between to promote air circulation) and continue the drying in a shady, but breezy area. This way, the sun isn't likely to scorch or burn the food, and fruit dries more evenly with less darkening and loss of flavor. It's worth trying wherever you have fairly low humidity, high temperatures and considerable wind during the drying season.

Building a Solar Dryer

Like a cold frame or greenhouse, a solar dryer catches and intensifies the heat of the sun under glass or plastic so that the temperature inside is higher than that outside. Ventilation is part of the design: Cool air comes in through ventilators at the bottom; as it heats up, the air rises, passing over the food and taking up moisture; the hot, moisture laden air escapes at the top. The solar dryer is a useful device to use in areas where days are dependably sunny, but temperatures are too low for open air drying.

A solar dryer should be placed where sunlight will fall directly upon the sloping glass or plastic surface for as many hours as possible each day. That means moving it two or three times a day to keep dryer windows in direct sunlight. Check the food every hour or two, at first, and stir to help it dry evenly.

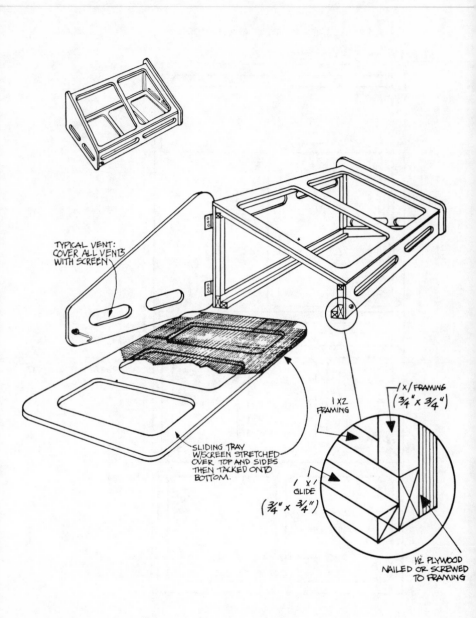

TYPICAL VENT:
COVER ALL VENTS
WITH SCREEN

SLIDING TRAY
W/SCREEN STRETCHED
OVER TOP AND SIDES
THEN TACKED ONTO
BOTTOM.

1 X 2
FRAMING

1 X 1 FRAMING
($\frac{3}{4}$" X $\frac{3}{4}$")

1 X 1
GLIDE
($\frac{3}{4}$" X $\frac{3}{4}$")

$\frac{1}{2}$ PLYWOOD
NAILED OR SCREWED
TO FRAMING

Figure 12
Solar Dryer

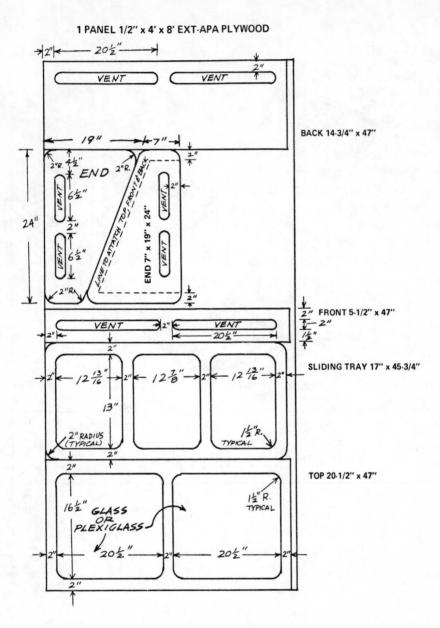

Figure 13

Solar Dryer
Plywood cutting diagram.

When the sun goes down and the dryer interior has cooled, cover the ventilators with plastic sheet or tarp and bring the dryer indoors. The next morning you can set it out again and continue drying.

The plan we show (see Figure 12) was designed for the American Plywood Association and it can be made from a single 4×8′ sheet of ½-inch exterior plywood (see Figure 13 for cutting diagram). It has a big tray for food that's easy to slide in and out. The vents are covered with nylon netting to keep out insects.

Materials needed:

1 sheet (4×8′) of ½-inch plywood (recommended A-C, B-C Exterior, or Medium Density Overlay APA grade-trademarked)

26 linear feet 1×1″ wood strips (actual dimensions of 1×1″ wood are ¾×¾″)—or you can rip 13 linear feet of 1×2″ wood

10 linear feet of 1×2″ lumber, for framing (actual dimensions are ¾×1½″)

8 square feet of ⅛-inch or 1/16-inch clear sheet or film plastic, or glass

Plastic mirror mounts for fastening glass or plexiglass to top (if you use film plastic, just staple it to under side of top)

12 feet ¼-inch gauge nylon netting to cover vent holes

8 square feet fine gauge nylon netting for tray

2 butt hinges, 2×3″

1 screen door latch

Urea resin glue

6d finishing nails, or #6 screws 1½ inches long

Cutting and Assembly

Before you begin, study Figure 12 carefully to make sure you understand all details.

Draw dryer parts on plywood panel, following the

layout in Figure 13. Use a straightedge and carpenter's square for accuracy and a compass for rounded corners. Be sure to allow for the width of saw cuts when you plot dimensions.

For hand sawing, place plywood face up. For inside cuts, start the hole with a drill, then use a coping saw or keyhole saw.

For hand power sawing, place panel face up. For table sawing, face down.

Cut ¼-inch nylon netting in sections 3 ½ inches wide to cover ventilator holes. Staple or thumbtack over vents.

Cover top "windows" with glass, plexiglass or plastic film.

Cut 1×2″ lumber for framing; rip the top blocking lengthwise to proper angle (see dotted line on drawing of end panels) so that sloped top will rest firmly on frame. Assemble frame, including the tray glides.

Attach plywood to framing using glue and nails or screws for extra strong joints.

Cover tray with a double thickness of fine nylon netting, to hold food.

CHAPTER VII

Packaging and Storing

If drying food is a way to preserve it, then it follows that dried food—if it is to stay preserved—must stay dry. That means packaging it properly, in airtight containers, hermetically sealed. A plastic bag closed with a twist-tie is not enough. . . it is not vapor-proof. (See packaging suggestions that follow.)

Dried food is siccative. It wants to drink back from the air, the moisture you dried out of it. Your packaging job is to prevent that—to prevent any reabsorption of moisture. But first, you should make sure that food really is dry and ready to be stored. This is a step called conditioning. . . like a final inspection.

Conditioning

When you take food from oven, dehydrator or sun tray, chances are it will not be evenly dry. Small pieces will be dryer than larger pieces, even on the same tray. And in a dryer or oven, the food dries faster in some spots on the tray.

To condition dried food, put the pieces of fruit or vegetable in a heavy-duty plastic bag (or use two regular bags, one inside the other), seal tightly and refrigerate for at least 1 day for vegetables, 2 days for fruits. If there's moisture in some of the food, this conditioning step will distribute it evenly throughout. Check again for dryness. If vegetables are limp, or fruits show moisture when cut and squeezed, spread them on drying trays again and heat them in a 150° F. oven for 30 minutes. Cool and package immediately.

Heat treatment for insects. All fruits and vegetables dried in the sun or open air should be heated before packaging, to destroy insects and insect eggs. Spread the food pieces on trays no more than 1 inch deep and place them (no more than two trays at a time) in a preheated oven, 150° F. Heat for 30 minutes. Cool, then package immediately.

Packaging

Glass jars, metal cans or boxes with tight fitting lids and plastic freezer cartons all make good containers. Heavy-duty heat-seal plastic bags are acceptable. Coffee cans with snap-on plastic lids are fine if you put food in plastic bags first. You can seal them tightly by wrapping the joining area with plasticized pressure-sensitive tape.

Now a few precautions: Fruit that has been sulfured should be separated from metal. The reaction of sulfur fumes with metal causes color changes in fruit. So put it in a plastic bag before packing it in a coffee can. Or place a couple layers of plastic wrap over your glass jar before screwing on a metal lid.

Whatever containers you use, they should be immaculately clean by scalding and thoroughly dry. Pack the dried food into the container as tightly as possible without crushing, and seal to keep out moisture.

If you skipped the heat treatment for insects, put

packages of sun dried food into the freezer for 48 hours, to kill any possible insects or insect eggs. Containers and storage areas should, of course, be insect and rodent proof. Plastic does not deter insects or rodents—they chew right through it. Plastic-bagged food should be stored in the refrigerator or freezer.

Storage

Dried food should be stored in a cool, dry, dark place. Heat affects food quality. If you can keep your dried food cool, you can keep it longer. Many women tell us they store their dried food in the freezer. This isn't quite as strange as it sounds—food that's been dried takes less space and requires very little energy since there is very little water to freeze. It's the safest place to keep dried food.

Light is an enemy of dried food, causing it to fade and deteriorate. If you pack in glass or other clear containers, wrap them with foil or paper to block out the light. Or better yet, protect your dried food packages from light and changes in weather and humidity: stash them away in a large fiberboard container with a tight fitting metal lid.

Because they're low-acid, vegetables are more susceptible to spoilage than fruits, which have higher acidity to help preserve them. This is why it is especially important that vegetables be dried thoroughly and remain dry in storage.

All dried vegetables deteriorate during storage, losing vitamins, flavor, color and aroma. Carrots, onions and cabbage go downhill fast; their storage life is no more than 6 months. But some vegetables, under optimum storage, will be good for a year. You'll find it helpful to label your food packages with the name of the product and the date of packaging.

Foods that seem "bone dry" when you package them

can spoil if they reabsorb moisture in storage. Check them every month or so, to see that they remain dry. Glass containers are good for storage because you can easily see if moisture is collecting on the inside. If you detect moisture or evidence of spoilage—odor or mold growth—discard the food.

CHAPTER VIII

Cooking with Dried Food

If your experience with dried foods is limited to apricots, prunes and raisins, you'll be pleasantly surprised to see how some of the others "come back" when you soak them. Your shriveled, wrinkled slices of apples, carrots, etc., will return practically to their original size, form and appearance. Assuming that you handled foods carefully during drying, and in storage, they will retain much of their aroma and flavor, as well as the minerals and appreciable amounts of vitamins.

Remember to check food often during storage, to see that it remains dry. If molds develop on stored fruits and vegetables, they should be discarded.

One pound of dried vegetables is the equivalent of 8 to 12 pounds of fresh vegetables; 1 pound of dried fruit, 4 to 8 pounds fresh. Or, roughly speaking, 1 to 2 cups of dried foods will serve 6 persons.

Dried fruits can be soaked and used in recipes for pies, cakes, breads and cookies; or cooked and served as a compote. Most dried vegetables are better used as ingredients—in soups, casseroles, sauces, stuffings and stews. While some of them might be cooked and served as side dishes, we think you'll find they suffer by comparison with fresh, frozen or canned vegetables. That's a matter of taste, of course. Some people prefer the different flavor obtained through drying—corn, for instance, and apricots.

In the pages that follow, we give you 50 recipes that use dried foods. They've all passed *Farm Journal's* Test Kitchen tasters.

Rehydrating Fruits

The time it takes to rehydrate fruits depends on the kind, the size of the pieces, and whether you use hot or cold water for soaking.

Add water just to cover; you can add more as needed. Don't oversoak. By oversoaking, you lose flavor and the fruit may get mushy or water-logged. Also, if soaking continues too long, fermentation spoilage will occur. Drying, you remember, does not destroy bacteria, yeasts and molds. When you restore the moisture and warmth they need in order to grow, they will start multiplying again. Rehydrated fruit should be refrigerated if not used promptly. . . within the hour. Some authorities suggest rehydrating in the refrigerator to prevent growth of microorganisms.

Cook fruit in the soaking water to retain nutrients. If you want to sweeten it, add sugar or honey near the end of cooking. But taste it—very likely you'll need less sugar than for cooking fresh fruit. The reason is, the drying process may change some of the starch in fruit to sugar. Add a few grains of salt, too, to bring out the natural sweetness of fruit. Just before serving, add some lemon, orange or grapefruit juice. It gives a fresh fruit flavor and adds Vitamin C to the dish.

If your dried fruit is to be used as an ingredient in baking, pour boiling water over the fruit in a bowl barely to cover. Cover with plastic wrap and let stand for at least 1 hour or until fruit is plump. If possible, use the soaking water in the recipe.

Rehydrating Vegetables

You can restore the water you dried out of your vegetables by soaking, by cooking in liquid, or a combination of both. The amount of water used for soaking and cooking should be as close as you can come to the amount the vegetables will take up. It is better to add more water during cooking, than to start with too much water.

Place dried vegetables in a bowl or saucepan; add boiling water to cover. Cover with plastic wrap and soak until vegetables plump—anywhere from 20 minutes to 2 hours, depending on vegetable, size of pieces, etc. There is danger of spoilage if vegetables soak too long at room temperature. They should be refrigerated if not used within the hour.

Greens, cabbage and tomatoes do not need to be soaked. Put them in a saucepan, add enough water to keep them covered and simmer until tender.

To cook other vegetables, bring them to a boil in the soaking liquid and simmer until done. Let excess water evaporate during cooking.

Cooking time will range from 10 to 30 minutes, depending on vegetable. Like fresh vegetables, dried vegetables lose flavor and texture if you overcook them.

With a good variety of dried fruit and vegetables in your storeroom or freezer, you can experiment finding new ways to use them. Look through the recipes that follow for ideas. . . then try using your dried foods as ingredients in some of your own favorite recipes.

EASY MINESTRONE

1½ qts. boiling beef broth
½ c. dried green beans
½ c. dried carrots
½ c. dried green pepper
½ c. dried onion
½ c. dried zucchini
½ c. dried celery
½ lb. ground beef
1 (1 lb.) can tomatoes, cut up
1 (1 lb.) can red kidney beans
½ c. small shell macaroni
1 clove garlic, minced
1½ tsp. mixed Italian seasoning
1 tsp. salt
¼ tsp. pepper
2 c. water
Grated Parmesan cheese

Pour boiling beef broth over green beans, carrots, green pepper, onion, zucchini and celery in large bowl. Cover with plastic wrap. Let stand 1 hour.

Brown ground beef in Dutch oven. Drain off excess fat. Add undrained vegetables, tomatoes, kidney beans, macaroni, garlic, Italian seasoning, salt, pepper and water. Bring to a boil; reduce heat. Cover and simmer 20 minutes or until vegetables are tender. Ladle into bowls; sprinkle with Parmesan cheese. Makes about 3 quarts.

TOMATO RICE SOUP

2 c. boiling water
½ c. dried onion
¼ c. dried carrots
2 beef bouillon cubes
1 lb. ground beef
1 (1 lb. 12 oz.) can tomatoes
2½ c. water
1 tsp. salt
1 tsp. dried parsley
½ tsp. chili powder
1 bay leaf
⅓ c. regular rice

Pour boiling water over onion, carrots and bouillon cubes in bowl. Cover with plastic wrap. Let stand 1½ hours.

Brown ground beef in Dutch oven. Pour off excess fat. Add undrained vegetables, tomatoes, water, salt, parsley, chili powder and bay leaf. Bring to a boil; reduce heat. Cover and simmer 35 minutes. Add rice; simmer, covered, 15 more minutes. Makes about 2 quarts.

CHILI CON CARNE

1½ c. boiling water
½ c. dried onion
¼ c. dried green pepper
1 lb. ground beef
1 (1 lb.) can red kidney beans
1 (8 oz.) can tomato sauce
1 (1 lb.) can tomatoes, cut up
1 tblsp. chili powder
1 tsp. garlic salt
½ tsp. salt
¼ tsp. pepper

Pour boiling water over onion and green pepper in bowl. Cover with plastic wrap. Let stand 1¼ hours.

Brown ground beef in Dutch oven. Add undrained soaked vegetables, kidney beans, tomato sauce, tomatoes, chili powder, garlic salt, salt and pepper. Bring to a boil; reduce heat. Simmer, uncovered, 1 hour. Makes 4 to 6 servings.

CORN CHOWDER

1½ c. scalded milk
½ c. dried corn
6 strips bacon, diced
1 tblsp. flour
2 c. milk
2 c. sliced, pared potatoes
¼ c. crumbled dried onion
1 tsp. dried parsley
1½ tsp. salt
⅛ tsp. pepper
1 c. heavy cream
Paprika

Pour 1½ c. scalded milk over corn in bowl. Cover with plastic wrap. Let stand 4 hours.

Cook bacon until crisp. Remove and drain on paper towels. Pour off pan drippings, reserving 2 tblsp.

Place 2 tblsp. pan drippings in 3-qt. saucepan. Stir in flour. Cook, stirring constantly, 1 minute. Add undrained corn mixture. Cook over medium heat, stirring constantly, until thickened.

Add 2 c. milk, potatoes, onion, parsley, salt and pepper. Bring to a boil; reduce heat. Simmer, uncovered, 25 minutes or until potatoes are tender. Stir in cream. Heat well. Serve bowls of chowder topped with bacon bits and sprinkled with paprika. Makes 4 to 6 servings.

ONION PARSLEY CHIP DIP

1 (8 oz.) pkg. cream cheese, softened
½ c. dairy sour cream
2 tblsp. crumbled dried onion
½ tsp. dried parsley
2 beef bouillon cubes, crumbled
Potato chips, pretzels or crackers

Beat together cream cheese and sour cream until smooth. Stir in onion, parsley and bouillon cubes. Chill well.

Serve with potato chips, pretzels or crackers. Makes 1⅓ cups.

CREAMY MUSHROOM SPREAD

1 c. dairy sour cream
3 tblsp. chopped dried mushrooms
2 tblsp. crumbled dried onion
½ tsp. dried parsley
¼ tsp. salt
⅛ tsp. pepper
Celery or crackers

Combine sour cream, mushrooms, onion, parsley, salt and pepper. Cover and chill at least 2 hours. Delicious as a filling for celery or spread on crackers. Makes about 1 cup.

BEEF CARROT RAGOUT

2 c. boiling water
2 beef bouillon cubes
½ c. dried carrots
¼ c. crumbled dried onion
2 lbs. stewing beef, cut in ½″ cubes
1½ tsp. salt
¼ tsp. pepper
¼ c. cooking oil
1½ c. water
½ tsp. thyme leaves
1 clove garlic, minced
1 bay leaf
3 c. cubed, pared potatoes (½″)
2 tsp. dried parsley
1 tblsp. flour
¼ c. water
1 tsp. bottled sauce for gravy

Pour 2 c. boiling water over bouillon cubes, carrots and onion in bowl. Cover with plastic wrap. Let stand 1 hour.

Meanwhile, season beef with salt and pepper. Brown beef on all sides in hot oil in Dutch oven. Add 1½ c. water, thyme, garlic and bay leaf. Bring to a boil; reduce heat. Cover and simmer 45 minutes.

Add undrained soaked vegetables, potatoes and parsley. Continue to simmer, covered, 30 more minutes or until meat and vegetables are tender.

Combine flour and ¼ c. water. Stir into boiling liquid. Add bottled sauce for gravy. Cook 2 minutes. Makes 6 to 8 servings.

GROUND BEEF SKILLET

2 c. tomato juice
½ c. dried onion
½ c. dried green pepper
½ c. dried celery
1 lb. ground beef
1 (15 oz.) can tomato sauce
2 c. water
8 oz. small elbow macaroni
1 clove garlic, minced
2 tsp. salt
1½ tsp. chili powder
½ tsp. oregano leaves
⅛ tsp. pepper
½ c. shredded sharp Cheddar cheese

Bring tomato juice to a boil in small saucepan. Pour over onion, green pepper and celery in bowl. Cover with plastic wrap. Let stand 1 hour.

Brown ground beef in large skillet. Add undrained vegetables, tomato sauce, water, macaroni, garlic, salt, chili powder, oregano and pepper. Bring to a boil; reduce heat. Cover and simmer 20 minutes or until vegetables and macaroni are tender. Top each serving with shredded cheese. Makes 6 servings.

ZUCCHINI BEEF SKILLET

1 c. boiling water
1 c. dried zucchini
1½ lbs. ground beef
2 tblsp. dried onion
1 tsp. dried parsley
½ tsp. salt
¼ tsp. garlic salt
1 (8 oz.) can tomato sauce
1 (12 oz.) can Mexicorn

Pour boiling water over zucchini in bowl. Cover with plastic wrap. Let stand 30 minutes.

Meanwhile, brown ground beef in 10" skillet. Add dried onion, parsley, salt, garlic salt, tomato sauce and undrained Mexicorn. Stir to mix.

Add undrained soaked zucchini. Bring to a boil; reduce heat. Cover and simmer 25 minutes, stirring occasionally, until zucchini is tender. Makes 6 servings.

CHEESE-STUFFED HAMBURGERS

1½ lbs. ground beef
¼ c. crumbled dried onion
2 beef bouillon cubes, crumbled
1 tsp. dried parsley
3 oz. Cheddar cheese, cut in ½" cubes

Combine ground beef, onion, bouillon cubes and parsley. Mix lightly, but well. Shape beef mixture into 6 patties, pressing about 6 cheese cubes into the center of each. (Be sure cheese is completely covered.)

Fry beef patties in large skillet over medium heat, turning as needed when browned (about 15 minutes). Makes 6 servings.

STUFFED BEEF LOAF

1½ c. boiling water
¼ c. dried carrots
3 tblsp. crumbled dried onion
1 c. boiling water
⅓ c. dried mushrooms
2 tblsp. crumbled dried onion
2 lbs. ground beef
½ c. dry bread crumbs
1 tsp. dried parsley
2 tsp. Worcestershire sauce
2 tsp. salt
3 eggs
2 c. soft bread crumbs
½ tsp. poultry seasoning
¼ tsp. salt

Pour 1½ c. boiling water over carrots and 3 tblsp. onion. Cover with plastic wrap. Let stand 1 hour.

Pour 1 c. boiling water over mushrooms and 2 tblsp. onion. Cover with plastic wrap. Let stand 1 hour.

Drain carrots and onion, reserving ½ c. liquid. Combine ground beef, dry bread crumbs, parsley, Worcestershire sauce, 2 tsp. salt, eggs, drained carrots and onion and reserved ½ c. liquid. Mix lightly, but well. Place on double-thick square of greased aluminum foil. Shape into 14×8″ rectangle.

Drain mushrooms and onion. Combine with remaining ingredients. Spread over meat; roll up like a jelly roll from long side. Seal edge. Fold foil on top and ends. Place on rack in shallow pan.

Bake in 375° oven 1 hour. Open foil; bake 15 minutes or until brown. Makes 6 to 8 servings.

EGGPLANT CASSEROLE

2 c. boiling water
2 c. dried eggplant
1 lb. ground beef
2 tblsp. crumbled dried onion
⅛ tsp. pepper
1 tsp. dried parsley
1 (1 lb. 13 oz.) jar meatless spaghetti sauce
8 oz. mozzarella cheese, shredded

Pour boiling water over eggplant in bowl. Cover with plastic wrap. Let stand for 1 hour.

Brown ground beef and onion in medium skillet. Add pepper, parsley and spaghetti sauce. Bring mixture to a boil.

Drain eggplant. Layer ½ of eggplant in 11 × 7 × 1½″ baking dish. Spread with ½ of meat sauce. Sprinkle with ½ of cheese. Repeat layers.

Bake in 350° oven 30 minutes or until bubbly. Makes 6 servings.

BEEF AND CHEESE CASSEROLE

1½ c. water
¼ c. dried carrots
1 lb. ground beef
1 tblsp. butter
¼ c. crumbled dried onion
2 (8 oz.) cans tomato sauce
1 tsp. salt
¼ tsp. pepper
1 c. dairy sour cream
1 c. cream-style cottage cheese
8 oz. medium noodles, cooked and drained
1 tblsp. dried parsley
1 c. shredded Cheddar cheese

Bring water to a boil in 2-qt. saucepan. Remove from heat. Add carrots. Cover and let stand 1 hour.

Bring to a boil; reduce heat. Cover and simmer 20 minutes or until carrots are tender. Drain; set aside.

Meanwhile, cook ground beef in melted butter in skillet. When meat begins to turn color, add onion. Continue cooking until meat is well browned. Stir in tomato sauce, salt and pepper.

Combine sour cream, cottage cheese, noodles, parsley and carrots; toss gently to mix.

Alternate layers of noodle mixture and meat in greased 3-qt. casserole, beginning and ending with noodles. Sprinkle with cheese.

Bake in 350° oven 30 minutes or until bubbly. Makes 8 servings.

CHICKEN IN TOMATO SAUCE

1 c. boiling water
½ c. dried mushrooms
¼ c. dried sliced onion
¼ c. dried green pepper
½ c. flour
1 tsp. salt
⅛ tsp. pepper
2 (2½ lb.) broiler-fryers, cut up
⅓ c. cooking oil
2 (14½ oz.) cans Italian tomatoes, cut up
1 (8 oz.) can tomato sauce
1 tsp. oregano leaves
½ tsp. basil leaves
1 bay leaf
1 clove garlic, minced
2 tblsp. water
Hot cooked rice

Pour boiling water over mushrooms, onion and green pepper. Cover with plastic wrap. Let stand 1 hour.

Combine flour, salt and pepper in plastic bag. Add chicken, a few pieces at a time, shaking to coat with flour mixture. Reserve remaining flour.

Brown chicken, a few pieces at a time, in hot oil in Dutch oven. Remove chicken as it browns. Place chicken back in Dutch oven. Add undrained soaked vegetables, tomatoes, tomato sauce, oregano, basil, bay leaf and garlic. Bring to a boil. Reduce heat and simmer, covered, 1¼ hours. Skim off fat. Remove chicken.

Combine remaining flour mixture and 2 tblsp. water. Stir into hot mixture. Boil 1 minute. Serve with rice. Makes 6 to 8 servings.

SAUSAGE AND POTATO PIE

1½ c. boiling water
½ c. dried mushrooms
¼ c. dried green pepper
1½ lbs. potatoes, pared and quartered
   (5 medium)
1 tsp. salt
1 egg, beaten
½ c. corn flake crumbs
2 tblsp. crumbled dried onion
2 tsp. dried parsley
1 lb. bulk pork sausage
1 (10½ oz.) can mushroom gravy
2 tsp. cornstarch
1 c. shredded Cheddar cheese

Pour boiling water over mushrooms and green pepper in bowl. Cover with plastic wrap. Let stand one hour.

Cook potatoes with salt in water until done. Drain well and mash. Add egg; blend well. Add corn flake crumbs, onion and parsley; mix well. Spread mixture in greased 10″ pie plate.

Brown sausage in 10″ skillet. Remove and drain on paper towels. Pour off fat. Place sausage in skillet.

Drain vegetables, reserving 1 tblsp. liquid. Add drained vegetables and mushroom gravy to skillet. Combine cornstarch with 1 tblsp. reserved liquid. Stir into sausage mixture and bring to a boil. Pour into potato shell. Sprinkle with cheese.

Bake in 400° oven 25 minutes or until golden brown. Makes 6 to 8 servings.

ITALIAN SAUSAGE AND VEGETABLES

> 2 c. boiling water
> ½ c. dried mushrooms
> ½ c. dried green pepper
> ¼ c. dried sliced onion
> 2 lbs. Italian sweet sausage or pork sausage
>   links, cut in 4″ lengths
> 2 tblsp. water
> 1 (14½ oz.) can Italian tomatoes, cut up
> 1 (6 oz.) can tomato paste
> ½ tsp. oregano leaves

Pour boiling water over mushrooms, green pepper and onion in bowl. Cover with plastic wrap. Let stand 3 hours.

Place sausage with 2 tblsp. water in 10″ skillet. Cover and cook over medium heat 10 minutes.

Remove cover. Cook sausage until well browned on all sides, turning frequently (about 10 minutes). Pour off excess fat.

Drain soaked vegetables, reserving liquid. Add vegetables, ¾ c. reserved liquid, tomatoes, tomato paste and oregano to skillet. Cover and cook 30 minutes. Makes 8 servings.

PORK CHOPS WITH MUSHROOM GRAVY

2 c. boiling water
1 c. dried mushrooms
⅓ c. dried onion
6 pork chops, ½" thick
½ tsp. salt
¼ tsp. thyme leaves
⅛ tsp. pepper
1 beef bouillon cube, crumbled
½ c. light cream
1 tblsp. flour
2 tblsp. water

Pour 2 c. boiling water over mushrooms and onion in bowl. Cover with plastic wrap. Let stand 1 hour.

Season pork chops with salt, thyme and pepper. Brown pork chops in 10" skillet. Remove pork chops.

Add undrained mushrooms and onion to skillet. Stir in beef bouillon cube. Place chops on top. Cover and simmer 1½ hours or until tender.

Remove pork chops and keep warm. Stir cream into cooking liquid. Combine flour and 2 tblsp. water. Stir into hot liquid. Cook over medium heat until slightly thickened. Do not boil. Makes 6 servings.

HAM-STUFFED POTATOES

6 Idaho baking potatoes, about 5" long
½ c. boiling water
¼ c. crumbled dried onion
1½ c. diced cooked ham
½ c. chopped green pepper
1 tsp. dried parsley
½ tsp. salt
¼ tsp. pepper
2 c. dairy sour cream
½ c. finely shredded Swiss cheese

Bake potatoes in 400° oven 1 hour or until done.

Pour boiling water over onion in bowl. Cover with plastic wrap. Let stand 1 hour.

Drain onion; set aside.

Cut off tops of potatoes. Scoop hot potato out of shells with spoon. Break up potato with fork (do not mash). Combine hot potato, drained onion, ham, green pepper, parsley, salt, pepper and sour cream. Toss lightly, but well. Pile potato mixture back into shells. Place on baking sheet. Sprinkle with cheese.

Bake in 400° oven 15 to 20 minutes or until golden brown. Makes 6 servings.

HAM STEAKS WITH FRUIT

8 dried peach halves
2 c. water
12 dried pitted prunes
¼ c. brown sugar, firmly packed
2 tblsp. cornstarch
½ tsp. ground cinnamon
½ tsp. dry mustard
2 whole cloves
2 tblsp. lemon juice
1 tblsp. butter
2 fully-cooked ham steaks, about ½" thick

Combine peaches and water in 2-qt. saucepan. Bring to a boil; reduce heat. Cover and simmer 20 minutes or until tender. Add prunes; cook 5 more minutes.

Combine brown sugar, cornstarch, cinnamon, mustard and cloves. Stir into hot fruit mixture. Bring to a boil; simmer 2 minutes, stirring constantly. Add lemon juice and butter.

Broil ham steaks 4" from source of heat, 2 minutes on each side. Serve ham steaks with hot fruit sauce. Makes 4 servings.

TUNA SPAGHETTI SAUCE

1 c. boiling water
¼ c. crumbled dried onion
¼ c. dried green pepper
1 (1 lb. 12 oz.) can Italian tomatoes
1 (6 oz.) can tomato paste
1 tsp. salt
½ tsp. oregano leaves
½ tsp. basil leaves
¼ tsp. ground nutmeg
¼ tsp. pepper
¼ tsp. sugar
1 (7 oz.) can tuna, drained and flaked
Hot cooked rice

Pour boiling water over onion and green pepper in bowl. Cover with plastic wrap. Let stand 1 hour.

Whirl tomatoes in blender a few seconds until smooth. Combine tomatoes, tomato paste, salt, oregano, basil, nutmeg, pepper, sugar and undrained soaked vegetables in 3-qt. saucepan. Bring to a boil; reduce heat and simmer, uncovered, 50 minutes. Add tuna; simmer 10 more minutes. Serve over rice. Makes 4 to 6 servings.

LAMB SHANKS WiTH FRUIT

4 (1 lb.) lamb shanks
1½ tsp. salt
⅛ tsp. pepper
2 tblsp. cooking oil
2 c. orange juice
1 c. water
½ tsp. ground ginger
½ tsp. ground cinnamon
8 whole cloves
1 tsp. grated orange rind
12 dried pitted prunes
2 tblsp. cornstarch
¼ c. water
2 oranges, peeled and sliced

Season lamb with salt and pepper. Brown on all sides in hot oil in 12″ skillet. Pour off excess fat. Add orange juice, 1 c. water, ginger, cinnamon, cloves and orange rind. Bring to a boil; reduce heat. Cover and simmer 1½ hours or until tender.

Add prunes and cook 5 more minutes. Remove lamb. Stir combined 2 tblsp. cornstarch and ¼ c. water into hot liquid. Bring to a boil; cook 2 minutes. Add orange slices; heat well. Discard cloves. Makes 4 servings.

RATATOUILLE

6 c. boiling water
2 c. dried eggplant
1 c. dried zucchini
1 c. dried onion
½ c. dried green pepper
2 cloves garlic, minced
¼ c. cooking oil
1 (1 lb.) can tomatoes, cut up
1 tblsp. dried parsley
2 tsp. salt
½ tsp. basil leaves
⅛ tsp. pepper

Pour boiling water over eggplant, zucchini, onion and green pepper in bowl. Cover with plastic wrap. Let stand 1½ hours.

Drain vegetables, reserving ¾ c. liquid.

Saute garlic in hot oil in 3-qt. saucepan 1 minute. Add drained vegetables, ¾ c. reserved liquid, tomatoes, parsley, salt, basil and pepper. Bring to a boil; reduce heat. Cover and simmer 30 minutes. Uncover and continue cooking until vegetables are tender and juice is thickened, about 10 minutes. Makes 8 servings.

ITALIAN-STYLE VEGETABLES

6 c. water
1 c. dried zucchini
½ c. dried corn
½ c. dried carrots
½ c. dried green beans
½ c. dried onion
¼ c. dried green pepper
1 (1 lb.) can tomatoes, cut up
1 beef bouillon cube
2 tsp. salt
1 tsp. oregano leaves
¼ tsp. pepper
2 tblsp. butter

Bring water to a boil in Dutch oven. Remove from heat. Add zucchini, corn, carrots, green beans, onion and green pepper. Cover and let stand 1 hour.

Drain vegetables, reserving 1 c. liquid. Combine drained vegetables, 1 c. reserved liquid, tomatoes, bouillon cube, salt, oregano and pepper in Dutch oven. Bring to a boil; reduce heat. Cover and simmer 30 to 35 minutes or until vegetables are tender. Add butter; stir until melted. Makes 12 servings.

ZUCCHINI AND TOMATOES

    1 c. boiling water
    1 c. dried zucchini
    1 (1 lb.) can stewed tomatoes
    ½ tsp. salt
    ½ tsp. oregano leaves
    ¼ tsp. basil leaves
    2 tsp. cornstarch
    1 tblsp. water

Pour 1 c. boiling water over zucchini in bowl. Cover with plastic wrap. Let stand 30 minutes.

Combine undrained zucchini, tomatoes, salt, oregano and basil in 2-qt. saucepan. Bring to a boil; reduce heat. Cover and simmer 15 minutes or until zucchini is tender.

Combine cornstarch and 1 tblsp. water. Stir into vegetable mixture. Boil 1 minute. Makes 4 to 6 servings.

PARSLIED BUTTERED CARROTS

    1(10½ oz.) can condensed chicken broth
    ½ c. dried carrots
    ¼ c. dried onion
    1 tblsp. dried parsley

Add enough water to chicken broth to make 3 c. Bring to a boil in 2-qt. saucepan. Remove from heat.

Add carrots and onion. Cover and let stand 1 hour.
Bring to a boil; reduce heat. Cover and simmer 20
minutes or until carrots are tender. Sprinkle with parsley. Serve in chicken broth. Makes 6 servings.

EASY CARROT BAKE

---

1 (10½ oz.) can condensed chicken broth
1 c. dried carrots
½ c. dried onion
¼ c. dried celery
1 (10¾ oz.) can condensed cream of celery
  soup
⅛ tsp. pepper
¼ c. corn flake crumbs
1 tblsp. melted butter

Add enough water to chicken broth to make 2½ c.
Bring to boil in 2-qt. saucepan. Remove from heat. Add
carrots, onion and celery. Cover and let stand 1 hour.

Bring to a boil; reduce heat. Cover and simmer 30
minutes or until vegetables are tender. Drain vegetables, reserving ⅓ c. liquid.

Combine ⅓ c. reserved liquid, celery soup and pepper. Stir in drained vegetables. Turn into greased
1½-qt. casserole. Sprinkle with combined corn flake
crumbs and butter.

Bake in 350° oven 25 minutes or until bubbly. Makes
6 servings.

COUNTRY SUCCOTASH

**1 qt. water
1 c. dried green beans
1 c. dried corn
½ c. dried onion
1 tsp. salt
¼ tsp. pepper
½ c. light cream
1 tblsp. butter**

Bring water to a boil in 2-qt. saucepan. Remove from heat. Add green beans, corn and onion. Cover and let stand 1 hour.

Bring to a boil; reduce heat. Cover and simmer 20 to 25 minutes or until vegetables are tender. Drain. Add salt, pepper, light cream and butter. Heat thoroughly over low heat. Makes 6 to 8 servings.

OLD-FASHIONED GREEN BEANS

**3 c. water
1 c. dried green beans
½ c. dried onion
1 c. cubed, cooked ham
¾ tsp. salt
¼ tsp. pepper**

Bring water to a boil in 2-qt. saucepan. Remove from

heat. Add green beans and onion. Cover and let stand 1 hour.

Add ham, salt and pepper to undrained soaked vegetables. Bring to a boil; reduce heat. Cover and simmer 20 to 25 minutes or until beans are tender. If you wish, add a little butter. Makes 6 servings.

PICKLED CARROTS

7 c. water
2 c. dried carrots
1 c. dried onion
½ c. dried green pepper
1 (10½ oz.) can condensed tomato soup
⅔ c. sugar
⅔ c. vinegar
½ c. salad oil
1½ tsp. salt
1 tsp. prepared mustard
1 tsp. Worcestershire sauce
½ tsp. pepper

Bring water to a boil in 3-qt. saucepan. Remove from heat. Add carrots, onion and green pepper. Cover and let stand 1 hour.

Bring to a boil; reduce heat. Cover and simmer 20 minutes or until vegetables are tender. Drain.

Combine tomato soup, sugar, vinegar, oil, salt, mustard, Worcestershire sauce and pepper; mix well. Add drained vegetables. Cover and refrigerate at least 24 hours, stirring several times. Serve as a salad or relish. Makes 8 cups.

SWEET AND SOUR GREEN BEANS

6 c. water
2 c. dried green beans
1 c. dried onion
½ c. sugar
½ c. vinegar
¼ c. water
2 tblsp. salad oil
2 tblsp. chopped pimiento
1½ tsp. salt
¼ tsp. pepper

Bring 6 c. water to a boil in 2-qt. saucepan. Remove from heat. Add green beans and onion. Cover and let stand 1 hour.

Bring to a boil; reduce heat. Cover and simmer 20 to 25 minutes or until vegetables are tender. Drain.

Combine sugar, vinegar, ¼ c. water, oil, pimiento, salt and pepper. Pour over beans in bowl. Cover and refrigerate 24 hours, stirring several times. Makes 12 servings.

GREEN BEANS WITH MUSHROOMS

6 c. water
2 c. dried green beans
⅔ c. dried mushrooms
¼ c. chopped, toasted almonds
2 tblsp. butter
1 tblsp. lemon juice
¾ tsp. salt
⅛ tsp. pepper
⅛ tsp. rosemary leaves

Bring water to a boil in 2-qt. saucepan. Remove from heat. Add green beans and mushrooms. Cover and let stand 1 hour.

Bring to a boil; reduce heat. Cover and simmer 20 to 25 minutes or until vegetables are tender. Drain.

Add almonds, butter, lemon juice, salt, pepper and rosemary to drained vegetables. Heat thoroughly. Makes 6 to 8 servings.

WINTER CORN PUDDING

¾ c. dried corn
2 c. dairy half-and-half, scalded
2 eggs, slightly beaten
2 tblsp. chopped green onions
2 tblsp. melted butter
1 tblsp. sugar
1 tsp. salt
⅛ tsp. pepper

Rinse dried corn. Add to dairy half-and-half. Cover and let soak about 4 hours.

Combine undrained corn mixture with eggs, onions, butter, sugar, salt and pepper. Pour into greased 1-qt. casserole.

Bake in 325° oven 35 minutes or until a knife inserted in center comes out clean. Makes 6 servings.

ONION MUSTARD BUNS

2 c. milk, scalded
2 tblsp. sugar
2 tblsp. crumbled dried onion
2 tblsp. cooking oil
1 tblsp. prepared mustard
1½ tsp. salt
¼ tsp. pepper
1 pkg. active dry yeast
¼ c. lukewarm water
6 c. sifted flour
1 egg
2 tblsp. crumbled dried onion
¼ c. water
1 egg, beaten
2 tblsp. water

Combine first 7 ingredients. Cool to lukewarm.

Dissolve yeast in ¼ c. lukewarm water. Add yeast and 2 c. flour to milk mixture. Beat until smooth. Add 1 egg; beat well. Add enough remaining flour to make a soft dough. Knead on floured surface until smooth and satiny, about 10 minutes. Place in greased bowl. Cover and let rise until doubled, about 1½ hours.

Divide in half; let rest 10 minutes. Pat each half into 9″ square; cut in 9 portions. Shape into buns; place on greased baking sheet. Flatten with palm of hand. Let rise until doubled, about 30 minutes.

Combine 2 tblsp. onion and ¼ c. water; let stand 5 minutes. Brush rolls with glaze made by combining 1 egg and 2 tblsp. water. Sprinkle with onion mixture.

Bake in 375° oven 20 minutes or until golden brown. Makes 18 buns.

APRICOT SWIRL BUNS

1 (13¾ oz.) pkg. hot roll mix
¾ c. lukewarm water
¼ c. sugar
1 egg, beaten
¾ c. dried apricots
1½ c. water
3 tblsp. sugar
½ tsp. ground cinnamon
1 tblsp. melted butter
Orange Frosting (recipe follows)

Dissolve yeast from mix in ¾ c. lukewarm water. Add yeast, ¼ c. sugar and egg to mix; stir well to blend. Cover and let rise until doubled, about 45 minutes.

Combine apricots and 1½ c. water in 2-qt. saucepan. Bring to a boil; reduce heat. Cover and simmer 15 minutes or until tender. Drain, reserving ½ c. liquid.

Puree hot drained apricots with reserved ½ c. liquid in blender until smooth. Combine pureed apricots with 3 tblsp. sugar and cinnamon; mix well. Set aside.

Roll dough on floured surface to 15x10″ rectangle. Brush with butter. Spread with apricot filling. Roll up like jelly roll from narrow end. Cut in 12 slices. Place in greased 13×9×2″ baking pan. Let rise until doubled, about 45 minutes.

Bake in 350° oven 30 minutes or until golden. Cool 5 minutes and frost with Orange Frosting. Makes 12.

Orange Frosting: Combine 1½ c. sifted confectioners sugar, 1 tblsp. soft butter, 1 tsp. grated orange rind and 2 tblsp. orange juice; mix until smooth.

CRUMB-TOPPED PRUNE KOLACHES

1 (13¾ oz.) pkg. hot roll mix
¾ c. lukewarm water
¼ c. sugar
1 egg, slightly beaten
1 c. dried pitted prunes
1 c. water
2 tblsp. sugar
¼ tsp. ground allspice
1 tblsp. lemon juice
1 egg, beaten
Crumb Topping (recipe follows)

Dissolve yeast from mix in ¾ c. lukewarm water. Add yeast, ¼ c. sugar and 1 egg to mix; stir well to blend. Let rise until doubled, about 45 minutes.

Combine prunes and 1 c. water in 2-qt. saucepan. Cover and simmer 5 minutes or until tender. Drain, reserving ⅓ c. cooking liquid. Puree hot prunes in blender with reserved ⅓ c. liquid until smooth. Stir in 2 tblsp. sugar, allspice and lemon juice.

Divide dough in 12 portions. Shape into rolls; place on greased baking sheet. Flatten with palm of hand. Make a hole in center of each, leaving ½″ rim. Fill with prune filling. Brush rolls with 1 beaten egg. Sprinkle with Crumb Topping. Let rise until doubled, 45 minutes.

Bake in 350° oven 15 minutes or until golden brown. Drizzle with your favorite confectioners sugar icing while warm. Makes 12 rolls.

Crumb Topping: Combine ⅓ c. brown sugar, firmly packed, 2 tblsp. flour and ½ tsp. ground cinnamon. Cut in 1 tblsp. butter until crumbly.

CINNAMON PEAR MUFFINS

2 c. sifted flour
¼ c. sugar
3 tsp. baking powder
1 tsp. salt
1 egg, beaten
1 c. milk
¼ c. melted butter
1 c. snipped dried pears
1 tsp. grated orange rind
2 tblsp. sugar
¼ tsp. ground cinnamon

Sift together flour, ¼ c. sugar, baking powder and salt into bowl.

Combine egg, milk and butter. Add to dry ingredients, stirring just enough to moisten. Stir in pears and orange rind. Spoon batter into greased 3″ muffin-pan cups, filling two-thirds full. Sprinkle with combined 2 tblsp. sugar and cinnamon.

Bake in 400° oven 20 to 25 minutes or until golden brown. Cool 5 minutes; remove from pan. Makes 12.

SPICY APPLE PIE

6 c. boiling water
3 c. dried apples
Pastry for 2-crust 9" pie
½ c. sugar
1 tblsp. flour
1 tsp. ground cinnamon
½ tsp. ground nutmeg
1 tblsp. lemon juice
3 tblsp. butter

Pour boiling water over apples in bowl. Cover with plastic wrap. Let stand 1 hour.

Meanwhile prepare pastry.

Drain apples, reserving ½ c. liquid. Combine drained apples, sugar, flour, cinnamon and nutmeg. Arrange in pastry-lined pie plate. Combine ½ c. reserved liquid and lemon juice. Pour over apple mixture. Dot with butter. Adjust top crust and flute edge. Cut vents.

Bake in 400° oven 40 minutes or until apples are tender. Makes 6 to 8 servings.

APPLE CRUMB PIE

10 c. boiling water
5 c. dried apples
¾ c. sugar
1 tblsp. flour
¾ tsp. ground cinnamon
¼ tsp. ground nutmeg
⅛ tsp. salt
9″ unbaked pie shell
¾ c. unsifted flour
⅓ c. brown sugar, firmly packed
6 tblsp. butter

Pour boiling water over apples in large bowl. Cover with plastic wrap. Let stand 1 hour.

Drain apples, reserving ½ c. liquid.

Combine sugar, 1 tblsp. flour, cinnamon, nutmeg and salt. Stir in ½ c. reserved liquid. Combine mixture with drained apples. Arrange in pie shell.

Combine ¾ c. flour and brown sugar. Cut in butter until crumbly. Sprinkle over apples.

Bake in 400° oven 50 minutes or until apples are tender. Makes 6 to 8 servings.

APPLE/RAISIN PIE

3 c. water
1⅓ c. dried apples
2 c. sugar
1 c. butter
4 eggs
1 tblsp. flour
¾ tsp. ground cinnamon
¼ tsp. ground nutmeg
⅛ tsp. salt
½ tsp. vanilla
1 c. raisins
1 c. coarsely chopped pecans
10" unbaked pie shell

Bring water to boil in 2-qt. saucepan. Remove from heat. Add apples. Cover and let stand 1 hour.

Bring to a boil; reduce heat. Cover and simmer 10 to 15 minutes or until apples are tender. Drain.

Cream together sugar and butter until light and fluffy. Add eggs, one at a time, beating well after each addition. Add flour, cinnamon, nutmeg, salt and vanilla; beat well. Stir in raisins, pecans and drained apples. Spread in pie shell.

Bake in 350° oven 1 hour or until knife inserted halfway between center and edge comes out clean. Makes 8 servings.

FRIED APPLE PIES

1½ c. dried apples
3 c. water
¼ c. sugar
2 tblsp. lemon juice
½ tsp. grated lemon rind
½ tsp. ground cinnamon
⅛ tsp. salt
⅛ tsp. ground nutmeg
3 c. sifted flour
1 tsp. salt
1 c. shortening
6 tblsp. cold water
1 qt. cooking oil

Combine apples and 3 c. water in 2-qt. saucepan. Bring to a boil; reduce heat. Cover and simmer 35 minutes or until apples are tender. Drain. Puree hot drained apples in blender until smooth. Combine pureed apples with sugar, lemon juice, lemon rind, cinnamon, ⅛ tsp. salt and nutmeg; mix well. Set aside.

Combine flour and 1 tsp. salt in bowl. Cut in shortening until crumbly. Sprinkle 6 tblsp. water over surface; stir until moistened. Shape into ball. Divide in half. Roll each half into 16″ square on floured surface. Cut in 16 (4″) squares. Place scant 1 tblsp. apple filling in center of each. Fold over into triangle. Dampen edges and seal. Press edge with tines of fork. (Keep pies covered with damp cloth until fried.) Repeat with remaining dough.

Heat 2 c. oil in 10″ skillet to 375°. Fry pies until golden brown, turning as needed. Drain on paper towels. After frying 16 pies, pour off oil. Add remaining 2 c. oil; heat as before. Fry remaining pies. Makes 32.

APPLE PIE PIZZA

6 c. boiling water
3 c. dried apples
1¼ c. unsifted flour
1 tsp. salt
½ c. shortening
1 c. shredded Cheddar cheese
¼ c. ice water
½ c. powdered non-dairy "cream"
½ c. brown sugar, firmly packed
½ c. sugar
⅓ c. unsifted flour
¼ tsp. salt
1 tsp. ground cinnamon
½ tsp. ground nutmeg
¼ c. butter
2 tblsp. lemon juice

Pour boiling water over apples in bowl. Cover with plastic wrap. Let stand 1 hour.

Combine 1¼ c. flour and 1 tsp. salt in bowl. Cut in shortening until crumbly. Stir in cheese. Sprinkle water over surface; stir until moistened. Shape into ball. Roll into 15″ circle on lightly floured surface. Place on baking sheet; turn up edge making ¼″ rim.

Combine non-dairy "cream," brown sugar, sugar, ⅓ c. flour, ¼ tsp. salt, cinnamon and nutmeg. Sprinkle half over crust. Cut butter into remaining mixture until crumbly; set aside.

Drain apples. Arrange on crust by overlapping them. Sprinkle with lemon juice. Top with crumbs.

Bake in 450° oven 20 minutes or until crust is golden. Serve warm. Makes 12 servings.

DANISH APPLE BARS

10 c. boiling water
5 c. dried apples
3 c. sifted flour
1 tsp. salt
1 c. shortening
1 egg yolk, beaten
Milk
1 c. crushed corn flakes
½ c. sugar
1 tsp. ground cinnamon
1 egg white, beaten until stiff
Vanilla Icing (recipe follows)

Pour boiling water over apples in bowl. Cover with plastic wrap. Let stand 1 hour.

Sift together flour and salt into bowl. Cut in shortening until crumbly. Add enough milk to egg yolk to make ½ c. Add to flour mixture; mix until moistened.

Divide dough in half. Roll out half of dough on floured surface to 15×10″ rectangle. Place in 15½×10½×1″ jelly roll pan. Sprinkle with corn flakes.

Drain apples, reserving ¾ c. liquid. Arrange apples on crust. Pour reserved ¾ c. liquid over apples. Sprinkle with combined sugar and cinnamon. Roll out remaining dough to fit top. Cut vents in top. Moisten edges of dough with water; seal. Spread egg white over top crust.

Bake in 375° oven 45 minutes or until golden brown. Drizzle with Vanilla Icing while warm. Makes 12 servings.

Vanilla Icing: Combine 2 c. sifted confectioners sugar, 1 tsp. vanilla and 2 tblsp. milk; mix until smooth.

COUNTRY APPLE CRISP

6 c. water
3 c. dried apples or pears
¾ c. quick-cooking rolled oats
¾ c. brown sugar, firmly packed
½ c. unsifted flour
½ tsp. ground cinnamon
½ c. butter

Bring water to a boil in 3-qt. saucepan. Remove from heat. Add apples. Cover and let stand 1 hour.

Bring to a boil; reduce heat. Cover and simmer 10 to 15 minutes or until apples are tender. Drain. Place apples in greased 8″ square baking pan.

Combine oats, brown sugar, flour and cinnamon in bowl. Cut in butter until crumbly. Sprinkle oat mixture over apples.

Bake in 375° oven 30 to 35 minutes or until golden brown. Serve warm or cold. Makes 6 servings.

STRAWBERRY LEATHER

5 c. halved strawberries
¼ c. sugar or honey

Place strawberries, 1 cup at a time, in blender. Puree strawberries until smooth. Stir in sugar.

Line two 15½×10½×1″ jelly roll pans with plastic wrap. Secure edges with tape. Spread fruit puree evenly in pans.

Place in 150° oven to dry. Leave oven door ajar approximately 4″. Place candy thermometer in back of oven. Check temperature periodically to be sure it is correct. If necessary, turn oven off for a while to reduce temperature. Rotate pans every 2 hours. The leather is dry when the surface is no longer sticky. (Drying time is 6 to 12 hours.)

When dry, remove from oven. Remove plastic wrap. Let cool completely. When cool, rewrap in plastic wrap by rolling up like a jelly roll.

Leathers can be stored at room temperature for 1 month; in refrigerator for 3 months and in freezer for 1 year. Makes 2 leathers.

Apricot, Plum, Peach or Nectarine: Wash and cut up 3 lbs. fresh fruit. Remove pits. (No need to pare fruit.) Proceed as above.

Strawberry Rhubarb: Cook together 3 c. cut up rhubarb, ¾ c. sugar and ¼ c. water until tender, about 8 minutes. Do not drain. Puree with 2½ c. halved strawberries. Proceed as above, using 2 tblsp. sugar.

Apple Cinnamon: Wash, core and cut up 3 lbs. apples. (No need to pare.) Do not use hard baking apples. Puree apples as above, adding ¾ c. water. Stir in ¾ c. sugar and ¾ tsp. ground cinnamon. Proceed as above.

PRUNE/PEACH UPSIDE DOWN CAKE

⅔ c. butter
1⅓ c. brown sugar, firmly packed
1 (1 lb. 13 oz.) can sliced peaches, drained
20 dried pitted prunes, cooked and drained
⅔ c. shortening
1 c. sugar
2 eggs
2 tsp. vanilla
3 c. sifted cake flour
3 tsp. baking powder
½ tsp. salt
1 c. milk

Melt butter in 13×9×2″ cake pan. Sprinkle brown sugar over melted butter. Arrange peaches and prunes in pan.

Cream together shortening and sugar until light and fluffy. Add eggs, one at a time, beating well after each addition. Beat in vanilla.

Sift together cake flour, baking powder and salt. Add dry ingredients alternately with milk, beating after each addition. Spread batter carefully over the top of arranged fruit.

Bake in 350° oven 50 minutes or until cake is done. Cool 5 minutes. Turn out on serving plate. Makes 16 servings.

FRUITED CUSTARD CAKE ROLL

Custard Filling (recipe follows)
¾ c. sifted cake flour
¾ tsp. baking powder
¼ tsp. salt
4 eggs
¾ c. sugar
1 tsp. vanilla
Confectioners sugar
½ c. chopped stewed apricots
½ c. coconut
¼ c. raisins
¼ c. chopped maraschino cherries

Prepare Custard Filling.

Sift together cake flour, baking powder and salt.

Beat eggs until light and lemon-colored (about 5 minutes). Gradually add sugar, beating well after each addition. Beat in vanilla. Fold in dry ingredients. Spread in waxed-paper-lined 15½×10½×1″ jelly roll pan.

Bake in 375° oven 13 minutes or until done. Turn out on dish towel dusted with confectioners sugar. Roll up from narrow side. Cool 10 minutes.

Stir apricots, coconut, raisins and cherries into Custard Filling. Unroll cake. Spread with filling. Reroll and cool completely. Dust with confectioners sugar. Refrigerate until serving time. Makes 8 servings.

Custard Filling: Combine ⅓ c. sugar, 2 tblsp. flour, ⅛ tsp. salt and 1 c. scalded milk. Cook, stirring constantly, until thickened (about 5 minutes). Stir in 1 beaten egg; cook 1 more minute. Stir in 1 tsp. vanilla. Cool completely.

SPICY APPLE CAKE

6 c. water
4 c. dried apples
2 c. sifted flour
1¼ c. sugar
2½ tsp. baking powder
1 tsp. salt
⅓ c. shortening
¾ c. milk
1 tsp. vanilla
2 eggs
1 tblsp. sugar
2 tsp. ground cinnamon
½ tsp. ground nutmeg
⅓ c. chopped pecans

Bring water to a boil in 3-qt. saucepan. Remove from heat. Add apples. Cover and let stand 1 hour.

Bring to a boil; reduce heat. Cover and simmer 10 to 15 minutes or until apples are tender. Drain and cool.

Sift together flour, 1¼ c. sugar, baking powder and salt into large bowl. Add shortening, milk and vanilla. Beat thoroughly at medium speed 3 minutes. Add eggs, one at a time, beating well after each addition.

Combine 1 tblsp. sugar, cinnamon and nutmeg. Spread half of batter in greased and floured 13×9×2″ baking pan. Cover with drained apples. Sprinkle with pecans and half of sugar/spice mixture. Spread remaining batter on top; sprinkle with remaining sugar/spice mixture.

Bake in 350° oven 40 to 45 minutes or until cake tests done. Makes 16 servings.

MIXED FRUIT COBBLER

4½ c. dried fruit*
4½ c. water
2 tblsp. cornstarch
¾ c. sugar
½ tsp. ground cinnamon
1½ c. sifted flour
2 tsp. baking powder
3 tblsp. sugar
¾ tsp. salt
¼ c. butter
¾ c. milk

Cut up dried fruit. Place fruit and water in 3-qt. saucepan. Bring to a boil; reduce heat. Cover and simmer 15 minutes or until tender.

Combine cornstarch, ¾ c. sugar and cinnamon. Stir into hot fruit mixture. Pour into 11×7×1½″ baking dish.

Sift together flour, baking powder, 3 tblsp. sugar and salt. Cut in butter until crumbly. Add milk; stir just until moistened. Drop by spoonfuls over top of fruit mixture.

Bake in 400° oven 25 minutes or until golden brown. Makes 6 to 8 servings.

*Note: Any dried fruits can be used.

FRUIT SUNDAE SAUCE

1½ c. dried mixed fruit*
2 cinnamon sticks
12 whole cloves
3 c. water
1 (11 oz.) can mandarin oranges
2 tblsp. cornstarch
¼ c. honey
½ tsp. vanilla
Vanilla ice cream
Toasted coconut

Combine mixed fruit, cinnamon sticks, cloves and water in 2-qt. saucepan. Bring to a boil; reduce heat. Cover and simmer 10 minutes or until tender. Remove from heat. Drain fruit, reserving 1½ c. liquid. Cut up fruit. Discard cinnamon sticks and cloves.

Drain mandarin oranges, reserving liquid. Combine cornstarch with reserved mandarin orange liquid. Combine cornstarch mixture, 1½ c. reserved liquid and honey in 2-qt. saucepan. Cook, stirring constantly, until thickened (about 5 minutes). Add fruit and mandarin oranges; heat. Remove from heat; cool slightly. Spoon into dessert dishes. Top with scoop of vanilla ice cream; sprinkle with coconut. Makes 8 servings.
*Note: Any dried fruits can be used.

HOT FRUIT COMPOTE

**1 c. dried pear slices
1 c. dried apricot halves
¾ c. sugar
5 c. water
2 tblsp. lemon juice
2 cinnamon sticks
10 whole cloves
1 c. dried pitted prunes**

Combine pears, apricots, sugar, water, lemon juice, cinnamon sticks and cloves in 3-qt. saucepan. Bring to a boil; reduce heat. Cover and cook 15 minutes. Add prunes; simmer, covered, 5 more minutes. Remove from heat and cool in pan.

Remove cinnamon sticks and cloves. Serve topped with vanilla ice cream, if you wish. Makes 8 servings.

Index